Not Privileged To Know

This is a work of fiction. Names, characters, places and incidents are products of the author's imagination, or are used fictitiously, and are not to be considered as real. Any resemblance to actual events, local organizations, governments, or persons, living or dead, is entirely coincidental.

Copyright © 2014 by William Rockwell
ISBN 13: 978-1494746582
ISBN 10: 1494746581

Second Edition

BOOKS BY BILL ROCKWELL

Not Privileged to Know

Generation "Z," Birth of the Zompire

Heaven's Conflict, The Rise and Fall of Angels, A Novel.
Lucifer conspires to do the seemingly impossible, to destroy God. God assigns St. Michael to defend Heaven. The stage is thus set for the most significant confrontation ever with the sovereignty of God's Throne at stake.

Coming:

A Detective Murph Mystery, Death of the Innocents
Someone's murdering women who have undergone a recent abortion. As the body count increases, a more sinister plot emerges, one that affects Murph personally. How will he deal with it, and can he find the killer before he suffers a tragic loss?

Generation "Z," Vampire War
Damon and Gabriella pursue the vampire council, but, this time, the vampire fiends are prepared for the zompires. They have learned their weaknesses, and have set a trap. Will the zompires fall prey to the vampires and their zombie horde, leaving all humanity at risk, or will they rally, and prevail?

Heaven's Conflict, The Fall of Man
Satan makes good on the threat he made to trigger humanity's final destruction. He starts in the Garden of Eden by attacking Adam and Eve where he finds them most vulnerable: their pride. God directs His loyal Archangels to intervene on mankind's behalf, leading to another confrontation between the forces of Good and Evil.

http://billrockwell.net

3

THE TWINS: ZODIAC SIGN: GEMINI

Versatility is a great keyword for this dual sign. Expressive and quick-witted, the Gemini presents two distinctive sides to his or her personality, and you can never be sure with which one you're going to come face-to-face. On one hand, the Gemini can be outgoing, flirtatious, communicative, and ready for fun, fun, fun. Yet when the other twin is present, you can find this air sign contemplative, serious, restless, and even indecisive. Both twins are able to adapt to life's circumstances well, making them wonderful people to know. Things are never boring when a Gemini is on the scene.
(**Provided by** Astrocenter.com)

Horoscope for 'today':

Have you recently lost some faith in the future, Gemini? Isn't it time to do something about it, especially where your personal life is concerned? You could find the answers to these questions if you'd take a second look at the quality of your close relationships. Who knows? Love might give you back your enthusiasm for life.
(**Provided by** Astrocenter.com)

IDENTICAL TWINS: Two offsprings produced from a monozygotic (single egg) pregnancy.

Say to wisdom, 'You are my sister!'
Call Understanding, Friend.
Proverbs 7:4

"Be careful what you wish for,
you may receive it."
Harpers Monthly
W.W. Jacobs

CHAPTER 1

Washington, D.C.

As Detective Hank Wu mulled over the four unsolved murders jamming his caseload, his troubled expression grew. All had occurred within the last five days. Were they related? He didn't know. He had no suspects and few clues. Worse, instinct told him he hadn't seen the last of the violence.

New York City
Five days ago

As Corinne Day's stomach tightened into a painful knot, she grimaced. "Why aren't you returning my calls, Monica? What's wrong? Where are you?" Without warning, her throat constricted. She gasped for air. Her trembling hands dropped the patient's chart, and shot to the collar of her blouse. She struggled to unbutton it, succeeding only after three attempts. Once successful, she flapped the collar frantically. It didn't help.

Breathless, she rushed to the ancient window of her third-floor office. Rubbing the sweat from her chest, she leaned out as far as she dared. The crisp autumn breeze stung her as she attempted to gulp the life-giving air. She couldn't. The tightness in her throat worsened. She began panting, and immediately felt lightheaded. Her head pounded in rhythm to the horns blaring below; she thought it might explode, raining its contents down onto the street. Sweat soaked her long, ginger hair, and poured down her neck. Flashes of light and floating lines suddenly burst before her eyes, blurring the parade of cars coasting along Fifth Avenue, their drivers ignorant of the drama unfolding above them. Darkness crept over her as her view of the street narrowed to a mere pinpoint. Tears welled in her eyes. She tried to grip the windowsill tighter, but her hands had cramped into fists. Lightheaded, she teetered back, then forward, nearly falling through the window, only her shoulder striking the frame preventing the fatal plunge. *Help me, Monica! Oh, God, please help me!*

Anxiety attacks linked to her psychic connection with her identical twin weren't new to Corinne. She had experienced their discomfort many times since the link first manifested at age ten. Monica had been playing on a ledge above a river that fateful day, searching for her favorite wildflowers, lilacs; she loved their aroma. Despite warnings from her parents, she had gotten too close to the edge when a rock beneath her foot lost its grip, and plunged into the ravine, carrying the young girl with it on its journey toward the water below. As Monica fell, her leg became entangled in a shrub, breaking her fall, as well as her leg. Unconscious, she dangled twenty feet above the roaring river.

At her home about a mile away, Corrine had experienced the shock of the slip, the terror of the fall, and the pain as her sister's leg became entangled, and then snapped. Unlike her sister, Corrine had only become lightheaded, and hadn't lost consciousness. Terrified, she ran to her mother who, after hearing her daughter's story, assured her that she had merely been daydreaming. However, Corinne knew deep within her that something terrible had happened to Monica. She hunted for her sister, eventually finding her predicament.

After the rescue and several other shared experiences, the twins realized that they were joined by more than common parentage and birth date.

As the teenage years had approached, the young girls had discovered that this bond forced each to experience not only the other's physical sensations, but emotional ones as well. The confusing and intertwined feelings made both of them giddy at first as they used the connection to share feelings, and then bitter when they sought solitude from the problems of teenage life. Finally, each experienced a reluctant acceptance once they realized, as adults, that they had something unique, a bond with a sibling most people would love to have, but in reality could never experience.

Now, as Corinne's symptoms subsided and the tension left her body, her muscles relaxed, enabling her to open her hands to grip the windowsill, and breathe easier. She gulped the wonderful tasting air. Her vision improved. She sighed as her mind cleared. *Oh, thank God, I can breathe again! Monica must be safe, not in danger any more. Maybe she had only been frightened, not in real physical danger. I bet it probably had something to do with that damned job of hers, but whatever the cause, I guess we're both fine...for now. Come on, Monica, call, and reassure me...now, please.*

Leaving the window open, she returned to her desk, and, with shaking hands, picked up the patient's chart. He had been referred to her for physical therapy following knee-replacement. As the preeminent physical therapist in the practice, she had always been assigned the most difficult patients, and this one proved no exception. Like her, he suffered from anxiety attacks, and standard physical therapy had, unfortunately, increased their frequency until they had hampered his recovery. He had consulted a psychiatrist; however, these sessions had been unsuccessful. Knowing that Corinne had an additional degree in psychology, the psychiatrist had referred the patient to her, hoping she could formulate a physical therapy program that would provoke less apprehension.

A sudden sense of dread poured over her. Her hand shot to her throat again as the choking feeling returned. She slammed the chart onto the desktop. "Damn! Get a hold of yourself, Corinne. There's no reason to panic. Monica's fine. Calm yourself." She closed her eyes, rubbing her fingers against her temples, and mumbled, "Control, control, control."

Finally, after forcing herself to take several deep breaths, Corrine dialed Monica's cell phone. After three rings, her voicemail answered. Frustrated, Corinne pressed her intercom button. "Did you get in touch with Monica yet?" she asked the clinic secretary with the little breath she could muster. "All I keep getting is her voicemail. Any luck with her other numbers?"

"No, Corrine, there's been no answer at her apartment. I left a message on both the answering machine at her office and on her cell phone, but she hasn't returned the calls. Do you want me to keep trying? Are you okay? You sound short of breath."

"I'm fine, and yes, please keep trying. If you get her, I need to speak to her immediately. So, interrupt me no matter what. Thanks."

Forcing herself to breathe slowly and deeply, Corrine disconnected from the intercom. She used her cell phone to call her boyfriend.

Paul answered on the first ring. "What's up?"

"I had another one of those anxiety attacks. You know, the ones I told you about."

"Oh, yeah, you mean where you and your sister feel what the other is going through. Right? Are you okay? You don't sound too good."

"I felt absolutely terrible a few minutes ago, but I'm feeling a little better now. I'm really worried about Monica though. She's either in great danger, or is distressed over something. I feel…well…I think…maybe she's discovered something in one of her investigations that has upset her. I can't explain it. It's simply how I feel."

"Oh? Discovered what? Can you tell?"

"No, we can't read each other's mind. I simply know something upset her. Maybe she's in danger. I'm not sure. I haven't been able to reach her. I'm really worried."

"Now, don't go worrying yourself, Corinne. I'm sure if she's anything like you, she can handle herself."

"Oh, she can handle herself better than I ever could. You're right there." Despite her concern, Corinne couldn't help but smile. Monica had become a private detective, finding herself in many tight situations before, and had always emerged unscathed. Corinne admired her fortitude in the face of danger, although she hated experiencing her sister's fear with each episode.

"I'm sure when I finally get in touch with her, she'll laugh at me for being overly concerned again. She'll explain the problem, maybe a friend in trouble, or something upsetting about one of her cases. Whatever it is, she'll assure me she's okay, and chide me for overreacting." She lost the smile. *Who am I kidding? My heart is telling me Monica is in trouble. So, until proven otherwise, I have reason to worry.* "But that doesn't make me feel any better right now. I guess I'll always worry about her."

She took another deep breath, clenching her eyes. She had to admit it aloud. "I need her. I can't live without her." She dropped her voice to a mere whisper. "I know it's probably wrong, but it's true. I need her."

She expected Paul to say something reassuring. He didn't. The silence cut her.

Her voice became staccato. "I'm really frightened this time, Paul. I can't explain it. I feel…well…different than before…more upset than ever. It's got me worried…that she may not be…all right this time."

"Would it make you feel any better if I checked with some of my sources down in Washington? I can have them try to find her. I'll have them check where she is, what she's been up to, that sort of thing. I'll even have them check the hospitals and police headquarters to be sure nothing bad has happened."

"Could you, Paul? I know it's a lot to ask, but you've got better contacts down there than I do."

"Consider it done. I'll give them a call right now, tell them to drop everything, and find your sister. They'll report back to me later today. I'll get back to you as soon as I know something."

"Thanks, Paul. You're a sweetheart." As she started to disconnect, a sudden thought struck her. "By the way, the feelings I'm having are really intense this time. That may mean Monica is close. I wonder if she might be here in New York."

"I'll check on that too, Babe."

As Corinne disconnected, she picked up the chart, trying to concentrate on the patient's case, but her heart still raced, and her stomach remained taut. She frowned. *I can still sense your apprehension and fear, Monica, and that really worries me. What's happening to you, Dear Sister?*

Paul stared at the phone. "I can't believe it. Of all the sister acts in town, I had to become involved with psychically connected twins…and I had to end up with the one with all the psychological hang-ups who can't even treat herself…great with psycho patients, but her own problems…they're a total mystery to her. I must be as crazy as she is to stick with her." He sighed again, and dialed his contact in Washington. "I'm afraid I have another job for you, Kevin."

Washington D.C.

Senator Richard Edmond's speech, outlining his vision of the future had attracted the attention of many supporters, and one scheming, bloodthirsty dissident. The roar of the crowd drowned his final, "Thank you, and good night." The senator, surrounded by his bodyguards, forced his way through the crowd, stopping at every opportunity to shake an outstretched hand. He burst from the building and into a crowd of thrilled, cheering supporters. He waved in every direction, ensuring that even distant followers would receive his appreciation.

Senator Edmond grinned. These pre-campaign rallies had jump-started his Presidential run more successfully than he had imagined. His goal drew nearer with each passing moment. He knew he had the support of many in power in his political party. However, the road to the White House would not be without obstacles. His major opposition would come from another high-ranking senator, Frank Stern. Senator Stern also had loyal supporters and rich financial backers. More than that, he boasted as good a political record as his own. Political surveyors had already picked Senator Stern as the leading candidate in the upcoming race. Senator Edmond hoped to change that opinion with these rallies.

On a rooftop across the street, breathing shallow and slow to steady his aim, an assassin searched the crowd through the telescopic sight of his rifle, determined to end Senator Edmond's campaign before it had begun in earnest. The assassin watched the senator offer another wave before the jubilant crowd, and then squeezed the trigger.

Senator Edmond's head slumped forward, his mouth opening wide with the bullet's impact. Blood burst from the wound as the second bullet struck above his right eye. The senator's limp body fell into the arms of his wife who screamed, and collapsed under his weight. Several supporters tried to shield the senator from further assault by throwing their bodies over his. Others, terrified of being shot, ran for cover.

Two of the senator's bodyguards, guns drawn, rushed the building that housed the shooter, as the figure on its roof withdrew from sight. By the time they charged onto the roof, the shooter had disappeared. Looking down, the bodyguards mournfully watched as ambulance attendants rushed their lifeless Presidential candidate away from the scene.

CHAPTER 2

New York City

Except for the monologue of the TV reporter, recounting the events leading up to Senator Edmond's assassination, silence filled the motel room. "The assassination of one of the leading Democratic candidates for President of the United States, Senator Richard Edmond, occurred last night as he left a large political rally in Washington DC. We have been trying to reach the other likely contenders, but, so far, none of them have made themselves available to us. A massive hunt for his killer is being conducted along the entire eastern seaboard."

Senator Frank Stern had seen the same report three times. He wore a frown. "What does the damn media want me to do? Do they really expect me to proclaim that Dick's assassination is terrible for both our country and the Democratic Party?" He threw up his hands. "That's obvious! Do they expect me to scream that Senator Edmond had been a fine man? Everyone knows that too."

He turned to Paul who remained silent, as he leaned forward, trying to hear the reporter over Frank's ranting.

"Do they really expect me to tell the world that I'm the leading contender in this race that I always have been, and always will be? Don't they know that already?" He stood, and began pacing in front of the TV. "What do they expect me to tell the public, vote for me because I had been so gracious after my opponent's assassination?" He lowered his voice. "The American people are smarter than that; they'd see right through my words. They'd know I'd be taking advantage of the situation. The media can't really expect a statement so soon after his assassination, can they?" He pointed at the reporter, babbling on about Senator's Edmond's career. "Can't they respect the family, give them a chance to get over the initial shock before expecting me to make any kind of statement?" He stood in front of the TV, running his fingers through his thinning hair. He then grabbed a handful. "I don't know what to do." He

12

released his hair, which now stood upright, resembling that of some mad scientist. The action removed any appearance of decorum. Not hearing any answers to his questions, the fifty-year-old senator plopped down onto the couch, feeling twice his age. He closed his eyes, and took a deep breath. "What do you think? Should I do what they want?"

Paul Camarazza glared at the senator. When it came to political decisions, Senator Stern usually made up his mind quickly and with political precision. Paul had never seen him so indecisive. *Could he have something else on his mind, something more important than his Presidential campaign? I hope not, but it really doesn't matter. If Frank can't make up his mind, I'll do it for him.* "It wouldn't hurt to do exactly that." Paul poured Frank another Mojito. "Someone did you an enormous favor by killing off your competition. Why not take advantage of it?"

With a large frame, Paul towered at least five inches over the six-foot tall senator, and weighed in at over two hundred and fifty pounds, although more fat than muscle. His bulk, along with his stern facial expression, screamed for respect and obedience, things he demanded, and always received. He had used his imposing façade, bellowing voice, and business acumen to claw his way to the top of his family's import-export company. He would force Frank to listen to him one way, or another.

Senator Stern feared neither Paul's size nor his authority, although he owed his present Senatorial office to Paul's efforts and his monetary backing. "Oh, come on. You can't be serious." He accepted the Mojito, and took a large gulp.

"Why not? It's a great opportunity to advance your career."

"I can't. Maybe in that corporate world of yours, you could jump on such an opportunity, but I can't take the risk politically, not if I'm going to make a run for President. It could backfire. The voters might be offended if I took advantage of the situation. I might not even survive the firestorm of negative publicity. I'd be crucified."

"Only if you make it appear that you're out to take such an advantage."

Senator Stern tilted his head. "What do you mean?"

Paul knew what the tilt meant: 'Tell me what to do, and I'll do it.' *It's so easy to control people when you know how.* He smirked. "Well, instead of talking about your reactions to the assassination and *your* personal plans, you could simply denounce the murder. All the other would-be candidates will do the same thing anyway when they get over the initial shock, and finally come out of hiding, but you have to appear to be only concerned with Senator Edmond's family, his constituents…all the American people for that matter. The public will eat it up. Besides, if you're the first to do the noble gesture, all the others who make similar statements will appear to be followers and imitators. You'll come off as the compassionate leader, the one who's best equipped to lead America in dealing with future crises as its President."

"That's still taking advantage." Senator Stern shook his head, and closed his eyes.

"Of course it is, but only because we know the real reason behind your announcement. In the viewpoint of the public, and even the news media, you'll have put aside your differences with Senator Edmond, and would be simply coming across as displaying your true emotions, feelings from your heart and soul…if you deliver the speech with as much emotion as you can muster…maybe even shed a tear or two. It'll make you appear more human and more sympathetic in the public's eyes. Believe me; they'll remember you and your gesture when they vote."

Senator Stern thought it over for a few, long moments before speaking, his mind struggling with the likely consequences of Paul's proposal, both advantageous and adverse. He sighed, and then stared at Paul with eyes devoid of emotion now that he had made his decision. "I suppose you're right. I'll call our publicity chairman. He'll know the best way to approach our announcement, and should be able to help me make sure I nail the emotional part of the speech."

"Good idea. I'm sure he'll agree with me. While you have him on the phone, check on your girlfriend…I mean fiancée. I'm disappointed she didn't come with you on this trip. See if he knows what she's up to. Tell her I miss her."

"Can I use this desk phone? I left my cell phone in the car."

"Sure, help yourself. I've got another call to make anyway. I'll use my cell phone from the bedroom."

Senator Stern began dialing the number. "Speaking of girlfriends, where's that physical therapist friend of yours? What's her name? Corinne, isn't it? I still want to meet her. This is the first girlfriend you've had this long without an introduction. Is that who you're going to check on?"

"No, it's business. Don't worry though. You'll meet her soon enough. We can't afford to have you associated with me right now. It's bad enough the police are always erroneously associating me with my relatives in the mob without you getting sucked into the fray. You know I

14

try to keep my distance from their criminal activities, but the press won't buy that any more than the police. If they ever connected you to me through my girlfriend, you'd never hear the end of it. No matter how innocent the association, it would be misconstrued, and would give the opposition something to use to attack you, and maybe even end your career. That's the last thing I'd want to cause. Simply having you stop up here could prove disastrous if someone saw you. I don't want you taking any more unnecessary chances, especially involving me. So, you'll have no contact with my girlfriend until after the election. Go make your call. I want you out of here before some nosy reporter catches you."

"Hi, Ed." Senator Stern rubbed his eyes to the point he saw twinkling lights. *Events are proceeding faster than I expected, faster than I anticipated, and maybe faster than I can handle.* He blinked, and the twinkling lights disappeared. "Are you watching the news about Dick's assassination?"

"Yes, Frank, it's the only thing on any channel. It's terrible. I can't believe what's happened."

"Same here." Senator Stern stared at the bedroom door. *I wonder who Paul is calling. Does it have anything to do with my campaign? I have to be extremely careful. This could be the biggest risk of my career, but, if successful, could lead me right to the White House.* "He and I disagreed on almost everything, but I didn't want him out of the race this way. That's why I'm calling. How do you think I should handle this? No one has made any statements to the press yet. Should I be the first to denounce the killing, express my feelings for his family and his constituents, for the entire *nation* for that matter? Will that give the impression I'm a leader, or mark me as an opportunist?"

"I've been sitting here wondering exactly that. You're now the undisputed head of the party. I think that leader should be the first to make a statement. It'll make you appear to be the strongest politician in the country, as you said, a leader. I don't think anyone will accuse you of being an opportunist, if you're careful in what you say. Expressing your feelings is the right thing to do, and you might as well be the first to do it. So, where are you now?"

"I'm in New York City. I could make a statement to the press in about half an hour. I know what to say. There's no time to have the text edited by your whole committee. I'll be careful."

"Okay, but why don't you call me back before the press conference to read it to me?"

"I had hoped you'd say that, Ed. Stay by the phone. I'll call you back in a few minutes."

Paul whispered into his cell phone so Senator Stern wouldn't hear. "Kevin, any problems with our business there?"

"No, Boss, everything went fine….no problems."

Paul beamed. "Good. Did you locate Corrine's sister? Is she still there in Washington? Corinne is worried about her, and keeps bugging me about her whereabouts."

"Nope, maybe Corinne is right. Maybe she's in New York."

"She's apparently as unpredictable as her sister. Maybe she'll check in with Corinne if she's here, and Corinne can stop bugging me. One can only hope."

"Do you want me to keep looking for her?"

"No, I have more important things for you to do here. So, you'd better come back to New York." *I don't like the way things are going with Frank's campaign, or with Corinne's problems. I don't like all the complications. I don't like it at all.*

CHAPTER 3

Chuck Florentino burst into the motel room in Washington, and froze, realizing at once that he had made a huge mistake. Not fifteen minutes earlier, he had left his partner, Jim Wyman, to get some beer and smokes. Everything had seemed fine at the time, everything except Jim, that is. Jim had been acting strange, complaining nonstop that they shouldn't have had to make the trip from New York, and that Paul had overreacted. Much to Chuck's annoyance, Jim had continued the tirade after they had checked in. His nonstop chatter had made Chuck wonder if he had started using drugs again, but a quick search of the room had revealed nothing. Annoyed with Jim's behavior, Chuck had decided to go for an extended walk, spending much of the time worrying about Jim's sobriety, but trying to give his partner the benefit of the doubt. *Maybe it's not drugs. Maybe Jim has something else on his mind, something he'll confide to me when he's ready.*

Upon returning, Chuck had found the door ajar. He remembered closing it when he left. *Jim would never leave it open, even if he were expecting company, even a drug supplier. Jim's a pro. He knows better.* Chuck's eyes explored the room, searching for any sign of Jim, or danger. Nothing. His heart raced, the hairs on his neck bristled. He ventured farther into the room. "Jim?" He dropped the two, over-stuffed grocery bags carelessly on the bed. One tore on impact, as the six-pack split the paper, the sound ripping the silence of the room. He listened for any hint of his partner. Still nothing. The stillness of the room returned. He unbuttoned his jacket, and pulled out the Glock semi-automatic pistol he always carried for just such a situation.

He advanced into the room, eyes and ears searching for any signs of danger. Then, he spotted Jim's muscular body between the two beds, blood oozing from the wound in his chest, soaking his tee shirt.

The squeak of a door hinge suddenly shattered the silence. Chuck whirled. Coming from within the bathroom, he spotted the barrel of a gun, looming large against the white door, a slight shake noticeable at the weapon's tip. He raised his gun, but too late. He saw the flash as he pulled his trigger, his shot striking the door, but missing its human target. As the bullet slammed into his chest, he shook his drooping head. *Careless, very careless!* His gun bounced on the floor as he toppled lifeless across Jim's body.

The killer threw a bag of cocaine next to the bodies, and then, using a black marker, crossed out a hastily scribbled "NY," on the bathroom mirror, and rushed out of the room.

The world of his dream consisted of an alley filled with felines, screaming in unison. They snarled at him, fangs exposed, their backs hunched, hackles raised. Even the deafening ringing of the church bells could not drown out their screeching. Without provocation, they suddenly attacked him, their sharp claws ripping at his pants. Seeking shelter, he ran toward the church with its many spires, hoping it would offer him solace and protection. However, the attack worsened, the swipes of their claws becoming more accurate, their numbers increasing until they blocked any hope of escape.

He wondered if the cats were mentally communicating his whereabouts to every other feline in the city, recruiting them in an effort to overpower him. He kicked one of them away, but another even more vicious attacker replaced it. He finally fought his way to the stairs of the church. Safety loomed only a few feet away. The sounds of the church bells intensified, the sound reverberating through his skull, giving him an instant, pounding headache.

Paul awoke with a start. *Where am I?* Reality fought hard to rise from his dream, to silence the bells, only creeping back into his consciousness one small baby step at a time. His wide-open eyes refused to recognize the darkness surrounding him. The church bells finally morphed into the ringing of his phone. Realizing he had been awoken, he checked the illuminated readout on the digital clock: 1:30 AM. Still groggy and only half awake, he groped for the receiver.

"Yeah," he mumbled before the phone reached his ear.

"Sorry to bother you at this hour," the female voice said, "but I had to speak to you."

"Sage?" Her voice jolted him to alertness. He fumbled for the light switch, shielding his eyes from the brightness. "Where are you, and where have you been? I've had Kevin searching for you. Why didn't you answer your cell phone?"

"I had some personal business to take care of. I needed some privacy. I turned my cell phone off."

"Oh? What kind of business?"

"Tom asked me to go with him a few weeks ago. We were picking out a surprise birthday present for his father. I'm not going to tell you what it is. You're going to have to wait until his birthday celebration later this month. That's why Frank didn't know how to find me either."

"Well, I've already sent Chuck and Jim down there to check on Corinne's sister, and try to find you. Frank and I were worried about you."

"I appreciate that, and that's why I'm calling you so late. Chuck and Jim are dead."

"What?" Paul sat upright. "What happened to them?"

"I'm not one-hundred-percent sure." Her voice became lower, less defensive. "All I know is that Chuck called me earlier. I had turned my cell phone on by then. He told me to meet him in their motel room around ten, but when I arrived, the police were there. I managed to mingle with the crowd, and found out that they had both been shot."

"Shot? Do they know who shot them, and why?" Paul rubbed the sleep from his eyes.

"The police don't know. They think it may have been an organized crime hit, or a drug buy gone sour."

"Organized crime? They've got to be wrong. That makes no sense."

"I'm only telling you what I heard. They mention organized crime, and some kind of message written on the mirror in their motel room. I don't know what it says."

"What about the drug angle? Any idea what evidence they have for that?"

"I overheard one detective mention they found a bag filled with a white powder they think is cocaine. So, maybe Jim had gone back to using. Maybe something went wrong when he tried to make a buy, but I can't be sure."

"Maybe, but I don't buy two of my associates shot by a drug dealer. It makes no sense. Those guys were street wise. They knew better than to take any chances." He lowered his voice as he thought aloud. "Why would anyone want to kill two of my men on an innocent trip to check on Corinne's sister...and you, Sage? Can you think of anything that might connect your recent disappearance from cell phone contact with the murders?"

"No, nothing. I know how important I am to Frank's campaign effort, and wouldn't do anything to jeopardize that. I love him as much as he loves me."

"Okay. Let's assume the police are right, for now, and it was a drug dealer who killed them, because the organized crime angle makes no sense at all. The police probably won't expend much effort to find their killer. They'll assume Jim and Chuck were junkies, and file their case away, probably expend their efforts on some rich missing wife down there. It's sad. I think I'd better come down myself to do some investigating on my own. I'd like to meet with you as soon as I get there. Maybe you can fill me in on what else has been happening in that God-forsaken excuse for a city we call our Capital. I'll be on the next plane." He paused, trying to decide what needed to be done upon his arrival. "No, wait a minute. On second thought, I'll have Kevin drive me so I'll have my own set of wheels there. I'll call you when I arrive. You stay with the senator until then. He needs you with him with the hullabaloo about that assassination."

"Do you think that's a good idea, I mean coming down here? If the police are right, and it wasn't a simple drug buy gone sour, you could be in danger. They shot two of your associates. They may have some reason we don't know about, maybe to do with your businesses in New York. They may come after you simply because those two worked for you. I'm really worried you might be walking into danger."

Paul growled. "I think the police are wrong. It couldn't have been a mob hit. Those men were innocent employees of my legitimate business. As far as I know, they have no connection to anything illegal. Besides, I only decided to send them down yesterday. So, no one from any so-called crime family should have known they were even there. As far as drugs, Chuck assured me last week that Jim hadn't been using anymore, and his performance has been exceptional of late. So, there shouldn't have been any drugs in their room. None of it makes any sense, but if something fishy is going on, something that is making someone so nervous that they'd dare shoot my innocent men, I want to know how they knew about their trip, and why they killed them. I don't trust the police to do a thorough investigation, at least not one up to my standards."

"I'm still worried about you. Why not send someone else? Don't take any unnecessary risks."

"No, I'd better go down myself. I'm not willing to risk any more of my employees. It'd be better if I handle it."

"Okay, I'll wait for your call. Meanwhile, I'll try to learn more about the murders."

"No," Paul snapped. "Don't do that. I don't want you poking around. Someone might wonder what Senator Stern's fiancée is doing snooping around a supposed drug-buy-gone-sour. I'll do all the investigating when I get there. You're Frank's fiancée. Act like it by sticking with him. He really needs you now. Don't even tell him I'm coming down, or what happened to my men. It'll only upset him."

"Okay. I'll be waiting for your call though."

As Paul disconnected, he pushed a red button on his nightstand. In less than ten-seconds, Kevin barged into the room, gun at the ready, aimed at the bed, his eyes scanning the room for intruders. Although shorter than average, Kevin weighed in at over two hundred and sixty pounds, all of it muscle. He wore only boxer shorts, and resembled a contestant in the Mister Universe contest, ready to flex his well-trained muscles for the eyes of the judges. He bore a scar on his cheek that extended from his right eye to the corner of his mouth. He had acquired it in a fight during his two-year jail term for robbery before Paul had recruited him as his chauffeur. Kevin soon became Paul's best employee, developing the loyalty and tenacity of a bulldog, and avoiding any run-ins with the law. After a bullet, fired by a disgruntled employee, smashed Paul's knee, Kevin became Paul's bodyguard and, eventually, his personal assistant. His huge hands now dwarfed his automatic pistol, his eyes now focused on Paul for any hint of the reason for the emergency summons.

Paul waved him to the chair at the foot of the bed once Kevin relaxed, having found no imminent threat. "Chuck and Jim were murdered tonight in Washington." Paul climbed out of bed, and began pacing the floor.

"Murdered?" Kevin's voice had a gravelly and deep quality, his scar pulling his mouth to the right with each word. "I can't believe it. Any idea who did it?"

"No! The dumb police have labeled it either an organized crime hit, or a killing during a drug buy. Had you talked to them recently?"

"I talked to them before they left, and they didn't expect any trouble. No one knew they were there in the first place. I know I didn't tell anyone."

Paul stopped in front of Kevin. "That's right, you and I were the only ones who knew where, when, and why they were going. It had to be someone they ran into in Washington. Maybe they met someone they knew at the airport."

"Like Sage?"

"Yeah, like Sage." Paul resumed his pacing, this time slower, more deliberate, as he mulled over the events in his mind. "But why would she kill them. She hardly knew them, and looking for her was a secondary reason for their trip. Besides, she never struck me as a murderer, but you never know with someone like her. Maybe she simply discussed their visit with someone who had it in for them, or maybe she didn't have anything to do with it at all. Of course, that's giving her a huge benefit of doubt." He stared at Kevin. "Do you know if Jim had begun using again?"

Kevin set the safety on his gun. "Not as far as I know. He's been clean for over a year now. Chuck's been keeping him honest."

"That's what I thought. I've got a bad feeling about this. I think we'd better go there ourselves to find out exactly what's going on, and who's behind it all."

"Okay. Just the two of us?"

"No, I'd like Corinne with us." Paul stopped pacing. "I'm sure she'd love the opportunity to check on her sister, and, besides, I'd like her company while we're there, a mini vacation along with the business. We'll keep her away and out of trouble for safety's sake, only do dinners, and sleeping together. Of course, she may not want to leave. You know how dedicated she is to that clinic of hers. I'm sure she has patients she has to see, patients who can't do without her. They'll hold her here. On the other hand, maybe, just maybe, my wanting to accompany her will be just the excuse she needs to leave. She's really connected with that twin of hers. Maybe I can convince her. We'll see." He paused, staring at Kevin, finally smiling behind wide-opened eyes. "I know. I'll let her drive my Lamborghini. She might go simply for that. I'll broach the idea with her later today."

"Are we going to visit Senator Stern while we're there?"

"No way! He's getting a lot of media attention after that stirring speech about Senator Edmond's assassination. No, he's got enough to do organizing his campaign. I don't want to add to his burdens. There'll plenty of time to party with him once he wins the Presidency."

"How about Sage?"

"Oh, we're definitely going to talk to her. I've got this nagging feeling that she's up to something, and it's something that's not in Frank's best interest. Something's going on between those two that's not good, and I'm afraid whatever it is might torpedo Frank's campaign. I'd like to prevent that, if at all possible. Maybe I can fix whatever the problem is, but we'll see. Meanwhile, let's get some sleep. We've got a lot of planning to do tomorrow."

As Kevin departed, and Paul extinguished the light, he stared at the ceiling he knew hung above him, but that he couldn't see. "I think I'd prefer those ringing bells and cats to what may await me in Washington. Who killed them, and why?"

A disturbed sleep finally overtook him, placing him again on the steps of the church, only this time, no cats surrounded him, instead Chuck and Jim stood at the entrance of the church, motioning for him to join them inside. That worried him even more.

CHAPTER 4

As Corinne walked the final three blocks to Dr. Gunther's office, she pondered the message she had found awaiting her that morning at the Physical Therapy and Rehabilitation Center. "Corinne, I need to talk to you first thing today. Extremely urgent! Please meet me in my office at 10 AM. Dr. Steven Gunther."

The Center's secretary had already taken the liberty of rescheduling her 10 AM patient, adding that Doctor Gunther had not mentioned anything concerning the subject of the meeting.

Corinne wondered why the Chief of Staff of the hospital had asked to see her. *It could only mean one thing: something has gone terribly wrong in my department, and either I'm to blame, or they want me to fix it pronto. Otherwise he would have simply called, emailed, or texted me.*

She knew Dr. Gunther well since they had battled over their many differences concerning hospital policies, physician-nurse interactions, and the operation of the Center. Despite their differences, Corinne had worked with Dr. Gunther to save the Center when it ran into economic difficulties. With great efforts by everyone involved, they were able to revive the Center, and turn it, once more, into a profitable, patient friendly and caring facility. Such a summons from him, especially one signed so formally, usually meant a problem, or the need of a difficult favor. Corinne wondered which had moved him to action this time. *Either means more stress for me.*

On her trip up Fifth Avenue, she lingered at some of the street vendors, browsing their wares of books, sunglasses, and knock-off purses. She had ample time to get to Dr. Gunther's office, so she paused frequently, but purchased nothing. The light breeze streamed through her hair like a lover's fingers. She lifted her head so the wind could strike her more fully, something she adored. She always found it refreshing, invigorating and pleasing. She loved Autumn with its crisp days, replete with bright sunshine whose radiance would become obscured only occasionally by a few wispy clouds. She enjoyed walking the city streets almost as much as she enjoyed driving Paul's sports car. The speeding car provided exhilaration. The walking provided the serenity she often needed. Both gave her a much-appreciated feeling of freedom.

As she approached the hospital, Corinne paused, again trying to deduce the reason for the summons. *Could it be that Dr. Gunther and the hospital board have finally decided that they don't need me anymore? Are they going to try to dislodge me from my position at the Center as they've tried before? If so, I'm ready for another fight...a fight I fully intend to win.*

Although her phone had not rung, she pulled it out to check its display: no message from Paul. She sighed. *I had hoped you would have called by now with good news about Monica....no such luck!*

Her thoughts turned to Paul once more. He had been the one man who had accepted her for herself: a woman afraid to express emotions, yet a woman who still desired a lasting relationship with a man who appreciated her intelligence and her achievements, even if those had been aided, or even at times orchestrated, by her twin. He never questioned how she acted, whether she happened to be reserved, or forward, moody, or giddy, or changing on the spot like a chameleon, instead, allowing her to be herself, her true self, never asking why she had behaved as she did. She loved him for that. After several dates, she had told him about Monica, their connection, and the problems it had caused. He had understood. She had expected him to. She appreciated how understanding he could be. She couldn't wait to introduce him to Monica.

She sighed, her mind focusing once more on the hypothetical problems she might encounter in her upcoming meeting with Dr. Gunther. *I need your help again, Monica. I pray you are now totally out of danger, and are around to guide me once more in the next phase of my career...whatever that may be. Please help me take the right path.* She took another long look at the striking facade of the hospital, took a deep breath, and stormed into the building.

Although Corinne had arrived ten minutes early, Dr. Gunther's secretary ushered her into his office immediately, without saying more than a cordial "Hello." The small size of the room always amazed her. Today, even Dr. Gunther appeared diminutive, hiding behind both the enormous computer screen and his rectangular 'in box' filled to eight inches above its sides with rashly torn open letters and patient charts that hadn't as yet been converted to electronic files. Many yellow sticky notes protruded from these charts, marking pages that required the doctor's attention before being scanned.

He stood as she entered, but didn't smile as he hastened to greet her. "Thanks for coming." He had a high-pitched voice, unexpected from his portly physique, replete with a belt worn below a wad of fat, a crop of disheveled blond hair and jowls that would have made a Tom turkey proud. "Please be seated. I'm so glad you could free up the time to see me."

Corinne sat, and began drumming her fingers. "What's so important that you got my receptionist to cancel my morning appointments?" *There's always been something about you that's made me uncomfortable, something that's bothered me beyond your chubby looks. Someday I'll discover exactly what that something is. Maybe today is that day.*

A large smile split his face as his eyes decreased to slits. His resulting appearance, resembling a sinister Jack-o'-lantern, caused Corinne to shutter. She halted her finger drumming, and folded her arms across her chest, as she awaited his explanation. *What are you up to, You Devious Man?*

He pointed a stump of a finger at her. "Ah, getting right to the point, I see. You haven't changed in years." He cleared his throat. "I received a phone call early this morning from a colleague of mine, Dr. Brian Filmore...you know, my friend in Washington." When Corinne shrugged, he waived his hand in the air dismissively. "No matter. Anyway, he has a patient that he's having a great deal of difficulty helping. The patient has shown resistance to all approaches to physical rehabilitation for his injured knee. Brian thinks it's not necessarily his injured knee that's the problem. The patient is a prominent lobbyist in Washington. He has some overlying psychological problems, and is fighting Brian every step of the way. Brian says he won't even discuss what the problem involves, but he's guessing it has something to do with Washington politics. Maybe he doesn't want to give the appearance of being injured, disabled, or weak to the politicians in power down there...something like that." He paused, continuing when Corinne didn't comment. "Anyway, Brian can't get him to agree to any program of physical therapy, or even counseling for his underlying psychological problem." He closed his eyes for a few seconds. "He insists he doesn't have any psychological problems, and his knee will be fine, if he's allowed to do his own exercises at home."

"We all get those difficult patients occasionally." Corinne lowered her arms, folding her hands in her lap, "They all think they know more than us thanks to the internet, TV talk shows and those awful ads for pharmaceuticals, describing all the benefits of a drug, and then listing every side effect ever seen. Those things empower them with only superficial medical knowledge, not enough to make an unbiased medical decision in their own case. Your friend's patient may fall into that category."

Her heart rate slowed, and her breathing eased. *I guess this meeting isn't about terminating me, or a clinic problem after all. If Dr. Gunther only wants advice on patient treatment, then this should be a short and easy meeting, but could have been easily handled over the phone. I guess I overreacted though. What's wrong with you, Corinne? You've had your back up all morning, even before Dr. Gunther summoned you. Maybe your reaction to Monica's distress has put you more off kilter than you realized. Monica is probably laughing at your uncharacteristic indiscretion right now.* She sighed lightly, hoping Dr. Gunther wouldn't notice.

"That may be true, but this patient isn't any ordinary patient. Besides being a prominent lobbyist, he's a close friend of mine…Brian's too. He has a wicked temper, and has been in trouble with the law because of it. There's no problem with that this time, though. The other person threw the first punch, and neither party is filing charges. Anyway, during the fight, he injured his knee so badly that they needed to do a full replacement of the joint. Jason, that's our friend's name, had previously injured the knee in a skiing accident, and had thought of getting a partial knee replacement anyway. He underwent the total replacement three weeks ago, spent some time in a local physical therapy facility…one not as good as yours, obviously…but, as I said, is refusing any further treatment despite the fact he doesn't have full range of motion in the knee. Brian's afraid he might never be able to walk correctly, go skiing, play tennis, or hoops with his children again. We think he doesn't understand the long term implications of his injury, and the surgery he underwent."

"Interesting, and unfortunate for your friend, but what does all this have to do with me?"

"When Brian told me the story, I immediately thought of you. With your extensive background and training in physical therapy, nursing, and psychology, and with your excellent management and great interpersonal skills, I thought you might succeed where others have failed." He paused, and then added, "We want you to go to Washington to help treat our friend. Convince him to undergo physical therapy at their facility…using a program you will design for him, of course."

She took a deep breath, and stared directly into Dr. Gunther's brown eyes, trying to discern any hidden motive, but, as usual, couldn't read anything from his expression. *Very tempting offer. The case does sound interesting, and I probably can help him, but do I really want to leave New York right now? I have so much going on in my life here, both at the clinic and with Paul. On top of that, I sensed that Monica might be here in the city anyway. I could leave town only to end up missing her visit here. On the other hand, she would have called if it were a social visit; of course, if business, she might not. Who knows? She might be back in Washington already. If I accept his offer, I get to go there, and can surprise her, and probably learn what had upset her. Maybe. Maybe. Maybe. Oh, God, I don't know what to do. I need more guidance, more encouragement, before making any final decision. I think I'll put him off for now.*

"Your offer is very tempting, but I know for sure they have good physical therapists in the nation's capital. Some of the best are there, dealing with war injuries. I can't imagine they would have much trouble handling any difficult patient, including your friend."

Dr. Gunther brought a bent finger to his wide chin. "True, but several have already tried, and failed. I thought that if you went down, spent some time with him, preceded by a glowing letter of introduction about your unique professional skills from me, our friend might be amenable to seeing you, and ultimately agree to follow your advice. I think you'll succeed where others have failed."

"That's a long shot. I would bet those other therapists tried their best. There's no guarantee I'll do any better."

I've got to convince her. It's so important to me and my future. I'll have to appeal to that huge ego of hers. "True, but you have skills they don't. I've seen you manipulate patients, your colleagues, and even our hospital administrators to get them to do what you think is best, even if they had vehemently disagreed with you at the outset. You're our friend's best chance of literally getting back on his feet. I'd come with you to do the introduction personally, but I'm too busy with hospital duties…you know, finance meetings, curriculum meetings, the upcoming hospital recertification…those sorts of things. I couldn't possibly consider leaving. But you…"

"But, nothing," Corinne snapped, her voice loud, her fists clenched in her lap. She took a deep breath, and relaxed her fists. *Control, control, control.* She struggled to project a steady and calm voice. "Do you really think I've got nothing better to do but mosey down there to treat your friend, and ignore my duties here?"

"Of course not." Dr. Gunther waved his arms in the air again. "Please, don't take offense, Corinne. I know how busy you are, and how important your presence is to your Center. Believe me, I have no ulterior motives. My friend with the knee replacement saved my life years ago, and I owe him, and want him to receive the best possible treatment despite his resistance to both the physical and psychological approaches." He paused, took a deep breath before speaking. "Now, I'm asking you to help him as a personal favor to me." He paused again, waiting for Corinne to say something.

Corinne remained silent.

"I'll owe you a return favor in the future. You can count on me to reciprocate; you know that. I'll even sweeten the deal by picking up all your expenses while you're down there. Do I have to get down on my knees to beg? I will, if you want me to."

"Wow, you'll pay even in view of the hospital's dire economic condition and upcoming recertification problems? You must really want me to go." *It would be great to go, to look for Monica, but I've got to consider all the ramifications of leaving the city for several days, my patients, Paul, my scheduled meetings. They're all important, but I'm really worried about Monica, and it's a great opportunity to find her, a gift really, a gift I guess I shouldn't refuse.* "I guess, if you're that desperate, you really must owe your friend a lot."

"You'll never know the depth of that debt, Corinne. How about it? Will you do it as a favor to Brian and me…and our friend? He really needs your input. If you fail, at least we can say we tried our best…your best. Will you go? Please."

Corinne leaned forward, and pointed a finger at him. "I suppose, but not for the reasons you think. I could care less about what you owe your friend."

Corinne stood, and walked to the window, avoiding eye contact with Dr. Gunther. Instead, she gazed out at the building not ten feet from the hospital. *I prefer the view from my window; at least I can see the street. I guess I could reschedule my patients for next week. Other ther-apists could see those whose treatment can't wait. I would have to cancel my date with Paul. He had said he really wanted to go to that perfor-mance, but I'm sure he would understand.*

Dr. Gunther awaited her decision with his fingers crossed under his desk.

She turned from the window. "I'll go at your expense, but only to help the patient. My guess is that your Doctor Filmore may have been too rough, too direct in his approach. If you truly believe a gentler touch...my touch...will make a difference, I'm willing to give it a try. Who knows? Maybe I can get through to your friend." She resumed her seat. "Is there anything else you wanted to see me about? I've got a busy schedule today, thanks to you."

"No, that's everything. I'll call Dr. Filmore to tell him you're coming, and I'll write that referral letter for you today. You can fly out later tonight after your patients. Do you want me to make the arrange-ments for the flight and hotel room?"

"No. I'll make my own, if you don't mind. I may decide to drive down. It's only a five hour drive."

"The way you drive, I'll bet you do it in three."

"Maybe. I'll call you when I get back, or from Washington, if I have any problems."

Doctor Gunther extended his hand. "Thanks again, Corinne. You don't know how much this means to me."

Corinne huffed as she walked to the elevator. *That turned out to be easier than I expected. Didn't need your input this time Monica, and now, I'm free to look for you. I pray you're safe, and we have a wonder-fully peaceful and uneventful reunion.* As she pushed the elevator button, their last upsetting connection clouded Corinne's mind. *Come on, Mon-ica. Don't let me wait any longer. I'm still worried. Call me.*

As soon as Corinne had closed the door, Dr. Gunther mumbled, "Forgive me, Corinne, but I had no choice." He dialed his cell phone, smirking as he awaited the completion of the call.

CHAPTER 5

Corinne marched back to her office in half the time, arranging lunch with Paul along the way. He sounded upbeat as he told her to pick the restaurant, and that he would meet her at the clinic.

Paul arrived fifteen minutes early, and busied himself by flipping through one of the magazines in the waiting room. He found an article concerning the growing crime problem in New York.

"Sorry to keep you waiting." Corinne entered the waiting room wearing a knee length, blue skirt, white blouse and high black boots with short heels. She stretched her arms up as she pulled on her matching blue jacket. Her breasts, in sharp contrast to her slim waist, were plentiful, and put an extra stretch on the buttons of her blouse as she donned the jacket.

Paul closed the magazine, and stood. His mouth fell open, as his eyes examined her from head to foot. "Wow! Don't let any of your horny patients catch you wearing that outfit. I might get more competition than I can handle."

"I doubt there are many men you couldn't handle, but thanks anyway."

"My pleasure. I still wonder why you let me hang around you in the first place. Not that I'm complaining, mind you. It's simply that you're so beautiful." He put his arms around her and, as he did so, he dropped the magazine in the wastebasket behind her. "And I'm so…"

"You're so full of it that I can't believe anything you say, You Upstart Casanova. A Romeo you're not, but keep trying. The effort is appreciated, no matter how much bullshit it contains. As to why I let you hang out with me, maybe it's because I admire those dark suits you're always wearing."

"Or maybe it's my dark side that attracts you. You're always trying to analyze me, trying to find out what makes me tick, what constitutes that dark side, the side that does so well in the business world. I sometimes wonder why you didn't become a psychiatrist rather than a nurse and physical therapist."

"I will admit I do enjoy psychology, but I fell in love with nursing, and later with the challenge of physical therapy."

"Is that what I represent to you, a challenge? A difficult patient, recovered from his physical ailment, and now someone to analyze. Is that what I am to you?"

Corinne pushed him away in mock protest. "Huh, I don't see you as a patient of any type now that you've recovered from your injuries...thanks to me, I might point out." She took a deep breath, and placed both hands on her hips. "Although your dark side does interest me, I have not been trying to analyze you, or change you. I know better than that. That doesn't work in any relationship that's going to last. If I tried that on you, you'd leave faster than if I told you I worked as an undercover agent from the treasury department assigned to check the last seven years of your tax returns." She smiled. "Besides, your dark side is offset by a much lighter personality, the one that loves opera, ballet and Broadway shows. It's a side you try to hide, but you've allowed me to view it, and become a part of it. I appreciate that."

"Oh, you see me as your sugar daddy, huh?"

Corinne punched him in his chest, feigning anger. "No, of course not. You know better than that. I never see any hint of that dark, serious, business side when we're together, and believe me we all have a dark side of one type or another. The nuns in my grammar school used to emphasize that the Devil tries to get into each of us to play with that dark side. He attracts us with empty promises, and deceives us into thinking he could give us anything we want."

Paul chuckled. "Well, excuse me, Sister Corinne. I didn't know you were so religious."

"I'm not now, but I used to be." Corinne's eyes and mouth became sullen, her speech slow and deliberate. "Almost became a nun way back when. My sister even encouraged me. She said I always tried to be a 'goody-two-shoes,' out to help every kid I ran into, but, no, I decided on medicine instead. I figured I could help peoples' minds and bodies more than helping their souls, I guess." She paused, looking Heavenward. "It was one of the few times I didn't listen to her advice. I often wonder if I made a mistake. I guess I'll never know."

He chuckled. "I'm glad you didn't. I would hate the thoughts of dating a nun now, but are you saying I don't have a soul, that I am the Devil incarnate, ready to swoop down upon you with my sports car, black suits, and gorgeous smile to attract you to my dark side?"

A bright twinkle jumped into Corinne's eyes, as she fluttered her eyelashes teasingly at him. "Of course not, but you're a different person when I'm with you. I prefer that person, not the one who functions so well in that corporate world of yours."

"But suppose my dark side comes out someday. What then?"

"I guess that could happen, and I probably will hate it if it does, but I can't imagine you'd be all that bad."

"Oh, really? Maybe red horns will suddenly sprout through my scalp, and I'll start dragging my tail around behind me. What will you think then?"

"Then, I'll know I made a mistake for believing in your good side, and I'll be mad at myself for not seeing right through you."

"But would you leave me, or stick with me?"

"That depends on whether you stick me with those horns, or your pointed tail, and how much I get hurt in the process of your transformation into the Devil." She paused, took another deep breath. "I guess I'm in for the long run, and if I'm not hurt too much, I'd take the dark side with the light." She took another deep breath before continuing. "Through all my experience in the field of psychology, I've learned that personalities are package deals. They don't come a la Carte."

She kissed him so gently he barely felt her lips. He loved the feel of her thick lips, the passion that emanated from her light blue eyes, and especially her light touch which usually drove his desire through the roof. This time, however, she didn't have loving on her mind. She poked her stiff index finger as hard as she could into his chest, her eyes wide and ablaze with seriousness he had never seen before. "But let me warn you, Mister. I'm not really the forgiving nun I almost became. So, you better not hurt me too much, if you know what's good for you. Do you understand?"

"Perfectly, Miss Corinne, 'My Boss Forever,' Day." Paul assumed a sheepish grin. His hands flew into the air, fingers shaking, as though fear coursed through them.

"Now, enough philosophy and psychology! Let's eat. I'm starved."

Corinne had picked an upscale restaurant that offered excellent cuisine on Tenth Avenue. She ordered veal Marsala with al-dente pasta. Paul had chicken Florentine. The luscious fragrances of garlic, parsley and rosemary percolated through the air, stimulating their taste buds. Corinne passed on the wine, choosing sparkling water instead. She sampled Paul's Chablis though. Its flinty flavor and aroma more than complemented the meal; it enhanced it. Elvis serenaded them with "Love Me Tender," through hidden speakers above their heads. Corinne hummed the tune.

"I love this place." Corinne rested her chin on both hands, elbows on the table, her eyes riveted on Paul.

"It's not your usual choice for lunch." Paul sipped his wine. "You must have something horrific to tell me at these prices."

Corinne's eyes remained glued on him. "Is it that obvious?"

"It's easy to see something's on your mind. Is it your sister?"

"She's part of it. My anxiety is totally gone, but I still haven't heard from her, and she's still not answering her cell phone. That's unlike her, and it worries me. Did your contacts find out anything?"

"Afraid not, but they'll keep looking, I promise."

Corinne took a deep breath, and blew it out slowly before speaking. "The head of the hospital asked me to go to Washington to consult on a friend of his as a patient."

"Let me guess. You're going to combine the patient visit with the search for your sister."

"Yes, exactly! I've got to check on Monica for myself. I can barely sense her. That's happened a few times in our lives, but this time, I'm worried because of the intensity of the reaction yesterday. I've got to go. I have to know if she's okay."

"I'm guessing that means our weekend plans are cancelled. Correct?"

"I'm afraid so." Corinne lowered her head, her eyes perusing her partially eaten meal. She moved the pasta around with her fork, piling it at the edge of the plate. "Sorry."

Paul laughed. "There's nothing to be sorry about." He used his bent index finger to raise her chin until their gazes met. "I understand. After all, you're worried about Monica. There'll be other weekends and other concerts. I'll give the tickets away. No use wasting them, and I really don't want to go to the concert without you. When are you leaving?"

Corinne smiled at Paul's understanding. "Right after lunch. I've cancelled all my patients this afternoon. I'm going home to pack, and then I'm going to drive down. I knew you'd understand."

"Sure you did. That's why I got the 'You're terrific, Paul,' at the office, and then this place for lunch. So, not only do I have to be gracious enough to understand, I get to pick up the tab for the meal. You're sneaky, Corinne."

"My plans had nothing to do with lunch."

"Right." He took a big gulp of his wine. "You say you're driving. Care for some company? We can take my sports car. I'll even risk my life, and let you drive."

"That would be great, but what about all that work you're always telling me you have to do?"

"Oh, someone will cover for me. I'll see to that. I was actually going to ask you to accompany me to Washington. I have some business there that needs my attention."

Paul studied his wine, swirling it as he spoke. The color was pleasing, and fit the fragrance perfectly. "I can keep you company on the trip down, and I'll have Kevin drive the Rolls. That way, I'll have some decent transportation in Washington while you're playing Kamikaze with my Lamborghini. I'll even pick up all your speeding tickets again."

"Paul, you have to understand that I may not be able to spend much time with you." Corinne's expression turned serious. Her hands gripped his across the table. "I mean, I'm going to be extremely busy, both working for Doctor Gunther and looking for my sister. I'd love to be with you as much as possible, and we can try to get together if you come, but I can't promise anything. Work and my search have to come first."

"Maybe I can help you search, and I'm sure we'll manage to spend at least a few minutes together, maybe another expensive lunch, or a few intimate moments at night before bed. That would certainly be better than working here all weekend without ever seeing you. I'll settle for whatever I can get." He slid his chair around the table, placing it next to hers. He leaned forward until their lips were almost touching, their eyes locked in a mutual, loving embrace. "Even a few minutes with you will be worth any inconvenience, or price."

"Oh, Paul, it's not fair to use flattery against me." As their lips were about to touch, she added, "Okay. You win. We'll go together."

CHAPTER 6

The ride to Washington proved terrifying. Corinne had pushed Paul's Lamborghini hard, slowing to the speed limit only when forced to because of traffic. She swerved around cars, and constantly talked about her twin. Most of the time, her eyes were on him, not the road; Paul couldn't fathom how she avoided the other cars. He swore she never once applied the brakes. Petrified, Paul had shut his eyes for most of the trip. He had prayed, something he had sworn off long ago.

Paul paced the hotel room, pausing only long enough to snuff out his cigar. He lit another. His stomach still lurched two hours after they had arrived. He rubbed his abdomen. It hurt. He burped up acid. *I should have flown rather than risk my life with her. The woman is a driving menace; I should report her to the DMV so they would revoke her license. The roads would be safer. I would be safer.* He popped another antacid. It didn't help. He studied his cigar. He had started smoking again, a habit he thought he had licked.

Corinne's driving had only added to his concerns. Unanswered questions jumped through his mind. *Who would dare kill two of my men, and why? Did drugs really fit into the answer? What about Corinne's sister? Where was she, and was she truly in trouble as Corinne suspected? Could he find her before something happened to her? How would Corinne react if not, and what about Sage?* He grimaced. The image of Sage, possibly sleeping with the senator's son infuriated him. *What could she possibly be thinking? Doesn't she realize such a relationship would destroy Frank's run for the White House?* He took a long drag on the cigar. He popped another antacid, and then sucked on the cigar once more. Neither helped him, nor brought him any satisfaction. "Damn it all! I wish I had some answers."

"What's the matter?" Corinne asked as she towel dried her hair.

After a brief bout of coughing, Paul finally spoke. "Oh, I thought I'd be able to conduct some business while we were down here, but one of the people I'm supposed to meet isn't anywhere to be found."

"I thought you came here to be with me. You said we would have a few minutes together. Remember? How about now?"

Paul reached for her. He wrapped his arms around her slim waist, and drew her moist lips to his. He felt hypnotized by her glowing sapphire eyes. Subtle, and alluring facial features, including prominent cheekbones, and a diminutive cleft chin, added to her beauty. Her body still steamed beneath the robe from her shower. Smelling her freshness stimulated him more than he could control, but her kiss sent his desire into the stratosphere. *Not now! I need to concentrate on work.* "You were the one who said we might not have a lot of time together. Remember?"

"Well, I've got a few minutes before I have to leave." She talked with her lips brushing his cheek. "We could make the best of it."

He fought the urge to whisk her to bed. "Not now; I'm not in the mood. My mind is on business at the moment, and my business here is important."

She squeezed him, brushing her lips lightly against his, causing his whole body to stiffen. "And I'm not?"

He held her at arm's length. "Of course, you are! That's why I came, but I hoped that while you were with your patient, I could get some work done." His heartbeat quickened; his knees weakened. He almost hated his physical reaction to her in this provocative mood. No woman had ever affected him as much as this seductress, and yet she could be so cold, so distant at times. He didn't understand her, and, right now, he didn't really care. Trying to regain control, he looked over her shoulder at the phone, wishing it to ring.

She caught the change in his gaze. "I can see that your mind isn't on me at all." She tightened the belt of her robe as she walked toward the bathroom, each step deliberate, slow, and with an exaggerated hip movement.

It drove his desire even higher. He clenched his fists, digging his nails into his palms.

"I'm going to get dressed, and head for the hospital. I'm supposed to meet with that patient today. One of us had better get some work done on this trip. Maybe you'll be in the mood later. You'd better hope I still am."

He inhaled, trying to quell his passion. He bit his lip. "Oh, don't get mad, Corinne. Of course, I want to be with you, but I'm annoyed right now because of the way my associates are behaving, or misbehaving, I should say."

"Your dark side is showing again, Paul. Have some patience."

"Yes, Nurse Day. I'll try to be brighter. Isn't that the word you used? I also promise to be more attentive to you, My Beautiful Caregiver, as soon as I can. Now, am I forgiven?"

Corinne flashed her eyelids at him as she entered the bathroom. "Maybe. Let me think it over. Meanwhile, I'll let you take me to dinner and a show tonight. I hear there are some great ones playing. It'll make up for the concert we're missing in New York."

"That's fine," Paul yelled through the door. "How late are you going to be at the hospital?"

"I don't know. I'll have to call you later. After the hospital, I want to check on my sister. I'm still trying to reach her. There's no answer at her apartment, her office, or on her cell phone. I'm worried sick about her. I hope she's not out of town on a case, or hurt somewhere. I can't get over the feeling that something's wrong."

"Now, don't go worrying yourself over nothing, Corinne. I'll bet she's here in town, and doesn't want to be disturbed. You and I have been in that position. Remember last year, Las Vegas? We turned off our cell phones for more than a few days." When Corinne didn't respond, he added, "I'm sure she's fine. She'll show up, don't worry. In any case my associates will keep looking for her."

"Well, if we do find her, I'll try to get her to come with us tonight. Okay?"

"That would be great. You know I'm dying to meet her."

The phone finally rang.

Paul ran to answer it. "Yeah," he said, breathless.

"Hi, Paul." Senator Stern sounded as breathless as he.

"Frank? What's up, and how the hell did you know I'd be at this hotel?"

"Your secretary told me. Listen. Something's happened."

"What?" Paul closed his eyes so tightly that the muscles of his forehead and cheeks hurt. *The last thing I need now are more problems, especially concerning Frank.*

"I've been followed by some private investigator. Her name's Monica Day. She's got some pictures of me that could be damaging."

"What kind of pictures?" Paul glanced at the bathroom, hoping Corinne wouldn't come out to ask who had called. *Great! Corinne's sister is now mixed up with Frank's problem. How am I ever going to straighten everything out?* He grabbed his aching stomach.

"Apparently, she's been taking pictures of almost everything I do. So, she's probably got shots of you and I together...not good for my image, or your businesses. Who knows how long she's been following me? She may even have caught us on our trips to Vegas and Atlantic City. God only knows what else she has, but don't worry, I've got plans to take care of the problem."

Paul's eyes sprang open. *Oh, no! I can't afford any more mistakes. I don't even want to hear his plan. He's not thinking straight.* Paul's voice grew louder. "That's not a good idea." *I've got to stop him before he does something we both might regret, but I've got to be careful not to add to his fear.* He forced his voice to quiet. "Let me handle it. I have all sorts of connections at police headquarters, and I may have a connection with your Monica Day. You'd be surprised how I know her, but that's a story for another time. Besides, if I get caught meddling with her, there won't be as much of an uproar. You have to stay clear of her. It's the best for your campaign. Catch my drift?"

"Oh, I hear you, but I think I have a much safer way. It's foolproof."

"I don't want you to do anything," Paul shouted. Fearing that Corinne may have heard his bellow, he listened at the bathroom door, heard a hairdryer blasting, and breathed out audibly into the phone. When he again spoke, he forced his voice to be deliberate and low, and staccato. "Listen to me. You stop whatever you were planning, right now. I'll take care of the detective. You're too much in the spotlight. Let's not ruin everything you've worked on so long by overreacting. You keep your nose to the political grindstone, and enjoy the company of your beautiful girlfriend."

"That's another thing. I don't even know where Sage is. Haven't seen her since..."

"Since when?" Paul interrupted, covering his eyes with his hand, and shaking his head. . *Why did I ever get involved with both a stupid senator and that dumb broad?*

"Since a few nights ago. I think there's something wrong with our relationship, but I have no idea what. She's not acting the same toward me. It really bothers me."

"Maybe it's PMS, or something similar, something temporary. You know how fickle these women can be."

"Maybe, but I doubt it. She's changed, and I don't know why."

"Listen, I wouldn't worry about that right now. We have bigger issues confronting us."

Senator Stern paused before speaking again. "I guess, but it seems to me that everything I had planned is coming unglued."

"Now, you listen to me, Mister Future President…remember those are the high stakes we're pursuing…we can handle *anything* that comes along. Trust me, everything is going to be fine. I'll handle the private detective my way, and I'll track down Sage for you. I'll find out what's bothering her, and, if I can, I'll even fix it between you two. You two are perfect together. I don't want anything to interfere with that."

"Wow. Could you do all that for me?"

"Sure. Corinne is going to be at the hospital most of the day. I'll spend the day fixing your life for you, but I want you to promise you'll stay put, and let me do the work."

"Well…" Another long pause followed while Senator Stern considered what Paul had offered, followed by a deep sigh of acceptance and relief, "…I suppose you're right. Okay. We'll do it your way. I'll wait to here from you. I'm in my office, but call me on my cell phone in case I have to leave for some reason."

"Good. I'll be in touch." After hearing the phone "click," Paul slammed it onto its cradle. "Damn you, Sage!" After a brief pause, he added, "Damn you too, Senator! Neither of you know what you're risking by your reckless actions. We're talking the highest political position in the country and the most powerful in the world, and you two are playing games that could ruin everything." He relit the cigar, and watched the smoke encircle his head. *I really detest these things, but, right now, they're my only solace.*

Paul's cell phone rang as Corinne headed out the door. She blew him a kiss. He returned the gesture as he retrieved his cell phone from his shirt pocket.

"It's me," the female voice said.

"Sage," he yelled. "Where have you been? What are you up to? Where the hell are you? You said you were going to stay with the senator until I called. He's looking for you."

"I know. Something came up."

"Something came up?" He took a deep breath. "Come on, Sage. Nothing could have come up that is more important than the man you love, the man you're supposed to be helping achieve the Presidency. Don't you realize the consequences should your actions ever get out to the news media? They'd eat it up, and both of you along with it."

"Sure, I understand perfectly. You don't have to worry about me though. I'm doing everything I'm supposed to, including sticking close to Frank. Honest."

His closed his eyes. His voice calmed. "Now, why is it I don't believe you?"

"Because you spend too much time around people who lie."

"That may be, but you better not turn out to be one of those people. You better not disappoint Frank. Where are you now?"

"At Frank's home. I arrived only minutes ago. He's real happy to see me. I told him I had some shopping to do. Don't worry, he bought it, and, besides, it's true. I'll show you what I bought when we meet, if you want."

Paul relaxed. Maybe Frank could salvage his campaign after all. "At least you're where you should be. I want you to meet me at the Essex hotel, room 843 in one hour. I'd like to discuss what's going on between you and Frank. I told him I'd try to straighten out any apparent problems. So, please come here as soon as possible."

"This place is crawling with reporters right now. One of them followed me on my shopping errands. It's too risky to leave. They're liable to see the two of us together. Besides, Frank wants me to be with him right now."

"What's all the fuss?"

"His advisors want Frank to make another statement about the assassination. I think the press wants him to say something about his candidacy. I talked to one reporter. He said the press thinks he'd be a fool not to make his move now before anyone else does. They expect him to grab as much political power and support as he can. The publicity generated is going be worth millions. It might even ensure his victory. Frank's not so sure, though. I'm trying to help him decide what's best."

"Okay. In that case, you'd better stay there with him. He'll want you by his side, if he does make that announcement."

"That's what I figured. Do you want me to call you when they leave?"

"Yeah, as soon as they leave. I need to talk to you without Frank present. Please remember what's at stake."

"I know, Paul. Believe me, I know. Don't worry. I'll stay with Frank. His worries about me will be all gone in the next week, or so. You'll see."

"Why a week?"

"I told you. Tom and I have been making big plans for his father's birthday. We don't want anyone else to know, especially Frank. It'll ruin everything we have planned. We should have it all arranged by next weekend. Then, things will be back to normal around here. Frank will be happy, and will be able to concentrate on the Presidential race. You'll see."

"I hope you're right. We're all counting on you."

"Frank is coming. Got to run. Bye."

Paul closed his cell phone, pausing for only a fraction of a second before opening it again. With a snarl, he pressed a speed dial button. "Kevin, get over to the hotel right away. We've got some more work to do today."

CHAPTER 7

Corinne had no difficulty negotiating the corridors of the Veterans Hospital on her journey to Doctor Filmore's office. Arriving exactly at her appointed time, she knocked once. A squeaky, male voice immediately invited her in, calling her by name.

Dr. Filmore stood as she entered. As they shook, Corinne noted his small and weak hand, almost flaccid in her grip. *It's no wonder you're friends with Dr. Gunther. You even look alike.* He stood a full six inches shorter than Corinne, and had a rotund body with a stub for a nose. He wore Coke bottle glasses that barely hooked over his protruding ears. *You resemble the mad scientist's assistant from every horror movie I've ever seen.* Her mind flipped through a list of several congenital deformities, but couldn't match his features with any Latin title. She would have to discretely ask Dr. Gunther about his friend's strange appearance when she returned to New York.

"I'm so glad you could come, Miss Day." Dr. Filmore's voice rose in pitch almost as high as that of Dr. Gunther. "Dr. Gunther, Steve, has told me so much about you, and how good you are with patients. Let's hope my patient benefits from your experience." He escorted her to one of the overstuffed chairs, gently gripping her elbow in the process. He released her arm only after she had been firmly seated.

"I certainly hope I can help him, Dr. Filmore, but sometimes a tender approach doesn't always work, even for me."

After resuming his seat, he gaped at Corinne. She squirmed, refusing to look directly at him. His eyes drifted downward. The simple green dress she had donned made no attempt to hide her figure or her shapely legs.

I'm not sure I've ever seen a woman as beautiful as this one. Steve's always been a good judge of beauty, that's for sure, but I'd better get back to the work at hand before I get too distracted. "Possibly, but I'm sure you'll succeed where the rest of us have failed. You have so many…" he paused, searching for the appropriate words, "…talents beyond what we have offered him. You have a unique perspective of a patient's medical and psychological problems. I'm sure you'll succeed. Maybe after you've seen the patient, we could discuss what techniques you used to convince him to cooperate over a cup of coffee. I'll buy."

"Okay." Corinne eyed him, wondering if the small man's interest truly centered on her success with his patient, or simply on her. "I assume you have your patient coming in today. Tell me all you know about him."

"Ahem. Okay. His chart is on my computer." After a few keystrokes, he turned the computer screen so both he and Corinne could see it. "Dr. Gunther and I became friends with the patient many years ago on the local golf course. He is, or rather, used to be, a much better player than either of us, almost professional. Do you play golf, by the way, Miss Day?"

"No, I never took it up, and please, call me Corinne."

"Fine. Dr. Gunther filled you in on most of it. The full reports of the fight, and knee replacement surgery are there for your inspection. Our problem with him started after surgery. He tolerated the pain…or seemed to, anyway. For no reason we could ascertain, he started giving our therapists a hard time. He refused all efforts to help him. He can walk, but with a limp that, if not corrected, will damage the bony structures attached to his artificial knee. Ultimately the artificial knee will be damaged. It'll need replacement, and probably bony reconstruction of his leg, a much more complicated surgery. We want to prevent that."

"Does he understand the consequences of not following your treatment plan?"

"It seems he does, but he's a stubborn man who is used to getting his way. He thinks he can order his body to fix his gait by sheer will, I guess."

"That's exceedingly stupid."

"You and I know that, but he doesn't. We told him as much, and he walked…I should say limped…out of here, grumbling that we didn't know what we were talking about."

"I guess the direct approach is not going to work on him."

"No, I wouldn't tell him he's stupid, if I were you. We tried that once, and it backfired on us, scaring him away. There has to be a better way to get through to him."

"Don't worry, I'll be more tactful. I see that his chart indicates he's not married."

"Is that important?"

"Well, if he has someone in his life, a wife, a girlfriend, or any close friend, I might be able to use that person as a lever to give him a reason to succeed. That person may provide the impetus for him to cooperate, and try harder. I could then use that person as his at-home personal trainer, so to speak."

"Good idea. I hadn't thought of that. He certainly won't do it for me, now that he feels I've attacked him. He'll probably never want to play golf with me again." He leaned back in his chair, searching his mind. "If memory serves me, he had a male buddy who visited him several times. I think I've even seen him at the golf course. I've never been introduced to him though."

"That would be perfect."

"I'll call the patient, and ask him to bring that friend with him. As an excuse, I'll tell him I saw them together in the hospital, that I saw him on the golf course, and am anxious to meet him. I'll suggest the three of us have a drink later. I'll clue his friend in on what we're trying to do. After that, you can instruct him on what you need him to do at home."

"That'll be perfect. It's a little deceptive, but not unethical. Sometimes, we have to outsmart our patients for their own good."

"Exactly!" He stood, and walked to the window, staring at the downtown traffic. "It's now up to you and your talents, Corinne."

"I hope I can live up to your expectations, Dr. Filmore."

"You can print out anything you think you might need, and please, Corinne, call me Brian, at least when we're alone. I don't want to stand on formality either."

"Okay, Brian," Corinne scrolled through the chart, deciding after reading most of it that printing it would not prove helpful.

She stood. "I'm going to head…" Suddenly, Corinne froze. She grabbed the desk for support. She felt lightheaded. The room began a dizzying spin around her. Sweat began to stream down her forehead. It burned her eyes. *Oh, no! Not again! Not here! Not now!* Her hands began to quiver. She stared at them. She didn't recognize them. They couldn't be hers. Her skin should be a ruddy tan. The hands before her had ashen, lifeless skin. Her vision blurred. She tried to focus on the computerized chart, trying desperately to get her mind focused on the reality in front of her, but this couldn't be reality. Monica's image appeared on the screen, and then lifted off the computer. Monica opened her mouth to scream in terror, but no sound emerged. As Monica's eyes slowly closed, the image settled back into the monitor, and a cloud streamed across the screen, blurring the image. Then, with the same rapidity that it had appeared, the apparition vanished, and so did Corinne's brief connection with her sister.

Corinne felt an overwhelming desire to run from the office, as fast, and as far as she possibly could.

CHAPTER 8

Corinne's compulsion to flee continued to build until she could no longer control the urge. She simply had to get out of that office, away from the walls now impinging on her from all sides, and into the fresh air. She tried to run, but couldn't. In fact, she couldn't move at all. She could hardly feel her legs. Her heart pounded. Her mind became clouded, adding to her terror; she couldn't concentrate on anything. *Where am I? What's happening to me?*

With great effort, she turned her head toward Dr. Filmore. The exertion increased her dizziness. His blurred image stood before the window, still admiring the view, unaware of her panic.

She shook her head, trying to clear it. It didn't help. Instead, the effort produced severe pounding from temple to temple. Darkness began to overshadow her. She tried to take a step. Her legs refused to move. Her calf muscles cramped. She shook her head again, amplifying both her dizziness and the pain. She forced one hand against her forehead, the effort bringing spasms to the muscles in her arms. Her head pounded. She had to do something about it before it crushed her brain, her intellect. She forced both palms against her temples to rebuff the pounding, the effort only intensifying it.

She felt nauseated. A dull pain developed in the pit of her stomach, increased in strength, and then radiated as a crushing pain into her chest. She dropped her hands to her sternum. With lightning speed, the pain shot to the left side of her jaw. Breathing became more difficult, each breath promising to be her last.

She tried to concentrate on her present location, but her thinking became increasingly fuzzy. *Where am I, an office? What am I doing here? Oh, yeah, Dr. Filmore…his patient. Oh, God! What's happening, a heart attack? What's wrong? What the hell is going on? Oh, God! I feel so sick. Help me, someone…anyone. Please! Dr. Filmore, Brian, please!*

"You can see from the chart that he received the best this hospital could offer."

Corinne could barely hear Dr. Filmore's voice. It sounded far away, and much too faint to distinguish his words.

"Do you want a cup of coffee while I make that phone call?"

Filmore! What's the matter with you? Keep your coffee, You Twerp. I need help, not a damn cup of coffee. You couldn't keep your eyes off me a few minutes ago. Now that I'm in trouble, you refuse to even look in my direction. Turn around. Can't you see I'm sick? I need help...now. Oh, please, Dr. Filmore. Brian, look at me. Help me. Please.

Tears began to stream down her cheeks, taking the tiny amount of makeup she wore with them. Her nausea increased. The room spun faster, adding to her disorientation. She opened her mouth in an attempt to scream. Nothing. Total silence now enveloped her. She felt totally alone and helpless. *Oh, my God, I'm dying.*

Corinne watched in horror as the already blurred contents of the room glowed red. She blinked her eyes. The red hue morphed to white, the brightness stinging her eyes. She grabbed her chest as another episode of excruciating pain pierced it, front to back this time. Almost immediately, another crushing pain seized her, emanating deep within her chest. Her breathing ceased. *Oh, my God! My heart!* As her left arm dropped to her side, she felt numbness race down its length, rendering it useless. She forced a breath, her effort producing a barely audible wheeze. It doubled her pain. A tremor spread over her body. Total darkness began a relentless descent upon her. Her body became limp.

"Have you given any further thought to having coffee with me, Corinne," Dr. Filmore asked as he turned back toward her. Seeing Corinne's terrified expression, and her limp body heading for the floor, he rushed toward her. "Corinne, are you all right? What's the matter?"

She tried to answer, but still couldn't get her trembling lips to form any recognizable words. The room rocked beneath her. She watched Dr. Filmore's approach in slow motion. She could see his lips moving, but still couldn't hear a sound. Her body collapsed under her. *Oh, God, I'm dying.*

After what seemed a full hour to Corinne, Dr. Filmore reached her, catching her limp body as her knees finally collapsed totally. His voice remained miles away.

"It must be these bright lights. It's awfully hot in here, isn't it? Come on. Let's sit down for a few minutes."

As he carried her to the couch, she gasped for air, the inrush burning her parched throat. She tried to remain conscious, forcing herself to remember...*an office, a patient. That's it, a patient and a doctor.*

Dr. Filmore placed her on the couch, elevating her feet. Checking her pulse, he found it rapid and shallow, consistent with the paleness of her skin. "Corinne? Can you hear me?"

Her normal ruddy color began to return as her pulse increased in volume, and slowed its horrific pace. She rubbed her chest, finding the entire area tender, the pain only partially abated. As her vision began to clear, she reached up with shaking hands, and grabbed the back of Dr. Filmore's neck, drawing him closer to her. Her body still trembled. Tears flowed down her cheeks in torrents. She clung to him until the room finally stopped spinning, and her lightheadedness faded.

"Can...barely...hear...anything. What...the...hell...happened?" She gasped for air between words. "I...can't...remember."

Dr Filmore regarded her with clinical precision and detachment. "I think you were about to faint." Corinne released her grasp on his neck. He lowered her until she once again rested on her back. "It probably became too hot in here, that's all. Your pulse is returning to normal. You'll be all right now."

"I had...so much...pain."

"Maybe we should get you to the Emergency Department for an ECG, and have you examined right away. Has this ever happened to you before?"

Corinne's mind finally cleared, and began filling in the gaps left by the episode. "Yes, it happened last...in New York." She tried her legs, finding them stiff, but movable. "But this seemed much worse...the pain...the fear." She started to sit up, but Dr. Filmore pushed her back down.

"Take getting up slowly, Corinne. Don't want you fainting again."

She braced herself on one elbow. Her headache faded. "It's all right; I'm feeling better. Thank you." Her eyes opened wide, her voice squeaky from her weakened state. "It's not me. It's my sister, Monica. Something's wrong...terribly wrong."

Monica Day eased her Chrysler to a halt in front of her office building. She jumped out of the car, snapping her head toward the corner she had negotiated only moments before. No cars had followed her. She checked the other end of the street. Nothing moved. She climbed the steps in the front of the building two at a time, pausing at the front door to check the street once more. Convinced she had not been followed, she tried the door, confirming it remained securely locked, as she had left it.

Her latest case, which consisted of a supposedly simple data gathering exercise, had taken a turn she had never expected. It made her jumpy. Still sensing danger, she entered the building, her hand unlatching her purse, exposing the Colt automatic she always carried.

She climbed the wooden stairs to the second floor, wincing each time one of the stairs creaked under her weight. As she mounted the empty landing, she noticed a light beneath the door to the office next to hers. She knocked hard to ensure her neighbor heard her.

The door opened slowly, as a pair of eyes peaked out. She recognized them as belonging to John Zachary.

"Monica, I wondered when you'd be back. Are you here to catch up on some work like me?"

"Have to, unfortunately. I stopped by to thank you for your tip about Sage. I flew to New York, and you were right. That woman really isn't what she makes herself out to be. The information is exactly the sort of thing I've been looking for."

"Great! I knew I could be of some service to you one day. That's why I moved into this building in the first place. Did you know that?"

"Really? That's news to me. What do you mean?" She studied his eyes. Did that twitch of his eyelid indicate a lie would be forthcoming? Did she detect a hint of nervousness in his voice? How many times had he lied to her already? She had not really trusted him since they had first met, although she couldn't put her finger on what bothered her about him. He had given her a good tip, but had refused to reveal his source. How far could she trust him?

"Well, I didn't tell you before because I thought you'd think I was crazy, maybe even a stalker. I'm not, believe me." He bowed his head, his eyes peaking over the top of his wire rimmed glasses. "Truth is, I spotted you following Sage one day. I knew Sage from New York many years ago. I knew she had to be up to no good. She never is. When I later found out you were a detective, I moved my office here to keep track of your investigation, and thought maybe I could help you in some way."

"So, that's why you showed up while I tailed her last week."

"Precisely." He raised his head, smiled and pointed a finger at her. "That way, I could tell you who she is, and could help you. I knew I could help."

"Well, I do appreciate it. Your tip led me to information that will prove helpful to me, and distressing to my client, I'm afraid."

"Glad to be of help."

"I still am curious about your motive, though. Why do you want to help me? Do you expect a reward, or some compensation? What are you after?"

He lowered his eyes again. "I'd rather not say." He spoke barely above a whisper. "Please don't ask me anymore."

Monica did not want to pressure him. He had been a good source, and didn't want him clamming up on her. To change the direction of the conversation, she glanced down the hallway. "Tell me, has anything unusual, or suspicious happened around here in the last day, or so?"

"Nothing I noticed." His gaze following hers toward her office. He then glanced into his office, checking for intruders, but found none. "Why do you ask?"

"Oh, I've had a few things stolen from my office recently, nothing major, or important, though. Happen to you?"

He scrunched up his thin nose, the motion raising his glasses. "No, but I'll keep my eyes open when you're not around from now on. I'll pay special attention to your office. I'll let you know if I see, or hear anything. Maybe I should have your cell phone number in case I catch someone snooping around."

"Sure, good idea." She placed her laptop case on the floor. She reached into her purse, pushed aside the Sunday newspaper, and extracted a business card. She handed it to him. "My cell phone died while on my way to New York. So, you couldn't have called me anyway, but I've got a new one now. Phone number's the same. Thanks for agreeing to keep an eye on my office. I really appreciate it. Talk to you later, John. Don't work too hard." Retrieving her laptop, she headed down the hallway.

"Maybe we both should consider an intruder alarm system. I'll look into it, and get back to you with some quotes."

"Thanks. I'd appreciate that."

She didn't really suspect John of breaking into her office. She imagined the little man as more the informant type than thief, but she had been wrong about people before. She made a mental note to keep him on the top of both her suspect and informant lists.

After John closed his door, Monica pulled her gun from her purse, flipping the safety off in one fluid motion, and walked the remaining distance to her office. Opening the door, she stood, legs apart, and gun at her right shoulder, ready for a confrontation. She saw no one. She entered, reconfirmed that no intruder hid behind either the door, or desk, and locked the door behind her. Using the same cautious technique, she checked her coat closet. Only a rack of familiar coats greeted her.

"No one home today, I guess." She placed her gun in the top drawer of the desk, and then laid the newspaper, her purse, and the laptop on its glass surface. "But it sure as hell looks as if my phantom intruder visited again." Who could it be, and how does he get in…pick the lock…use a key? She checked all the drawers, none of which had a lock. "Humph. This time he took my notebooks…even the unused ones…and my phone directory. Last time he pinched personal photos, this time notebooks. I don't get the connection. What's he after? Taking personal effects doesn't make any sense. They're not worth anything." She stood, scanning the room for anything that might have been touched by the thief. She clenched her fists. She looked up at the ceiling. "I'll catch you one of these days, You Meddlesome Thief. No one takes anything from me without asking… and without paying the price. Your days are numbered, Phantom. I'm going to set up a camera to catch you in action. That should give me your identity." She raised her fist at her imaginary foe. "I wonder if you picked the locks on my file cabinets, and stole anything from there?"

She stood, turning toward her cabinets. The newspaper headline caught her eye. "POLICE BAFFLED BY KING GEORGE MOTEL MURDERS."

"What's this? Those files can wait." She retrieved the newspaper. The article told the story of the discovery of the bodies, identifying the motel room number, the probable time of death, their names, and the current police theories on the murders, as explained by Detective Hank Wu of the Washington detective bureau. The article ended with a plea from Detective Wu for help from the public, and a phone number for contacting him.

"Oh my God!" A wave of excitement flooded her body. "That's where I took those photos. I actually have photos of the killer." She took a pad from her pocket book, and wrote the victims' names: 'James Wyman, and Chuck Florentino' in large letters. After reading of their possible connection with the New York mob, she added: 'Probably New York crime family,' adding under this, 'Sage Browning! Senator Frank Stern! Senator Richard Edmond!??? Camarazza family! Corinne!'

"Of course," she screamed, "that's the connection I've been looking for." She paused for a few seconds, allowing her mind to digest the facts. "My God! What the hell did I get myself involved in?" Another thought struck her. "I've been used. Corinne. Damn it! We've both been used. Oh, Corinne, I've endangered both of us."

She retrieved her cell phone from her purse, and dialed the number mentioned in the article.

CHAPTER 9

When the call from Monica Day came into the 104th Precinct, Detective Hank Wu had been adding some finishing touches to his preliminary report on the case of the mob-style murders of the two New York hoods. Thus far, there had been little progress made toward its solution. Wu, frustrated by the number of unsolved cases stacking up in his workload, slammed his fist onto his desk. The other officers in the room looked over to see what had happened. Satisfied Wu hadn't directed his anger at them, they resumed their own work.

A tall, muscular man, Wu usually dressed in light gray suits with matching tie. His slim waist with broad shoulders and chest always required the services of the Big Men's Shop's expert tailor for alterations. He currently had his jacket wrapped around the back of his chair, tie loosened, and white shirt unbuttoned at the collar. He had an overly round face with a pleasant smile, and the women on the force had tagged him as "ruggedly handsome," and "definitely eligible," but none of them had been able to corral him as a permanent boyfriend. Despite his large frame, his manners were always those of a gentleman with an even disposition; however, he could be gruff to both suspects and fellow officers when the need arose, or when tired and frustrated, which reflected his current disposition.

Wu had spent the night, and this unusually quiet Sunday morning studying the details of the murders, but getting nowhere. Open pizza boxes with curled pieces of pizza covered the file cabinets against the wall. Half empty cups of soda were spread around the room. Steam rose from the coffee cup near his right hand. The two windows in his office were open a few inches, allowing a cool breeze to blow into the room, refreshing the otherwise stuffy air.

Spread open before him were two large folders, containing the deceased men's rap sheets. They both had long lists of arrests and convictions, covering everything from assault to attempted murder. Each had served time in the state penitentiary, but their records had remained clean for several years. Both were known members of the Camarazza crime family.

They had arrived Thursday on an early morning flight from New York City, and had immediately checked into the motel. What they did the rest of the day, and why they had come to Washington remained a mystery. Their murders had been reported to 911 operators at 6:15 PM by the front desk clerk who had heard a shot, but couldn't provide any other useful information. The cocaine found at the scene seemed to imply it may have been a drug buy gone sour, but the crossed out 'NY' on the mirror implied a different, more heinous scenario. Wu thought it might be a warning to the Camarazzas to stay out of the Washington crime scene. Wu's concern over the mob connection increased when Paul Camarazza, a relative of the known head of the New York crime syndicate, blew into town soon after the murders. Although never convicted of any crime, Paul Camarazza had been suspected of being intimately connected to the criminal side of his family. Wu wondered if he were truly a legitimate businessman, or whether he used that as a cover for his underhanded activity. The possibility of the latter bothered Wu greatly.

He walked over to the large dry board that occupied one wall of the office and wrote:

1-a drug buy?

2-the beginnings of a mob war over territory?

　　　NY crossed out: ? connection

3-a personal vendetta against one, or both men?

　　　Inside or outside of mob?

James Wyman-murdered-drug addict-

　　? NY Camarazza family

Chuck Florentino-murdered-? NY Camarazza family

Paul Camarazza-??? Connection???

Wu turned from the board as Sergeant Doyle bolted into the office.

"What is it, Doyle? What's the matter?"

"There's a PI on line one for you about the article in the paper. She sounds scared."

Wu grumbled, threw down the grease pen, and tore through the pile of papers and folders until he uncovered the phone. "Detective Wu here."

"Detective Wu?" the shaky female voice said. "Oh, thank God! This is Monica Day. I'm a private investigator. I have to meet with you right away to discuss those two murders at the King George Motel." The words were spoken much more rapidly than Monica had intended, but she couldn't control either the excitement, or fear racing through her.

"Oh?" Grabbing a pencil, Wu scribbled her name on the back of Wyman's chart. "Have you got some information for us?"

"Well, yes, but I've discovered there's much more involved in the case than those murders, and it's much too big for me to handle. I'm way out of my league. You see, it involves…"

"Hello. Miss Day? Are you still there?" Wu glanced over to Doyle, and shrugged, wondering what had happened to his connection with the PI.

The "click" of a key, opening her office door interrupted Monica's conversation with Wu quicker than if the line had been severed. It also cut off her breath. When she could finally breathe, she gasped once.

"Who's there?" she asked her voice now raspy, weak and dry. "Is that you, John?" No reply. The barrel of a .22 caliber pistol inched its way through the doorway. "What the…?" Monica dropped the phone, and yanked open the top drawer, reaching for her gun. She touched the cool metal at the same time that the .22 fired.

The bullet struck Monica in the chest. Her chin dropped as she fell backward, her heart exploding, spilling its life-giving blood into both her lungs. Her weight on the back of the chair caused it to roll to the right, spilling her body onto the floor. The blood from her wound coursed over her breast, each drop increasing the puddle accumulating on the floor.

The killer closed Monica's cell phone, grabbed the newspaper, her notebook, laptop, and purse, and ran from the office.

Wu heard a moment of silence, ruptured by a shallow gasp, a few nondescript utterances, and finally, the clinking of the dropped phone. Next came a single gunshot and a dull thud. In Wu's mind flashed the sight of a falling body.

"Hello, Miss Day?" He covered the mouthpiece. "Doyle, trace this call, and make it fast."

Doyle reached for his phone before Wu had finished his sentence.

"Hello, Miss Day. Are you there?" A loud click followed by a dial tone filled Wu's ear. He looked at Doyle hopefully.

"Not long enough for a trace."

Wu slammed the phone down onto its cradle, and jumped to his feet, grabbing his jacket in the process. As he ran toward the door, he yelled, "Get her address. Radio it to me, and get a patrol car there fast." He ran out the door before Doyle's phone reached his ear.

CHAPTER 10

Wu's car had barely exited the Station garage when the message crackled over his radio. "Monica Day's office is listed as 154 Benning Road. It's near Capitol on the East side of town. There's a patrol car in the neighborhood that'll be there in a few minutes."

Wu made a quick U-turn in front of a car driven by an elderly woman whose eyes opened so wide Wu thought he could see right into her soul.

She cursed him, as he placed the flashing light on his roof, and sped off. "These young upstarts don't know enough to give a senior citizen the right of way," the woman said, her shaking hands gripping the wheel with all her might. "Even the police don't give us any respect."

"I tried calling her office," Doyle said above the scream of the siren, "but there's no answer."

After slowing at a large intersection, Wu's car sped through it, barely missing a car whose driver had not heard the siren, nor seen the flashing lights. Wu swerved, blasting his horn, and burned rubber to get back up to speed. *No time for apologies, or explanations.* His eyes remained riveted on the road ahead. "Tell the patrol car I should be there in about five minutes," Wu screamed into the mike. "Make sure they don't touch anything."

"Will do. A man named John Zachary called 911 to report he heard a shot in Day's building. He said he'd be waiting for you."

The drive actually took only three minutes, thanks to light traffic and no other near misses. As he approached the row of offices that lined Benning Road, he noted the two patrol cars that had, indeed, arrived before him, their red lights flashing at the entrance to number 154. Wu reached into the inner pocket of his bulky sport jacket, and flashed his badge at the officer, standing guard at the entrance.

"It's up on the second floor," the officer said.

Wu took the stairs two at a time, preferring not to wait for the elevator. Not even puffing upon reaching the second floor, Wu knew he could easily have done several more flights without problems; he prided himself on his fitness. He headed down the hallway toward an open door. The sign on its frosted glass window read: "Monica Day Detective Agency."

He stopped at the door to examine the scene within. Other than the two police officers, nothing in the office appeared to be out of order, no sign of either a struggle, or a hurried search. It appeared neat, neater than his office had ever been. It had hardwood floors and scant furniture. In one corner stood a small computer table with the largest monitor Wu had ever seen, a keyboard, mouse, and a wireless printer. Alongside the computer table sat the tower unit, its power light dark. An open cabinet with empty shelves stood in the opposite corner. Two small tables occupied the other corners of the room. A row of gray, metal file cabinets stood against one wall. The only closet in the room had its door ajar, exposing several heavy coats within. The shade on the lone window rested at the half-open position, adding natural light to the fluorescent bulbs illuminating the room.

"Over here, Detective," the officer kneeling behind the desk said. His partner stood over him, writing in his notebook.

Wu could barely see the top of the officer's head behind the massive desk, whose surface appeared much more organized than his. He noted the phone, sitting in its cradle, a few pencils and pens in a ceramic coffee mug, and a small digital clock with the correct time. There were no files, or masses of papers anywhere. *A neat and organized private detective, maybe obsessively so. You're neatness didn't help you in the end, though, did it? What, exactly, were you going to tell me, Miss Day?*

The victim, presumably the same Monica Day, lay on her right side with her right arm partially caught under her torso, and her left arm hanging loosely behind her back. She had been shot once in the chest. Her curly red hair had become glued to her shoulder with blood. Her chair lay behind her on its side.

"There's a gun in the open drawer there. My guess is that the killer shot her before she could reach it."

"Did you touch anything?" Wu asked.

"No, we found the door open when we arrived. I've already called for the CSI team and coroner."

"Good. What about this John Zachary fellow who reported hearing the gunshot?"

"He's the only other person working in the building at the moment. The responding officer from the other car is with him in his office down the hall. Zachary claims he heard the shot, and then saw someone running down the alley alongside the building when he looked out his window. He then came here, and found the victim. We checked the alley, but couldn't find any evidence, no gun, no footprints, nothing at all. It leads to the street behind the building. We didn't have enough time to check if anyone on that street noticed the perp running out of the alley, but we could do that for you if you want."

"Thanks, I'd appreciate that. I'm going to see what Mr. Zachary has to say. Make sure one of you stays with the body until the CSI team arrives."

When Wu walked through the open door of John Zachary's office, he found the man pacing the floor, wringing his hands together. Sweat poured down his ruddy brow, as if Wu had been grilling him hard under bright lights, and he were the only suspect in the murder.

Wu flashed his shield. "I'm Detective Wu, Mr. Zachary."

Zachary's short frame jumped off the ground when Wu spoke, his arms flailing in front of him. When he finally composed himself, he lowered his hands, and gaped at Wu, scrunching up his nose to adjust his glasses.

"Could you tell me exactly what happened, please?" *I wonder what the heck that contorted facial expression means. Strange man, nervous, maybe too nervous.*

Zachary paused before answering. He took several deep, wheezy breaths, and began in a whiny voice, "I came in today to work on some tax forms, trying to get a little ahead on next week's work…you know how it is…when I heard a shot from down that way." His hand trembled as he pointed down the hallway toward Monica's office.

"Did you hear anyone come into the building before the shot?"

"Well, no. When I work, nothing disturbs my concentration. So, I didn't hear anything before the shot."

"You heard the shot though," Wu prompted. "Then what?"

"I heard someone running down the stairs, but I didn't get to the hallway fast enough to get even a glimpse of him. Maybe it's better that way. He could have shot me, I suppose." He pointed toward a window.

"Anyway, I went to that window to see if I could spot him outside, and, sure enough, a tall man in a raincoat and hat ran down the alley, and took a left onto Maplewood...that's the street behind this office building."

"Could you tell anything about the man, his approximate height, the color of his skin, hair, anything that could help us identify him?"

"No, all I can say for sure is that he wore a gray raincoat and gray hat. I can tell you that much, but he never looked back, so I have no idea what he looked like. I couldn't estimate his height; I'm good with numbers, but not at guessing heights. Honest. He may be of average height...maybe. That's all I saw. I called you people right away. Then, I went toward Monica's office...found the door open. She usually keeps it closed and locked when she works...and there she lay...dead."

"Which phone did you use to call 911, the one in her office?" Wu wrote everything Zachary reported in his notebook.

"Oh, no, I came back here. I didn't touch anything...too afraid." He began to pace the floor again.

Wu grabbed his shoulder as he walked past, stopping him cold. Zachary grimaced. His knees were shaking, matching the rest of his body.

"Did you know her?"

"No, I tend to keep to myself. I even work alone. I don't know anyone in the building. I need my privacy. I wouldn't want to see my name in the newspapers, or on TV. Does it have to be?" Zachary spoke quickly, the wringing action of his hands matching the cadence of his speech. He turned toward his chair, hoping, Wu figured, to sit before he fainted.

"That depends."

"On what?"

"On whether you're telling the truth, and how cooperative you are during our investigation. Don't leave town. We're going to talk to you again, probably several times."

"Oh, please hurry," Zachary whispered as he approached his chair.

"Excuse me? What did you say?"

"Praying for Monica, that's all." He lowered his head, and closed his eyes as he plopped, more than sat, in the chair.

As Wu left the room, he turned to one of the officers, now standing outside Monica's door. "Make sure the CSI team goes over Mr. Zachary's office too. Something doesn't feel right. I don't trust him, or his story." He glanced back at Zachary's still-opened door. "As a matter of fact, I think you'd better stay with him. We're not through with him yet."

CHAPTER 11

Upon returning to the PI's office, Wu found the officer who had been bending over her body, looking out her window at the alleyway and street below. "CSI team is here." He smiled the conspiratorial smile of comrades sharing some mutually kept secret. "What do you think of our witness? A real nervous ditty, isn't he?"

"Yeah, and I don't believe all he's telling either. I'm going to want a full run down on him before we eliminate him as a suspect. He wouldn't be the first perp to call in his own shooting."

Wu knelt alongside the body once more, being careful not to kneel in her blood. He had seen many dead women during his twelve years on the force, but none as gorgeous as this one. Even sprawled on the floor in her own blood, she looked invitingly attractive. The curves of her cheek flowed unerringly into her delicate chin. Her pale, silent lips were slightly parted, as if she wanted to speak, wanted to tell him who had invaded her office to end her life so abruptly.

He moved a wisp of her hair that had fallen across her eyes, eyes that would never see the light of day again. Wu sighed. *What a waste of life, of a beautiful woman, no less! Even in death, this woman has a radiance that speaks of a refined, young woman with a contagious, exuberant personality, one that probably allowed her to handle herself in any social situation from a formal affair to a meeting at a local bar.* "You know, she looks familiar to me." He allowed the wisp of hair to return to its pre-disturbed position.

"Yeah, I know what you mean. I thought the same thing a few minutes ago, and I finally figured out who she resembles."

Wu looked up impatiently at the officer whose long pause irritated him. "Well, who do you think she resembles?"

"That woman who's had all that publicity in TIME and in those gossip newspapers my wife always buys. You know, the one who won that humanitarian award a while back for something about how she cared for patients and for saving some medical center at the same time, if I'm remembering right. They made her out to be a superwoman. It made headlines in all the papers a while back. My wife kept shoving her picture at me every chance she got, telling me that there were still some decent people left in the world, unlike all the criminals I'm always telling her about. She had the same name as our deceased PI…Day. Maybe they're sisters. I remember her name because my wife is still telling me that I should call her…claims anyone who straightens out some hospital using psychology could straighten me out. She thinks I'm crazy…my wife that is. Maybe she's right. I must be crazy for staying married to her. Anyway, that's who this dame reminds me of, the beautiful superwoman from the papers."

"Humph. Except this one's dead, but you're right about the resemblance. I do remember the piece on her. She certainly looked good in those photos. This one's even more beautiful than that, though. Maybe they are sisters. There's definitely a strong resemblance, and, with the same last name, it doesn't take much to make the connection. Wait a minute." Wu jumped to his feet. "Those articles said something about the woman being involved with someone with a jaded past, but who? Was it some gangster in New York? Yeah, I remember now. She hung around with Paul Camarazza."

"Right on. Good memory. Rumor had it that he had the hots for her, and spent a lot of time with her. I thought there had been some talk about their getting married, but I never heard any more about that. So, my guess is they never tied the knot. If they had, I'm sure those same newspapers and magazines would have been all over it." He sighed. "Wouldn't you think that someone with her beauty and education could have found a better catch than someone with possible mob connections? There must have been other men attracted to her, men with a little more character than the likes of Paul Camarazza. I tell you, there's no accounting for tastes in this crazy world."

"I wonder how Camarazza fits into all of this?" Wu asked, stroking his chin. "I don't believe much in coincidences. Having his girlfriend's sister killed while we're investigating the murders of two men who worked for him is stretching reality. They have to be connected somehow."

"I doubt if they are. Wouldn't it be stretching things an awful lot…I mean blaming a New York executive, even one with suspected mob ties, simply because some murdered woman resembles his girl-friend?"

"Maybe," Wu said, totally unconvinced, "but my thoughts were centered on Paul Camarazza and the deaths of his men not even an hour ago." Wu looked down again at the body. "What did you stumble onto, Miss Day? What did you get yourself mixed up in, something involving the mob side of the Camarazzas? You said you were in over your head. Did it involve Paul Camarazza? Did he figure in your murder some-how?" He sighed deeply. "Oh, how I wish you had called me a few minutes earlier."

The desk phone rang. Wu calmly took out his handkerchief, and used it to pick up the receiver so he wouldn't disturb any fingerprints.

"Hello."

"I need to speak to Monica Day," the excited female voice said. "It's an emergency."

"Who's calling, please?" Wu took out his notebook and pen.

"It's her sister. Please, tell me she's okay. Please, let me speak to her." The voice now quivered with every syllable.

Wu pictured her crying, sobbing between sentences. What connection did this sister have to the murder? Wu decided to ask his own questions before answering hers. "First, tell me, are you the Miss Day from New York that's dating Paul Camarazza?"

"Yes, but what's that got do with anything? Who is this anyway? Where is my sister? What are you doing in her office? Something is wrong, isn't it?"

Wu's eyebrows rose almost a full inch. He wrote the time of the call in his notebook, adding the fact that the sister had called. "Now, calm down, Miss Day. This is Detective Wu from the Washington Detective Bureau. There's been an incident at your sister's office. Are you in Washington? If so, could you possibly come down here right away?"

"Oh, my God," Corinne screamed. "I knew it. She's dead, isn't she? I knew it. I could sense it. She's gone."

For the second time in an hour, Wu heard a distinctive click, fol-lowed by a dial tone as the sister hung up. He placed the receiver gently on its cradle, wishing she would call back so he could speak to her again. *I still have a ton of questions in need of answers.* "I don't believe it." Wu pointed at the dead woman. "This really is the sister of the woman we were talking about."

As if in response to his wish to reconnect with the sister, the phone rang again, startling both the officer and Wu. "I'll bet that's her calling back. Hello."

"Am I speaking to Detective Wu?" the deep male voice asked.

"Err…yes." Wu's jaw dropped in surprise faster than if the dead woman had sat up to answer her phone.

"This is Special Agent Collins from the FBI"

"The FBI?"

"That's right, the FBI. I understand you're heading the investigation into the murder of the Private Investigator, Monica Day."

"That's correct, but how did you know about her murder? She's only been dead a few minutes. The investigation hasn't really begun in earnest yet."

"Never mind that. You must stop your investigation immediately. We've got to talk in private…now…before one more word gets written down in that notebook of yours."

Wu looked around, searching the room for a hidden camera that might be recording every movement for the FBI, but found none. "What do you mean stop the investigation? I can't do that. Besides, the FBI doesn't have any jurisdiction over a simple murder case."

"You listen to me, Detective. This isn't a simple murder case. You stop your investigation right now, and meet me at your captain's office in fifteen minutes, or you'll find out exactly how much jurisdiction I have over this whole affair. Understand?"

"No, I don't understand," Wu yelled, his skin turning a bright red with each passing second. He gripped the phone tighter with each word. "Talk to me now. Tell me what's going on."

"Not over the phone!" Collins screamed to match Wu's volume. "Do what I say, and do it now. Leave the other police officers there to preserve the scene if you must, but you leave now. Meet me at your HQ."

Again came the click, and the dial tone, the third time a caller had hung up on Wu in one day. This time, he slammed the phone down as hard as he could, not really caring at this point if he disturbed any fingerprints. He immediately regretted his action. Wincing, he addressed the officer. "I've got to go to headquarters. Keep an eye on things until I get back."

"You're not seriously thinking of stopping the investigation, are you?"

"Not on your life! Until I'm told what is going on with the FBI involvement in my case, or am relieved by the captain, I'm in charge, and I say the investigation continues."

Wu stared at the victim, digesting all that had happened, trying to regain control of his emotions. Once he had calmed himself, he turned to the officer. With a determination born of years of training and experience, and a grim, but defiant expression, he growled, "But, in case they do interfere somehow, tell the CSI team I need them to rush their investigation, and finish here as quickly as they possibly can. Okay?"

"You got it."

"Oh, and I need you to do one other thing for me. Don't let anyone else answer that phone. It's haunted."

CHAPTER 12

Wu soared back to headquarters, itching for a showdown with Special Agent Collins. He had no idea how the FBI could possibly be involved with this case, but he wouldn't allow their interference to hinder its progress...no matter what authority Special Agent Collins thought he had. *A murder investigation is a local matter under local control, not a federal matter. I wonder if the Camarazza family's influence even extends to the FBI. Could the Camarazzas be manipulating Special Agent Collins? Could they be behind all three murders and a cover-up too? If so, he'll meet his match in me; I won't allow any interference...from the mob, or FBI.*

Wu found his progress slow amid heavy traffic. He pounded his fist on the wheel when a slow motorist hampered his advancement through an intersection. He scowled, not at the motorist, but at the disturbing thoughts scrambling his mind. *What had the PI discovered that so upset her that she called on a Sunday? She had said it concerned the motel murders, so maybe she saw the newspaper article, but she also said it involved much more than the murders. How much more, and what had she gotten involved with that became too big for her to handle? How did the murderer manage to shoot her while she spoke to me...a mere coincidence, or planned to prevent her explaining the reason for her call? Maybe the murderer had been waiting for her to phone someone, but if so, how did he know she would call me then? Could the room be bugged after all? If it were bugged, had the FBI bugged it, or did the Camarazzas, or someone else, and why?*

How did the sister know that something had happened to her, and how could she call that soon after the murder? That can't be a coincidence...to many coincidences!

Where did Paul Camarazza fit into all this? Could he really be an innocent participant, caught up by accident in the murder of his girl-

friend's sister, or did his family perpetrate the whole affair, and, if so, had he known about it? Could he actually be involved in the murder?

How had the FBI known of the murder only minutes after it had happened? If they had bugged the room, why not simply tell me that, and give me the recordings to help catch the murderer? How could Special Agent Collins order a halt to my investigation with no explanation, and over the phone, no less? Will my captain back me, or him? I've got a ton of questions and no answers, but I'm sure as hell going to get some before this day ends.

When Wu finally stormed into Captain Patelli's office, he found Special Agent Collins, sitting with his arms folded, and wearing a huge frown that could scare the most savage bully at any high school in the city.

"Hello, Detective Wu. I'm Special Agent Collins."

Wu froze in his tracks, his mouth agape. *How the hell did he get here already? I wanted to talk to the captain alone, before the FBI could pull any more surprises on this case. I guess I should have called him, but I thought a face-to-face with him would be better.*

The thirty year old, thin, clean-shaven Special Agent stood. He had an elongated face, replete with a squared off chin and long nose, and sported neatly cut, thick, blond hair. His dire expression remained unchanged as he extended his right hand.

Wu made no effort to shake it. "How the hell did you get here so fast? More importantly, who the hell do you think you are, J. Edger Hoover? What gives you the right to order me off this case? Furthermore..."

"Calm down Wu," Captain Patelli ordered, "now!"

Wu marched to within inches of Collins. He stared defiantly into his deep blue eyes. Wu's fists were clenched at his side.

"Back off immediately, Wu. He's on our side." The captain tore his reading glasses off as he jumped to his feet. Shorter than both men by a good six inches, with thinning, light brown hair, the captain bore a multitude of wrinkles, each line a story of some hardship during his long police career.

Neither Collins nor Wu budged. Neither spoke.

"Back off, both of you," Captain Patelli yelled, as he rushed toward the two men. He forced his way between them. "Now, Wu! I mean it. Back off!"

Wu took two steps back, fists remaining balled, and now shaking, at his side. "All right, Captain." He refused to take his steely eyes off his opponent. "But someone had better explain to me what this outrage is all about"

"Special Agent Collins is here to explain it to you." The captain resumed his seat, but kept his eyes glued on his angry detective, unsure what he might do after he heard Collins' explanation.

"You see," Collins said, his voice steady and firm, "your chief witness in Miss Day's murder, John Zachary, is in our witness protection program."

"So, that's how you knew of the murder so fast," Wu said.

"That's right. Before Zachary...and that's not his real name, obviously...called in the shooting to 911, he called the US Marshals assigned to protect him. They called my office to tell me what had happened. Zachary called me after you left his office to give me your name, and then provided me with the woman's office phone number. I called you from my car on my way here. So, I had no trouble arriving before you."

"You certainly don't waste any time, do you?" Wu grabbed a chair from against the wall.

"Can't afford to under the circumstances. Once he had identified himself to your department, I thought it better to give you one shot at him before I stepped in. Then, I had to stop your investigation temporarily until we talked. Did his information prove helpful?"

"Not really, but what do you mean by 'one shot?'"

"I mean you can't use him as a witness in this case. You can't even use his new name for that matter."

"And why not?" Captain Patelli asked.

"Because your witness is wanted by some big underworld figures that are after him for testifying against them. Releasing his new name probably wouldn't do any harm, but if one picture, or even a description of him, ever managed to appear in the news media, he'd be a dead man, and I would have failed at keeping him safe. Listen, the US Marshals and FBI worked together on Mr. Zachary. We went to a lot of trouble to have him disappear once and, we'll do it again, but we're not going to have all our work with him undone by getting him killed. That's not how the witness protection program works." He sighed.

"Do you really expect us to stand by, and do nothing as you take my only witness without a fight?"

"That's exactly what I expect, and that's exactly what you're going to do. You and your department simply have no choice. You said it yourself. This is a simple murder case. From what Zachary told me, the victim's a small time investigator, probably killed by some husband she had been tailing, or someone she pissed off during one of her investigations. Under the federal rules of the witness protection program, the safety of our witness supersedes your criminal investigation. Besides," he continued, his eyes bouncing back and forth between Wu and Captain Patelli, "the marshals already have Zachary in their custody, and are relocating him as we speak."

Captain Patelli nearly jumped out of his seat. "What? By whose authority?"

"Mine, and if you don't think I have the authority, check with Judge Jacobs. Here's her number." He tossed a card toward the captain. "She'll back up everything I told you. Now, if you'll excuse me, I have other work to do."

"Special Agent Collins," Wu said, as Collins took a step toward the door, "by any chance is one of those big underworld figures Zachary testified against a member of the Camarazza family, maybe a guy named Paul Camarazza?"

Collins froze in his tracks, turning toward Wu, lips curled in contempt. He stuttered as he spoke. "I'm not at liberty to say." Collins voice became slow and angry. "Why do you ask?"

"A hunch. His family name seems to be coming up a lot today, that's all."

"Keep your hunches to yourself," Collins warned in a loud voice, "and, by the way, other than the judge, no one is to know of this conversation, and all the officers who have had any contact with Zachary are to be sworn to strict secrecy. Understood?"

Both the captain and Wu nodded as Collins left the room, slamming the door behind him.

"Captain, I don't like it. I don't like it at all."

Sergeant Doyle stood by, and watched the FBI agent leave. He then stuck his head into the office after knocking only once. "The dead woman's sister is here. I put her in your office."

"Thanks," Wu said. "Tell her I'll be right there."

"There's more," Doyle said. "One of our informants called to say the sister arrived in town with none other than Paul Camarazza, you know, the suspected New York hood." He inhaled, and then blew the air out fast. "You should see the car she's driving. It's a red Lamborghini

Contauch. If the car thieves don't steal it before she leaves, I may take it myself." The sergeant laughed as he closed the door.

"She got here fast," Captain Patelli said.

"Yeah, everything about these recent murder cases seems to be moving fast, maybe too fast."

"What do you mean?"

Wu explained the two phone calls he received in Monica Day's office. "It's eerie. It made me think the murder had been advertised in the morning papers."

"Do you think the sister had anything to do with that murder?"

"Don't really know yet, but I intend to find out." He glanced at the captain, and sighed, "I'd love to interrogate that Camarazza boyfriend of hers."

"So, that's the reason behind the question to Agent Collins about Camarazza. From his reaction, I think you hit a nerve."

"That's what I thought too. Now, I have to find the connection between the murders and the Camarazzas." He moved his head in the direction of his office. "I doubt if she's going to be much help. Those same tabloids made her out to be an absolute 'air head' outside of medicine. They say she's brilliant in medicine, but naïve and stupid otherwise, a bad combination, but she must be both, if she hangs around with a Camarazza, even if he really isn't directly connected to his family's mob activities, which I sincerely doubt, by the way. Anyone who runs a supposedly legitimate corporation that's probably owned by the mob has to be involved with them somehow. And any woman who hangs with that corporate executive has got to have a few screws loose, or be involved in the underworld up to her pretty, little neck. I'm betting it's a little of both. Either way, I'm going to find out everything she knows about this whole affair."

"All beauty and scrambled brains, someone who loves those fast cars Doyle mentioned, and maybe the high-class partying, plus easy access to drugs, huh?"

"That's my guess. Normally I wouldn't be looking forward to interviewing someone with those credentials, but I suspect she may hold the key to both her sister's murder, and the murders of the two hoods who worked for Paul Camarazza."

"Remember, right now, she's not a suspect. She's a nurse, a respected professional, as you describe her, not a criminal. Treat her with respect, as you would any other person of interest. Don't go after her as if she's guilty of murder. Don't take your distrust of Special Agent Collins out on her, unless she gives you a reason. Got it?"

"In my book, she's simply another suspect, and I treat them all the same. They're guilty until I say otherwise."

Captain Patelli sighed. "I can see another complaint being filed now."

Wu paused at the door. "By the way, Captain, Special Agent Collins said he only put a temporary stop to my investigation. I assume that now that he has John Zachary, or whatever his real name is, in his custody, I can proceed with my investigation under my own authority again."

Captain Patelli slammed his fist down hard enough to make the papers and pens on his desk jump. "You presume right. No one takes you off this case but me. Understood?"

"Understood, Captain." He then headed toward his office, and his confrontation with the deceased's sister.

CHAPTER 13

Corinne sat unmoving, her chin resting on her chest, her eyes closed. Tears that had long ago streamed down her cheeks left tortuous tracks in their wake, marring her makeup. She barely raised her head as she heard Detective Wu enter the room. *I can't look at him, at anyone concerned with Monica's murder for that matter, even a policeman, not yet anyway. Eye contact is only going to bring back the tears and the pain, the memory of Monica, and the connection with her I've lost forever. I can't go through that upheaval so soon again, not without Monica. Oh, I feel so alone. I doubt if I'll ever be able to face another human being again.*

She sniffed several times. *How many times have I met death during my nursing career, hundreds probably, and how many times have I told relatives of the deceased to be strong, to stretch to find their inner strength, to seek God's help if they were religious, to do all they could to bear with the heartbreaking news? I've always known that this advice fit exactly into the family's need, helping them to achieve some resolution to their sadness, to reach closure. How empty those words and directions seem to me now.*

"How do you do, Miss Day? I'm Detective Wu. I spoke to you on the phone from your sister's office."

Corinne didn't bother standing. *I don't have the strength to stand any more. My legs are weak. They're shaky. They won't offer any support.* She merely extended an ashen hand.

Wu accepted the icy hand. "I'm sorry about your sister." He sat, never taking his eyes off the young beauty before him, not sure how he wanted to approach the interview. *Although I usually have sympathy for the victim's family, in this case, I'm not sure I can. This woman presents a unique challenge. Is she simply the victim's sister, or, as is more likely, simply a gangster's girlfriend, maybe not worthy of sympathy, and maybe guilty of conspiracy in her sister's murder? I need to find out which.*

I have two active cases that are probably related. Both have a connection with the New York Camarazza crime family. Two victims worked for one of the Camarazzas, and a third had a sister that dated Paul Camarazza. Could the New York mob be making a move to spread their influence into DC? Are these murders the beginning of many more to come my way? Was this woman's sister investigating the Camarazza family? Had she stumbled on their planned move into DC? Did that get her killed? Did it involve Paul Camarazza directly, or merely his murdered men? Was he more than the corporate executive he pretended to be? Could he have killed his girlfriend's sister? Would this sister know it, if he had? Could she be naive enough to be totally innocent of all of this, of her boyfriend's possible involvement? I doubt it. Could she be the murderer herself? I've got to find out how much she knows, no matter how hard on her I have to be to get the truth. To hell with the captain's warning! I need information to solve these murders, and I need it now, before the FBI maneuvers me totally out of the picture, or this erupts into a bloody mob war. I'll press her hard. The reward should be worth it. The victims demand it. I demand it. But how do I go about getting that information in the most efficient manner? That, I'm not sure of...yet.

He continued staring at the beauty before him, weighing his options. He knew that her connections with the Camarazza family would make her less than cooperative and probably antagonistic anyway. *I wonder where Paul Camarazza is now? Why isn't he here consoling his girlfriend? Maybe I can get to him through his girlfriend, attack her connection with Camarazza, get her mad enough to open up, and maybe give up what she knows. Maybe I can even get Paul Camarazza mad enough at me for verbally attacking his girlfriend to come out of hiding, and tell me about his family's connection with the murders. It's a bold plan, fraught with possible problems and complications, but one I think might yield the best results, if it doesn't get me killed first.*

"Thank you," Corinne said in a barely audible, hoarse voice.

Wu studied her in detail. She wore black heels with dark nylon stockings below a dark green skirt with small, sparkling flecks of silver. Her chest heaved with each breath beneath her pale-yellow blouse. Wu had all he could do to avoid staring at her breasts, trying to force their way through the restraining clothes. Ringlets of hair partially blocked her face. *What I can see reminds me of one of those classic Greek statues I've seen on TV. She has so much beauty; what a waste to spend it on Camarazza.*

"Please call me Corinne. Can you tell me...what happened to my sister? The officers wouldn't let me into her place. They wouldn't tell me much either."

"That's normal police procedure. We can't afford to have anything disturbed. It's an active crime scene. We have to preserve any evidence. As to what happened, all we know for sure at the moment is that someone shot her a few minutes before you called."

Corinne's tears began to flow again. She made no attempt to wipe them away. Wu offered her a tissue. She accepted it, but simply crushed it in the palm of her hand. Her mind felt numb, unable to comprehend anything at the moment, not even what to do with the tissue.

"May I ask you what made you call your sister at that particular time, and why you hung up on me so quickly? You said you knew something had happened. How did you know that?"

Corinne sniffed once, and blew her nose into the tissue so delicately it barely moved. She raised her head, forcing herself to look at Wu. Through her tears, his image appeared blurred. "We're identical twins. We often shared...each other's experiences. That's the only way I can explain it." More tears flowed from her eyes. This time, she wiped them away, having accepted another tissue.

"So, you had one of those 'experiences' before you called?"

"Exactly. I felt...fear, tension, and then pain...real pain... I've never felt that bad before. Then, I lost total contact with Monica. I could sense nothing. I felt alone for the first time in my life...a truly frightening experience." She wiped her nose again. "I knew something had happened, but I didn't know exactly what. When you confirmed that something had happened to her, I couldn't speak. I nearly collapsed. That's why I hung up so hastily. I couldn't believe Monica had died, but I really already knew it...here." She pointed to her heart, sobbing as her tears returned anew.

Wu shook his head in mock sympathy, his frown exaggerated by protrusion of his lower lip. "That sounds terrible. So, let me get this straight. You had one of your 'experiences' that you and your sister shared, so you make the call to her office to check on her?"

"Yes, but, as I said, I'm afraid I already knew she had...died."

"What were you doing when you had your 'experience'?" Wu continued to write down the details in his notebook between fleeting glances at Corinne.

"I'm a physical therapist. I had been reviewing a chart on the computers at the Veterans Hospital on the other side of town. The experience came on fast, and nearly…killed…me."

"Was there anyone with you at the time who could vouch for your story?" Wu watched her eyes for any hint of a lie.

Corinne sat up with a start, her expression a mixture of both sorrow and surprise. Wu's chin dropped. Her beauty surpassed that of any Greek statue he had ever seen; it exuded perfection. It made him gasp. *I can't believe that two such beautiful women have crossed my path in the same day, in the same hour for that matter…even if one had been murdered. I don't understand how these twin beauties could possibly have totally different alliances, one a private detective, sworn to uphold the law, the other allied with a possible super-criminal.* He looked down at his notebook to get his mind back to his questioning. *I wonder what details this twin has left out of her story, and what ugliness lay behind her beauty, ugliness that had somehow allied her with none other than Paul Camarazza. Had Camarazza threatened her, or had she join him willingly?*

"What are you implying?" Corinne watched as he raised his head, his expression that of a smug lawman out to trick the guilty party. *Could this idiot really think I could have anything to do with Monica's death? Didn't he hear me say that Monica and I were intimately connected? How could I hurt my twin? I couldn't. Hurting Monica would mean hurting myself. We were more than twins, more than two women who were identical physically. We were one.* She snarled at Wu. *I can't believe this. He thinks I murdered my own sister.*

CHAPTER 14

Wu paused before speaking, still staring at the beauty before him. Finally, he took a deep breath. "I'm not implying anything…really." He picked up a pencil, and rotated it along its length using his fingers as a fulcrum. "It's simply that we need to know the whereabouts of everyone at the time of her murder."

"In that case, you should check with Dr. Brian Filmore at the Veterans Hospital. He presented the patient to me, and we were formulating a plan of treatment when I felt…Monica." Overwhelming exhaustion suddenly gripped Corinne. *I can't continue much longer without some sleep. I wish Wu would finish his inane questioning. I need answers, not an accusatory inquisition. I want to leave…now. I have arrangements to make, a funeral to organize, people to call, grieving to do…alone.* More tears burst from her eyes.

"Was there anyone else around," Wu asked, as he wrote Dr. Filmore's name in his notebook, "maybe your boyfriend, Paul Camarazza?" He raised his gaze to meet Corinne's.

Corinne nearly bolted off the chair, barely stopping at its edge, her eyes ablaze. *How could you bring up Paul? You remind me of all the other dumb cops I've ever met; you're all wrong about him.* "Paul? What the hell does Paul have to do with any of this?"

Wu pointed the pencil at her. "You tell me. I hear he's in town."

"So what! He's here because of me, nothing more. He came to keep me company, not to kill my sister, if that's what you're implying."

"Company, huh?" Wu studied the pencil, and then pointed around the room with it. "I don't see him accompanying you right now."

Corinne slammed her fist into her lap. *I'd like to slam my fist on the top of your stupid head. Maybe that would beat some sense into you. Leave Paul out of this.* "Only because I couldn't find him. He didn't answer my phone call. I left him a message. Until he gets it, he won't know anything's happened…that I need him."

"Then, you don't know his whereabouts at the time of the shooting, do you? You have no proof that he's innocent of your sister's murder."

"No, of course not. He didn't accompany me to the hospital. He had no reason to be there. You can't possibly believe he's involved in this. He's got nothing to do with Monica's death. You've got to believe me. He's got no reason to hurt my sister, much less kill her. He's never even met her." *Corinne leaned forward. Maybe, if I can convince him of Paul's innocence, he'll back off a little. I wonder if that's even possible...probably not. No policeman is ever going to believe Paul is innocent of anything, not with his family connections. It's not in their blood, or training.* She sighed. "Why do you people only look for the bad side of everyone?"

Wu's eyes opened wide. "Oh, he has a good side? I wouldn't have guessed that, not from what I've heard about his family. Now, let's cut the bull, Miss Day, and try being truthful for a change." He tented his fingers in front of him. *I hate the idea of the Camarazzas possibly moving into my city, and I'm damned tired of being jerked around...by both Camarazza's girlfriend and the FBI. She must know more than she's letting on with her history with the Camarazzas. I'm sure she has the information, the key I need to solve these murders, and I want it. I guess I need to push her even harder.* His tempo increased, as did his volume. "Tell me about Paul Camarazza. What are his plans? What's he really doing in Washington? What does he know about your sister's murder? What's the real reason for his absence? Is he afraid to answer my questions? Believe me, he's not the saint you think he is."

Corinne stood, her fists clenched at her side. "I can't believe you. Here I am crushed at my sister's death, and all you're interested in is my boyfriend. You haven't heard a word I've said." She turned to leave. "When you're ready to believe me, we'll talk again...maybe."

"I'm sorry, Miss Day. Please stay." *I guess I pushed too hard, too quickly. I alienated her, instead of tripping her up. I made a mistake; I miscalculated her volatility, and I probably caused her more pain than I had intended. I lost focus, allowing my anger at Camarazza and my run in with Special Agent Collins to rule me. The captain warned me to be respectful, go slow, but no, I had to do it my way. I let my anger blind me to this woman's pain. My tough approach failed miserably. I failed miserably. I wish I could blame it on her ridiculous story of having some psychic connection with her sister, but, truthfully, the fault lies with me. I overreacted, pushed too hard, too soon. I really expected her to become increasingly nervous, defensive, and angry enough to slip up. She didn't. She's become defensive, and so angry at me that I'm about loose her. I have no right to hold her, and, if she leaves, I've lost any opportunity to gain whatever information she may possess about her sister's murder. She appears to be simply a grieving sister, nothing more. I am both stupid and insensitive.*

She returned to her seat, staring at him through her sorrow and anger, making him regret his actions further.

Wu lowered his head. *I wonder if I'll ever be able to interview her without anger flaring between us. I doubt it, but I have to try to salvage something from this interrogation, find out what I can from her, if not for her sake, then for her murdered sister's and mine.* "Please forgive me, Miss Day…Corinne. I apologize. I get carried away at times." He gazed at her, but didn't see any change in her expression. "Please, forgive my thoughtless words. I'm not accusing you, or your boyfriend of anything at the moment. It's simply that his name has been coming up a lot lately, and it made me wonder about his involvement."

"Well, there is no involvement," she yelled, leaning forward until nose to nose with him, hoping he couldn't possibly misunderstand. She stared deep into his eyes. *Is there a soul in there? I can't be sure, but I doubt it.*

Wu held up his hands in defeat. *I have to act fast if I hope to salvage anything useful out of this interview.* "Okay, let's assume that for now. I won't bring his name up again. Please, sit down. Try to calm yourself. We're getting nowhere yelling at each other. We're both after the same thing, a quick resolution to your sister's murder. Let's try a different area. What do you know about your sister's friends? Who are they? Did she ever discuss any of them with you?"

Corinne paused before answering, waiting for her deep, rapid breathing to slow. When she tried to speak again she found her voice hoarse and much weaker from yelling. "To tell you the truth, I never met many of them. I hardly ever came down here, and Monica hardly ever came to New York."

"Are you telling me you two never visited at all?"

"No, of course not. We tried to get together for our birthday, even for only the day, but I have a busy practice and a lot of hospital responsibilities. So, any extended visits were out of the question. On top of that, I do a lot of traveling, both for pleasure and business, conventions, speaking engagements, consulting, that sort of thing. So, it is…used to be…difficult for us to connect."

"Consulting?"

"Yes, consulting on patients." She paused, and lowered her head. "That's what I was doing when I felt…ill…when I had the last connection with Monica. As I said, I hardly ever got the chance to get to Washington." She raised her head, pushed her hair back. "This trip and that consult came up unexpectedly only a few days ago. Monica didn't even know I made the trip. I tried her cell phone several times yesterday, but only got her voice mail. She never answered any of the messages I left. I thought that she may have gone away for a few days, and had turned it off."

"So, you were consulting with this Dr. Filmore. Is that why you came to Washington?"

"Yes. I thought I said that already."

"But this is the first time you were asked to consult here in Washington?"

"Yes."

"Okay, then, did you usually keep in touch with your sister by phone?"

"Yes, I said that, didn't I? Whenever I got the chance, I'd call her, or vice versa."

Wu continued to write the details. "Did you talk to her in the last few weeks, before your failed attempts?"

"Why, yes, I talked to her last week. She sounded fine at the time."

"Did she happen to mention any of her friends, or her plans at that time?"

"No, we talked about a Broadway play I'd seen, and then she told me about an opera she attended here. She never mentioned any friends. What's all the interest in Monica's friends?"

"I'm looking for some leads. Did you two exchange letters?"

"Oh, yes, whenever we could. We used e-mails mainly; I'm not into texting. I think the last e-mail I received from her came about three weeks ago, and, no, she didn't mention any of her friends then either."

"She worked as a private detective. Did she happen to mention her current case, who or, what it involved, or any enemies she may have had, people who were upset with her investigations, anyone who may have had it in for her?"

Corinne looked down at her hands, folded in her lap. "No, Monica never talked much about her work, and never mentioned any enemies. She would tell me whenever she had been successful on a case, but wouldn't talk about particulars. I guess she felt discussing her client's business would be unethical, against her professional ethics, I guess. Do you think she could have been killed because of her involvement in one of her cases?"

"The thought had crossed my mind."

"Maybe she kept some kind of record. Did you check her apartment and office?"

"Of course. There were no personal things there, no purse, cell phone, camera, nothing. On top of that, all her file cabinets were empty. Someone removed every piece of writing paper and any memory sticks she may have had. Even the hard drive of that dinosaur of a computer has been erased. The lab boys are working on it now trying to recover anything she may have saved there, but they don't have much hope. The murderer went to a lot of trouble to destroy all her records, and took anything that could be used to record information. Makes me think one of those case files named the killer."

"Well, she never talked to me about her cases. Sorry, I can't help you there."

"Hmmm. So am I." Wu leaned back, thought for a few seconds. *Should I push again? Will she break down again? I don't want to hurt her anymore, but I'm getting nowhere. How much of her reaction has been an act? I have to try one more time; hope it works this time.* "Did she happen to mention any men she may have been seeing socially, dating? Had she fought with any of them, had a recent break up, any problems at all?" Wu's frustration grew, his muscles tightening to the point that his cheeks hurt; his teeth ground together. His police instinct still told him Corinne knew more than she professed. *She'd better open up soon, or I'm going to lose it again, and probably lose all cooperation from her forever.*

"As a matter of fact, she had become secretive about her current love. She broke up with her last boyfriend over a year and a half ago when he transferred to Tokyo because of his job. She told me they were never serious anyway. As far as her new boyfriend, she told me she had become serious with him, but didn't want to tell me anything about him yet. She said she wanted to surprise me. I thought it might have been

82

some famous rock star, sports hero, or politician. I'm afraid I don't know any more than that."

Frustrated, he threw up his hands, his mouth agape, revealing coffee-stained teeth. He rolled his pitch-black eyes toward the ceiling.

Corinne wondered if he were about to have a seizure. She waited, and felt a little disappointed when he didn't.

"Oh, great," he shouted, his voice reverberating through the thin office walls, attracting the attention of the other officers in the adjacent room. "You expect me to believe that you're identical twins with some kind of crazy mind connection, but you don't know anything about your sister's friends, her job, or even her boyfriends. On top of that, your gangster boyfriend happens to be here when she's murdered, but you have no idea where he is at the moment? It seems there's an awful lot you don't know about. Are you sure you're not holding out on me, Miss Day?"

"Why the hell would I hold out on you?" Corinne shouted louder than Wu. "I want my sister's killer caught as much as you do, maybe more. I'm telling you the truth. My boyfriend is not a gangster. He's a respected businessman who's got no connections with the gangster element in his family. He avoids that like the plague. As to my sister's murder, maybe, if you'd go ask some people who knew her here instead of harassing my boyfriend and me, you'd get the answers to your dumb questions. Now, if you're not going to arrest me for lack of knowledge, or some other stupid thing you've invented in that empty head of yours, I'm leaving this place right now."

"Oh, you're free to go whenever you choose, Miss Day, but I wish you'd be a little more cooperative, and stop acting out the beautiful, dumb-lady-nurse routine."

"Dumb-Lady-Nurse?" Corinne opened her mouth in disbelief, her eyes closed involuntarily in an attempt to wipe out the hateful man in front of her. It didn't work. "Is that what you think of me? Is that the impression I've given you in this short interview? Is that all the compassion you have for the sister of the victim? It's no wonder they call you 'dumb' cops. You fit the description of 'dumb' better than I do!"

"Oh, I fully agree. I'm sure you're smarter than I am. You've got the degrees to prove it. That's why I think you could be more informative…and cooperative. I don't buy your act, not one bit. I can't believe that anyone who has the smarts to become a nurse, a physical therapist, and get her story all over the nation's magazines can be as naïve as you make yourself out to be. It's a great act, but I don't buy it. I agree with you. You're too smart for that. But I'm not dumb enough to fall for such an act."

"Act? What act? I came down here to talk to you, to find out what happened to my sister, to help you in any way I could, and all I've gotten from you is abuse. I have been cooperative. I'll bet you don't even know the meaning of the word. I've answered every question you've asked to the best of my knowledge. I may not have had all the answers, but that's not my fault. It happens to be the truth, and you can take it, or leave it. If you want me to be more informative, then ask me questions I have at least a small chance of answering. I have cooperated with you more than I should have, Detective Wu. I should report you to your superiors. I think I will."

Corinne jumped out of her seat, and headed for the door.

"Before you take your pert body out of here, Miss Day, one more question. Did your sister have a temper like yours?"

Corinne spun around, now convinced that a devil dwelt within Wu, maybe Satan himself. "Find out for yourself," she yelled. "You're the detective. Maybe you'll find she had a temper, and could act as angry as you've made me. Good luck with your investigation. The way you're pursuing it, you're going to need it."

As she stormed out of the room, Wu yelled, "As soon as the lab boys are through with your sister's things, we'll give you a call."

She stopped at the door, her shaking hand gripping the doorknob for support.

"Does that mean you're finally going to let me into my sister's apartment and her office? Are you really going to return all her things too? Aren't you afraid I'm going to find something you missed, and, being as uncooperative as I am, keep it from you?"

"There's nothing there to find. The lab boys have been over every inch of it already, but, if you do find something, I fully expect you to give me a call." He extended his hand in her direction, a business card with his contact information sticking between the fingers. "As I said, when we're finished with your sister's things, we'll return them, if they're not needed for our case."

She ripped the card out of his hand, and threw one of her cards at him.

"You can reach me on my cell. If I do find something, maybe I'll begin my own investigation. Then, we'll find out how dumb I really am."

"Ha! Stick to looking for answers to your patients' medical problems. Leave the detective work to us. Your sister's an example of what can happen when private citizens get mixed up in something they shouldn't. And remember, your sister's private investigator license doesn't extend to you, even if you two are dead ringers. I suggest you leave town right after her funeral, and let the professionals handle the case."

"And I suggest you change your attitude, You Pompous Ass."

Corinne stormed out of the office, slamming the door as hard as she could behind her. *Where are you Paul? I need you, not to accuse you of anything, not even simply to tell you about that stupid detective's accusations, but for comfort, to reconnect with the friendly, caring person I know you are. I need you to hold me, love me…right now. I need you to console me, but even more than that, I need you to help me adjust to being the only remaining twin, to being alone, to hurting so much inside. Help me, Paul. Help me, Monica. Help me, please…anyone!*

"For a beautiful and supposedly smart woman," Wu muttered to Corinne's back through the closed door, "you're either the most naïve woman I've ever met, or you're involved up to your gorgeous eyes." He squinted, and huffed. "I intend to find out which, Miss Corinne Day, aka Paul Camarazza's Moll."

As Corinne stormed out of the building, she wiped her tears, and lifted her head high. *No more self-pity, Corinne, not while Monica's killer is still on the loose.*

CHAPTER 15

Corrine drove Paul's Lamborghini as fast as traffic would allow, running yellow and newly-turned red traffic lights as if they were green. Tears continued to flow down her cheeks, blurring her vision. *I wish the tears were capable of totally blocking the pain I feel, but I guess that wish isn't about to come true.* She slammed her foot to the floor, pinning herself to the contoured seat. She screamed, a scream of frustration, of pain, of desperation. It didn't help. She trembled from head to toe, making her think she would jump out of her skin. *I'm ready to abandon this useless life; it hurts so much. I'm ready to give it all up, my career, everything I find pleasurable in life, even my relationship with Paul. I need to end my misery; I'm ready to die. Life has lost all its attraction and meaning.*

The faster she drove, the more her stomach ached. A sudden wave of nausea rolled over. Her stomach quaked. She tasted the bile as it rammed its way into the back of her throat. She swallowed hard, wishing she had some water to quell the burning. She became light headed again. The road ahead blurred. She fought the urge to vomit. *What the hell! Soiling the car doesn't matter. Even choking to death doesn't matter. Nothing matters any more.*

As slower drivers got in her way, the compulsion to scream again grew until she could control it no longer. "Get out of my way, All Of You," she yelled, her eyes closing for a split second as the scream reached its peak. As she finally pulled ahead of traffic, she added, "I hate the whole damn world and everyone in it. You better stay out of my way." *I've never been this angry before. I've never allowed myself to experience uncontrolled rage like this because I've always been afraid...no, sure... that Monica would experience the same thing, that she would think I were in some kind of trouble, that I couldn't handle the situation, and call me, a wasted call, really...and wasted emotional sharing on both our parts. I always thought Monica would think less of me be-*

cause of that. So, I hid behind my emotional facade. I thought of it as a better approach to living...for me, anyway. At least, that's what I believed, what I hoped, but now Monica's gone, really gone...forever. I no longer have to worry about Monica experiencing my emotions. The emotion freeway is now open, but that freedom doesn't provide me any solace....none at all. No! I may be able to get angry, feel frustration, or express any emotion for that matter, without suppressing our connection, without worry that Monica would experience my emotion, but that doesn't help now, nothing helps. Catharsis doesn't work for me; it never has. Besides, I have an even bigger problem: I'm alone. I'll never experience Monica's feelings...never...nor draw on our connection for the critical guidance I need...in everything from my career to my personal choices and experiences. No information or help is coming along that one-way road from Monica to me. I'm truly alone for the first time. How can I survive? How can I deal with the world without our private connection? Monica always knew how to advise me, not only on which emotions were appropriate, but also on what decisions I should make, which road to follow...always, but always no longer exists. Monica's been murdered, and with her my self-confidence and direction has been killed, as if I had been the one who had been shot. I wish I had. What can I do to survive alone, without her supportive phone calls, emotional guidance, and her love? I have absolutely no idea.

My bravado with Detective Wu was a fraud. I knew that then, and now, I'm sure. I don't feel brave, only filled with apprehension...no, filled with dread. I don't want to face life alone,..worse, the truth is that I can't face life alone, can't do anything alone for that matter. Oh, Monica, I'm totally inept without you. Investigate your murder alone? I have to be kidding. I can't be an investigator. I have no idea what to do with my own life without you, much less delve into yours. I can't, no, I won't go there.

Oh, God, what might I find if I look? Could I deal with whatever I uncovered? Could Wu be right? Could Paul be involved somehow? Could I be in danger of losing Paul so soon after Monica? No, it's impossible. It's simply not true. It can't be. What Wu proposed is preposterous. What do I do now, end my life, and end the pain? She let out a quick puff, took in another. *I can't live without Monica. Monica, what should I do? Tell me, please. I need to escape from everything happening in my life, to go as far away, as fast as I can.*

She floored the gas pedal as she screamed. The car lurched, obeying her command, rushing to the next intersection, as if racing toward the checkered flag for a photo finish. She slowed only long enough to avoid sideswiping a delivery truck, zooming away as soon as she had cleared it. The driver of the truck gestured in anger as she flew past. Corinne didn't bother to respond, keeping her eyes on the road ahead instead.

The whole world is against me. Oh, God, help me! Even You have abandoned me. She glanced at her shaking hands, hands she had once used to pray to God. *I don't even know if I can pray anymore. Would it matter? Would He listen to me, a lost soul? I don't know. Why should He?* She glanced at the dashboard clock. *I hope Paul is back in our suite by now. I need him more than ever. Maybe he can help me. Oh, Paul, please be there. Please help!*

She had to swerve into the oncoming lane to avoid a pedestrian. Finding herself traveling headlong toward a tractor-trailer, she realized she had been pushing both the car and herself too hard. She swerved back into her own lane, avoiding both pedestrian and truck by mere feet. She tapped the breaks.

"Slow down, Corinne. Having an accident, or killing an innocent old lady is going to get you nowhere fast, and committing suicide isn't the answer either. Monica wouldn't want you to; you know that, but who else can I turn to now? Paul is the only one, I guess. Paul will be waiting for me. He'll know what's best. He'll know what to do. That's what lovers are for."

As she slowed to a more civilized pace, she leaned back. She hadn't realized she had been hunched over the wheel, her muscles in knots. She forced her arms to relax, gripping the wheel with only her fingertips, taking advantage of the car's sensitive steering. She flexed her neck from side to side, listening to the cracking the motion produced.

She allowed her mind to wander, trying to avoid any invading mental pictures of her sister's death. Instead, the interrogation by Detective Wu suddenly crystallized before her. *That damn cop is totally wrong. 'Act,' my foot. I'll bet he had planned to get me mad enough to say something I didn't want to say, maybe something that would implicate Paul. Why, You Sneaky Dog, You, that's an old psychology trick: get the subject so mad that their unconscious mind blurts out what it's been hiding from the logical, conscious mind. However, there's nothing for me to blurt out. I'm not hiding anything, You Dumb Cop. Wait till our next meeting. My guard won't be down quite as much then. I'll make sure of that. I'll show you how an expert handles an interview. I'll be interrogating you. I'll show you how much it hurts.*

She slammed her fist on the steering wheel. It didn't help, but she didn't sense any of the pain she thought she should have from the impact. She looked at her uninjured hand, took several deep breaths, and headed for her next turn. "Get a hold of yourself, Corinne. Control, control, control."

She abandoned her car in front of the hotel, and ran into the lobby without waiting for the claim check. The parking attendant chased her through the lobby, but couldn't catch her before Corinne managed to squeeze between the closing doors of the elevator.

The ride to her floor proved to be both quiet and prolonged, with the elevator stopping at every floor, increasing both her anxiety and her desire to jump into Paul's arms. By the time she reached the eighth floor, Corinne caught herself hyperventilating. "Stop it, Corinne." When the elevator doors opened, she hastened into the hallway, still breathing rapidly. "You can handle this." *Who am I kidding? I know I can't, not alone.* She bawled openly again as she swiped her keycard.

Paul could hear Corinne's crying through the door. "Got to go, Kevin. Corinne's here. I'll call you later."

Corinne bolted through the door, her blouse tear soaked, her skin ashen.

"Corinne, what's wrong?" He took one step in her direction, but, by then, Corinne had covered the distance, and had jumped into his outstretched arms.

She gasped between sobs. "It's Monica. She's dead."

"Dead? Oh, Honey, I'm so sorry." He hugged her hard for several seconds, allowing her to bawl without interruption. He then led her to the couch. "Sit down. Tell me what happened." He handed her his handkerchief.

"She's been...murdered...in her office." She finally raised her gaze to Paul's. She saw sympathy, kindness, and love, exactly what she needed.

"Do the police have any idea who did it?"

"No, but the stupid detective I talked to thinks you had something to do with it."

"Me? Ha! That figures. They're all narrow-minded when it comes to my family and me. And why would I want to kill my girl's sister? Did he happen to explain that?"

"No, of course not." She hooked her hair behind both ears, exposing more of her redden cheeks. "He's simply looking for any suspect he can accuse. He probably doesn't even care if the person he accuses is guilty, or not."

"You're probably right. He sounds like a real stupid cop."

"Boy, is that the truth. Wait until you meet him. He's all muscle and no brains." She lowered her head, images of Wu flashing in her mind. "He's got no personality to speak of either." She paused, mopped more tears, and then related her interview with Wu. "He might trick others, but not me. I'm too smart for him. I still can't believe he tried to get me to implicate you. Ridiculous! I didn't say anything about you, by the way."

"That's because there's nothing for you to say. All the same, I think I'd better avoid him if I can. He's got no clues, and he's on a fishing expedition. I could end up being the fish-in-season."

"That's true; so avoiding him is probably a really good idea."

"What did the cop say happened to your sister?"

Corinne lowered her head, the hair she had adjusted dislodging to again cover her face. She didn't bother fixing it. "Well, after her...murder...someone stole everything from her office. They've got no idea why, maybe to cover their tracks. Anyway, the police have no clues to who...murdered her. I think he suspects I knew more about her murder, maybe that I'm even involved somehow. That's probably why he treated me with so much hostility."

"Enough about him, Corinne. I'm more concerned about you, about how you're handling your sister's loss." He held her at arm's length. "Are you going to be okay? Want a drink to settle you down?"

"Scotch, please, and I guess I'm okay on the surface; inside, I'm not so sure. I can't believe this is all happening." She looked to the ceiling. "Oh, Monica, sweet Monica, I miss you so much already, your voice, your advice." She then watched Paul as he went behind the chest-high bar, and retrieved the liquor and drink glasses. The mirror behind his head reflected the back of his always impeccably combed hair. The pride he took in grooming it usually made her smile. It didn't this time.

"I hurt so much inside. I'm exhausted." She closed her eyes, resting her head on the back of the couch as Paul poured her drink. "I felt Monica's trouble, and shared her pain when she died. I've never experienced a worse connection with her. I guess it...her death...I guess I should have expected it to be the worst, but I had never thought of her...dying, or losing our connection permanently."

She closed her eyes. "From the beginning, I hated that connection, and now I wish we had never had it. I'll never be the same. I'll never get those awful physical sensations associated with her death out of my mind. Oh, Monica, I'm so sorry." The tears began to flow again. She didn't bother wiping them.

"Here's your drink." He held it in front of her, and waited for her to lift her head, and open her eyes.

"That damn policeman's got me all riled up." Corinne took the drink, and raised it to her lips. The liquid tasted good, but burned all the way to her empty stomach. The nausea returned. "I wanted to kill him. I hope I never see him again."

Paul headed for the bedroom. "Unfortunately, that kind never give up. Take it from someone who's dealt with the bums a lot. Once you have a run in with them, you're branded as one of their targets, even if you're innocent." His raised his voice while in the bedroom. "Oh, yeah, you'll have to deal with him again, I'm afraid, but maybe I can help you next time, whether I'm there, or not."

She took another sip, worsening her nausea. She didn't care. "Next time, I won't be so nice to him." She placed the drink on the coffee table, and reclined on the couch. "He's an idiot. I'll treat him worse than he treated me. After all, I'm the victim's sister, not a suspect. He should have been more sympathetic. I'll make him pay for the way he attacked me."

"Try to calm down, Corinne." Paul covered her with the blanket he had retrieved from the bedroom. "Forget the dumb cop. Take a nap. I've still got some calls to make. I'll make them from the bedroom so you can rest. We'll talk more later." He kissed her lightly on her cheek, noting that her breathing had already become more shallow and regular. "Call out if you need anything. I'm here for you."

Paul started dialing the number before he had reached the bedroom. He lit a cigar as he waited for Senator Stern to answer.

"Frank. It's Paul. The private eye you were worried about is dead."

"I know. Ed Jackson told me what happened. Seems he hired the detective to follow me. He thought a preliminary investigation into my background would prepare us for anything the opposition might eventually uncover. I wish he had informed me at the outset of her investigation. I wonder if she discovered our connection before being murdered."

"It doesn't matter now. I want you to stop worrying. Everything is under control. We're prepared to handle anything the opposition does discover, including our innocent relationship. Believe me, we've prepared for everything, including a nosy detective, or two."

"I hope you're right. I guess I should be mad at Ed and his committee for hiring her, but then again, he is my campaign manager, and the committee is only looking out for the party's best interest. I heard they didn't find anything at the detective's office though...I mean, anything mentioning me. You hear different?"

"No. I guess the police are stymied. I'm sure they'll discover you were her last case. So, be careful what you say to the detective investigating the murder. He's already trying to make some kind of connection between the dead woman and me."

"What connection?"

"That detective turns out to be my girlfriend's identical twin."

"Wow. Okay, I'll be careful. Don't want to get you in trouble either."

"I'm more worried about your career than my reputation. I want you to be careful when they talk to you."

"Don't worry. I know how to handle these policemen. Is there any news on Sage? I'm still worried about her."

"Yes, and it's all good. It seems Sage and your son are planning some kind of surprise for your birthday. That's what all the secrecy is about. I couldn't find what they were planning, but I'm sure it'll be harmless. I'll keep an eye on Sage for you, though, but I wouldn't worry about it anymore."

Senator Stern sighed, relief saturating his voice. "Boy, that is good news. I guess I overreacted. I'll pretend I don't know anything about the surprise when she shows up. Thanks for the reassurance."

"No problem. That's what friends are for. Besides I owe you for allowing me to guide you on your way to the White House."

"You remember to keep that in mind when it comes time to pay up." Senator Stern chuckled, knowing full well he owed Paul for everything he had, rather than the other way around.

Paul's voice became dead serious. "Don't worry, I will."

Paul opened the bedroom door about an inch, checked that Corinne still lay on the couch, then closed the door silently, and pressed a speed dial number on his cell phone. Kevin answered on the first ring. Paul got right to the point. "What do your informants know about the investigation of the PI's murder?"

"Well, since I talked to you a few minutes ago, I learned that the FBI are involved now."

"What the hell are they doing shoving their noses into a simple murder?"

"I think it has something to do with a man they whisked from the office complex right after the murder."

"What man?"

"Josh Zbronski...although I hear he now goes by the name of John Zachary. That's the name they gave him in the witness protection program."

"Josh Zbronski!" Paul almost yelled the name. He covered his mouth with his free hand, and then checked on Corinne again. She hadn't moved. "Wow, Zbronski. My cousins have been looking for that SOB ever since his testimony put two of them in the federal pen, and almost put me there too. Damn good thing we have the best lawyers and accountants in New York. They'd love to know where he is. Are you sure it's him?"

"I'm pretty sure. I couldn't get close enough to see him clearly, but my informants swear that's who it is, and that his name is really Josh Zbronski."

"Find out where they've taken him," Paul ordered, "and get back to me."

"Right, boss. It'll be my pleasure. I think it may be a little difficult to find him, though. The police don't even know where he is. The FBI turned him over to the Marshals again for relocation. My informants don't know where they've taken him, but they're looking. If they don't find him, I'll do my best to do the job myself."

"You always do." Paul imagined Kevin's smile growing at both the assignment and the complement. "I'll see if I can get the information from my other sources. Keep me informed. Good work, Kevin."

CHAPTER 16

The dinner dishes had been removed from the table when Senator Frank Stern finally dismissed the servants for the night. The dinner had been scheduled as a political planning session with Senator Edwin Jackson weeks before; however, the events of the past week caused both men to have additional reasons for wanting the meeting. As a result, an uneasy silence existed through much of the meal. They each now waited for the other to speak first. Senator Stern thought Ed looked more drawn and tired than usual. Senator Jackson thought the same of Frank. Sage Browning, the only other dinner guest, poured water into her glass from a large, crystal decanter, and offered a refill to the others. They both refused.

"I should be mad at you, Ed. I mean, having me followed without even giving me a heads up. Suppose I did something nasty, or stupid."

An older man, Ed exhibited a pure white mustache and graying hair. Of medium build, he had a small face covered with a number of wrinkles that made him appear even older than his actual age of sixty-four. He wore a black dinner jacket with a white shirt and striped green tie. He stood, and moved his chair closer to his host. His chronically painful hip caused him more discomfort than usual this evening. He fidgeted, trying to get comfortable in the wooden chair. "Let's say that I know you better than you know yourself. You're not capable of any dire deeds."

"Oh? I might surprise you someday."

"I doubt that. You're too straight laced for anything too sordid. In any case, tonight, I want to make sure you really understand why I hired that detective." Ed lowered his head, staring at the white linen tablecloth. He cleared his throat before speaking again. "You've got to believe me I had no intentions of casting aspersions on your character." He raised his head, staring at Frank until he turned toward him, and their eyes met. "We want the people voting for the best candidate...you. I had to be sure nothing came out that would make them think twice. That's why I hired that detective, and that's why I'm here explaining myself to you."

"And here I thought you came here for my company," Sage said, pretending to pout.

"That too," Senator Jackson said, amending his statement, and saluting the pretty woman with his empty water glass.

Sage used her small mouth with full lips to blow Senator Jackson a kiss. Her young age of twenty-eight had never bothered either senior senator, and her pert body and dark-brown hair, set into a mass of curls that bounced when she walked, had always been a welcomed addition to both of their homes. She always felt comfortable in their company, and enjoyed joking with them, even though she knew she planned to use both of them for her own purposes.

"Explain your thinking to me as much as you want, if it'll make your conscience rest easier," Senator Stern said, smiling wider, "but I still reserve the right to be mad at you."

"Maybe you've got every right to be mad, but the truth is, I knew for sure that the detective wouldn't come up with anything."

"Then, why hire her in the first place?" Sage asked, taking another drink of her water.

"Because the other side will dig as deep as they can to come up with something to damage Frank's character. I thought this detective might uncover that small piece of forgotten something that could be used against us before the competition did. Then, we would be ready for their attack, and have our answer prepared well in advance."

"And what, exactly, did you learn from her?" Senator Stern asked.

Senator Jackson lowered his head, and took several deep breaths before answering. "Unfortunately, not much. Up to last week, she reported nothing unusual. This week, she died before she could give me a report." Tears began to form at the corners of his eyes.

Sage placed a comforting hand on Senator Jackson's arm. "Are you all right, Ed?"

Senator Jackson wiped the tears away with his napkin. "Forgive an old man for crying. I'm afraid I…got to know her a little too personally. I…admired her. So, for me, she's not simply another private detective who got killed in the midst of some investigation. Remember, I hired her; it was my investigation. Suppose she died because of that hiring. I may be guilty of her death."

"It's okay, Ed. We understand how you feel, but you shouldn't blame yourself. Her death may have nothing to do with you. Tell me, though, what happens when the press discovers she had been investigating me? What do we do then?"

"I don't think that's likely. All of her records have disappeared. The police have no idea who, or what her investigation involved, and I'm not about to tell them, that's for sure."

"Did she work with anyone, a partner for instance?" Senator Stern asked.

"No. She worked alone."

"Well," Senator Stern said through a huge sigh of relief, "the whole affair seems to be all wrapped up nice and neat now. Doesn't it?"

"Do the police have any leads to her murderer?" Sage asked.

"No, their only witness reported seeing the back of the murderer as he ran away, but couldn't identify him. Now, he's been whisked away by the FBI"

"Why the FBI?" Sage asked.

"He's in their witness protection program. They were the first on the scene; so, they covered him until the Marshals could arrive. Apparently the man testified against some mobster years ago. The Marshals took him to one of their safe houses in Georgetown until they can resettle him with a new identity."

"A safe house," Sage said. "Isn't that a place where they hide a person who's in danger?"

"Yes, it's usually a home, or some hotel room far away from crowds, a place the bad guys can't find."

Sage leaned toward Senator Jackson. "You mean this witness is at the safe house now, and the DC police can't even interrogate him?"

"Unfortunately, that's correct. I'm sure the police would love to learn as much as they could from him, but the witness protection program takes precedence. The FBI and Marshals are committed to protecting him, even from the police. They don't trust anyone with their witnesses. It's the only way to keep them alive."

"Boy, I'll bet the police would pay a lot to know where that fellow is," Sage said, staring into her water.

"The mob would pay more. I mean, here's a guy they've probably been trying to find for years. He's accidentally a witness in a murder case, and is immediately taken away to this safe house in the North part of the city where they'll never find him. It's got to be frustrating for the mobsters."

Sage raised her gaze to Senator Jackson. "You mentioned Georgetown. Are you saying you know where this safe house is?"

"Well, yes, I do." *Oh, no! I wasn't supposed to tell anyone I even knew that. Damn me anyway. Oh, well, too late now. I might as well explain my reason for knowing.* "You see, I wanted to talk to this man myself. I wanted to make sure he couldn't really give us…the police…any further information. Her murder really upset me; I really feel guilty. I didn't want to let him get away without the opportunity of talking to him, even for a few minutes."

"How did you find out where they've hidden him?" Senator Stern asked.

"I called my friend, Michael Higgins, the director of the FBI. For security reasons, even he didn't know which safe house the Marshals had moved him to, but he found out as a favor to me. He owes me."

"So, you went there already?" Sage asked, disappointment creeping into her voice.

"No, I haven't had the chance yet, but I will soon. I have to hurry because they'll move him once they make up their minds where they're relocating him permanently."

"This is exciting." Sage leaned over the table, and rubbed her hands together. "The FBI, Federal Marshals, the safe house, a murder…I've never been involved in a real murder case before. Where is the safe house? You mentioned the North section of Georgetown. I'm familiar with that part of town. I go there quite often. Maybe Frank and I can go with you to meet this witness. Wouldn't that be exciting, Frank?"

Senator Jackson shook his head behind a deep frown, and then glanced at Senator Stern. "Oh, I can't tell you that, Sage for obvious security reasons. It's dangerous for too many people to know its location. You realize that, don't you?"

Sage frowned. "No, I don't. How about if I promise not to shoot him, and cross my heart at the same time?" Sage ran her index finger across her chest, drawing a large cross. "Come on, Ed. I really want to go."

Senator Jackson smiled for the first time that evening. "Ha! You're something else, Young Lady, but, no, I can't let you come. Sorry."

"Well, if that's the way you're going to be, I'm leaving." She exited the room, and then stood beyond the doorway, listening intently.

"Don't go away mad, Sage," Senator Jackson yelled. "I won't sleep all night."

The two men shared a laugh.

"You should have told her. Now, she'll bug me all night to get the whereabouts of that safe house from you. There'll be no living with her."

Senator Jackson glanced at the open doorway to be sure Sage had truly gone. "Well, the FBI are planning to move him the day after tomorrow anyway. That's when I've been given permission to question him, immediately before that move. Promise you won't tell her until then?"

"I promise." Senator Stern crossed his heart in a mock imitation of Sage. "But do tell me so I can tease her with it until then. Of course, I won't tell anyone else. You know that. I'll wait until I'm sure the time has passed, and the witness has been moved. Then, I'll tell her the address, and she can go there to search for him all she wants. I won't tell her when they're moving him. I'll play dumb, and pretend I didn't know for sure. She'll be furious at me when she discovers he's gone, but she deserves to be punished for trying to force you to give her the address. We'll play with her a little, have a little fun with her, if that's okay with you. She'll laugh with us later over the whole affair when it's over."

Senator Jackson thought it over for almost a full minute. "Okay. He's at 124 Two-Sixty-Fourth Street. The house is owned by one of the Marshal's relatives. It's not used frequently because of that, but the owners are out of town for a few weeks, and under the circumstances, they decided it provided the safest emergency relocation spot."

Being careful not to make a sound, Sage turned, and tiptoed upstairs.

The phone on the nightstand rang, startling John Zachary. He picked it up on the first ring. *That can't be for me. They told me not to answer the phone. No one is supposed to know where I am, but I have to talk to someone, anyone other than a Federal Marshal. They're boring, and this isolation is driving me nuts. I'll talk to anyone at this point. I have to be careful, though; I mustn't reveal where I am. I'll be very careful. I always have been.* He lifted the receiver to his ear. "Hello."

"Hello, Mister Zachary," the female voice said. "This is Corinne Day, Monica's sister. We need to meet."

Zachary listened carefully to her instructions. "I'll be ready. Be here in a few minutes, and park in front of the next house, but right near our driveway. I'll come out to meet you." He hung up the phone, and stood motionless for several minutes. He had expected Monica's sister to contact him eventually. He thought she would find him as easily as Monica would have, same blood, same perseverance, same genetics. *I'm doing the right thing, I'm sure.* His hands began to shake. His heart pounded. He closed his eyes. He sucked in several deep breaths. *Yeah, it's the right thing...maybe.*

He glanced at the door. His protectors were there. *On the other hand, maybe it's not a good idea, but I do feel bad about Monica's death, especially since I gave her the lead that put her onto Sage's real identity and background in the first place. Maybe that information had something to do with her murder. I want to tell her sister how sorry I am for that, maybe even help her in her investigation. Oh well, we're only going to talk for a short time. No real harm in that, but how do I get by my guards. I've got to figure a way to slip by them for a few minutes.*

"I think I know a way," he muttered. Picking up the phone, he called the pharmacy. "This is John Zachary. I need a refill on my prescription of blood pressure medicine. I have the prescription number right here. It's 2196375."

"Hold on while I check it on our computer," the female technician said. "The computer says it's okay to fill the prescription. Your co-pay will be forty dollars. We can have it ready in about an hour."

"That will be fine. I'll send someone by to pick it up. Thank you."

He headed toward the family room to con the Marshals.

Zachary found Phil sitting on the couch reading the morning paper. "Where's Jake?"

"He's taking a shower." Phil kept his gaze glued on an article on a bank robbery that had taken place the day before. "He should be finished any minute now. He's been in there forever." He glared at Zachary. "I heard the phone ring. Who called? You know you're not supposed to answer it. That's our job. We don't want anyone even recognizing your voice, much less figuring out where you are. Don't do it again. I'll cut the cord, if you do."

"I know I shouldn't have, and I am sorry, but the pharmacy down the street called. I called them when we arrived to see if they could fill my blood pressure prescription. I forgot to tell you. They're a chain, so, I can get my prescription filled at any of their stores thanks to their computer system. Anyway, they called to say my prescription is ready. I know you guys won't let me go. So, I wondered if you'd pick it up for me. I really need it. The doctor wants me on it every day. I've only got one pill left, and I'll need another for later today."

"Well, I'm not sure that's a good idea, but, if you need it...okay. It sounds like Jake's finally out of the shower. I'll let him know where I'm going. If the phone rings again, don't answer it, and if anything else happens out of the ordinary, let him know right away. Remember, it's your life that's at stake here. You can't afford to do anything stupid."

"Oh, don't worry. I wouldn't think of it. I enjoy living too much."

Phil walked to the bathroom, and rapped on it twice. "Jake, I have to run to the pharmacy for our guest. Don't take forever drying yourself. I warned him to behave himself. I'll lock the door, but I need you to get out here as soon as you can. Babysit him until I get back."

"Okay. I'll be out in less than a minute anyway. You don't have to wait. Tell Mr. Scaredy-Cat I'll be right there to hold his hand, but make sure he knows enough to stay put."

"He does. Don't you, Mr. Scaredy-Cat?"

"Oh, yeah." Zachary cowered into the corner of the couch, pretending to be terrified of being left alone for any length of time. He picked up the newspaper. "I think I'll sit, and read until Jake comes out."

"Great, but don't throw out the paper while I'm gone. I'm not finished with it yet. Be right back."

As soon as Phil had closed the door, Zachary headed for the back door. He peered out, checking the surroundings. Nothing moved. Encouraged by his audacious plan's apparent success, he stepped out, and peeked around the corner of the house, spotting the rear of Phil's car as it sped down the street. Ducking back behind the house, he counted to five to give Phil enough time to make the corner, and then ran to the front of the house to await Corinne.

She said she'd be here right away. Where is she? Doesn't she realize we don't have all day? Jake will be looking for me any minute now.

He ventured a little further into the front yard, wringing his hands together. He scrunched up his nose, adjusting his glasses so he could see

Corinne's approach more clearly. He knew he risked being spotted by Jake, but the position brought him closer to where he had told her to park.

From a rooftop down the street, the assassin sighted John's head in his telescopic sight. He had a clear shot since Zachary had cooperated, and moved away from the house. Now, he wouldn't have to use the decoy car he had parked down the street with his girlfriend sitting behind the wheel, posing as Corinne, to lure him out. He aimed immediately above Zachary's right ear. When his target stopped his nervous trek toward the sidewalk, pausing to look up the street, he pulled the trigger.

The bullet snapped Zachary's head to the side, and he fell to the ground, bouncing once on the hard lawn. A second round struck him in the back of his head, jerking the head off the ground, and spurting blood over the grass around it.

The front door flew open, and Federal Marshal Jake Tangee darted out with gun pointed at the rooftop directly across the street. Seeing no sign of the shooter, he scanned the adjacent homes. No shooter. He ran to Zachary, but didn't have to check the man to know that they had failed to keep their charge alive. Most of his skull had been blown away, and his brains were scattered over the lawn.

The assassin snickered at the Marshal's frustration. He then packed his rifle in its case, and headed for the safety of the fire escape at the rear of the building.

CHAPTER 17

The long funeral procession finally came to a halt near a pair of giant oak trees at the edge of Oak Hill Cemetery. In front of the open grave stood one folding chair, protected from the light drizzle by a brown canvas canapé. The edge of the canapé flapped briskly in the gushing wind, snapping in the cold air, mimicking the distant claps of thunder.

Corinne sat motionless in the stretch limo, watching the rear door of the hearse. Her tears returned, as the pallbearers began to remove the gray, metal casket. The rain bounced off its shiny surface in tempo with the sound of the rain upon the limo roof, reminding Corinne of the times when, as children, she and Monica would lie under the skylight of their porch to watch the rain. Monica would always imagine patterns drawn by the accumulating water. Corinne, on the other hand, could never envision those patterns, seeing only the reality of the water droplets. "You're thinking is too literal, too concrete," Monica would say in reflection years later.

Now, Corinne smiled at the memory, as the tears rolled down her cheeks. *You were right, Monica. You were always right. I never did have any imagination. That part of our genetic inheritance went entirely to you. We're identical in every other respect except that. You rubbed that difference in as often as you could. I can still hear you screaming your favorite childhood expression: "You can't see anything beyond the end of our identical, nosy noses." Our private difference...our private little joke...a joke I'll never hear again.*

As she watched the coffin being suspended carefully above the gravesite, Corinne began to sob audibly. *Oh, how I wish I could see "beyond the end of our identical, nosy noses" right now. Maybe then I could make some sense out of your murder, some sense out of the abusive attitude of the police who wouldn't even allow me into your office for days after your murder, to say nothing of their non-stop, abusive questioning. God! They interrogated me as if I had murdered you. What did you get yourself into, Monica? You usually handled only small jobs, tailing cheating spouses, or investigating people's backgrounds for government, or private jobs, nothing major. I know for a fact that you usually avoided investigating violent crimes...at least that's what you promised me years ago. So, your murder should have had a low priority on the DC police agenda. Whether a jealous boyfriend, or an unhappy client murdered you, there's no reason for that much fervor to be put into the investigation, into grilling me, especially by an officer with Hank Wu's reputation for integrity and honor...at least, that's the background story I got from the policemen guarding your office. They praised him. None of this makes any sense.*

She sniffled, and then dabbed at her nose with a tissue. *Could I have helped you somehow? Did I fail you, Monica? Could I have done more for you, and, if so, what? Is it too late for me to do anything more, anything worthwhile? Oh, Monica, I miss you so much. Unfortunately, there is one thing Detective Wu had right. I should have come down here more often to see you. I'm so sorry, Monica, so sorry I couldn't do more for you, and that I didn't recognize your distress sooner. I should have rocketed down here as soon as I felt your distress.*

Corinne watched Monica's friends walk toward the gravesite, a sea of silent, black umbrellas, flowing across the cemetery. She spotted Detective Wu, walking among the throng. He carried no umbrella, nothing that might hamper his vision. He stood beneath one of the trees, using its branches for some protection while he attempted to write something on his little pad, protecting it by bending over, using his body as a shield.

Paul told me even more about you, Detective Wu. So, you're one of DC's top cops, been decorated several times, and usually headed up the investigations into the murders of dignitaries. Simple murder cases are usually left to the rest of the force, not their top cop. Why the hell are you putting so much effort into this case? I want Monica's killer caught probably more than you do, but I shouldn't have to take any abuse from you or anyone else connected with the police. Why are you so interested in my connection with Paul, and why the hell did you warn me to leave town right after the funeral? What the hell did you get mixed up in, Monica?

Corinne allowed her head to droop until her chin rested on her chest, her hair falling before her like a blanket. *I wish I could block Monica's murder from my mind's eye as easy as it is to block my tear-filled eyes with my hair. I don't understand any of this. Help me, Monica. Tell me what to do next.*

The limo driver suddenly opened her door. A gust of chilly wind brought Corinne back to the event at hand and her part in it. The limo driver handed her an open umbrella.

"Thank you." As she placed her foot onto the wet turf, the hem of her skirt fell into a murky puddle. *Monica would have thought to wear boots and pants, not this long skirt and dress shoes.* Using the limo driver's hand for leverage, she lumbered out of the car.

As she trudged toward the burial site, Corinne spotted Detective Wu speaking to a young man, who she recognized from Monica's wake as one of Monica's friends, although Corinne couldn't remember his name at the moment. The friend pointed to various mourners, as Wu continued to write.

"Of course," she mumbled, "he's getting the names of everyone here. Like a persistent, dumb cop, he can't even let the dead be buried in peace. Paul predicted you'd come, and that you would be itching for an opportunity to harass everyone here, all the mourners, especially him." She looked skyward. "You were right to stay away, Paul. You're a bastard, Wu." She knew full well that Wu couldn't hear her through the rain and at that distance. "What the hell is going on in your rotten mind, Wu? Why don't you come over here so I can tell you what I think of your approach to your criminal investigation method, You Escapee From A Psychiatric Ward."

Wu suddenly caught Corinne's eyes glaring at him. He stopped writing, and signaled Monica's friend to stop talking by holding up his hand. Corinne mouthed the word 'bastard,' and hoped he could read her lips as she approached her sister's final resting place.

As Corinne took her seat beneath the cover of the canapé with Monica's friends surrounding her, she glanced at the huddled crowd. She recognized most from the wake, but two were new to her. One, an elderly man with graying hair and a matching mustache looked vaguely familiar, but not from the wake. She had never seen the other, a young man with wire rim glasses and a full head of pure blond hair. Both wore raincoats, but neither used a hat or umbrella for protection. Through the rain, Corinne couldn't determine if either wept.

She returned her attention to the priest who had started the burial prayers, and who now sprinkled Holy Water on the already drenched casket. She tried to listen to his words through her sobs and tears…something about eternal life and final rest for Monica's soul. Corinne couldn't be sure, however. Despite being at her only sister's funeral, she couldn't concentrate on the priest's words, her only thought at the moment: a part of her had died when that bullet had ruptured Monica's heart. It had always been that way with them. They shared more than simply their looks and strange, psychic connection. They shared their hopes and dreams for the future, and, in a large way Corinne shared Monica's death, for she felt that a part of her had been whisked away as surely as if she had been in Monica's office when the murder weapon had been fired.

Corinne stared at the casket. She had several questions swimming around in her mind, searching for answers she couldn't produce, or even imagine. *Why hadn't Monica confided in me earlier if she had felt troubled? Why hadn't she given the slightest hint that she might be in danger when they last spoke? Why all the secrecy around her new lover?* Corinne didn't think it possible, but her tears suddenly increased, as did her loud sobbing. *How could I possibly get the answers to these questions without your help, Monica, without the help of the useless police, and without unnecessarily involving Paul? How?*

Suddenly, Corinne felt light-headed and warm. Sweat formed on her brow. She felt dizzy, and nauseated, her stomach and chest tight. Breathing became a chore. The world began moving sideways and vertically at the same time. She blinked her eyes; it didn't help. *It can't be Monica; she's gone. It's me. It's this funeral. It's everything. I'm losing it. Oh, Monica, I've never been confronted with a death I'm so intimately connected with before. I need you for guidance; I need you here…alive.*

Her heart pounded. She felt hot. She wished she could step out from under the canapé to let the cooling rain drench her. She clenched her fists around the Rosary Beads she had been handed on her way to the site by one of the mourners.

After what seemed like an eternity, the priest came over to her, offering his hand to help her stand. "I'm so sorry. Here, take this rose. Place it on Monica's casket."

Corinne took the rose with a shaking hand, walked to the edge of the casket with the priest gripping her elbow for support, and placed the flower upon her sister's casket as ordered. She touched the casket one final time, lowering her head toward the ground. "Goodbye, Sweet Monica, My-Beloved-Other-Self. I love you. I'm sorry this rose isn't your favorite flower, but I'm sure you'll find many beautiful flowers, including your beloved lilacs, in Heaven. Rest in peace, Sweet Sister. I'll find who did this to you...to us. I promise."

She walked slowly toward the limo, again under the cover of the driver's umbrella, her head still spinning, her temples throbbing, keeping pace with her heart. She thought she heard the funeral director speaking behind her. She turned her head to listen.

"Everyone is invited," the funeral director said, "to the home of Jacqueline Kant for a light lunch. Thank you all for coming. The Day family is grateful for all your support."

Ugh. The last thing I need is food. I'd never hold it down. As she approached the limo, the elderly man she had spotted earlier stepped in front of her.

"My condolences, Miss Day," he said, gripping her hand gently. As he squeezed, she felt the crunching of paper in her left palm. "Read this when you're alone," he whispered as he pretended to kiss her cheek. He then limped off, climbing into a large limo, parked two cars behind hers. Corinne watched him disappear into his car and then, climbed into hers.

Once the door closed, Corinne shut her eyes, and rested her head against the soft, leather headrest, taking several deep breaths, and sobbing as her tears returned.

A sudden, loud rapping on the window caused her to jump, her eyes snapping open in fright. Through the rain cascading down the window, she recognized Detective Wu, his face close to the glass. With a hand gesture, he signaled for her to open the window.

After a moment's hesitation, during which she clenched her eyes, she complied, finally staring at the detective through tearful eyes. "What do you want?"

"That man who stopped you." Wu had to yell to be heard above the noise of the rain beating on the roof. "He handed you something. What is it?"

Corinne threw her right hand open so quickly that the Rosary Beads that flew out actually struck Wu beneath his left eye. His eyes instinctively closed, as his head jerked backwards. When he again opened his eyes, the beads dangled by one slim finger only inches from him.

"Is this what you mean? Can't a mourner even give a set of Rosary Beads to me without you wanting to make a federal case of it? Can you see them? Do you want to examine them for secret compartments, or dust them for prints?"

He gently pushed her hand back into the limo, and then rubbed the area around his left eye that had been struck. No real damage had been done to either his skin or vision. "Now, calm down, Miss. Day. I'm sorry if I disturbed you, but I am investigating your sister's murder, and I'm not going to let anything slip by me. Besides, I want to know how he fits into all this."

"Well, why don't you ask him rather than harass me?"

Wu stood to watch the man's limo pull away. "Maybe I will. By the way, do you happen to know who he is?"

"No. Should I?"

"I wouldn't think so. Goodbye, Miss Day, and I am truly sorry for your loss."

Corinne closed the window, and watched Wu's broad back as he walked away.

"Excuse me, Miss Day," the limo driver said, his gaze glued to Corinne via the rearview mirror, "are we headed for the reception? I've been instructed to drive you wherever you want to go."

"Could we stay her for a minute or two, please?"

"Certainly, Miss."

Corinne quietly unfolded the paper she had held tightly in her left hand during her tirade at Wu. It read: "Your life is in danger. Meet me at your sister's office at two o'clock this afternoon if you want to learn more about her, and what started the investigation that may have led to her death. Come alone. Please destroy this note, and do not mention it to anyone! My position in this matter is delicate." He had signed it: "Senator Edwin M. Jackson."

Of course, he's the Senate majority leader and the President's right hand man. That's why I recognize him. I thought he looked familiar. She crumpled the paper. "We're not going to any reception, Driver. Take me back to the funeral home. I need my car. I've got something more important to do."

Wu watched Corinne's limo sit, unmoving for a few minutes, and then drive away. He toyed with the idea of following her, but opted to head for the police station instead. As Corinne's limo turned right out of the cemetery, he turned left, rubbing his cheek where the Rosary Beads had left a small, red welt. *She's feisty enough, but I'll never understand what attracted someone with her beauty and education to one of the Camarazzas in the first place? Could it have been his money, his looks, his fast cars, his position of power in the corporate world, maybe easy access to drugs through the rest of his family, or something else?* Wu drove below the speed limit, giving himself time to think, but arrived at the police station with no further understanding of the woman from New York.

As he walked into the station, he spotted Sergeant Doyle waving at him.

"Captain Patelli wants you to go to the lab before you do anything else." Doyle thumbed the direction for Wu as if he didn't know it already.

Wu entered the newly renovated, technically sophisticated lab, located in the basement with his expectations high. *Maybe I'll finally have something to go on, some lead to follow that will make some kind of sense in this senseless case.* "You wanted to see me? Good news, I hope. I trust you've got something off that computer, maybe the killer's name."

"I'm afraid not." Aaron Center pushed his thick, plastic glasses farther up his long nose. He had a crop of wavy brown hair deliberately kept long to cover his overly large ears. Young and tall, he was clean-shaven with prominent cheekbones and a protruding chin. He had unsuccessfully dated most of the available females in the department, making Wu wonder about his interpersonal skills. Although he had been on the force only a few years, he had quickly established himself as one of the best lab men in DC, and had gained the reputation of providing the best forensic evidence in the entire Northeast. He had helped solve many difficult cases, including many of Wu's. Wu hoped for that caliber of help today.

"Let's start with that computer." Center pointed to some equipment on his lab table.

The cover sat upright, forming a tunnel that bridged one side of his lab table to the other. Wu ignored the cover, and looked to the guts of the computer, sitting next to it. Like most people, Wu couldn't identify any of the interior parts of a computer, and had no interest in learning. He only glanced at it briefly, and then turned to Center.

"Someone sure knew what they were doing when they worked on that tower unit. That computer is an older model, but has a great IDE hard drive. In my preliminary report, I commented that the hard drive had been erased to clear the memory. It's worse than that. Someone did a low level format on it. You're not supposed to do that on that type of equipment. I doubt if the thing will ever work again. I took the hard drive out to see if I can get it to work with my equipment, but it won't. If you want, I'll try to fix it, but I really believe it's impossible. The thing's shot, and any information that may have been on the drive is corrupt, if there's any left at all. It'll be a total waste of time."

"Are you one-hundred-percent sure there's no chance of getting any useable data from it?"

"Absolutely."

"Then, forget it."

"Okay, I'll put the case back on, and send it back to you upstairs so you can return it to the victim's office. That's only part of the reason I called you down here, anyway."

Wu's fatigue and frustration had built up in him, making him irritable. He made no effort to hide it, growling at Center. "Well?"

"We went over every inch of both the victim's apartment and office. We found nothing, including no laptop computer."

"I got that report before. What are you getting at?"

"You're missing my point. In every investigation, we find something, a small clue, a partial fingerprint, a scrap of paper, or a strand of hair, something we can't identify, or maybe have problems identifying, but something. That something we find may not be totally relevant to the current investigation, but we usually find something." He turned to Wu. "Without that something, my job wouldn't exist."

"Are you telling me you found absolutely nothing at the scene we can use?"

"That's exactly my point."

"I still don't get it."

Center huffed. "There were absolutely no fingerprints anywhere in the victim's apartment, or her office. There should have been at least the victim's fingerprints somewhere. After all she worked there. Someone wiped the place clean, and I mean totally clean. There were no fingerprints on the glasses in the cupboard, on the desk, on the phone, on her empty purses, on the handles of the umbrella, even on her shoes. There were simply no prints to be found. I even checked the fluorescent lighting, the toilet seats, and under the tank lid where she had placed one of those deodorizers. No prints. There should have been some prints somewhere. I've never seen any place cleaned so efficiently."

"So, the murderer wiped the place clean. It's happened before, and it'll happen again. So what?"

Center spoke slowly. "Well, think about it. A woman with long hair lived there. Finding no hair in her hairbrush, or shower drain is unheard of, and downright impossible." He took a deep breath. "So, when I put it all together, there is a total lack of evidence. I've never seen anything like it. At the risk of repeating myself, there were no fingerprints, not one piece of paper, no hair, or fibers, an empty hard drive, all leaving nothing for me to analyze. The whole thing makes me think that whoever did it didn't want to take any chances that something might be found. My guess is that professionals cleaned the place, and, from what you told me about your arrival so soon after the shooting, they did it before the murder."

"Professionals?" Wu's head snapped toward Center. "What do you mean professionals...professional cleaners?"

Center shook his head much more vigorously than before. "No, I mean professional law enforcement officers, your colleagues to put it more bluntly. Listen, every place I looked for clues, someone had been there before, and had removed anything I may have been able to use as evidence. They knew exactly where I'd be looking, and made triple sure those areas were thoroughly cleaned."

"Law enforcement officers?" Wu eyes glowed with insight. "You mean the FBI. They became involved right after the murder."

"That's an excellent possibility. Although anyone from our own lab could have handled it too. The CIA has the knowledge and manpower also, but they're not connected to your case, as far as I know. Those Federal Marshals are high on my list." Center replaced the computer cover, screwing it back in place at its base. "I wonder what they were trying to hide, and why members of any law enforcement agency would want to do that in the first place."

"Why, indeed? I don't have a good explanation or answer to your questions, but I think I know someone from the FBI who does, if I can get him to talk to me."

CHAPTER 18

Sage wrapped her arms around his neck, and kissed him hard, immediately sensing his lack of response, his lips limp, almost lifeless, his body stiff. She felt none of the usual fire that had accompanied their embrace in the past. She pulled away, staring at his serious expression. It hadn't changed since she had approached him over fifteen minutes before.

"What's the matter, Hon? Don't you believe what I've been telling you?"

"No." His penetrating gaze never left hers. It offered no sign of belief, comfort, or the love that should have been there.

"Honest, it's the truth."

He placed his hands gently on her cheeks, allowing them to slowly caress her until they drifted down to the sides of her neck. She made no effort to resist. He pulled her closer, delivering a long, gentle kiss. It still lacked the passion of the past. During the kiss he reached into his left pocket, and removed a pistol. He placed its barrel against her right temple.

Sensing the cold steel, her eyes opened wide, her mouth opened in protest, but she never had the chance to utter a sound. He pulled the trigger. For an instant, her eyes opened wider in pain, the muscles of her cheeks pulling her mouth into a grotesque grimace. A microsecond later, her entire body became limp, her eyes closed forever. Her expression changed from that of extreme shock and pain to that of someone in tranquil sleep.

He held her up by her neck, and kissed her lips once more before allowing her body to slide down his. The chain around her neck caught on the pen in his shirt pocket, temporarily suspending her limp body against his, until the chain finally yielded to the pressure, and broke. Then, chain, medallion and body fell to the floor together, a heap of inanimate objects.

He reached down, took a final look at her beauty, burying it in the deep recesses of his memory for future retrieval, and picked up the chain and medallion. He placed them in his jacket pocket with the gun. He then lifted her, and carried her out of the room.

After retrieving her car, Corinne headed for Monica's apartment, located in the outskirts of the city in a quiet residential neighborhood. When she arrived, she found no policemen, or police barricades there to prevent her from entering Monica's fifth floor brownstone apartment; however, she hesitated at the doorway anyway, her hand shaking as she inserted the key into the lock.

She had dreaded going into the apartment. She had even bought new clothes for Monica to wear for the wake; it had been easier than facing Monica's personal things, things that would touch that part of her still linked to her twin, that part of her that still felt enormous pain. She knew she had to ultimately deal with them, but it remained a task she dreaded. Even now, her hands trembled as she reached for the doorknob. She remembered the last time she had been in the apartment. It had been over a year ago for a happy occasion...their birthday. Now, with no other avenue open to her and, forcing a false sense of courage on herself during the trip, Corinne had returned to collect her sister's things. Deep within her, she knew she wasn't up to the task, at least not so soon after the funeral. But no one else could do it, and waiting wouldn't make it any easier. During her ride, she had told herself she couldn't shirk the duty, no matter how much it hurt. "Besides," Corinne said aloud as added encouragement as she prepared to open the door, "I've got to start looking for Monica's murderer somewhere, and here is as good a place as any."

Corinne felt a tightening in her throat, making it difficult to both breathe, and swallow. "Some display of courage, Corinne. You're a fraud." Finally, with a loud sigh, she forced herself to push the door open, watching it sink slowly into the room until it struck the back of a couch, and started to close again. Corinne's hand reflexively pushed the door back against the furniture to keep it open.

Her jaw fell, the scene before her freezing her where she stood faster than if she had entered a meat freezer. Monica's clothes littered the living room floor, her size three dresses forming a rainbow of colors, leading from the couch to her bedroom and beyond. Several of her blouses had been thrown around the room, cluttering the couch, a table lamp, and the backs of two chairs.

She entered the room cautiously, fully expecting a burglar to jump out at her at any moment. Peeking behind the couch for the intruder, she spotted only the couch's cushions stacked one on another, ready to fall at the slightest disturbance. The couch's rich, embroidered fabric had been slashed in several areas, exposing the thick, white stuffing and shiny coil springs. Every picture had been removed from the walls, and had its backing slashed, the blade ripping through, and destroying the overlying painting, or print.

Proceeding to the bedroom, Corinne found it in a similar state of chaos, the rainbow of dresses ending upon the bed where they were joined by most of Monica's lingerie. Every dresser drawer had been yanked open, and appeared empty. Several had even been removed from the dresser, and now lay upside down on the floor, covering Monica's shorts, blouses, and nylon stockings.

Corinne pulled open the closet door, standing to one side, fully expecting the hordes of clothes to fall on top of her. None did. But the closet matched the disordered décor of the rest of the apartment. Monica's suits and dresses were piled against the rear wall, as if the clothes themselves were being used as a giant dam, holding back some teetering partition. She spotted a small, metal filing cabinet near the closet door. She opened each of its drawers. All were empty.

"Damn," Corinne yelled, leaning heavily against the doorframe. "Monica's gone, and the cops have made a wreck of her apartment." She kicked the filing cabinet as hard as she could, denting its thin, metal side, and almost toppling it. "Damn," she repeated, running toward the bed, and collapsing onto it, crying into Monica's clothes until she could cry no more.

Rolling over after a few more minutes of dry-eyed sobbing, she stared at the white ceiling fan with its fluted lights and five white blades for an extended period before finally forcing herself to get out of the bed. Standing with shaking knees in the center of the room, she surveyed the chaos once more. "Monica, please help me. Talk to me. You're the one with all the damn insight, not me." She closed her eyes, squishing the last drops of moisture from them like the final tear from her heart. "It hurts so much to lose you. A part of me has been amputated. Oh, God, it hurts so much. Monica, help me! Give me some guidance, some sign, please." She rubbed her palms into her temples, and looked up at the ceiling once more. *I wish I could see into Heaven, see Monica there, and speak di-*

rectly to her. I want to look into the eyes of the uncaring God who took her away.

"I know I'm the one who had always been so superficial, so naïve. I readily admit it, Monica." She allowed herself a fleeting smile. "A naïve nurse who thought she knew everything about psychology too. Can you believe it? Can you believe me? But outside of medicine, that's exactly what I am, Monica, a naïve woman, and you were the only one who realized it, the only one who could see through my façade. You were the only one who would go out of her way to guide me, to show me, to protect me, to help me.

"You know it's only been the last several years that I've felt comfortable on my own, and didn't have to call you with every personal problem I encountered." She snickered. "You don't know how many times I put down the phone after dialing most of your number. Can you believe it? I'm supposed to be the big shot physical therapist with the big psychology degree, the one with all the answers to everyone else's problems, but, in reality, I couldn't even handle my own. You were the one who always knew the true Corinne Day, the insecure twin. You were always the strong one, Monica. Now, you're gone. I need you now more than ever.

"How could you leave me? How could God take you away? I'm not sure I can handle this life without help. I've never had to be alone before. You were the power behind all my success in my career. Your guidance proved indispensable. I couldn't have done any of it without your guidance, your love, and your confidence. I could always sense your presence; I could always call on you for advice when I really needed it. I can't anymore. Help me, Monica. I need you now more than ever before. Help me, please."

Corinne forced herself to sit on the edge of the bed, her eyelids becoming as heavy as her legs and arms. *I'm not sure I'll ever be able to generate enough energy to stand again, much less clean this place, or try to discover who killed you. I know that if I had been murdered, the detective in you would have jumped on the investigation at once, and you wouldn't have quit until the murderer had been caught, but I wasn't killed, at least not physically. The opposite happened.* She lowered her head. *I now realize how much strength I drew from your mere presence, your voice, and our connection.*

"Did you suffer, Monica? Did you know you were in danger? Were you alone with the killer when you died? Did you experience the terror of your impending death? What am I asking? Of course you did. I felt it too. Oh, I can't believe you're gone! Could your death have been prevented? Could I have prevented it? What can I do about it now, Monica, investigate your death on my own? I can't do that. I'm not trained, and I'm afraid. Maybe Paul can help me. No, the police suspect him. They'll be watching for him. He can't help. It'd be too risky." She wiped some of the wetness off her tear-stained cheek, and examined her moist palm, wondering how many tears Monica had shed before she died.

"I'm sorry, Monica," she whispered with her head again lowered, her hair hanging down to her thighs, forming a cave before her, a cave she wished she could curl up in, and die, rejoining her beautiful twin for all eternity. "I should have called you more often. I should have been more open to you, more willing to listen to your problems, not only seek answers to mine. I should have visited you more frequently. I should have been here for you. Then, you might have told me about your problems. Maybe together we could have solved them before they escalated into your murder. Maybe, I could have helped you. Maybe, I could have saved you...maybe. I failed you. I failed me."

She snapped her head back, and again looked heavenward. "Damn! The insecure twin has done it again. Who do I think I'm kidding? I can't even help myself. How do I think I could have helped you? I must really be crazy."

She clamped her eyes shut for a full minute, trying to clear the fuzzy cobwebs from her mind. It didn't seem to make any difference. "Oh, Monica, my whole damn world is collapsing around me, and I don't know how to handle it, don't know what to do, don't even know where to start. Monica, I'm so sorry...for...failing you...for...everything. I'm so sorry."

She stood, her fatigue and dizziness causing her to stagger before she became sure of her footing. Still afraid of falling, she shuffled over to the bureau mirror, moving at a snail's gallop, her arms extended away from her body for added balance and leverage. The woman in the mirror looked haggard and withered, not the strong clinic-saving nurse type at all, and certainly not a person capable of attacking a murder investigation, much less solve one for a beloved sister.

"Get a hold of yourself, Corinne," she said aloud to her reflection as she wiped her face with a towel she found in a heap on top of the bureau. "This self-flagellation is not getting you anywhere, and certainly not helping Monica. You've got things to do, and a murderer to find. It doesn't matter if the police help you or not. It doesn't matter whether they spend all their time chasing Paul, as long as they don't actually arrest him for anything. Let them waste their time. What's important is what Monica meant to you, and what you're going to do to solve her murder. You can't let her down again.

"God may have abandoned you, punished you for your sins by taking her away, but you can't let any of that stop you. You simply can't let Monica down again. It doesn't matter what you know, or don't know about detective work. You need to follow the clues, and hand any evidence you find over to the authorities. No, wait a minute; it would be better to shove the evidence at Wu to show him how you solved Monica's murder on your own. No danger will be too great to confront to accomplish that. Come on, Corinne, stop playing the helpless idiot, and start doing something constructive. End of encouraging speech. There, don't you feel better?" She paused. "No, I don't. Who am I kidding? I'm still afraid. You're still a fraud, Corinne."

She threw the towel at her reflection, and turned toward the chaos in the room, wondering where she should begin. The sheer size of the task overwhelmed her. "Okay, let's start by cleaning the mess here." *Okay, Monica? We'll put everything back in its place, and then decide what to do with all your clothes, keep some, donate some and, well, whatever with the rest.*

She entered the closet. She began by picking up the pants and blouses piled high against the back wall. *You owned almost exclusively dark colors. I told you these looked boring on you, but, no, you wouldn't listen to me, wouldn't buy more fashionable items.*

"At least you had brightly colored shoes to wear with some of your dresses." She began rearranging the size six shoes neatly on their shoe rack. "Of course, I still can't believe you bought your dresses at department stores, and not designer shops. Ah, here's that Ralph Lauren original that Paul and I sent you. Now, that's a dress! I bet you never even wore it once, did you, Dear Sister Monica?"

Corinne had to make several trips between the two rooms, hanging the dresses neatly on the rack by color, and then placing the lingerie in the bureau drawers. She paused when she came across an overturned jewelry box, its contents splayed on the floor. She examined each piece as she placed it in the box. "This is costume jewelry. Monica, I don't believe it. For identical twins, we are...were...so different."

She next turned her attention to replacing the books, tossed in disarray on the floor in front of a small, wooden bookrack, pausing long enough with each book to read its title. When she came across a computer manual, her eyes opened wide in surprise. "A computer manual? I thought you hated computers, referring to them as the work of the Devil. Come to think of it, Detective Wu said you had a tower unit in your office. Why the hell did you have one in your office, especially since you were finally using a laptop? That makes no sense. Were you finally giving in to progress, and learning how to backup your laptop to the base unit?"

She flipped through the manual, finding an inscription on the inside cover: "To Monica, from Corinne: Computers can protect information as efficiently as safes. Use this guide for entry into the hidden files of the computer world."

"I never gave this to Monica. Besides, that's her handwriting, not mine. What the hell does it mean, Monica?" She searched the book for any highlighted areas, or other notes. She found none. She returned the book to the shelf. "Hidden files? Hidden from who? What's on them, and where are they hidden? Are those files sequestered somewhere on the hard drive of the tower unit in your office with a special password? Probably. Great! That's useless now. According to the police, all the files were erased, and the computer's not even working. If that's the clue you left, Monica, it's as useless as your tower computer now. I'm planning to ditch it."

She finished cleaning the apartment, carefully checking all the other books for anything else that might aid her investigation. She found nothing.

At one forty-five, she headed out the door, calling Paul on her cell phone. "Could you possibly meet me at Monica's office in fifteen minutes? Someone handed me a note at the funeral today. He claims he knows something about Monica that he says I need to hear. He'll be there at two."

"Sure, that shouldn't be any problem. Who handed you the note?"

"I'd rather not say over the phone. You'll find out when we meet him. I'll see you there in a few minutes. Thanks, Paul."

With the engine of the Lamborghini humming smoothly, Corinne headed for the meeting, running into heavy traffic right from the start. Frustrated, she arrived at Monica's office five minutes late. She expected to find Paul's Rolls there; it wasn't. She entered the building, climbing the stairs slowly, each step taking increasing effort. *I'm not sure I feel up to meeting an unfamiliar informant in the place where Monica had been murdered, especially after facing Monica's disheveled apartment.* Her hands began to tremble and cramp as she gripped the handrail. Her heart raced as if she were running up the stairs, her breathing became shallow, rapid, and difficult.

Finally arriving at the landing, she paused to peer down both ends of the hall. Nothing. She took a deep breath, and walked with shaky legs to her sister's office. She stopped short when she found the door ajar. She pushed it open, and watched it swing without a sound into the office. "Paul?" Both her lips and legs trembled. She fully expected someone to jump out at her. When she received no reply, she poked her head into the room, ready to pull it back at the first sign of danger. "Paul, are you in there?" Again, no reply.

She entered the office, still fearful of finding a hidden, silent assailant, or, maybe worse, a repeat of the mess she had found at Monica's apartment, her eyes scanning the room for any signs of danger. *Monica's killer hasn't been caught, and I certainly don't want to stumble upon him.*

There appeared to be no one, friend or foe, in the office. The interior, however, did resemble the shambles in Monica's apartment. Every drawer of her desk had been overturned onto the floor, and every picture had its back slashed. The only noise emanated from the fan in Monica's tower computer, sitting on the floor. The screen on the computer table shone a solid blue with no blinking cursor.

Advancing farther into the room, she spotted a lady's foot extending from behind the desk. Corinne gasped. The woman lay on her stomach, the entire right side of her head and her blouse stained red with blood that streaked from a gaping hole in her temple. As a nurse, she had seen dead bodies before, and had seen traumatic injuries far worse than the one before her now, but this unexpected death had occurred in Monica's office, the site of her murder. The image of the dead woman sent her pent-up emotions over the top before her clinical training could kick into gear. Corinne screamed.

Suddenly, mid-scream, large hands gripped her shoulders from behind. She gasped. She couldn't move. The strong hands crushed her shoulders, sending excruciating pain down both arms that went numb in an instant. Her already shaky knees buckled under her.

Oh, no, the killer is still here. He's got me. How stupid of me not to have waited for Paul. I don't want to die. Monica! Oh, God, no!

She struggled against her attacker, increasing her resistance to his pull, and trying desperately to yank herself free from his tight, relentless grip, but she proved no match for his strength, or his desire to restrain her. Her resistance only increased the pain in her shoulders. She couldn't break free.

The hands tried to spin her around. She twisted the other way. She fought harder, but found herself suddenly pulled against a large body, one she knew she couldn't defeat, even if she could break free. *This has to be the killer of that woman, maybe of Monica too. Is this killer going to be the last thing I see before eternal darkness?* As her scream became louder, she once again felt darkness begin to surround her. She struggled to stay conscious.

"Monica, help me," she screamed through trembling lips. "Anyone…please help me."

CHAPTER 19

Corinne had gone to her sister's office full of hope. She thought she would learn something about Monica's murder from Senator Jackson. Instead, she had walked into the arms of an attacker, and had potentially become the killer's next victim. Could Senator Jackson be the murderer? She didn't care at the moment. She found herself fighting for her life. Her attacker held her in his brutish hands, crushing her shoulders, preventing her escape. Now, she not only wouldn't learn anything about Monica's death, but she would join the killer's list of victims. She had no hope of escape. Pain shot through her shoulders. She twisted her torso against the grip, the strain increasing the pain so much that she thought her bones were about to shatter.

How could I have been so stupid to let the murderer get behind me? I sensed some kind of danger here, but stupidly ignored my own instincts, and entered the office anyway. I'm a fool. I should have listened to myself earlier, taken my own advice. I'm not ready to tackle any investigation. Ignoring my own admonition is going to cost me my life.

She screamed louder. Her voice cracked from the strain.

"Corrine. Corrine, it's me, Paul." He finally managed to spin the struggling Corinne. "Everything is fine now. Calm down. Stop screaming."

Corrine looked up, confirming his identity. His grip loosened as her body relaxed. She threw her arms around him, hugging him, her body still shaking uncontrollably.

Her voice quivered. "Oh, Paul, you frightened the hell out of me. I thought you were the murderer, about to add me to his list of victims."

"What happened? I heard you scream as I came up the stairs. That's why I came running, and grabbed you. What made you scream? What's going on?"

Corrine slowly pushed herself away from his embrace. She pointed her shaking finger at the far side of the desk.

Paul strained his neck to peer over the desk, careful not to release his embrace on the whimpering woman in his arms. "Oh, I see." His voice had a calm resolve Corrine couldn't quite fathom. Releasing Corinne, he walked around the desk for a closer look. Corrine clung to him, not wanting to get any closer to the body, but unable to release the arm of her protector. As they bent over the body, the sounds of several people running up the stairs filled the room. Paul reached for the gun lying beside the woman's head.

Corrine grabbed his arm. "No, don't touch it."

"Police," an officer shouted. "Don't move."

Corrine and Paul both turned toward the two police officers that had entered the room with their guns drawn.

"Don't move," the officer repeated.

One of the officers ran to their side. He placed his weapon against Paul's temple. "Take your hand away from the gun, and stand up slowly."

They silently did as they were told. Paul put his hands above his head, his fingers spread to show he held no weapon.

Corrine didn't raise her hands. Instead, she pointed at the dead woman. She sputtered as she spoke. "We arrived a few minutes ago, and found her,"

"Move away from the body," the officer ordered.

"But," Corinne began, stopping mid-sentence when Paul interrupted her.

"Quiet, Corrine," Paul whispered. "Let me handle this."

As they moved towards the wall indicated by the officer, Corrine spotted Wu, standing in the doorway.

"Good afternoon, Miss Day, Corinne." Wu waited until the officer frisked Paul. "From the Rolls Royce double parked outside and the large goon guarding it, I'd say this must be the infamous Paul Camarazza."

"That's right, and unless you really think we both killed that girl, and are ready to read us our rights, you'd better tell *your* goons to put their guns away, so we can tell our story."

"It's routine police procedure, Mr. Camarazza. Wouldn't want any weapons to suddenly appear while we question you. You can lower your hands as soon as the officer is finished frisking you."

Paul put his hands down, and straightened his suit as soon as the officer backed away. "How the hell did you happen to show up right after us?"

"We got an anonymous tip that something had happened here. I should've guessed you two would be involved."

"He's clean," the officer said, as he next went through Corinne's small leather purse.

"Get a female officer down here," Wu said to the officer when he finished checking the purse. "I want Miss Day frisked too."

"You can't believe I killed her." Corrine began sobbing.

"Why not? You didn't take my advice to get out of town. No, instead, you immediately get involved in another murder. Could be you found this woman searching your sister's office, and thought she had murderer her. So, you shot her."

"And where the hell would I get the gun?"

"Maybe from Mr. Camarazza here. I'm sure he'd do anything to help you."

"Oh, come on. You don't believe that, or we'd be under arrest already."

Wu knelt next to the dead woman. "Either of you know her?"

"No." Corrine hugged Paul tighter.

Paul remained silent, his expression blank.

Wu lifted his gaze from the body. "Well?"

"Of course not. Come on. Give me a break. The girl obviously killed herself before either of us got here."

"Or someone tried to make it appear that way," Wu said as he rose.

"Now why would someone do that?" Paul asked.

"You tell me. You seem to have all the answers."

Paul didn't comment. Instead, he simply stared at Wu.

"Why were you two here in the first place, and what were you looking for?"

"We weren't looking for anything. I came here after cleaning Monica's apartment. You guys had turned that place into a shambles; I suspect you were looking for clues. Fine, I understand the need for that, but, damn you, it took me forever to clean that mess. I came here fully expecting her office to look the same, not to kill some woman."

"We didn't do it. When our lab boys were through with their search, both this place and your sister's apartment were nice and neat, exactly as we found it."

"Then, I guess maybe she did it," Corrine said, pointing at the dead woman. "When I arrived, I found her... dead already."

"You said you cleaned your sister's apartment?"

"Yes, I had to. It resembled the aftermath of a tornado."

"You realize there may have been some evidence there we could have used to determine who trashed it, maybe even a clue to your sister's murderer. Why didn't you call us?"

"Because I thought you cops did it."

"Okay, calm down, Miss Day. Yelling isn't going to help. Did you find anything missing either at the apartment ,or here?"

"Couldn't say. I don't know what Monica had in the apartment in the first place. I told you I hardly ever visited her. As for the office here, I arrived only a few minutes ago. I haven't had a chance to look around."

"If you didn't know the office would be trashed when you got here, and that there would be a dead girl in it, why did you really come here anyway?" Wu asked. "I find it hard to believe you simply came to do office cleaning. Mr. Camarazza doesn't look to be the office cleaning type."

"Someone asked me to meet him here at two o'clock."

"Oh? Who?"

Corrine looked to Paul for guidance.

"You'd better tell him. It appears you were being set up to take the fall for this."

Corinne hesitated. *I really don't want to reveal the Senator's connection. He did ask me to keep our meeting confidential. Suppose he wasn't involved with this woman's murder, and really does have information about Monica's death. If I reveal his identity, will he still give me that information? Or did the senator really set me up? I don't know what to do.*

"Well?" Wu prompted.

"Okay. Senator Jackson handed me a note at the funeral. It said to meet him here at two o'clock because he had information about Monica's death, but he also asked me to not tell anyone about the note. However, under the circumstances, since you're the police asking, I don't think I have a choice but tell you, do I?"

Wu's mouth fell open. "The Senator? He's the one who told you to come here?"

"Yes."

"Why did he want to meet you here, and not at his office?"

"I don't know." *Why, indeed? If I knew the answer to that, I might be closer to understanding Monica's murder. As it is now, I don't know any more than you. The senator didn't show, and Paul and I were discovered over a dead body. Could the Senator really have set me up?* Her lightheadedness returned. Frustrated, she leaned heavily on Paul. *I don't feel so good. I need to lie down. I need sleep. I can hardly keep my eyes open. I wish I had eaten something earlier. I made a big mistake skipping lunch.*

"So, where's the senator now?"

"He never showed. Maybe he never will. So, I don't know."

Wu wrote everything into his notebook. "And now to you, Mr. Camarazza, what..."

"That'll be enough questions from you, Wu," Captain Patelli said as he entered the room at a trot.

Wu's jaw dropped open again. "Captain, what are you doing here?"

"Taking over this case."

"What? Why? I thought you were backing my investigation." His heart raced. *What does the captain think he's doing? He has no right to butt in on my investigation.* Wu threw an angry look at his captain.

The captain grabbed Wu's arm, and dragged him to the other side of the room, glancing at the body as they passed. "I'm taking over because the Commissioner wants it that way."

Wu's anger changed to disbelief. "The Police Commissioner? What's he got to do with this?"

"He's taken a special interest in this whole affair. He ordered me to take over, and that's what I'm doing." He hastened back toward Paul and Corrine, continuing to speak to Wu over his shoulder. "So, you can stop harassing these innocent people now. Get back to the precinct. You have other cases to keep you occupied."

"Innocent?" Wu protested, his voice louder than he intended. "How do you know they're innocent? We haven't even started the investigation into this woman's death."

"Because I've talked to the man you had tailing Miss Day here..."

Corinne straightened, her head snapping in Wu's direction. "You had me followed?"

"...and," the captain continued, staring at Corrine, "he reported never hearing a shot from in here. Also, I checked with the precinct. That anonymous call came in about the shooting prior to her entering the building. Mr. Camarazza came in after she did. They couldn't have done it."

"But..." Wu protested.

"But nothing! Things have changed since we talked last. I told you you're off the case; I'm in charge now, and that's the end of it. Now, get out of here. Let me finish my job." He pointed to the door.

Wu stormed out of the office, mumbling loud enough for the captain to hear the noise without being able to recognize any of the obscenities.

The office door slammed behind Wu, causing Corinne to jump, her nerves still on edge. She looked to Paul for answers. *What's going on? What's the captain up to?* She had grown to dislike Wu, but thought it wrong for his superior to take him off a case so abruptly. *Does it have anything to do with Monica's murder investigation? It all smacks of political innuendo, interference by someone in authority and a cover up of something, but what? I sure would hate it if I were unexpectedly pulled off the team treating one of my patients. Had the captain simply wanted the glory of closing the case, or could this be an elaborate trap, devised to put Paul and me off guard? They won't catch me, though. I'll keep my guard up, and Paul always does anyway.*

Paul answered Corinne's questioning stare by shaking his head. He no more understood what had occurred then she. In less than five minutes, they had both been accused of murder, and then exonerated, a new experience for both of them.

Captain Patelli began pacing the floor in front of Paul and Corrine, as if they were his audience, and he a Shakespearean actor about to perform his soliloquy. "As I understand this case, your sister had been investigating something, or someone, probably this murdered woman. Perhaps your sister discovered something incriminating about her. So, the woman shoots your sister before she can reveal what she found. Your sister probably had notes about her investigation, and maybe even some photographs. Who knows what? Your sister's murderer didn't have time to search the office thoroughly after she shot her because our patrol cars were already on the way. So, she returned today to find the information, but still couldn't find it."

Captain Patelli looked skyward. "I guess our witness couldn't identify the killer as a female because he only saw her from the back, and she wore a long rain coat and hat at the time."

He paused and placed a finger on his cheek, formulating the rest of the story before continuing. "Now, she doesn't want to be discovered, maybe risk going to jail, or worse. Who knows? Maybe the information about her, whatever it is, would have been so damaging to her that it represented a threat she couldn't live with if it were discovered. Maybe she worried about it being disseminated on the Internet. Who knows?" He took a large breath before continuing. "So, since she can't find your sister's hiding place, she begins to think the police may already have whatever it is, and are getting ready to act on it. Maybe she's worried the police are already looking for her. She can't take the strain. So, she decides to end her misery, and kills herself. Case solved." He folded his arms across his puffed-out chest, turned toward Paul and Corinne, his speech ended. "How does that sound as an explanation of the events at hand?"

Corrine's mouth stood agape. She didn't know what to say. She turned toward Paul, bewildered.

"It sounds fine to me, Captain," Paul said with a smirk. "In fact, it sounds perfect."

CHAPTER 20

Wu sat in his office, staring at the whiteboard, analyzing the facts of the case, or more accurately, his rambling thoughts on the case. He forced his eyes to focus on the words, trying to rearrange them into some kind of logical order that would point to the solution. *None of what's happened makes any sense, but I know the solution exists right there in front of my eyes, if I could only find the common denominator, but I don't see it. I'm missing something, something important, but what?* The names defiantly stared back at him:

James Wyman -NY Camarazza family - murdered
Chuck Florentino - NY Camarazza family - murdered
Monica Day - PI- murdered
Corrine Day - sister of PI - Nurse - Camarazza's girlfriend
Paul Camarazza - ? Connection
Senator Edwin Jackson - note to meet Corinne in PI's office-
    ? Connection
Witness –? John Zachary-? Real name -FBI informant-
    Unavailable for questioning
Dave Collins - FBI -? Connection.

Wu had more questions than facts on the board. His inside boiled for both being taken off the case, and facing the proposition he might never be able to find that solution. *That's never happened to me before. For that matter, Captain Patelli has always backed me, no matter what. I could always depend on him. What makes this time, this case, different?* He picked up a marker, and added:

Dead Woman - in PI's office -unidentified
    ? Suicide-? Murder.

Aaron Center stuck his head into Wu's office. "I understand there's been another killing at that PI's office. I'm on my way there now. I barely finished cleaning up at another murder scene when I got the call. Things are sure hopping these days."

"Come on in. I'm glad you stopped by. I need to talk to you."

"Sure. What's up?"

"I've been taken off the Day case."

"What? How did that happen? I thought the captain said you could continue your investigation."

"He's the one who ordered me off the case...at the direction of the PC"

"The PC? Wow! If that's the case, to whom do I give my new information?"

Wu pointed in the direction of the captain's office. "Give it to the captain. He's heading the investigation now, or, more precisely what's left of the investigation. That's what I wanted to talk to you about. I need a favor."

"Granted. You know I owe you big time for all the favors you've done for me. What do you need?"

"I want to follow this case, but from a distance. There has to be more to it than a couple of simple murders. I can sense it. It's eating away at me. I want answers, but I've got no way to get them now that I've been ordered to keep my hands off. So, I need a source of information. Let me know anything you hear about the case, preferable before you give any information to the captain. I want to be the first to see your lab results."

Center nodded, happy to be part of a conspiracy. "That's easy. If you're not in your office, I'll text you everything I find. Is there anything else?"

"That'll be plenty. Thanks."

Center paused at the door before leaving. "I can give you my first piece of information right now. I had stopped by to tell you anyway. The same gun killed Monica Day and your two New York hoods; the bullets match."

Wu wrote the information in his notebook. "That doesn't surprise me. You know, there's a gun lying on her office floor right now. It also wouldn't surprise me if it were the same gun used in all the killings. Let me know."

"You got it."

"By the way, you said you were investigating another murder. Anything I can help with?"

"Maybe. You know that FBI informant we were supposed to forget we ever saw?"

"Yeah, what about him?"

"He's dead. Someone shot him at the FBI safe house. Some safe house!"

Wu hustled to the whiteboard, picked up a marker, and added, "Murdered" next to the John Zachary entry. He stood with the marker pressed against his lips. *What the hell is going on here?*

Wu then added two more names:

Lawrence Sims -- Police Commissioner - ? Involvement
Captain Bill Patelli - ? Involvement

Corrine poured Scotches for Paul and herself at Monica's bar. Less than 24 hours had passed since their talk with Captain Patelli, the man with all the answers. *He might be right about the events leading up to Monica's murder, but I'm not satisfied with his flippant explanations about recent events. There are too many unanswered questions, too many loose ends and too many coincidences. How do all the events of recent days tie together? Did Monica's investigation really trigger everything? Did it involve the dead woman at her office as the captain said? What had Monica uncovered that could be so terrible that it got her killed, and drove that woman to suicide, if, in fact, she had killed herself?*

As a nurse, I understand that someone's thoughts of what might occur are often much worse than the reality of what actually takes place, and that these anxieties were what often drove people to desperate acts, including murder and suicide. So far, however, the police haven't uncovered the dead woman's real motive for either Monica's murder, or her suicide.

I am beyond dissatisfied with the conclusions of the dismissive police investigation, but what else can I do about it? I proved I couldn't be any kind of an investigator by my reaction of shock at discovering a dead body, and coming close to fainting again in panic when Paul grabbed me. She clamped her eyes shut. *Suppose I discovered some other grisly corpse, or, worse, some grisly detail about Monica's life, or her latest investigation? Could I handle it, or will I react again the same way I did this time, scared and blatantly incompetent?* She opened her eyes, eyes that stared off into space, seeing nothing but despair. *No, Wu had been right; I can't handle an investigation alone, but whom can I count on to help me, to guide me, or even show me where to begin? Everyone seems to be satisfied with the captain's explanation, everyone except me, that is.*

"I really need this drink. I can't believe what's happened these last few days. It's all a gigantic blur, a huge nightmare that won't go way." She leaned heavily on the bar. She fought back a tear. She then took a large gulp of her drink, the 30-year-old Scotch going down as advertised, smooth and without much of an initial kick. *That tastes great, nice and smooth.* She took a second, even larger gulp, then turned, and handed Paul his. He accepted it, but placed it on the coffee table without tasting it.

Corrine had changed into a loose fitting sweat suit. Even that couldn't hide the delicate curves that moved with a mesmerizing rhythm as she raised the glass to her lips, her small hands shaking with the effort.

Paul's eyes scrutinized Corinne. *She looks terrible. Her nerves are shot. I need to get her out of here, and back to New York for her own sake. I wonder if she's thought about going back yet? Time may be working against me. She looks like she's going to crack from all the pressure any minute now. So, I'd better handle her carefully, or she may lose it, and get defensive on me, even turn against me. If that happens, she won't do anything I suggest, especially leave. She looks ready to collapse right now. The strain of her sister's death has been too much for her. Come on, Corrine. Work with me here. There's a strong nurse in there somewhere. Hold yourself together long enough for us to get back to New York, away from this mess and back to our own reality.* He ran his fingers around the lip of his drink. "I've been thinking about that, Corrine. You're right; a lot has happened around you this past week. No wonder you're exhausted and confused, but the nightmare is over now. Everything is settling down." He paused, and waited for her reaction. When she remained inanimate, and said nothing, he stood, and approached her.

She watched him through half-opened eyes.

"I think it's not good for you to hang around here anymore. You've done all you possibly could."

"No, I haven't. I failed Monica, and I'll never forgive myself for that." The tear finally emerged, forming a rivulet down her cheek.

"You haven't failed her. There's nothing you could have done to prevent any of this. Besides, Monica is at peace now. There's nothing more you can do for her; you've laid her to rest." He took a deep breath. "So, I think you should go back to New York with me. Leave all these deaths behind. It's time for us to get on with our own lives. I'm sure your sister would understand."

"At peace?" Her voice trembled. "How can you say that? She's been murdered. How can she ever be at peace? How can *I* ever be at peace, ever rest?" The tears poured down her cheeks, turning the rivulet into a river. She took a step closer to Paul. *I should belt you for even thinking that, much less speaking it to me. It's a desecration of my sister's memory! Do I have to beat some sense into that thick head of yours?* "How can you be so insensitive to me, to my needs? You're supposed to care for me. I can't leave. I'd never forgive myself if I did." Corrine took another swig of liquor. This time it burned the back of her throat, making it difficult to speak properly. It triggered a coughing jag. "No, I won't leave yet. I can't leave yet. There's too much that I have to do."

Paul threw up his hands. "Like what?"

She wiped her tears with a handkerchief, and sniffed a few times. *Why doesn't anyone care about Monica's murder, and why doesn't anyone care about my feelings anymore? It's as if I'm not worth anything to anyone, including my boyfriend. Oh, how I wish you were here, Monica, to help me sort this all out, give me guidance, but I'm not going to let anyone, including the police, or Paul, stop me from looking into your murder, and getting some real answers. I'm certainly not leaving. Paul needs an excuse for me to stay? I'll give him several.* "Well, for instance, there's that patient I came here to see." She walked back to the bar. The woman staring back at her from the mirror looked old and haggard. She tore her eyes from the ugly apparition, choosing to look at the bar instead. "I've still got a lot of work to do with him. He needs a lot of help and guidance. I haven't completed his PT program yet, and I think I can formulate a plan that will get him to cooperate, and one that he'll agree to follow. I need to follow through on that plan with Dr. Filmore. You've got to understand my medical and ethical responsibility to both of them."

"Screw the patient and the doctor. They've got other therapists who can treat him. You showed them how to handle the case, gave them the direction they should follow. They should be able to take it from there without you now."

"I suppose, but there's still a lot I have to do with Monica's things."

"Like what?"

"I've got to find out about the lease on this place. I also want to go through her clothes and furniture. There are some things I think I want. I'll have them shipped back to New York. The rest I'll give to charity. Then, there's the will. I've got to see Monica's lawyer about that to see what Monica wanted done after her...passing." She turned toward the mirror behind the bar again to confront her reflection once more. *Could I really look that bad? There are a few more wrinkles in my brow. Is that a gray hair?* She closed her eyes to block out the image. *Appearances don't matter anymore. At least, they shouldn't; I can't let them anyway. I'm alone now, no longer a duplicate of another human being, no longer connected with Monica. I've never felt as lonely as I do this very minute, and it hurts more than I ever imagined.* She sobbed. Instead of her thoughts helping her to adjust to her situation, she felt worse. She turned her back on the reflection, keeping her eyes closed to shut out the world and all its ugliness. "I suppose Monica may have left some of her things to her friends. I hadn't thought of that before."

"You had other things on your mind."

"In any case, I simply can't leave now. There's too much to do."

Paul pulled her closer, and caressed her cheek. "Listen, Honey, all of this has been hard on you. I'm really worried about you, your health." He held her at arm's length. Her eyes remained half closed, fluttering a few times before fully opening. She wavered in his arms, making Paul believe she would fall if he were to let go. "There's no reason you have to do all this work by yourself. Go see the lawyer. Give him power of attorney to preside over Monica's estate. Let him arrange for the charitable contribution and the distribution of her things. Tell him what items you want. He can ship them to you. That's all you have to do. That way, you can come back to New York with me. It's time to go home."

Corrine pulled away slowly. She staggered, the alcohol taking effect. She paused to regain her bearings.

Paul's hand on her elbow steadied her gait. "Are you all right?"

"Too much Scotch and not enough food, I'm afraid. I haven't eaten much these last few days. I haven't slept much either." She sat down heavily on the couch, resting her head in her hands. "I'm sorry, Paul. I really need some time to think things over. I'm so confused right now." When he said nothing, she turned her spinning head toward him. "I have to stay. Now that the police have closed the case, there's no one else to look into it, to find if that woman really did it, and if not, then to find the real murderer." She took a deep breath, blew it out slowly. "Even if the lawyer agreed to do what you suggest, there's still the patient here, and despite what you think, the hospital will still want me in on his initial treatment sessions. I have to live up to my obligation to them. Besides, I'm not convinced that Captain Patelli's story about Monica's death really explains everything; it's too pat. So, I intend to do some snooping around on my own."

Paul sat next to her, gripping her hand firmly, so firmly that her hand actually hurt.

She looked deep into Paul's eyes, hoping to convince him with her facial expression since she had obviously failed with words. *I really need some time by myself to think things over. I'm so confused right now, but I know one thing for sure: I have to stay.*

"Snooping around on your own is not such a bright idea, Honey. As a matter of fact, it's downright crazy. The police know what they're doing. Let them do their job. If there is anything else to uncover, they'll find it, I'm sure."

Corinne's eyes opened wide. "Did I hear correctly? Did you say let the police do their job? What happened to the guy who used to say that all cops were corrupt, and out to nail anyone they could to close a case? What happened to the guy who once told me he never trusted any cops because they were only out to get as much for themselves as possible, and they didn't care who they hurt along the way?"

"Oh, he's still around. It's simply that, in this case, he thinks the police can handle it, that's all."

"Or maybe he's got his own selfish reason for wanting me to go back to New York with him?" Her speech became increasingly slurred with each word.

"Oh, come on, Corrine. That's the liquor talking, not you."

"Maybe, but it makes a lot of sense to me. Anyway, I'm not leaving, and that's final." She folded her arms across her chest, and yawned widely.

"Okay. Why don't you lay on the couch for now? We can discuss it after you've had a nap and maybe some food. I'll call you later today."

Corinne yawned. "Better make it tomorrow. I think I'll sleep until then."

Paul guided Corrine down onto a pillow, and covered her with an Afghan. He kissed her gently on the cheek as she shut her eyes. He paused at the apartment door. "Sleep tight, Honey."

Corrine listened to the sound of his fading footsteps. When she could no longer hear him, she sat up, and began to cry. She shook her head several times to clear the sleep trying to overtake her. "Maybe it is crazy, but I'm not crazy enough to leave here without finding out who really murdered Monica, and, maybe more important, why no one seems to care."

She leaned her head back on the couch, and laughed as the tears continued to flow down her cheeks. "And you're no help to me, Paul," she yelled at the door, "trying to get me to go back to New York before I'm done here." She placed the crook of her arm over her eyes to block out the light. "Besides, you should know by now that one drink may make me lightheaded, but it will never put me to sleep. I guess I proved I'm a much better actress than you think. I thought you'd never leave." She jerked her arm from her now wide-open eyes, ignoring the brightness, and forcing her eyes to search the ceiling for answers. "I wonder why you're so anxious for me to go back to New York with you. What's your real motive, Paul?"

She closed her eyes, and immediately succumbed to the sleep she had been fighting.

CHAPTER 21

A loud knock startled Corrine into consciousness. She rubbed her eyes with shaky hands, and then stood, the trembling in her knees matching the movement in her hands. Her body felt weary, and ached from the top of her head to the soles of her feet. She took a cautious step toward the door, her lead legs wobbling, causing her to almost fall. She paused, hoping to regain some strength and stability. It took longer than she thought it should have. She tried to focus her eyes on the door, but the image remained blurred. The distance she needed to travel seemed to stretch for miles. She sighed. *Oh, I am so tired. All I want is to go back to the couch and to the darkness and solitude of sleep.* She took a few deep breaths, her mind clearing slowly with the effort.

The knock recurred, louder this time. She sighed again. *I wonder if it's Paul? Oh, God, I hope not. Why can't everyone leave me alone?*

A third series of knocks, louder still and more persistent, rocked the door. She stumbled a few feet from the door, falling onto the door. Once assured her legs would support her, she pushed herself to a standing position, one hand gripping the door handle for support. She grinned at her success. She peered through the peephole. Detective Wu stared back at her.

"Go away." She threw the deadbolt to the locked position, and leaned her head against the peephole.

"I have to talk to you, Miss Day. It's important."

"Yeah, right," she mumbled. She stood in silence for several seconds, her head pounding. *I especially don't want to talk to you, Detective-Know-It-All.* "Go away. Nothing you could say to me could be that important. Besides, I'm too tired to listen anyway. Leave me alone."

"It concerns your sister. Please, let me in. Hear me out. I promise if you don't agree with what I say, I'll leave immediately, and won't bother you again."

Overwhelming fatigue gripped her. She banged her head against the door once, aggravating her headache. She allowed her forehead to remain pinned against the door despite the pain. She fought the nausea creeping up from her stomach. *I suppose...if he does have information about Monica...I should at least listen.* She unbolted and threw open the door in one fluid motion, turning her back on Wu at the same time. She staggered toward the bar. "Shit."

"Hello to you too. Do you always greet people that way?"

"Only those I abhor." Scowling, she poured the remainder of her drink down the wet bar sink. "Can I make you a drink?"

"No, thanks. I'll pass."

She checked the clock. It had only been a few minutes since Paul had left. She motioned toward the door with the empty glass. "You just missed Paul."

"I know. I waited until he left. I wanted to talk to you alone."

She forced a chuckle. "Yeah, I know, about my sister's death, but I thought you were off the case. Besides, your captain solved it. Didn't you hear? That dead woman did it."

Corrine sat on the couch, and invited Wu to join her, indicating the other end of the couch with a limp finger.

"That's exactly why I'm here." He sat on the edge of the cushion, and leaned forward, resting his elbows on his knees, allowing his hands to dangle.

Corinne hadn't noticed before how large those hands really were. His sleeves had retracted halfway up his arms, revealing large muscles, undoubtedly hewn from hours of lifting weights. *I'll bet that neat, navy blue jacket and white shirt are hiding large muscles that are flexing big-time to maintain your posture. Nice! By comparison, Paul has a large body, but isn't that heavily muscled, not even close. I've never dated a true athlete. Would making love to this man with such a hard, well-toned body be a better experience than that with Paul? Wait a minute! What am I thinking? This guy's the cop who gave me such a hard time when I first arrived. Maybe Paul is right after all. Maybe alcohol is affecting me more than I imagined.*

Wu sighed. "I don't believe that bull about her killing Monica, and then committing suicide any more than you do. There has to be more to it than that."

Corinne's chin dropped. *Did I really hear Wu say he agreed with me, or is the alcohol affecting both my judgment and my hearing?* "Why do you say that?"

"First, before we get to that, I want to apologize to you for the way I acted when we first met." He lowered his gaze to the floor, speaking softly. "I acted rudely. I attacked you unnecessarily and much too harshly. I now realize I should've been more sympathetic to your loss. Please give me a chance to explain why I overreacted." He made eye contact again, awaiting her response, nervously rubbing his hands together.

Do my ears deceive me? Did I really hear Wu apologizing...to me? You're full of surprises, aren't you? "You mean there's another side to the hard and harsh Detective Wu? You do have feelings? You surprise me. Explain away." She leaned back, and looked heavenward. "This should be good." She allowed her eyes to drift back toward Wu.

Wu's face reddened. "Let me start at the beginning, as I know it. A couple of days before your sister's death, we found the bodies of two men who worked for the Camarazza family in New York..."

"Now, that's the Detective Wu I know, ready to drag Paul's name into every crime in Washington. Why don't you accuse him of assassinating Senator Edmund while you're at it? His assassination occurred right before we arrived here too, you know."

"Hold it right there! Let me finish before you start yelling at me, please. I'm not accusing your boyfriend of anything...yet, and I certainly have no evidence that he had anything to do with the senator's assassination. I'm simply trying to present the facts, as I know them. Now, can I please continue?"

Corrine blew air through her pursed lips. "Okay. Go on. I'm listening."

"We had no leads, no suspects, and no real evidence. Then, your sister is murdered. Soon after, you and your boyfriend show up. I'm afraid I quickly jumped to the wrong conclusions. I really thought you were involved. I'm afraid I had made up my mind before you stepped foot into headquarters. I even told my captain that I considered you guilty until proven innocent."

"Me?" Corrine laughed. "But now you don't think that, right?"

"To tell you the truth, I don't know what to think anymore. I simply know your sister stumbled onto something too big for her to handle. From that point on, strange things have been happening." He sighed. "Someone's been pulling strings on the case, and directing what happens to it."

"Pulling strings? I don't understand. Who's doing that?"

"Don't know for sure. I suspect the FBI's involved somehow. They pulled my only eyewitness from me, and handed him over the Federal Marshals before I had a chance to interrogate him. They had placed him in their witness protection program under the name John Zachary. His office is right next to your sister's. Now he's dead."

"Dead?"

"Yeah, The FBI had moved him to a safe house, but someone shot him there. The FBI and Marshals don't have a clue to his killer, other than…well…now, don't get mad, and please, Miss Day, Corinne, please let me finish before you scream at me again." He took a deep breath, blew it out forcefully. "It turns out, he testified against Paul Camarazza over five years ago."

Corinne thought for a full minute before responding, trying to digest the information through her headache. *Could it be true? Could Paul be involved? Could Paul's crime family have ordered the man killed through Paul? It sounds plausible; it all makes sense, maybe, but would Paul, could the Paul I know, do such a thing? I doubt it. No, He couldn't.* "Paul? You think Paul killed him for revenge?"

"I don't know what to think at the moment, but not counting the senator you mentioned, we have five deaths, and at least four have some known connection with the Camarazza's." He counted them off on his fingers. "Two worked for him, one testified against him, and the murdered private investigator turns out to be none other than his girlfriend's twin. It wouldn't surprise me to discover he's tied in with the dead woman we found at your sister's office too."

Corinne sighed. "That's all coincidence."

Wu pounded his fist against his thigh. "I don't believe in coincidences, especially not this many."

"As far as Paul being here, I can tell you for sure that's a pure coincidence, despite what you think. As I told you, he's only here because I had a patient to see here."

"Did you ask him to come, or did he insist on coming,"

Corinne paused, staring deep into the Wu's black eyes. *This man knows how to probe for answers, I'll give him that much.* She thought back to her conversation with Paul at their lunch before their trip. Through the alcohol, the memory appeared vague. Finally, the words returned to her in crystal clarity. She leaned forward, her voice frail. "I guess you could say he insisted, but that doesn't prove anything. He's gone on other trips with me."

Wu shifted uncomfortably, trying to choose his words carefully. "Okay, let's look at it in a different way. How did you happen to be in Washington the day of your sister's murder? I mean, you told me that you hardly ever came here."

Corinne paused again before answering. Wu waited patiently.

What are you driving at, Wu? "Last Friday, the Chief of Staff at my hospital asked me to see a patient here in Washington. What possible connection could that have with my sister's murder and with Paul?"

"I'm not sure, but I'd love to know why they picked that particular weekend to ask you to come here."

"Oh, that's simple to find out." She reached for the phone. "I'll simply call the hospital to ask them that question."

"They'll probably tell you what they told me already, which is exactly what you said. That won't get us anywhere."

"Maybe, but I think I know a way to get at the truth." As she dialed the number, she cleared her throat.

Wu leaned back. *I wonder what she's got in mind. Maybe there's more to this woman than I realized. Maybe she is simply naïve, and not a part of the criminal world, but how could a person be that blind to the true nature of someone as corrupt as one of the Camarazzas? I think she really believes her boyfriend is an innocent businessman, incapable of the devious deeds the police have accused him of perpetrating. I hope she's strong enough to stand the shock when the truth finally surfaces.*

"Hello, physical therapy and rehabilitation office, Washington Veterans Administration Hospital, Kendra Dean speaking."

"Hello, Kendra," Corrine said in a good imitation of a deep southern drawl. "This is Becky Worthington from New York. I'm Dr. Gunther's secretary. Is Corrine Day there, by any chance?"

She spoke in a hushed voice. "No. Didn't you hear? Someone murdered her sister a few days ago."

"No," Corrine said loudly, feigning surprise, "how terrible! I've been out of town for a few days. I can't believe it. What a shame! What about the patient she's supposed to be seeing for Dr. Filmore? I mean, they went to so much trouble to get her there."

"Tell me about it. After we went to all that fuss to find a patient for her to examine, she doesn't even finish her evaluation. I mean, Dr. Filmore had to search all the records of almost every patient here to find one that would at least appear to be worthy of her so-called expertise, and then had to pretend he knew the patient, and needed her assistance, which

I assure you he didn't. Dr. Filmore hated to lie to her, but I guess he did it as a favor for your Dr. Gunther." She blew into the phone. "I really feel sorry for Dr. Filmore for having to lie. That's not his style at all. Guess it's not Miss Day's fault, though. She didn't know anything about it, and certainly didn't know her sister would be murdered."

"No, but I guess I've been away too long." Corrine continued to mimic the southern accent of the friend from Tennessee that she had known since her college days. "I'm missing something. What's all this about finding a patient? I thought Dr. Filmore had called our office, and specifically asked for Corinne to help with this patient. That's not what happened?"

"Not as I understand it. All I know is that your Dr. Gunther got a call last Friday from a guy in New York, and that got the ball rolling. He related the plan to our Dr. Filmore."

Corinne's eyes shot open. She almost gasped into the phone. "A guy from New York? What guy, another doctor from one of our New York hospitals?" Corrine slid to the edge of the couch, her eyes staring at the wall blankly, seeing nothing.

"Oh, no, not a doctor, but some big shot executive type by the name of Paul…either Camarrina, or Camarazza…I'm not exactly sure. Things sure started moving fast after that call. I'd sure love to know what he has on your Dr. Gunther. He sure jumped when Camarazza, or whatever his name is, phoned, and he jumped again when Camarazza called him back a few minutes ago."

"He called again? What did he want this time?"

"You'll laugh at this one. The guy has changed his mind. Now he wants us to pull her off the case. We've been instructed to tell her we've got a program set up for the patient that's based on her preliminary recommendations. We're supposed to tell her we think it will work, and, therefore, we don't need her here anymore. Can you believe it? I heard Dr. Filmore after the call. He's madder than Hell right now. He hates being used, especially by some New York executive putting pressure on his friend up there. Anyway, I heard Dr. Filmore agree to do it. So, your Miss Day is going to be sent on her way, back to New York. Can you beat that?"

Corrine looked into the phone, her mouth opened wide, unable to speak for several seconds. "I don't believe it," she finally managed to mutter, the accent gone.

"I don't either, but that's exactly what happened. Do you want us to have Miss Day call you when we get in touch with her?"

"No," Corrine said, with full accent again, "I'll catch her later." Corrine disconnected, her eyes ablaze with anger.

Wu smiled slightly, a smile that reeked of: "I told you so!"

She turned to Wu. "You were right. Paul did orchestrate my coming down here, but I don't understand why?"

"Maybe you should ask him."

"Me? What about you? You're the detective. Why can't you ask him?"

"Because I've been ordered off the case. Remember, it's been solved already. According to my captain, there aren't any loose ends, but we know differently, don't we?"

"I guess so." She lowered her head. It began pounding again.

"That's the real reason I came down here, Corrine. I presume I can still call you Corrine?"

She spoke through gritted teeth. "I don't care?" *I really don't care what anyone calls me anymore, as long as it's not: "Paul's girlfriend." I never want to hear that phrase again.*

"Good. So, I need your help to prove that the captain's solution is wrong. I believe there's more to this case than even your boyfriend's involvement."

"He's not my boyfriend," she snapped, "not after what he did."

"Understood, and I don't blame you, but that doesn't get us any closer to solving your sister's murder."

"What will?"

"Well, I can't get involved in the investigation, at least not officially. Captain Patelli warned me I'd be walking a beat again if I didn't drop the whole affair. He'll be watching my every move, but you, on the other hand..." He let his voice trail off.

"Me? What do you want from me? I'm no detective. You were the one who pointed that out when we first met, remember?"

"True, and I do apologize for that remark too, but I feared for your life. Things were happening too fast. I thought you might get hurt if the killer had any inkling that you had some information that could lead to him, maybe something your sister had left you. That's why I had you followed, and why I told you to get out of town. I thought it best if you didn't get involved at all. But now, I think differently. Now, I think you have to get involved."

"You were afraid for me? You really do have many sides, don't you?" She paused to take several deep breaths before speaking again. "Strange as it may sound, I do agree with you. If I want the truth revealed, I have to get *involved*, as you put it." Before Wu could interrupt her, she snapped her head toward him. "However, to be honest, you were right when you said I had no qualifications to lead an investigation. I don't know the first thing about being a detective. Look what happened at my sister's office. I could have been walking right into a trap, right into the killer's arms. No, I'm not qualified in the least to do any investigating, especially involving a murder. I'd be insane to even try."

"I'll teach you what you need to know, work with you, and supply any information we need from the precinct. I still have my contacts there. No one will know we're working together."

"But wouldn't I be at risk again if the killer thinks I've begun investigating the case?"

"Possibly, and unfortunately, I can't provide you with a tail this time. You'd be on your own, but I would be your backup, ready to come to your aid. Of course, I can't promise I'll be there at a moment's notice. I do have a full caseload to work on, and I have to keep up appearances at the precinct. So, you'd be on your own most of the time. I think you'll be able to handle it, though."

"You're asking a lot." *I did want to investigate Monica's murder, and, deep down inside, I had already decided to do it on my own, but I'm afraid, not of the danger, that doesn't bother me...actually, at this point, I really wouldn't care if the murderer killed me...at least it would end my pain, my loneliness...but I fear failure more than anything else. What do I do if I find nothing, no killer, no reason for the murder, nothing at all? Do I admit defeat, and return to New York with my tail between my legs, beaten by Monica's murderer?* She closed her eyes. *I suppose it could even be worse than that. Suppose something evil about Monica got her killed, something she hid from me the way I hid many of my emotions from her. Could I take the shock? Probably not. I'm not even handling the revelation about Paul very well. No, I don't think I can do any of it. It's too much for me to handle.*

"I never said it would be easy, and you're one hundred percent correct when you say it could be dangerous, but you don't have to take any unnecessary risks. It would, however, be better if you could defend yourself. Your sister had a gun. Do you know how to use it?"

"Yes, I do."

"Then, I suggest you carry it, and forget I ever suggested that, since you don't have a license." He paused to let her think. He couldn't read her unchanging, flat facial expression. *She looks exhausted. What will she decide, investigate and risk death, but have a chance of solving her sister's murder, or opt for the safety of New York? What will be her reaction to her boyfriend's involvement, and what influence will it have on her decision?* "What do you say? Want a crack at solving your sister's murder? It's the only way we'll ever know the truth."

Corinne rested her head on the back of the couch, and stared at the ceiling, as if Monica would appear there to provide an answer, a direction to follow. "If we don't work together, I suppose the real murderer gets away. Right?"

"Precisely."

Corrine thought only for a second longer. *I have no choice. I owe it to Monica and myself. I have to pursue the truth, no matter where it leads me, or what the consequences are.* She rolled her head so her gaze rested on Wu. "You're on, Detective Wu. I had planned to do it on my own anyway, but I could use your help."

"Please, call me 'Hank.' That way, if anyone sees us together, we can appear to be dating."

"Dating?" she yelled, her headache immediately intensifying again, causing her to wince. "That's not part of the deal."

"It's only for looks, Corrine."

She clamped her eyes shut. "Right, only for looks."

A knock at the door interrupted their conversation.

Corinne rushed the door. "If that's Paul, I'm going to kill him, and don't try to stop me." She swung the door open without looking through the peephole.

"Hello," the man said, displaying a badge as he spoke. "I'm Special Agent Dave Collins from the FBI. I'm looking for Detective Wu. I understand he's here."

CHAPTER 22

Corinne had hoped Paul would be the one standing at her door, begging entrance and forgiveness. She would have loved to give him a verbal thrashing and maybe a physical one too. Both disappointment and surprise flooded her body upon finding an FBI agent there instead.

"I'm in here," Wu yelled, bouncing off the couch. "What the hell do you want this time? Are you going to try to screw up my private life too? I'm off-duty. You can't tell me what to do on my own time."

Collins finally tore his gaze from Corrine long enough to see Wu standing with his fists clenched at his side. "I'm here to talk, that's all. Your captain told me where I could find you. I have some information you may find useful." He regarded Corinne who blocked his way. "Mind if I come in?"

"Oh, I'm sorry. Please, by all means."

Collins entered, sliding past Corinne. He carried a large, brown leather attaché case.

"How the hell did Captain Patelli know I came here?"

Without speaking, Collins walked past Wu to the sliding glass doors, and peaked through the curtain, disturbing it as little as possible.

"What's the matter, Collins?" Wu asked. "Afraid you were tailed?"

"No, but maybe you were."

"No one tails me without my knowing it."

Collins waved him to the window, relinquishing his place. Imitating Collins, Wu peaked out the slider. He saw no one there. There were cars parked on both sides of the street, but they all looked empty. His eyes then focused on a blue Ford van with no window in the rear, similar to the ones used for surveillance by his own police department.

"A little paranoid, aren't you, Collins?" Wu turned from the slider to find Collins busying himself checking behind a picture of the New York skyline taken at sunset.

"I don't think so." Collins held up a dime-sized metal disc.

"Oh, shit!" Wu began his own search for other bugs in the room. He found one more under the coffee table. Collins found another beneath the mirror behind the bar, another in a lamp.

"The van," Wu mouthed silently.

Collins pointed towards the door.

Wu gave him a "thumbs up'"as they headed out of the apartment.

"You wait here, Corrine. Special Agent Collins and I have a few things to settle in private. We'll be right back." Wu put a finger to his lips, and pointed to the bugs, now bunched on the coffee table like loose change.

Corinne silently mouthed, "Okay," and headed toward the window to see what had started the search of the room.

Wu and Collins approached the van carefully, each silently signaling the other his intentions with hand motions. Wu took the lead with Collins close at his heals, continually searching the area for any lookouts who would warn the van's occupants of their approach. They reached the back of the van without being spotted. Both pulled their guns.

Wu nodded to Collins, and grasped the handle of the rear door. *How could I have allowed this van to tail me? Whoever's inside has a lot of explaining to do, if they survive.*

Wu yanked the door open, and stood in a ready position with feet spread, and both hands gripping his weapon. Collins stood behind him in a similar stance with his gun pointing over Wu's shoulder.

"DC Police! Freeze," Wu yelled. His mouth fell open as he relaxed his stance, and lowered his gun. "What the hell are you doing here?"

Aaron Center, who had frozen at Wu's command, now relaxed. "Oh, thank God it's only you! I thought I had locked that door. I guess I'm getting careless in my old age."

Wu climbed into the van. "You're avoiding my question. What the hell are you doing here?"

"The Captain sent me. He wanted to know what you're up to. I've been following you all day."

"Told you." Collins holstered his weapon.

"Shut up."

Center eyed Collins as he climbed into the van. "Who's he?"

"FBI. Forget about him. I want to know what you're doing here." He didn't give Center a chance to answer. "I never saw you following me. You're no field agent. You're a lab tech. How the hell did you do it?"

"The captain ordered me to keep tabs on you. He said he had no choice but to use me. You see, well, I guess, this assignment is off the record, so to speak. I mean, you're not suspected of any criminal activity, but the Captain wanted to know what you were up to for some reason he wouldn't share with me. As to how I did it, I used electronics. I put a bug in your holster. I simply followed your signal."

Wu tore off his jacket. "Where?"

Center reached under the belt holster, and removed a pin, its head about twice the size of a normal straight pin. He held it up. Wu grabbed Center's shirt, and lifted him, ramming his head into the roof of the van. Center dropped the bug, and reached for the top of his throbbing head.

"You Son of a Bitch!"

"Don't hurt him, Wu." Collins grabbed Wu's arm. "I think he's on our side."

"You could've fooled me." Wu dropped the terrified lab technician back into his chair. "I suppose you're the one who put those bugs in Day's apartment too."

Center adjusted his rustled shirt. "Yes."

Wu growled. "Give me all the recordings, and I mean everything for the entire day. Erase anything saved to a hard drive. Don't fool with me anymore. I don't care what the captain's orders are."

Center's voice trembled as he spoke. "I wouldn't have used these recordings against you, I swear. I would have covered for you, if I had discovered anything incriminating, honest, but I had to follow you. I had to collect something to give to the Captain. Those were his orders."

"Screw the captain." Wu scrutinized Center's every move as he collected all the data sticks, and erased the files on the computer. "You were supposed to keep me informed, not spy on *me*." Wu grabbed Center's collar. "Come on, you're coming with us."

Center remained silent as Wu yanked him out of the van, and onto the pavement.

Wu glared at Center. "Lock the door, this time. You never know who might drop in on you."

Wu leaned on the rear of the elevator, as he scowled at Center. He still had most of Center's lapel gripped in his clenched fist, ready to toss him to the ground at the first sign of any resistance, but his captive knew better, and remained passive. Wu refused to let up the pressure of his restraint; he didn't care if he hurt the delinquent lab tech. *I've embarrassed myself in front of Collins because of you. Not only had I not thought about checking Corinne's apartment for bugs, but I also had you, one of my own men, manage to place a tracking device on me...and I had to be informed about it by Collins. Damn embarrassing.*

As each floor went by with a high-pitched ping from the elevators control panel, Wu became redder, the furrows on his brow deepened, and his grip on Collin's lapel tightened until all the blood drained from his hand. *What is Corinne going to think of my offer to help her in the investigation when I can't even protect myself from my own men? Would either Corinne or Collins ever trust me again? I screwed up royally.*

When they arrived at the apartment door, Wu pushed Center against the hall wall. Collins winced, as Center's head bounce off the wall. The ensuing thud rolled down the empty hallway.

Wu leaned toward Center. "You wait out here, and don't even think about listening at the door."

Center froze, his arms limp at his side, his head turned, avoiding Wu's glare. "Yes, Sir."

After explaining the lab technician's presence in the hallway to Corinne, Collins turned to Wu. "A little rough on him, weren't you?"

"He deserved it. He's playing both sides of the fence."

"Maybe, but aren't you doing the same thing? I mean pretending you're finished with this case, and investigating it on your own."

Wu grinned. "Oh, haven't you heard? There is no more case to investigate. My captain solved it before the body had even gotten cold."

"Oh, I heard, but you're still investigating it anyway, aren't you?"

"Now, why would I do that?"

"Because you're the best damn detective in town, that's why, and it's not your style to let any murder investigation get away from you that easily, to say nothing of the murderer. Besides, you think there's more to this whole case then a couple of simple murders, don't you?"

Wu took two steps towards Collins, his fists clenched again. "What if I do? It's none of your business."

Collins put his hands up in a surrendering posture. "Calm down. You might find I happen to agree with you, but I'm not so sure we should discuss that sort of thing in front of your lady friend here."

"And why not? My sister is one of the murder victims."

"That doesn't mean you're not involved in all this somehow."

Corrine's hands trembled as she fought the urge to strike out at him. *I'm beginning to hate cops, all cops.* "I'm getting extremely tired of being accused of things I'm not guilty of committing." She took one step toward Collins. "If you've got some proof, arrest me. If not, get out, and let Hank and I get on with our investigation. We don't need you."

"Hank and you? My, we are chummy."

Wu growled. "Cut the bull, Collins. What we do together is none of your business."

"That's true, but I don't appreciate being manipulated, and, from the way you reacted at your lab tech, you don't either, but that is exactly what happened to both of us, and now we're being treated like yesterday's garbage. We've apparently lost all our usefulness to our respective bureaus."

"We? What happened to you?" Wu asked.

"I've been transferred to California. Mind you, I've been here for fifteen years, but now, all of a sudden, the West Coast can't do without my experience and wisdom. It's crap, I tell you."

"I don't understand. Who's manipulating you two, and why?"

"I wish I knew. Any ideas, Wu?"

"No, but to be honest with you, that's why I'm here. I'm trying to get Corinne to volunteer to do a little detective work for me, be my eyes and ears, that sort of thing."

"You're assuming she's not already involved in all this up to her eyeballs. If you're wrong, that could be an extremely dangerous mistake, especially if these killings do turn out to be a string of related events."

Collins regarded Corinne, studying her reaction, hoping for some hint of her involvement. He detected none. Instead, Corinne's expression remained serious and determined. "Assuming you're not involved, Miss Day, you should consider that you could be the next target, especially if you get too close to the murderer's identity. Are you sure you want to risk that?"

Corinne glared at Collins. "I don't think I have any choice, not if I want the real murderer caught anyway."

Collins paused for a full minute, his gaze bouncing between Wu and Corinne. "You have to understand my position in all this. These murders fall under local jurisdiction, not Federal, not mine." He turned to Wu. "I came here to try to help you, to tell you what I know, but I'm still leery about telling her everything." He moved his head in Corinne's direction once more. "How do we know she's not working for her boyfriend, Paul Camarazza? Everything we say could go right back to him."

"Corinne's learning that her boyfriend is not the angel he pretends to be, and that's putting it mildly. I trust her now."

Collins smirked. "How sweet, disgusting, but sweet nonetheless! Okay, it's your life on the line, Wu, not mine. What I came here to propose is a temporary truce between us. What do you say we tackle this investigation together?" He sighed. "I guess that *we* would now include you, Miss Day. Maybe we can make more sense out of it if we pool our resources."

"I thought you were going to sun yourself in California."

"I am, but I still have access to all the information in the FBI files. I can tap anything we need to help us in the investigation. I may be able to help even from the West Coast."

"Great," Corinne said, "but where do we start?"

"Right here. Tell me what you know about your sister's involvement in all this. Any idea who, or what she had been investigating?"

"We don't know. All her records were stolen."

"And destroyed," Collins said, "I know."

"How do you know they were destroyed?"

Collins lowered his eyes.

"Of course," Wu exclaimed, suddenly seeing the obvious. He threw his arms up in total frustration. "You destroyed them, didn't you?"

CHAPTER 23

Wu glared at Collins, his accusatory index finger only inches from the FBI agent. "I hate people who abuse their authority, and you've proven to be exactly such a person."

Collins swiped Wu's hand away. "Now, wait a minute, Wu. Don't think you can push me around the way you did your lab man. Like him, I followed orders, nothing more."

"You mean it's true?" Corinne asked, hands on her hips. "The FBI not only seized my sister's files, they destroyed them?"

"Now, stop it, both of you. I surrender. It's against my better judgment, but I'll tell you exactly what happened. We cleaned her apartment out the morning of her murder."

Corinne yelled her question. "But why?"

"We had orders straight from Director Higgins."

Wu blew out noisily.

Collins took one step toward Wu. "Listen, when the Director tells you to do something, especially when you think it's legitimate, you don't question, you do it. That's my job."

"Maybe. What cock and bull story did he hand you?"

"That the PI had stumbled onto something that could jeopardize national security. I couldn't get him, or the judge to tell me any more than that, even after her murder. 'Still a case of national security' he told me." He fidgeted with the combination lock on the attaché case as he talked. "Director Higgins instructed us to search for, and confiscate, every file folder, piece of writing paper, photograph, computer storage device…anything that could convey information, and not to read, or even look at any of it. We were to be kept totally in the dark. They didn't want any chance of any information leaking. So, we were all kept in the dark."

"Then you were the ones who destroyed the computer hard drive too?" Wu asked.

"We reformatted it. That destroys the information on it, not the disk itself."

"Well, I've got some news for you. According to our lab, your guys did a low level format on an older computer, whatever that means. That damaged the hard drive permanently. It has something to do with the type of hard drive the computer had. Anyway, it's fried."

"I didn't know that. I did what I had been instructed to do, format the drive so no one could retrieve any files." He glanced at Corinne. "Sorry. I really didn't know."

"Too late for that now." Corinne turned her back on Collins.

"What did you do with the paper files you took from her cabinets?" Wu asked.

"They all went immediately to the incinerator. I took them there myself. Nothing survived."

Wu clamped his eyes shut. "Shit."

"Didn't Director Higgins give you any small hint as to what Monica had found?" Corinne wheeled around on the balls of her feet as she spoke.

"No, none. We were told that she didn't know the significance of what she had in her possession, and that destroying it would end the problem."

Wu stared at Collins. "I presume you did all of this without a search warrant."

"No, of course not. FBI agents don't break the law. We had a search warrant. Judge Jacobs issued it."

"Maybe I could talk to that judge to find out what he knows," Corinne said.

"The judge is a woman. I've already talked to her since the murder. I asked her specifically why she issued the search warrant. She claims she had been presented with strong evidence that what the PI had discovered could indeed jeopardize national security, the same words Director Higgins used. Anyway, lives were at stake, as she put it. She wouldn't say more than that. She sounded sincere, though. I'm not sure she knows much more, but you're welcome to try to get more out of her. I'll give you her contact information."

"That search warrant couldn't have possibly given you the authority to destroy what you found," Wu said. "That's illegal. What you had could have been construed as evidence."

"You're right there. Director Higgins took that responsibility himself. At least, that's what he told me, and then, later, the original search warrant disappeared, and no one knows what happened to it."

"Didn't you become more suspicious after the murder?" Wu asked.

"Of course. We clean the PI's place out, then she's murdered, the search warrant disappears, and I get booted across the country. Suspicious? I felt used. I should have suspected something earlier when John Zachary called to tell me of your sister's murder. I'm afraid I pulled Wu's only witness right out from under him before he had even begun his investigation."

"Hank told me about him. They murdered him at some safe house, right?"

"Correct. He moved into your sister's building a short while ago. He originally had an office on the other side of town. He told us he needed a change. Now, I wonder if he moved there to get closer to your sister. Maybe he learned about her investigation, and wanted to get involved, either to help her, or maybe to stop her. I wouldn't put either past him."

"Any idea who killed him?" Wu asked.

"No, but you guessed right earlier. He had testified against Paul Camarazza in New York a few years ago. My guess is they learned his whereabouts, and executed him. That's another thing I'm not proud of. We should have protected him better."

Corinne held her breath. *How could I have been so blind to what Paul has done...what he did to me? How long has he been using me, since our first meeting? Some insightful nurse I turned out to be!* She felt lightheaded once more. Her skin became pale. She suddenly felt faint. She plopped onto the couch, and leaned against its soft back, trying to regain her composure, to make sense out of all this senselessness. She covered her tearful eyes with her arm, trying to block out all the dreadful news being presented to her. "How could Paul do this to me?"

"I'm sorry, Miss Day, but I know that your boyfriend must be deeply involved in all of this. So, listen carefully. If you intend to follow Wu's advice to investigate this case, you'd better be prepared to learn a lot more about Paul Camarazza that might both surprise and hurt you."

She accepted a handkerchief from Wu. "I thought I knew him so well. I'm usually pretty good at judging people. I can't understand how I could have been so blind."

"He's a great user of people, if you believe his rap sheet," Wu said, taking a seat next to Corinne.

Collins had been watching Corinne's reaction to the news concerning Camarazza. Her reaction surprised him. "You're either the most naïve woman I've ever met, or a very good actress, Miss Day."

Wu's head snapped in Collin's direction. "Are you still stuck on her being involved? She's been through a lot these last few days. Give her a break."

"It's my suspicious nature, I guess." He opened his attaché case, and removed a voice recorder. "I'll show you what I mean." He placed the digital recorder on the coffee table, tapping it as he spoke. "I have something you two should hear. We don't know for sure how they learned the location of the safe house, but I suspect we have a major leak somewhere in the FBI, or among the Federal Marshals."

"Or maybe your director told them," Wu said.

"That unsettling thought had crossed my mind, although he denied any knowledge of Zachary's whereabouts at the time of his murder. I had made it a point not to tell anyone which house we were using, but he is the Director after all, and there are ways he could have found out." He held up one finger for emphasis. "However, I can't see Director Michael Higgins, career FBI man, giving that information to anyone who could use it to harm someone, especially a person in the witness protection program. It's not his style. He's one hundred percent loyal US law enforcement agent. No, he's not the leak. He's even started his own investigation to find out how the information got out. He's working with the head of the Federal Marshals. They swear they won't stop until they find, and plug, the leak. I wish them luck. Moles are hard to find."

"Maybe the killer overheard your Director Higgins discussing it with someone he trusted," Corinne said.

"Possible, I guess. You'll have to keep that in mind during your investigation. Don't trust anyone, and watch what you say." He pointed to the bugs on the table. "You never know who might be listening. As to Zachary, I can't tell you how they found him, but I can tell you that he died at eleven fifteen Tuesday night, and I can show you how they got him to go outside so they could kill him. We have a tap on the phone line into all our safe houses that records all calls. Unfortunately, it's not monitored all the time. It's simply a recording device; we're thinking of changing that now. Anyway, this conversation occurred immediately before Zachary snuck outside. We back checked the call, and the caller used a disposable cell phone. It's untraceable. Listen carefully."

He pressed the play button, and watched Corinne's reaction.

"Hello, Mr. Zachary?" The female voice sounded muted, making her difficult to understand. "This is Corinne Day, Monica's sister. We need to meet."

"I can barely hear you," Zachary said.

"I must talk to you immediately. It concerns my sister's investigation."

"Well...I don't know. I'm not supposed to talk to anyone. They're afraid the mob may find me. That's why they're hiding me. They're not letting me meet anyone."

"But I have to see you. It's a matter of life and death. Listen, I'm calling from my car now. I'll meet you outside the back door in a few minutes."

"Well...I still don't know...they told me to stay inside."

"Yes, I'm sure they did. They won't let me talk to you for even a few minutes, but I must speak to you. My life may be in danger unless I can go over some of my sister's notes with you, and make some sense out of them. Oh, please say you'll meet me."

"How did you know where they had taken me?"

"Detective Wu told me. He said it would be all right to talk to you, if you can get away from the Marshals for a few minutes. Please say you'll help me."

"Well, okay. I'll be right out...as soon as I can give these guys the slip for a few minutes."

Collins switched off the recorder.

"That's not me!" Corinne yelled.

"And I couldn't have told anyone about the safe house. I didn't know its location."

Collins ignored Wu's comment, and continued to stare at Corinne. Corinne returned his glare. "I never made that call!"

"That should be easy to prove. Where were you Tuesday night between eleven and eleven thirty?"

"Tuesday, that's the day of my sister's wake. I stayed here that evening with...Paul. He left about eleven thirty."

Collins stared wide-eyed at Corinne. "Your alibi is Paul Cama-razza? That's rich, a crook as an alibi. Of course, you realize that's not going to look especially good in court, but you, on the other hand, have provided Mr. Camarazza with a great alibi. He used you, Miss Day."

"It appears that he's done it to you again." Wu patted Corinne's hand.

Damn! No, not again! "Shit!"

"There is another way of proving that's not you on that recording," Wu said, as he headed for the door. He found Center still pinned against the wall. "Get your ass in here, now!"

Aaron Center entered the apartment with his head lowered, fully expecting the worst from the detective he had betrayed. Wu grabbed him by the shoulder, pulling him to the bar where Collins had moved with the recording.

Wu waved Corinne over to the bar with his hand.

"This is Aaron Center, one of our lab boys, and the person who's been spying on me all day. This is Corinne Day." Wu then pushed him onto the couch, and replayed the recording.

"Do you think you can identify that female voice?" Wu asked.

"We want it checked against Miss Day's voice first."

Both Corinne and Wu scowled at Collins.

"You can keep that recording if you need to. I have another copy. Can you match it to Miss Day's voice?"

"Maybe. It sounds muffled. The woman is obviously trying to disguise her voice. She probably spoke through a handkerchief. I suppose we could try matching voiceprints. I can't promise anything, but I'll try. I'll need a sample of Miss Day's voice. You can put it on the end of the recording."

"Good. Do a decent job, and I might forget you were spying on me."

"You can count on me."

"We'll see about that, and as far as the Captain goes, I went to a movie alone tonight and then straight home. Right?"

"Right you are."

"Before I kick you out of here, have you got any other useful news for me about this case?"

"Yeah, as a matter of fact I do. You were right about that .22 pistol we found in the PI's office next to the dead woman. It not only killed her, but it's the same weapon used to kill those two hoods, and the PI."

"There's the connection I've been looking for. That gun connects the supposed suicide to the Camarazza family shootings. Now, all the deaths have some connection with your boyfriend."

"That doesn't surprise me in the least," Collins said.

A tear appeared at the corner of one of Corinne's eyes. "Oh, no, we're back to that again?"

"Damn right we're back to that again," Collins said, slamming his fist down on the bar. "It's time you understand that Paul Camarazza is a dangerous man. He's involved in this all the way up to that impeccably combed hair of his, and, if that's the case, he'll stop at nothing to protect himself. Keep that in mind, and maybe you'll be able to come out of this alive."

"Thanks. I didn't know you cared."

"I don't."

"Enough of your bickering, You Two. Have you identified the dead woman yet, Center?"

"Yup, her name's Sage Browning, age twenty-eight. She's lived here in Washington for the last five years working for Senator Frank Stern."

Wu's eyebrows rose in surprise. "Senator Stern?"

"Sure, the one they've been talking about running for President. Seems this Browning woman is his fiancée, and, according to my sources, they were planning to get hitched soon."

"Why would she want to kill herself?" Corinne asked.

"Don't know the answer to that one yet. The Captain seems to think that she had a falling out with the senator after she found the PI investigating her, and both she and the senator were afraid of some dirt coming out because of her investigation. So, she kills the PI, and then herself when she can't find the evidence the PI had incriminating her."

"Only the Captain would dream up something to fit the facts…without evidence to support his case, of course." Wu covered his eyes with his hands, trying to block out the image of his Captain, expounding his explanation to his underlings.

"The M.E.…." Center looked toward Corinne, but saw no hint of recognition. "…that's the medical examiner…puts the time of death between nine and eleven Wednesday morning. We checked her hands for gunshot residue…nothing. She hadn't fired a gun. So, I guess you were right. It wasn't suicide. She also had a red mark around her throat that we can't explain."

"She had been strangled?" Wu asked.

"No, the autopsy showed no evidence of strangulation, but we found a thin red line around her throat about here." He drew a line with his index finger across his Adam's apple. "The M.E. described it as more of a light bruise, or scrape. Apparently, it didn't compromise her airway, and probably happened after she died."

"A necklace, maybe," Corinne offered.

"That's possible, but we didn't find one with her body."

"Maybe the killer took it after he killed her," Corinne said.

"Maybe. Anything else, Center?"

"Only that the Captain told me to ignore the gunshot residue results. He said GSR testing is too unreliable, and that he had closed the case successfully anyway. He also said he didn't want it reopened, period. He told me to file the information away, and forget it."

Wu huffed. "That's our current Captain Bill Patelli, The Sleaze Ball."

"Ha!" Collins shook his finger at Wu. "You should have more respect for your superiors, but in case you're right about him, and he is involved in this cover-up, I would suggest we not tell him about the recording, or the necklace mark, or anything else we uncover, at least for now. We're not really withholding evidence from him since the case is closed in his opinion anyway."

"Right." Wu walked to within inches of Center, and poked his index finger into his chest twice for added emphasis. "Do you understand that?"

"Oh, I understand. Believe me, I understand."

"You'd better," Wu warned.

"I also think that it might be a good idea to match Sage's voice prints against that recording also."

"Oh," Corinne said, "you mean you're finally going to admit that might be someone else's voice? How big of you!"

"Watch it, Miss Day. I'm still not convinced you're totally innocent, you know."

Corinne laughed once. "What're you going to do, arrest me? Then, there'll be no one left to investigate this mess. Wake up, Mr. FBI. I want this solved as much as you, maybe more."

"We'll see."

"Matching Sage Browning's voice to that tape might be a little harder than you think," Center said. "At least with Miss Day here, she's around to speak into the microphone. I'm not sure where we can get a voice clip of the dead woman, but I'll try. Maybe someone recorded her saying something cute when she and the senator attended some rally somewhere. Anything else I can do to help?"

"How about getting us a list of long distance phone calls for Sage Browning, my sister, Senator Jackson, and Senator Stern, including office, home and cell phones for the last month or so?"

"What's the idea of the phone records? Do you suspect something we're not seeing?"

"I don't know for sure. Call it a hunch. Maybe we'll get lucky, and one of the calls will give us a direction to go in, maybe give us a hint at what Monica had been working on, who she talked to, that sort of thing. I figured we might as well check on the senators and that Browning woman as well. They all have to be connected somehow."

Collins closed his attaché case. "That's not a bad idea. There's no way you're going to get a search warrant to do that legally, but I think I can coordinate with Mr. Center here to get him the computer access he needs that can't be tracked back to him or us. I have a few favors I can call in at the Bureau's call center. Give me your cell phone number, Mr. Center, and I'll contact you later."

"I think I'll add Wyman and Florentino's motel phone to Corinne's list," Wu said.

"Any idea where you're going to begin what I'm going to call *our* investigation, Miss Day?"

"No."

"May I suggest that you begin at Sage Browning's wake, or her funeral? You'll probably at least run into Senator Stern there. Maybe you'll meet some of Miss Browning's other friends, and, who knows, maybe some enemies too. Sometimes killers have a morbid curiosity about their work. They sometimes attend the events they've set in motion."

Wu smiled at Corinne. "It's worth a shot. You meet the strangest people at wakes and funerals, you know."

Corinne threw a deadly look Wu. "That's not the least bit funny."

Wu lost the smile. *I wish, just this once, I had kept my big mouth shut.*

CHAPTER 24

Corinne spent the remainder of Thursday and all Friday morning in an uneasy sleep, plagued by a recurrent nightmare of Monica screaming for help, but being unable to locate her. Whenever she did manage to approach the sound of her voice, someone blocked her way. Once, it had been Detective Wu, another time Special Agent Collins. Paul had appeared more than once to stop her, as had both Senator Stern and Senator Jackson. Even Aaron Center appeared, wrapping Corinne in electrical wires, and refusing to let her continue her desperate search for her lost sister. Corinne awoke, drenched in sweat several times; however, each time she returned to the land of dreams, Monica's pleas returned, as did Corinne's unremitting and unrewarding search.

Corinne finally climbed out of bed at midday, made herself a light brunch, and read the newspaper she had found outside Monica's door. She read the obituary column first, discovering that Sage Browning's wake had been scheduled for that evening and the funeral Saturday morning.

The front-page headlines still concerned the assassination of Senator Edmond and the lack of progress by the authorities in the matter. The latest theory blamed radical terrorists for the act, although no group had come forward to claim credit for the assassination.

A picture of Senator Stern with Senator Jackson taken at a meeting on Capitol Hill took up a full quarter of the page. They were both smiling and waving. *What the hell do you two know about Monica's death?* Corinne tore through the rest of the paper, but could find nothing concerning Monica's murder. *Yesterday's news, I guess.*

As evening approached, Corinne combed Monica's closet for an outfit to wear to the wake. She decided on a pair of Monica's dark-blue pants, and adorned it with a wide black-leather belt above her hips. She picked a beige blouse with broad, brown, vertical stripes. She threw Monica's yellow jacket over her arm, and slipped on a pair of short brown heels to complete the outfit. As she headed out the door, she looked back, and tried laughing. Instead, she became choked up. "I always told you your clothes were best suited for wakes and funerals, Monica. I guess this proves it." She finally managed a small, but unsatisfying, smile.

Corinne opened up the Lamborghini when she reached an uncluttered part of the beltway around Washington, allowing the machine to do what it had been built to do, fly effortlessly past the speed limit. She whizzed past all the other cars on the multilane thoroughfare, weaving between the cars, slowing only when necessary, and only long enough to gain a further egress from behind some slower driver, whisking past at the first opportunity. She wondered, but really didn't care, if she would zoom past some policeman's radar gun.

Screw it. Let them try to catch me. I've got to blow off some steam. The judge will understand, I'm sure, if they catch me, that is.

Internally, she burned with frustration, feeling much like the high performance car under her: caught in slower traffic, obstructed and restricted on all sides. There were unseen forces preventing her from doing what she wanted to do most: find the true story behind Monica's death, and track down her killer.

I've made an uneasy alliance with Wu and Collins, but Monica's murder investigation has been closed by powers far above their heads, or government clearances. All of us agree that those same powers have instituted a major cover up, but had left no clues as to who's behind it, or why they did it. Who could manage such power so undetected? Wu insisted Paul had masterminded at least part of it. Of course, Collins agreed. I can't expect either of those cops to give the benefit of the doubt to anybody, especially Paul. He's automatically guilty in their eyes, but I'm still not convinced Paul knew anything about Monica's murder. I can't believe he's capable of hurting Monica. On the other hand, the rat had arranged my assignment in Washington, and then had gotten it cancelled. Why? What do the senators have to do with it? Tonight, I hope to get some answers.

She pushed the car harder. It responded without hesitation, leaping forward to even higher speeds, pinning her to the seat. The white lines on the road became mere specks as they zipped past. She gripped the leather steering wheel tightly, moving it only slightly to make the necessary adjustments to weave around the other cars on the highway.

Corinne had been concentrating on the road in front of her so much that she had not noticed the car that overtook her until she caught a glimpse of it out of the corner of her eye. A black Ferrari with darkly tinted windows, making it virtually impossible to see the driver, began passing her.

Corinne laughed. *Isn't that windshield illegal, Honey?*

The Ferrari pulled alongside, matching the Lamborghini's speed with expertise.

Want to race, huh? Okay, Honey, let's see what that tin can do against a real lady in heavy traffic. I should warn you though. I trained on the professional circuit a few years back, and learned quite a few tricks of competitive driving along the way. You haven't got a chance.

Suddenly, without warning, the Ferrari swerved toward her door.

"Watch out," Corinne yelled, instinctively turning her wheel away from the collision, and pushing the accelerator to the floor. Her car jumped out of the Ferrari's way, avoiding the collision by inches; however, Corinne now found herself hurtling toward the concrete barriers lining the highway. "Shit," she yelled, yanking the wheel to the left, narrowly missing the barrier, downshifting to regain control. She then sped toward the open road, aiming the sports car to the few open spaces between vehicles.

"Where are you, You Nut?" She searched all her mirrors for a glimpse of the Ferrari. "You need a driving lesson, and I'm precisely the person to give it to you. I'm tired of people pushing me around."

She finally spotted the Ferrari in the third lane, and shot toward it; however, as soon as she had established herself in the middle lane, the black demon again streaked toward her door.

"What are you doing? Are you insane? That's a dangerous and stupid move at these speeds." She again swerved away from the imminent collision. "What do you think you're doing, playing chicken, or are you trying to kill me?" *Wait a minute! That's exactly what you're planning, isn't it? You're deliberately trying to drive me off the road. Who the Hell are you, and, more importantly how, how do I get out of this one? What would Monica do? Monica, oh, please, help me!*

Corinne's aggressive attitude morphed to one of passivity and defense, as she tried to stay as far from the pursuing Ferrari as possible, trying to hide behind larger SUVs and minivans for protection. She could feel her heart pounding, racing like the pistons under the Lamborghini's hood. She gripped the wheel so tightly that her hands turned white. The muscles of her forearms ached. Her wide-open eyes searched the road for every opening through which she could possibly drive, openings barely large enough to allow entry but which she thought could lead to a possible avenue of escape.

She shifted in the seat, hunching over the wheel, hoping that would buy her more control of her car. *Come on, Babe. Don't fail me now.* Corinne's feet danced on the pedals as she piloted her car through the sluggish traffic. Spotting an opening as one car overtook another, she shifted, flooring the accelerator again. The Lamborghini's wheels screeched as it shot through the opening, missing both vehicles by mere inches, and raced past a long line of cars. She swerved several times to avoid collisions, leaning on her horn as she did so in a desperate attempt to warn the other drivers of her approach. "Move over, You Idiots," she yelled. "Get out of my way. He's trying to kill me."

The ever present Ferrari managed to stay in her rear view mirror despite her quick handling and alarming speed, its driver having no difficulty, or fear of squeezing his vehicle between cars to keep up with Corinne's pace and acrobatic driving. Several times she saw the Ferrari fishtail as it swerved around cars, but each time it recovered, and rocketed after her again. Twice more the Ferrari caught Corinne on her left, each time swerving toward her door as soon as it had regained its position. Each time, Corinne, aware of the Ferrari's presence, and now ready for its attack, launched the Lamborghini into a maneuver to avoid the collision, each time missing the impact by the narrowest possible margin. She tried using slower cars as shields, but the Ferrari always managed to out maneuver her to regain its attack position.

"You idiot," she yelled, wishing the Ferrari driver could hear her. "Leave me alone."

Corinne searched the road for a way to escape the ever-charging Ferrari. There seemed to be no place to hide from her pursuer, no way to outmaneuver the ever-charging automobile, and no police vehicle to offer her refuge. Finally, spotting an overhead sign for the next exit, she floored the gas pedal once more. *Come on, Babe. Give me all you've got. If we can't outrace that idiot, we'll outsmart him.*

She stayed in the middle lane, allowing the Ferrari to hover at her left rear bumper, but kept her speed up, effectively preventing him from overtaking her to launch another attack at her door. Every time he started to overtake her, she swerved partially into the other lane, driving him back and away from her. *It's only a temporary holding maneuver, I know, but I only need it to work for a short distance, a little while longer. Dear God, let this work!*

As the exit ramp approached, Corinne suddenly drove the car across the first lane, cutting off an older Cadillac. The driver of the Cadillac hit his breaks, cursed, and skidded, almost broad siding the Lamborghini. The Cadillac tires screamed as the car skidded in the first lane. Corinne found herself now headed at full throttle toward the exit ramp, exactly where she wanted to be; however, she had lost sight of her adversary. *Could he have changed direction when I did, imitating my seemingly outrageous maneuver? God, I hope not! Where is he?*

Indeed, the Ferrari had turned within a few seconds of Corinne's maneuver, trying to keep up with the Lamborghini. It swerved to avoid the Cadillac, turning almost ninety degrees, and skidding sideways down the middle lane, with tires spinning, screeching, and smoking as they sought traction. The car seemed to glide past the now stopped Cadillac, as if it were on ice. Its wheels continued to spin and smoke as the driver floored his accelerator, turning his nose toward Corinne. The Ferrari finally caught some traction, leaping forward in his pursuit, charging up the middle lane, attempting to recapture his preferred position on her driver's side.

Corinne, now flying in the first lane, and with no cars in front of her for at least one mile, checked her side view mirror to find the Ferrari still on her left and behind as they approached the oncoming ramp. *Come on. Keep up; push that sports car. I've got a surprise for you.* Corinne aimed her car directly at tip of the "V" formed by the concrete barriers that lined the left side of the exit ramp. *I hope I can time this right.*

As she approached the barrier, Corinne slowed slightly, allowing the Ferrari's hood to reach the level of her rear tire. She then turned the wheel slightly to the right, missing the barrier by inches. The concrete screamed past her window. The Ferrari driver, finding himself trapped behind and to the left of the Lamborghini and barreling toward the barrier directly ahead, veered to the left, barely missing the barrier, but also missing the exit, skimming along the shoulder of the road. Its driver cursed, and then swerved back onto the expressway, speeding away.

Corinne now faced a different, but possibly even larger dilemma than a pursuing Ferrari. Her speedometer read nearly ninety on a short ramp with a large curve at its end and a stop sign where the exit ramp "T"ed with another thoroughfare. She hit the brakes, and started to skid toward the barriers that lined the curve. As she flew toward the curve, she yanked the wheel to the right, flooring the accelerator at the same time. The Lamborghini's tires dug into the gravel lining the side of the road, the car shifting violently to the right. Corinne's head smashed into her driver's side window as she careened down the barrier. The crunching sound of metal scraping against concrete filled the air. Sparks flew across her window. The right side of the car rose off the ground. Only the shape of the barrier prevented the car from flipping over. When it finally righted, Corinne stomped on the brake pedal. The car slid through the stop sign, crossing the busy road as other drivers swerved to avoid the skidding sports car. The Lamborghini then mounted the opposite curb, bumping through some bushes, finally coming to a halt on the grass over one hundred yards from where it had first impacted the barrier. The impact with the curb, and sudden stop nearly smashed Corinne into the steering wheel. Only the seat belt and her extraordinary effort to brace against the crash prevented her impact with the wheel.

Corinne's whole body trembled. Her rapid and shallow breathing made her lightheaded. *Easy, Corinne! Control your breath. Don't hyperventilate.* Her breathing eased, as did her lightheadedness. *I wonder why the hell the air bags didn't deploy. Maybe Paul had them disconnected to get me killed. I wouldn't put it past him at this point.* Her left shoulder and head ached, but otherwise she felt uninjured. She peeled her hands from the steering wheel, unbuckled her seat belt, and reached for the door handle. The Lamborghini's door rose into the air like the wing of a huge bird. She started to get out of the car, one foot touching the grass before she realized how dizzy she felt, how clouded her judgment had become. *Wait a minute. What the hell am I doing? Where's the damn Ferrari?*

She looked over her shoulder at the now vacant exit ramp...no Ferrari. She pulled down on the door, both pleased and surprised that after the side impact it flowed so easily into its latched and locked position. Habit forced her to fasten her seat belt once again. Checking that she had free access to the road, and that all the cars she had sent sprawling had gone their own way, she gunned the engine, and popped the clutch. The tires dug into the ground, sending grass and dirt flying. Finding hard ground, the auto jumped forward over the curb, back onto the thoroughfare. Corinne ran the red light at the next intersection, increasing her speed, hoping a policeman would stop her for the infraction. None did. *Where the hell am I? How soon will my Ferrari-nemesis backtrack to find me again. I've got to get out of here while I can.*

Her hands still trembled. *That damned driver almost killed me. Don't want to run into him again.*

Afraid to stop to inspect Paul's car for damage, or even to ask for help, she slowed to a crawl only long enough to confirm that the car's GPS had adjusted to her detour. It had, and the female voice proceeded to guide her toward the funeral home. *At least the retrofitted GPS still works. Thank God for that!*

After a few forced, deep breaths, she finally started to breathe normally once more, but couldn't stop the trembling in her hands.

After parking under a light, she laid her head against the headrest, and closed her eyes. Exhaustion overtook her. She took a deep breath, blew it out forcefully. *God, he came close to killing me, too close.*

She finally mustered enough strength to climb out of the car. After scanning the lot for the Ferrari, she inspected the damage to the Lamborghini, rubbing her still shaking hand along the scrapes and dents that were once aerodynamically smooth curves. *Damn it! Paul will kill me. He loves this car, but, right now, I don't give a damn. He deserves more than simply a dented car.*

She then ran her hand along her throbbing temple. A small, hard lump had arisen in the area. She inspected her hand closely, but found no blood. She patted the car's injured side. "I guess we both got some scrapes this time. Thanks, Babe; I owe you one, and your repairs will be on me when we get back to New York, if I can afford them, which I sincerely doubt."

Still rubbing her forehead, she then forced her wobbly legs to carry her to the entrance of the funeral home.

CHAPTER 25

The ride to Sage's wake and her escape from the Ferrari had been harrowing. Corinne had barely emerged from the encounter with her life, both she and the Lamborghini surviving with only cosmetic damage. As she now walked to the funeral home, her mind finally cleared, her anger growing to replace the fear she had been experiencing. *Who the hell drove that Ferrari? Couldn't be Paul; he doesn't even own a Ferrari. Besides, he couldn't possibly drive as well as my attacker. Could it have all been a coincidence, a psychotic driver out to commit murder simply because I drove a competing sports car, or some other crazy, illogical reason? I doubt it. Coincidences don't kill in car accident fatalities, drivers do, and he came damn close to killing me. I could see the head-lines now: "CORINNE DAY, KILLED ON THE WAY TO A FUNERAL, HER OWN." Not funny, Corinne, not funny at all.*

Both Wu and Collins had warned her that her life could be in danger. She had accepted that as the possible cost of uncovering all the facts surrounding Monica's murder, and had even prayed for her own death so she could be reunited with Monica, but when the reality of death confronted her, she had been terrified, begging God and Monica for help, not knowing what to do, how to escape, or how to survive. *Did they intervene to help me, or had I escaped on my own? I don't know. I escaped, but only because I had outmaneuvered my opponent, beaten him to the exit ramp, and prevented him from following me. That maneuver saved me, but almost cost my life.* She looked Heavenward. *Maybe I did have some help after all, but I wonder if I could have done something different, quicker, or smarter to evade him? Next time, I'd better be prepared to anticipate the danger, and to defend myself better, or I will be joining Monica in Heaven.*

Once inside the funeral home, Corinne made her way to the ladies room, wondering how disheveled she looked. She hoped she could repair the damage, but decided it really didn't matter. She had survived. That's all that mattered at the moment.

She considered herself lucky when she found the ladies room unoccupied. She studied the disheveled woman in the mirror. Her hair looked only slightly ruffled, the natural curls stretched farther than usual. She ran a brush through it anyway. She winced as the bristles passed along her left temple. She felt the area again. The throbbing, golf ball size lump lay hidden beneath the mass of curls.

"What's the matter, Dear?" a voice said from behind her. "Have a headache?"

"Minor car accident on the way here. I bumped my head a little, that's all."

"You should go to the emergency room to have them do a CAT scan of your head. You never know what problems might develop later if you don't. You might have a concussion. There have even been people who have actually died from a slow bleed after bumping their head. Go to Emergency, and get checked out. Play it safe."

"I suppose you're right." Corinne placed the brush into her purse, and searched for the aspirin she always carried, as she smiled at the woman despite her headache.

"You look familiar. Haven't I seen you on one of those talk shows recently?"

"Probably, I appeared on a few. I'm a physical therapist. The name's Corinne Day. I'm flattered you recognize me."

"Now I remember. You saved some clinic. Weren't they going to rename the clinic after you?"

Corinne winced, her head now throbbing. "There have been rumors to that effect, but they're only rumors, nothing more. I'm hoping they don't do it."

Corinne judged the short, heavy woman to be older than she by a good thirty years. She wore a brown dress with no accompanying jewelry. Her hair had been dyed a bright shade of auburn, and hung loosely to her shoulders. Corinne sighed. *I really wish you hadn't recognized me. I don't have time for chitchat right now, and my head is killing me.*

"What you said impressed me," the woman said, "the way you helped all those clinic patients. You did save that clinic, didn't you?"

Corinne popped the aspirin into her mouth, and regarded the woman out of the corner of her eyes. "So they tell me, but it took a team of professionals to pull it off, not me alone."

"Yeah, I remember because my friend and I discussed the show afterwards. I think it's great what you did, whether you take all the credit or not. It's still great."

Corinne wished she had something stronger than aspirin, something with a faster onset of pain relief.

"How did you know Sage, Miss Day?"

"I didn't really know her, but my sister is the private detective she supposedly killed before she killed herself."

"Really? I didn't know the detective had a sister."

"It's been kept out of the news."

"Don't want the negative publicity, huh? Bad for your reputation and business, I suppose." She glanced over her shoulder to ensure no one had entered the room. "I'll tell you one thing, though. Sage didn't kill your sister."

"Oh? How do you know that?"

"I know because I know. Sage wouldn't kill anyone. I always found her to be one of the kindest and sweetest women I've ever met. She and the senator would have made a darling couple."

"Then, you knew them?"

"Of course, I'm Senator Stern's secretary. My name is Nellie Roget. I've been with the senator for years. Sage worked in our office. She and Frank hit it right off when she first arrived from New York."

"How long ago did Sage start work at the senator's office?"

"Let me think. She arrived about four, or five years ago. They started dating almost immediately. They spent every spare moment together. She's the best thing that ever happened to Frank." She lowered her voice. "He works too hard, too many hours, all those meetings, and all those last minute business trips. You never know when he's going to get time off. Sage could get him to relax a little, made him take a little more vacation. They were planning on marrying soon. I tell you, it's a shame." Nellie lowered her head until her chin rested on her chest.

"I imagine he's taking it hard."

"Dreadfully hard. He really loved her."

"I imagine all of Sage's other friends are here too."

"Well, at least all her coworkers. We were her friends, really. Sage tended to keep to herself, but we all loved her. I guess her closest friend, outside of Frank, would be Tom, Frank's son."

"The senator has a son?"

"Oh, yes, from a previous marriage. The senator's wife died about seven years ago in a car crash. Tom's twenty-nine, the same age as Sage." Nellie shook off Corinne's questioning expression with a swipe of her hand. "Oh, I know. The senator's old enough to be her father, but age didn't seem to make a difference with them."

"If the senator and his son are both here, I'd love to meet them."

"Sure, I'll introduce you, but I think this isn't the best time to talk about Sage and your sister. They're both pretty shaken up. Maybe you'd better wait until after the funeral."

"You're probably right. Could you set me up with an official appointment with the senator?"

"Sure." Nellie placed one finger alongside her chin. "Let's see. The funeral's tomorrow morning. Let's say 9 AM Monday morning. I'll pencil you in the appointment book, and I'll make sure he's available for you. It's the least I can do."

"Thanks, and I promise I'll go see someone about this head right after I leave here."

"Good. I hear you medical types make the worst patients. Let's go find the senator. I think I saw him going out back for some fresh air a few minutes ago."

Nellie dragged Corinne by the hand onto the back porch, and approached an elderly man in a brown suit and matching brown tie.

"Senator Stern, this is Corinne Day, the famous physical therapist. She's been on all the talk shows."

The senator extended his hand to Corinne. "Ah, yes, you're the sister of the private detective who died...ah...I can't remember her name?"

"Monica, her name's Monica." Corinne accepted his hand. It dripped with perspiration.

"Ah, yes. That's right."

"Then, you know about my sister?"

"Oh, yes, Ed told me about her."

"Ed?"

"Senator Edwin Jackson. He told me the entire story of your sister and Sage. It's so hard to believe all of this violence is really happening in our Nation's Capital, and that Sage is really...gone." He sobbed loudly.

Nellie put her arm around the senator, allowing him to lean on her for support.

"I'm sorry, Senator. Maybe this isn't the best time to discuss this, but I need to talk to you more about my sister and Sage. I'm trying to make some sense out of everything that's happened."

"I've already taken the liberty to schedule an appointment for her for Monday morning at 9, Senator. Is that all right with you?"

"That's fine, Nellie, but I'm not so sure there's much more for Miss Day to find out about her sister's murder. I've been told the police were very thorough."

"Oh, I've heard that story about my sister's murder, but I still feel they may have missed something, and I'm not at all satisfied with their conclusions. I've got to keep searching until I've discovered everything about the events leading to Monica's murder. Then, maybe we'll know the real reason for her death."

"And who did it," Nellie added. "We still can't believe Sage would do such a thing. Murder and suicide? I mean, what possible reason could she have had?"

"That's what I hope to find out."

"If you'll excuse me, Miss Day, my place is really inside...with Sage. I'm sure Nellie could provide you with more coherent information than I could at this stage. Maybe she could even introduce you to Senator Jackson."

"Sure I will. I see him standing right over there. Come on, Miss Day. I'll introduce you."

Edwin Jackson spotted the approaching women. He struggled to stand as they approached. He stared at Corinne. Corinne stared back, trying to read beyond his brown eyes, and refusing to break eye contact.

"Senator Jackson, this is Corinne Day, the famous physical therapist we've been hearing so much about on TV and in the papers."

"We've met, haven't we, Senator?"

"Briefly, anyway, but this makes it official. How do you do, Miss Day?"

"You set me up the other day, Senator, with that note you handed me. Why?"

"Perhaps we should discuss this in private. Could you please excuse us, Nellie?"

"Of course, Senator. Nice meeting you, Miss Day. I look forward to your visit to our office on Monday."

Senator Jackson began to walk toward the stairs. "Shall we take a little walk in the back yard, Miss Day, for some privacy?"

She grabbed his arm as he approached the stairs. "Can I trust you alone?"

"You can't really think of me as a danger to you. Can you?"

"A danger, probably not, but, in reality, I don't know what to think any more, or who to believe for that matter. Lies abound every-where. In your case, you never showed up for the meeting you set up. Instead, the police found me with Sage's body. I almost got arrested. Did you set me up for that, Senator?"

"Let's not talk here, Miss Day. You do deserve that explanation, but, again, not here. There'll be others on the porch here who will watch over you while we're in the yard. So, you'll be safe. Let's go." He climbed down the two steps to the grass, and lumbered toward the back fence, some fifty feet away with Corinne following a few steps behind. His limp seemed worse than the day of Monica's funeral, causing their progress to be slow. Looking back, he waved at several people on the porch. "Don't want any of them to come join us because they think I'm sick and in need of your medical skills. I've got to show them I'm fine, if we want to be alone."

Once they were out of earshot of the porch, Senator Jackson turned toward Corinne, taking a deep breath before beginning. "Did I hear Nellie say she already made an appointment for you with Senator Stern?"

"Don't change the subject," Corinne ordered in barely a whisper. "Answer my question. Did you set me up to take the blame for Sage Browning's murder?"

The senator hesitated before answering. "No, I had no idea her body would be there when I gave you that note. When I arrived for our meeting, the police were already there, and, I guess, so were you. So, I didn't go in."

"Didn't want to get involved, right?"

"I'm afraid so. I really wanted to keep my name out of any un-pleasantness that may have happened. Later, when I learned what had occurred, I thought you might be forced to tell the police about my note. I felt it would be better for both of us if I told them about our planned meeting. So, I spoke to Captain Patelli."

"How noble of you…after the fact, of course! Why do I get the sense you were more concerned about *your* hide than mine?"

171

"Come on, Miss Day. Give me a break. After all, I did call to admit that I had arranged the time and meeting place, but by then, they had figured out what had happened anyway. Captain Patelli assured me that they never really suspected you of anything." He paused, leaning heavily against the chain link fence.

Corinne thought he might collapse if the fence had not been there.

"Besides, it all fits. Sage killed your sister, and then committed suicide."

"Do you really think that's true? Nellie seems to think she wasn't the type to commit either murder or suicide."

"I have to admit that I didn't know her that well, but nowadays I'm not so sure anyone, including Nellie, can predict who would commit such crimes. With your medical training, you're probably more aware of that than I am." He stared at her. "You've got to believe me, I didn't set you up. I had no idea Sage's body would be there. I only wanted to talk to you."

Frustrated, Corinne threw her arms up. "Okay, I'm here now, Senator. What did you want to talk about?"

"Your sister. You remind me so much of her..." A single tear appeared out of the corner of his eye, and slowly coursed its way down his cheek. He quickly wiped it away with a single swipe of his hand, and sniffled loudly. "...I mean...I knew she had an identical twin, but I didn't know how much your looks would affect me."

Corinne's eyes narrowed to slits. "Affect you? What do you mean?"

He lowered his gaze. "Let me start at the beginning. I first met your sister about a year ago. I went to her office to hire her for a job. I'm afraid I unknowingly started her journey toward death." He sobbed openly, this time he allowed the tears to flow unimpeded.

"I don't follow you."

"Your sister died while working for me on that job."

Corinne began writing in her notebook. "What, exactly, did that job concern?"

"I hired her to investigate the backgrounds of Senator Stern and Sage Browning." He sighed deeply, and then continued sobbing.

"Why?"

Senator Jackson took a full minute to regain his composure before speaking. "As you know, this is the President's second, and last term. Senator Stern and Senator Edmond were the leading candidates in our party for nomination for the next election. I'm in charge of Senator Stern's election campaign. Senator Stern's a widower with one son. He met Sage a few years ago. She's a totally different kind of woman from his wife." He looked skyward. "Frank's wife had been quiet and introverted. Sage is anything but. She's outgoing, loved parties, drinking, that sort of thing. They started spending more and more time with each other, going off on long weekends together, and disappearing for days on end. It marked quite a change in Frank. I became worried that their relationship might pose a threat to his candidacy, if Sage's background contained something that could prove embarrassing. So, I had the FBI investigate her over a year ago. They found nothing."

"But you weren't satisfied?"

"That's right. Political opponents dig deeper and harder to uncover all the dirt. So, I wanted someone to dig that deep for me, and I asked your sister to do that for me. At the time, I thought I should also have her look into Senator Stern's background, not looking for any criminal activity, mind you, but to uncover anything the opposition could use as ammunition against him. As it turned out, I didn't need to do it for either one. I made a huge mistake." He huffed. "I chose your sister to do the job. Actually, an acquaintance, named Ross Martino, recommended her. He told me your sister would be perfect for the job. She'd done some work for him, I guess."

"You said you hired her over a year ago. Did she find anything in all that time?"

"Not that she reported to me. The last time I talked to her a couple of weeks ago she reported that she hadn't found much on either one. She told me Sage came from Connecticut originally, and moved to New York at the age of twenty-one. She got some sort of receptionist job there, and lived quietly, except for the parties, until she came here, and landed the job in Frank's office. She kept to herself mostly, had few friends outside of the office, at least none that your sister identified, anyway."

"Did you talk to Monica at all last week?"

"No, I had gone to California to give a speech. I stayed there until I received the news of her murder. I came home for...the funeral." He sighed deeply again, and clamped his eyes shut. More tears suddenly exploded from his eyelids, forcing their way onto his cheeks. He sobbed again.

Corinne had been concentrating on recording everything in her notebook, and hadn't noted Senator Jackson's latest tear burst. She looked up, pausing to study the crying man. *Although I really don't want to hurt you, if I'm going to get all the information I need to pursue my investigation, I'm afraid I have to continue my questioning, no matter how many tears it causes.* "How did you hear of Monica's death?" When he didn't answer, she prompted, "Did someone from Senator Stern's office call you?"

Senator Jackson dropped his hands, opened his eyes, and stared at Corinne. His eyes suddenly brightened, and the corners of his lips turned up into a hint of a smile. "No, my secretary called. You see, Corinne, she knew Monica and I had been dating."

CHAPTER 26

Corinne had started her interrogation of Senator Edwin Jackson with all the fury of a charging rhino. After all, he had been the one that had arranged the meeting at Monica's office that had gone so wrong. She had anticipated resistance and maybe even hostility from the senator that she knew had much to hide. She had been prepared for a fight, but it had never crossed her mind that he would declare that he had been dating Monica. When he announced it, she dropped her notebook and pen. "Dating her?" Her jaw fell, her charging rhino having collided with a brick wall. "You're the one?"

"Yes, I'm the surprise she had in store for you." More tears appeared. "I had asked her to marry me, and, fulfilling my wildest dreams, she had accepted. We were so happy. She couldn't wait to see your reaction when she told you." His expression became somber. "Oh, Miss Day, Corinne, I'm sorry I ever got her involved in all this." He turned to observe traffic through the neighboring yard, and wiped the tears from his eyes. He blew his nose softly. "I'm so sorry."

Having retrieved her notebook and her pen, Corinne shoved them into her purse as slowly as she could to give herself time to absorb what he had said. She flushed. *Oh, God! All the things I said to you. The last thing I would ever want to do is hurt my sister's lover, the man she intended to marry. I must be stupid, as well as blind and naïve.* "Senator, I'm the one who should be sorry. I need to apologize to you for the way I treated you. I simply didn't realize…"

"It's okay. You couldn't have known. I truly loved your sister. I wish I'd never given her that assignment. I'll never forgive myself for that. Oh, how I wish she had stopped her investigation before she discovered whatever caused Sage to murder her, instead of being so determined to get me what I had requested…" His voice trailed off as he added, "…useless information that caused me to lose her forever."

"That's Monica, persistent to a fault." Corinne placed one gentle hand on the senator's shoulder. "I mean, never giving up until she felt she had completed a job to her satisfaction. You couldn't have stopped her if you had tried."

"I suppose you're right, and I suppose we'll never find out what, if anything, she had discovered."

"I don't know about that. I'm going to keep digging until I get to the bottom of whatever's going on."

He stared at Corinne. Monica stared back at him, his Monica, the woman he had lost forever, the woman he had sent down the road to death. *I have to prevent that same thing from happening to her twin; I must protect her at all costs. I can't be responsible for both their deaths.* "Listen, Corinne, I'm already guilty of contributing to your sister's death. I don't want to endanger your life too. Do you realize you may be throwing yourself into the same danger, if you pursue your sister's investigation, or dig into her murder?"

"I've been warned about that several times in the last few days, and, believe me, I've discovered the danger is real, but that's not going to stop me. Nothing is. I'm determined to uncover what happened, what events led to the attack on Monica. I may not be a licensed private investigator, but I think I've got her determination, and I'm going to apply it to this investigation, the danger be damned, but thanks for the warning. I'll try to keep on my toes."

"Well, if you're sure this is something you must do, I'll back you the best I can. If there's anything I can do, please let me know."

"You could start by telling me about Senator Stern." Corinne retrieved her notebook and pen.

He paused before answering. "He's a good man, terrific family man, and a seasoned politician. He'll make a great President."

"That's enough of the campaign ad. When you cut through all that public image stuff, what's left? What's really under that façade? And what about those trips I hear he made? Remember, we're both after the same thing, and I won't leak anything to the opposition, or press, I promise."

He again paused before answering. *How much do I tell her? All of it, I guess. Monica would want it that way.* He took a deep breath before beginning. "Okay, Frank used to be quiet and reserved. We all used to think a little too quiet. Once he met Sage, he opened up, came to all the barbecues and parties with her. Everyone thought they were perfect together."

"What about the trips?"

"I can't help you too much there. I didn't keep that close a track on his personal life, although I had asked Monica to specifically find out about those trips. I didn't want to leave anything to be discovered by the opposition."

"And what did she uncover?"

"She never gave me any official report, but she called me once a month, always saying she hadn't found anything disastrous, including those trips. I really didn't think she would. Most of them turned out to be trips with Sage. She couldn't find anything on the others. So, I assumed neither would our opposition. You should check with Nellie. She might know more about them." He hung his head.

"Nellie mentioned Senator Stern had a son. Are they close?"

"Yes, Tom's a lawyer. He does a lot of work for his father's office."

"I understand he knew Sage. Did he approve of his father dating her?"

He raised his gaze to Corinne. "As far as I know. The three of them did a lot together, boating, fishing, sightseeing trips, that sort of thing. I can't imagine him not approving. Sage endeared herself to everyone."

"So I keep hearing: she wouldn't hurt a fly, much less murder my sister. I simply can't seem to buy into that image."

"You didn't know Sage as we did. She was, well, special. As for Tom, he's here tonight. If you want, I'll introduce you to him, but he's grieving almost as much as Frank. So, I wouldn't push him too hard tonight. Maybe you'd be better off questioning him more completely about Sage and his father next week, but it's your call."

"An introduction would be great." Corinne turned back toward the funeral home, and froze in her tracks like a hunter who suddenly spotted her prey. She stared at the man who climbed the steps of the funeral home.

"Okay, follow me."

Corinne hung close to the senator's back. She peeked around the doorway before entering to ensure her prey hadn't lingered there. He hadn't. She next spotted the man as he entered the viewing room where an open, gold casket presided over a quiet audience, both mingling together and sitting in groups, some in prayer, others talking softly.

"That's Tom over there. Come this way. I'll introduce you."

"Could you possibly go ahead, and tell him I'll be right there. I want to pay my respects first." Corinne made her way toward the crowd in the viewing room, pausing inside the door to sign her name in the guest register. She watched as the man she stalked knelt before the casket for a short time. She began her approach as he paid his respects to Senator Stern and the others who occupied seats near the casket. As he approached a vacant seat, Corinne intercepted him.

"Hello, Paul. What are you doing here?"

The sound of Corinne's sarcastic, pointed comment startled Paul. He spun toward the voice he knew so well. "Ah, Corinne. Hi." He fumbled to straighten his tie.

Corinne refused to back down. "Well, are you going to tell me what you're doing here?"

"I came to find you, if you must know." He encircled her waist with his arm. He led her toward the door. "Let's go outside. I'll tell you all about it."

When they reached the porch, she pulled away from his grip, and folded her arms across her chest, scowling as best she could. The full moon formed an eerie halo around Paul's head. Corinne smirked. *Devil's horns might be more appropriate for you.*

Paul checked to see who might overhear their conversation.

"Well, I'm waiting for an explanation. Care to try the truth for a change."

"It's the truth, Corinne. I came here looking for you. I tired your cell phone, the hotel, your sister's office, and her apartment, but when you didn't answer, I figured you might be crazy enough to come here."

"Crazy? Is that what you think I am for trying to solve my sister's murder?"

Paul took a breath, blew it out fast. "But it's been solved already, Corinne. The police are satisfied, and have closed the case. There's nothing more for you to discover. Let these people mourn in peace. Come back to New York with me. I'll even risk letting you drive again. Please." He reached for her shoulders with both hands.

He's at it again, but he's not going to manipulate me this time, or ever again. "Trying to dictate my life again, are you? You orchestrated this trip down here. You've been dictating my whole life. Well, it won't work this time, and don't even think of touching me." She batted away his arms. "Keep those probing hands off me. Understand?"

He didn't answer immediately, but did retract his hands, putting them in his pockets. He checked the other mourners to see if any had heard her warning. None had, or, if they had, they were ignoring the fighting couple, as none were looking in their direction. "I'm not sure I know what you mean."

"Isn't it true that you arranged for me to get that consult down here by pulling those long strings you seem to have attached to everyone around you? Admit it. Wasn't the real reason for coming to Washington that you had *business* to take care of while you were here, and that it had nothing to do with me, or finding my sister?" Her added emphasis on the word 'business' made it sound both dirty and revolting to her.

Paul stood quietly as the two other couples on the porch passed close to them to re-enter the funeral home. "Sure, I admit I pulled a few strings to get that consult for you, but isn't that what you're supposed to do, help people? You hardly talk about anything else."

"That's an exaggeration!" Her voice became loud and harsh. "Sure, you know I'll go anywhere to help a colleague with a difficult case, but not at the expense of that colleague's integrity, and certainly not with your unsolicited interference, especially if the reason for that interference is you own personal gain, not love for me, nor concern for the patient, nor that of my colleague."

He backed away one step. "Okay, I'm sorry. I'll make it up to you and to your colleagues, including the patient you saw."

"Let me guess. That patient didn't really need my expertise. Am I right?"

Paul lowered his head. "No, Corinne, you're wrong. Doctor Filmore assured Dr. Gunther he had found a patient that really had been giving him trouble, and he now thinks your plan is really going to help him. That patient will truly benefit by the program you set up for him. So, you see, the trip wasn't wasted. You did accomplish something." Paul looked up so their eyes met. "Listen, Corinne, I promise I'll make up for what you call my interference. I'll call everyone involved, all your colleagues here and in New York, and the patient, if you think that's necessary, and apologize for my interference. I really meant no harm."

"No, you won't call anyone." Corinne bounced her index finger off his chest in time with the cadence of her words. "You stay out of their careers, away from that patient, and out of my career and my life." She turned her back on him, and folded her arms across her chest. "How many other times have you tried to help my career, Mister Paul Butt-In-Ski?"

"None, honest!"

She placed her hands on her hips again, and lowered her head. Disturbing questions flooded her mind. *Could this truly be the first time he's interfered? Could he have helped save the clinic without my knowledge? Had he arranged for me to get all the credit? Am I as much of a fraud as him? Can I believe anything he says? I doubt it, but I've got to concentrate on the murder investigation, not my loathing of him. Nothing else matters now, not the clinic, the patient, or my career, past, or future. I've got to keep questioning him, try to tie him to Monica's murder, or clear him, if that's possible.* She took a deep breath, blew it out slowly. "So, why did you really arrange for me to come here? I want the truth, if you're capable of it. Did it have something to do with the two men who were killed here last Thursday? The police say they worked for you."

He waited several moments before answering. "Yes, they worked for me...well, they worked for one of my companies anyway. They were sent down here to get some information that their company needed for a new shipping technique it had developed. It will supposedly revolutionize the shipping industry. Anyway, their murders meant someone down here knew of our interest in the process, and were taking drastic measures to insure we didn't get what we were after." He paused.

"Continue. I'm listening."

"Thursday night, after I heard of the murders, I decided I needed to handle everything here personally. I admit I used your consult at the hospital as a cover to give me the appearance of simply being your companion. I didn't want the competition to know the real reason for my visit. I intended to secure the patent rights to the process right out from under them."

"You used me, You Bastard!" She slapped him hard, his head snapping to the side from the force of the blow, his cheek becoming instantly bright red, the marks of her fingers evident close to his ear. "Why didn't you simply tell me that, and then ask me to accompany you? I would have jumped at the opportunity to come here to find Monica anyway. Why go to all the trouble you did, all the lying and manipulation?"

"Because I didn't know if you'd go along with my plan, and because I thought you would be safer if you knew nothing about the whole project. It's one thing for me to put myself at risk from the same killers

180

who murdered my men, but it's an entirely different matter for me to put you at risk. I needed the competition to think you were simply my companion and nothing more. Don't you see you were safer not knowing?"

"Safer?"

"Of course, both you and I could have been next on their list, if they thought we were both down here after the process. As I said once already, I thought it better to have a legitimate reason for both of us to come down here, and, by not exposing the real reason, there wouldn't be any leaks either by you, or someone in my office."

I'll bet you're lying, making it up as you go along. "It doesn't sound any more believable the second time you proposed it, but continue with your fairy tale. How does all this tie in with the murders of my sister and Sage Browning?"

"As far as I know, it doesn't. The two incidents are not related at all. It's a mere coincidence that Sage killed your sister around the time that my men were murdered. It's coincidence, nothing more, and, before you ask, I have no idea why Sage would kill your sister."

Wu's words about coincidences ran through Corinne's mind.

"Besides, Sage killed herself because she felt so guilty about what she had done. She committed suicide. She wasn't murdered."

"I'm not so sure. It all seems to be more of a set up to me than reality. Someone wants all the pieces of the puzzle to fit perfectly, but they don't. They're being forced into positions they don't belong. There are too many unanswered questions."

"Questions? What questions?"

"There's the question of your involvement, for one thing. I find it hard to swallow that you came down here, using me in the process, simply to get some new patent rather than send one of those high-priced lawyers you always employ. How naïve do you think I am anyway?"

"Oh, Honey..." He reached for her.

She pushed him away again, gently, but firmly. "Back off!"

"I've told you the whole truth. Now, can't you forgive me for hiding my true motivation from you, now that you know the reason, the whole truth?"

"The whole truth? That's not the whole truth! What about the fact that you've had me pulled off the case? What's your excuse for that?"

Paul paused before answering, the pain in his cheek finally dissipating. "Okay, I'm guilty of that too, but I did it for your protection. You've got to get out of Washington. You may be in danger."

"From whom?" *As if I didn't know.*

"From those same guys who killed my men, for one. My plan isn't foolproof. You figured it out. They could too, and they may come after you once I leave. They may try to get to me by hurting you. There may be another danger. Suppose, for arguments sake, you're right, and someone did murder Sage. That means the killer may still be in Washington. Do you think he's going to do nothing while you poke your nose around, trying to discover something that will incriminate him? No, he'll try to stop you, permanently. Your life may be in danger."

Corinne turned, and leaned on the railing. *Yeah, maybe he'll try forcing me off the road again.* "In either case, I have to stay." She lowered her voice to a whisper. "I have no choice. I've got to find the truth about my sister's death." She turned back toward him. "I intend to find the whole truth, no matter what that may be, or what it costs me."

"Well, I wish you luck, Corinne, but I have to get back to New York. My business demands it. My task here is complete. I've left too many things unfinished in New York to stay here much longer."

Oh, no you don't. You're not leaving without answering a few more questions. "Before you go, I need some other information from you. Where you were when the murders took place."

"What?" His voice grew loud, louder than he had intended. "You sound more and more like those damn cops. They never quit, never give you a second chance." He threw his hands up in disgust. "Okay, I'll play your dumb game." He ticked off his statements on his fingers. "Let's see, you and I had gone out to dinner in New York the night my men were killed here in Washington. You should be able to attest to that. You picked the restaurant. Remember? By the way, I have no motive to kill my own men. If I were unhappy with their performances, I would have had their corporate bosses fire them, not kill them.

"Next, when Sage murdered your sister, I had been conducting business by phone from our suite. Don't you remember? Right after it happened, you came to our suite to tell me what had happened, and how badly the police had treated you. So, I didn't kill her. Besides, I certainly had no motive for killing my girlfriend's sister. I never even met her.

"As to Sage's death, you had called me only minutes before to tell me to meet you at your sister's office. If you remember, we found her together. I got there after you as a matter of fact, and the policemen following you confirmed the timing of my entrance."

I don't buy it. "You could have killed her, snuck out, and then waited for me to go in to make your appearance." Corinne studied his facial expression, looking for any hint of dishonesty. She saw nothing but a flat, disinterested expression. *You're apparently a good liar. You lied to me before, and I suspected nothing. Maybe I am more naïve, and vulnerable than I thought. I'll bet you're lying right now. I can't read you, but it doesn't matter anymore.* "I don't believe a word you're saying."

Paul's expression remained unchanged. "Oh, come on. Why would I risk being caught there with you if I knew Sage's body would be discovered with us? Remember, Detective Wu thought I had killed her, and wanted to arrest me on the spot. It's a good thing that his captain figured out what happened. He proved I didn't kill her." He threw up his hands. "So, you see, I couldn't have killed any of them."

"What about John Zachary's murder?"

"John Zachary? Who's that?"

Corinne referred to her notebook. "You may have known him as Josh Zbronski. That's his real name, according to the FBI."

"Josh Zbronski, the snitch from New York? He's dead? How does he fit into all this?"

"I understand he testified against you once."

"That's right. He worked as one our accountants. Some of our executives were doing something illegal, manipulating the books, I guess, and got caught. I got involved in the whole deal because I'm head of the corporation…guilt through association. You know how that works. Anyhow, Zbronski turned State's evidence, and then disappeared, but I had nothing to do with any illegal transactions. Did the FBI inform you that the charges against me were dropped in the subsequent investigation? So, I didn't have any reason to kill him, even if I knew his new name, or his whereabouts, which I didn't."

"He rented an office near my sister. Somebody shot him Tuesday night around eleven."

"My Dear Corinne, I believe you and I were together Tuesday night. I picked you up at five thirty for dinner. After dinner, we stayed together at your sister's apartment until a little after eleven thirty. You complained that you were tired, and wanted to be alone for the rest of the night. I went back to the hotel."

183

"If I remember right, you drove your Rolls. You could have sent Kevin to kill him."

"I had given him the night off. I have no idea what he did that night."

"Now that I think of it, I haven't seen him since. Where is he? I want to talk to him."

"I'm afraid he's back in New York already. He had a family emergency. I don't even know how to get in touch with him at the moment. I've tried calling his cell phone, but keep getting sent over to his voice mail. I've left messages, but he hasn't as yet returned my calls. Presumably, he's busy with that family emergency. However, as soon as he reports in, I'll have him give you a call."

Corinne scowled. "A convenient emergency, if you ask me."

"Please listen to reason. I didn't have any reason to kill any of them."

Corinne snapped her notebook closed. "Maybe, we'll see."

"You've changed, Corinne."

"You don't know how right you are."

"But it's not for the better."

Corinne squinted. "By the way, didn't I see you in a Ferrari earlier this evening?"

"Not me. You know I hate Ferraris. I prefer my vintage Lamborghini, or a big luxury Rolls Royce. I'm beginning to think the larger cars are a better investment. Besides, their size makes them safer in the long run."

"I know what you prefer. After all, I am driving your Lamborghini, but I could have sworn I saw you on the Beltway."

"Wasn't me"

Corinne studied his stone-cold expression, again failing to detect anything noteworthy. "Guess not. The Ferrari's driver came close to being as good as me. We had a little accident though. So, your Lamborghini got some scratches on it, nothing major, but you'd better check your airbags. They didn't go off."

"You don't have to worry about the scratches, Corinne, my insurance will take care of any damages, and I'll have my mechanic check the airbags. The important thing is that you're safe. Did the other driver sustain any injuries?"

"I don't think so. He disappeared after the accident."

"That should prove to you it wasn't me. I can't match your driving. Fast speeds actually scare me. I simply appreciate the looks of the vintage Lamborghini. I'm not good at driving it."

"Yeah, I've thought of that already. So, maybe I am wrong about you being the Ferrari's driver. It's not the first time I've been wrong about you, and I'm sure it won't be the last."

"I'll call you once more before I leave, in case you change your mind about coming back to New York with me."

"You do that, Paul." As she headed back inside the funeral home to meet Senator Stern's son, she added, "You do that."

CHAPTER 27

Corinne's meeting with Paul at Sage's wake increased her contempt for him. She no longer believed his dribble about how much he cared for her, how he only had her interests in mind, or how much sorrow he had expressed for his actions. *How deep were his claws into Monica's murder? For that matter, how deep have they penetrated my life? He's manipulated my every move down here, and I resent it. I wonder what other things he's interfered with in my life back in the City. I hate him for all of it, no matter his motive, or results. Interfere in my life, will you? You'll pay, Mister Big Shot. I'll see to that.*

She hurried down the hallway of the funeral home to her introduction to Tom Stern. As she turned a corner, she came upon Senator Ed Jackson, whispering to the man next to him like a movie director giving last minute instructions to his star. The non-stop motion of his hands emphasized each directive and its importance. When he spotted Corinne approaching, his expression morphed from serious to light and cheerful. He extended one hand in her direction with palm up.

"This is Corinne, Day, the woman I spoke to you about. Corinne, this is Tom Stern, the senator's son."

They shook. His palms were dry, the grip firm. His blonde hair matched the paleness of his skin.

"Hello. I came to offer my condolences."

"And to interrogate dad and me, right?"

"That too." *I wonder what Senator Jackson said to him, probably warning him to tell me nothing. I'm not so sure my sister's lover is on my side, despite what he claims.*

"Well, I must get back inside," Senator Jackson said, turning to leave. "I'll leave you two to talk. Remember what I told you, Tom."

They watched the senator limp away.

"What did he tell you?" Corinne asked through narrowed eyes. "Did he warn you to be careful what you tell the bitch?"

"Not in those precise words. I guess he's afraid I'll say something that will embarrass my father. Ed is my father's protector and chief advocate. He's going to make dad President one of these days. I'm sure of it."

"Well, I have no ambitions to attack your father, or you, and I'm not planning on interfering with any run for President. I can also assure you I don't plan on publishing anything you say. I'm not a reporter, looking for a juicy story. I simply wanted to talk to you about Sage and my sister, Monica."

"Sage. Sage. I'm going to miss her so much." He leaned heavily against the wall, his eyes drifting to the ceiling. He began to cry openly, making no attempt to hide the tears.

"I'm sorry about your loss."

He stared at her. "I'm the one who should be sorry." He lowered his gaze, and then closed his eyes. "Here I am wallowing in my own sorrow, and I haven't even acknowledged your loss." He raised his gaze to hers. "I am sorry about what happened to your sister."

"Thank you, but don't apologize. Believe me, I understand, but what I don't understand is why this all happened in the first place. I'm hoping that by talking to everyone who knew Sage and my sister, I may learn something about the circumstances surrounding their deaths."

"You mean you don't buy this story of murder and suicide?"

"No."

"Let's go where we can talk a little more privately."

"May I suggest the rear porch? I know it intimately."

He threw her a questioning glance. With a single wave of her hand, she motioned for him to follow.

They arrived to find the porch deserted. Tom walked to the railing, resting his hands there for support.

"What do you know already about this whole affair, Miss Day?"

"Only that Monica had been investigating Sage's background for Senator Jackson, and that, up to last week, she hadn't found much. Then, my sister is murdered, and her place is turned upside down by someone looking for something. I don't know what that something is at this point in my investigation, or if they found it. Next, I stumbled upon Sage's body in my sister's office." She sighed. "Unfortunately, that leaves a lot of gaps. Could you fill some of those in for me?"

"A few anyway. I suppose you want to know my whereabouts when your sister died."

"That'll do for starters."

Tom paused, pushing his glasses up hard.

Corinne waited silently. *I wonder if you're trying to decide where to start, or are trying to invent a plausible story. I wonder if I'll be able to tell the difference. I hope you're easier to read than Paul.*

Unseen by the two, a lone gunman sighted them in the crosshairs of his telescopic sight. He checked the rest of the porch. There were now two other couples that had followed Corinne and Tom onto the porch. The couples were talking at the far end of the porch. Tom leaned against the railing as he spoke. Corinne stood close to him, notebook and pen in hand.

The gunman placed the crosshairs on her temple. His finger pressed lightly on the trigger guard, not the trigger itself. The finger never moved, didn't even flinch.

"My father and I were at his house. We had some personal things to go over."

"Was Sage with you?"

"No, unfortunately, we both know where the police think she was, don't we?"

"Yeah, murdering my sister. Where do you think she really was?"

"Probably working. She always had some work to do, usually for my father, but I couldn't prove it."

"Do you happen to know Sage's whereabouts last Thursday night?"

"Last Thursday? Let's see." He stroked his chin thoughtfully. "Oh, that's easy; I attended a speech my father gave at the Kiwanis club. Sage should have been there with me, but had some work to do at her office. See, I told you she had become a workaholic. She never did show up that night, though. She said she got too busy, and lost track of time. She used that excuse more than once on me."

"What time did the meeting start?"

"Dinner started at seven with the speech and questions after that. We were there until almost eleven. Why do you ask?"

"I'm trying to get everyone's whereabouts straight in my head, that's all. The morning Sage died, where were you then?"

"At your sister's funeral."

Corinne struck her forehead with the heel of her hand. "Of course, I thought you looked familiar. I saw you there. Did you know my sister?"

"No, but Sage did. As you said, Ed had your sister investigating her background. I guess your sister had asked her some questions a few weeks back. I understand she had a clean record though, as you've already pointed out. Anyway, Sage thought we should go to the funeral."

"Sage attended the funeral? I didn't see her there."

"No, she wasn't there. She had something she had to do first. We were supposed to meet at the Church. She never showed. I went to the cemetery, hoping she would be there. She wasn't." He bowed his head, and closed his eyes. His breathing became deep, and irregular, punctuated by sporadic gasps.

"You were really fond of her, weren't you?"

"Yes. Sage, my father and I became close friends almost as soon as she joined dad's staff. We went on several trips together. The three of us hit it off, and ended up spending a lot of time together. She became an instant hit with almost everyone she met."

"Including you?"

"Yes, including me." He lifted his head. His eyes seemed to glow. "You couldn't find a more fantastic person, full of life and energy, wonderful to be with, and great for my father...and for me. She taught us how to enjoy life. I truly believe she had been sent to us by God to show us the good side of life."

"The good side? What do you mean?"

"She got my father to open up. Dad changed after mom died. He became too introverted, never went out, had no friends. He became depressed. He actually started gambling for the first time in his life, not to the point of addiction, though. Anyway, she brought him back to the real world, even got him to give up gambling. He became the dad I remembered from the good times with mom."

"I hear they fell in love, and planned to marry."

"Yes." He hung his head again, his voice a mere a whisper.

I wonder if there's more to their relationship. Could that be what Senator Jackson had been discussing with him, warning him to avoid mentioning? Maybe I can get him to ignore the senator's warning, and open up to me, confide in me, tell me the whole truth about Sage? I've got to try. "What's the matter? Was there something wrong with their relationship, or are you simply worried that your father may crawl back into the hole he hid in before she entered his life?"

He struggled to find the words to answer her, the words that would satisfy her, the words that would persuade her to leave him alone in his grief. His search failed. He sighed. "You're not a reporter, looking for a story, according to Ed. You've confirmed that. You're what you claim to be, a woman looking for answers to the events surrounding her sister's death, nothing more. Is that really true?"

"Yes, I'm simply a grieving sister, looking for the truth. I don't intend to publish anything I find, and I'm certainly no journalist, in any case. I wouldn't even know where to begin."

"The truth can be painful at times." He spoke slowly, staring at the moon as a veil of clouds sailed across it.

"True, but the truth is what I seek, what I want, what I must have, and I'll do practically anything to get it."

"I didn't mean only for you. The truth hurts me, but it could hurt dad a great deal more."

Corinne considered the young man as he studied the moon, mournful tears reappearing in both eyes.

"Listen, Tom. If you're afraid I'll use any of this against you, or your father, you're wrong. If there's a truth that I should know, please tell me. I promise I won't make it public knowledge. It'll stay between us. I swear I'm not out to hurt your father's political career, or yours."

He shifted his concentration to her, watching her carefully as she placed her notebook and pen into her purse, latching it closed with a slight click. He tried to read her eyes, her intentions, and, most importantly, her believability.

The crosshairs also followed the notebook, retuning immediately to Corinne's head with the closing of the purse. The killer's finger toyed with the weapon, alternating between the trigger and the guard, teasing the rifle's readiness before allowing it to dispense its deadly projectile.

"No notes." Corinne sat on a small bench, folding her hands across her chest as she awaited his decision. *I hope he trusts my discretion.*

Tom waited a few quiet minutes before he attempted an answer. The murmurs from the other people who had gathered on the porch and the distant roar of a car occasionally passing in front of the funeral home filled the air. Corinne smiled at him in encouragement.

"Okay, Miss Day. You're right. You deserve no less than the truth. Sage and I were in love."

"Sage and you?" The thought made her head spin.

"Yes, we found we had much more in common than she did with dad. We didn't plan it. We couldn't have even imagined it when we first met, but over time, we grew closer and closer, until the inevitable happened. We fell in love."

"What did your father say to all this? He must have been furious, or hurt a great deal, or both." *I can't imagine that scene, father and son discovering they were in love with the same woman, confronting each other like adversaries rather than family. I can't believe what I'm hearing.*

He didn't speak for another full minute. His lips trembled. "At first, he didn't even realize what had happened, that anything had occurred to change his relationship with her. Sage continued to do things with him. She really didn't want to hurt him, but eventually he caught the two of us together. I'm afraid it crushed him."

"Exactly when did he find out?"

"Last month. Sage and I have been trying to explain to him what happened between us ever since, but to no avail. I'm afraid we hurt him too much, especially when he learned we were planning on going away together."

"Away together? As in 'forever'?"

"Yes, as in 'forever.' We decided about two weeks ago. We even bought tickets to Europe for our honeymoon. Sage picked up the tickets from the travel agent on the Monday before she died. We were going to get married, and decide later where to live, where we wanted to start our lives anew, hoping nothing from our previous lives would follow us. We thought it best if we didn't live too close to dad, and as far as possible outside the American political realm for a while. We planned it so carefully; we wanted it to go so smoothly." Tears again streamed down his cheeks.

Corinne offered him a tissue. "Did your father try to stop you from going?"

"He tried to talk us out of leaving, tried to talk Sage into changing her mind, even tried to get me to stop seeing Sage, but his efforts proved powerless against our love. The more he pushed, the more we were drawn together. Sage and I were both determined to get on with our future together, and determined to go to Europe together. We both felt that if we were to disappear entirely for a while, then there wouldn't be as much of an impact on dad's political career. Of course, Ed thinks differently."

Corinne's mouth fell open in surprise. "Senator Jackson knew about you and Sage?"

"Of course. Dad confided in him. He always did."

"Was that what he wanted you to avoid telling me?"

"Yes."

"I'm glad you told me, Tom. It's a shock, but it helps me put some of the pieces together. Maybe when I have all those pieces, I'll be able to make some sense out of what appears to be senseless acts at the moment." She placed a gentle hand on his shoulder. "So, thank you for confiding in me. I won't violate your trust. I'm glad you told me."

"So am I." When the rear door to the funeral home opened, the motion caught his eye. "Right on time. Here comes Ed now to my rescue."

Corinne stood. "I guess that means we took too long to talk, and the interview is over. Thanks again, Tom. I may need to talk to you again later."

"Okay, but you must believe me. Sage didn't kill your sister, Miss Day. She couldn't have. She didn't have murder in her. I'm sure of that, and I don't believe Sage killed herself either. Please let me know when you find the truth. Like you, I need to know."

"I will. I promise."

The crosshairs shifted from Corinne to Tom, to Senator Jackson, and back to Corinne. As the trio walked silently back into funeral home, the gunman made his way to another part of the roof that overlooked the parking lot and the Lamborghini. As the gunman waited, he examined the car's fine, aerodynamic lines. *It would be a shame to put holes in such a beautiful sports car, or to splatter its bright finish with blood. I'll be careful with my shots when she approaches the car. No reason to rush the shot.*

CHAPTER 28

Corinne strolled to her car in deep thought, her head lowered. She plodded, buying time to piece together the facts she had collected at the wake. *First, Sage Browning, Monica's alleged murderer, had been Frank Stern's fiancée, but, instead, had made plans to elope with his son, Tom. Who else knew about that, and what did it have to do with Monica's death? Had Monica discovered the love triangle? Did Sage really kill Monica and then herself? No one, including me, seems to think so, except Captain Patelli and Paul, of course. On the other hand, no one seems to know Sage's whereabouts during any of the murders. So, where had she been, and what really happened? If Sage didn't kill Monica, who did, and, if she didn't commit suicide, who murdered her? Could the captain have been that wrong, or so influenced...no, probably pressured...by someone to deliberately distort the facts in order to squelch any further investigation? If so, did that implicate the meddling Paul again, or someone else in Washington like a high-ranking law enforcement officer, or maybe even a senator, or two? All I have are questions, questions, and more questions, and no real facts connecting them.*

Corinne kicked a twig, and watched it sail into the hedges that surrounded the parking lot. *I wish that twig really were the killer's butt, but I don't know who that is. I have too many suspects, and I'm not sure I've met the real killer, or killers yet, and that tears at my insides almost as much as the pain of losing Monica.* She retrieved the stick, and continued her journey, examining the twig as she walked. *I wonder what Senator Stern's involvement is? If Paul's number one, he's a close second on my list. He wouldn't even talk to me. Was he really simply crushed by the death of his loved one, or was he hiding something? Was that something the fact that his son had managed to take Sage away from him or some-*

193

thing totally unrelated? The answers to those questions, I'm afraid, will have to wait until our meeting on Monday.

Then there's Tom, Senator Stern's Son, the most talkative of the bunch, but how much of what he had said had been orchestrated by Senator Jackson? How much of what Tom said had some truth in it? How far would he go to protect his father's reputation?

Fourth on my list is Senator Ed Jackson. Of all the people for Monica to hook up with, she had to pick him. He's definitely not my type, but, then again, I thought Paul was my type... Corinne looked skyward. *...but I always had markedly different tastes than you, Monica. I have no trouble imagining that you really had loved him, though. He admitted to being your secret lover, your surprise for me. He claims to have loved you, but I keep getting the feeling that he is actively working to block my investigation into all the deaths. Oh, he certainly went out of his way to claim an interest in getting at the truth about your death, but he appeared to be doing his best to interfere with my every action, even going as far as directing Tom in what he should tell me. What else did Senator Jackson know? What else is he hiding?*

Then there's Paul...again. He's definitely not what he appears to be. He keeps showing up in all the wrong places, always claiming to know nothing about what's been happening, always claiming to be totally innocent, which I somehow now doubt. I certainly can't trust him anymore, and I simply won't trust him...ever again. I really wonder how much of his story is true, and how much he's invented for his own purposes...probably most, if not all of it. He's apparently an expert at weaving tales, and making them sound plausible...and, up to now, I've been dumb enough to fall for them. Enough!

"How do I make any sense out of it all?" She threw the stick toward the sky, and then fumbled to retrieve her keys from her purse as she approached the Lamborghini.

A loud popping sound rocked the air. It had come from over her left shoulder. Before she could react, the bullet shattered the windshield of the Ford Focus parked next to her. She instinctively froze, as if that would protect her from the gun's discharge, and the deadly lead it had sent. She quickly turned to look back when the second shot rang out, this time thumping loudly into the Ford's hood, the metal echoing the sound of the rifle. She could see the shape of a large man on the roof of the building across the street, taking aim in her direction.

Before she could make another move, a large pair of arms suddenly engulfed her, squeezed the air out of her, and slammed her to the ground, the cold asphalt hard and unforgiving, the heavy body above, relentless pushing her downward, trying to drive her deep into the ground. Her ribs bent until she thought they would finally yield, and crack under the pressure. She opened her mouth to scream, but couldn't produce a sound; her lungs had totally collapsed. She felt the hand move swiftly over her mouth, preventing her from screaming in any case.

"Don't move," a familiar voice said from above, as he released both his weight from her and his hand from her mouth.

"Get off me, You Oaf!" She gasped the delicious air that rushed into her lungs.

"Stay down," Wu said, as he pushed her against the ground once more. He crouched next to her car, aiming his gun at the now vacant roofline.

Corinne struggled to free her head from his grasp, and, finally managing to get the task done, sat against the Lamborghini, still gasping for air. "What in God's name do you think you're doing?" she asked between gasps. "You got me filthy. Look at this jacket. It'll never come clean. Where do you get off tackling me? You nearly crushed me to death. What are you doing here, anyway?"

"Saving your life." Wu kept his eyes fixed on the roofline.

"Bull shit!" She found herself yelling. "Look at me. I'm a mess." She hooked her hair behind her ears.

"Shut up, and get in the car before he starts shooting again."

"He won't, and I won't."

"Stop arguing, and get in the car. Meet me at your sister's apartment. I'm going after the shooter. I'll cover you while you drive away. Now, get going."

"Right, and if I'm not there, start without me."

"Be there. I've got some information for you."

"Okay, okay. I'll see you there. Good luck with your hunt."

The car door opened noiselessly, and Corinne slid into the leather seat. She pulled the door down and, as she started the engine, she watched Wu run across the street, gun still aimed at the rooftop. She gunned the engine, and popped the clutch, leaving rubber as she sped out of the parking lot and down the road to safety.

She pushed the car hard again, racing the lights, and scrutinizing every corner for the Ferrari, prepared to outrun it again if necessary. She sighed as she pulled to the curb at her destination, glad her adversary had never made an appearance. She slammed her hand against the steering wheel. *Where does Wu get off manhandling me?* She hurried out of the car, locked it, and tore up the stairs as if both the Ferrari and sniper were hounding her.

As she changed into a loose fitting sweat suit, she caught a glimpse of herself in the mirror behind the bar. *You're letting that cop get to you, Corinne.* She placed a cool hand against her burning, scrapped cheek. She went into the bathroom to apply cold water to the area. It felt good, but sent shivers down her body. She next inspected herself for any scratches that she may have suffered during Wu's brutish tackle. There were a few, but they could be hidden by carefully applied makeup. She touched her temple. Although still tender, the lump hadn't increased in size.

She picked up her soiled outfit, placing it in the sink to soak in cold water. *Damn cop thinks he's Rambo!* She winked at her reflection. *Hmm, but he is cute, a little rough and dumb even for a cop, but cute.*

She poured herself a Scotch as a knock broke the silence of the apartment. "Come on in." She sipped the liquor. "It's open."

"Should keep your door locked." Wu entered the apartment to find Corinne standing behind the bar. Even disheveled, her hair looked stunning as it glistened in the reflected light from the mirror behind her. *I can't read your expression. Is it friendly or hostile?*

"Saw you pull up outside." She pointed to the slider that led to a small balcony. "So, who do you think wants to kill me?"

"That's a good question. How about the murderer you're after? It seems to me he came pretty close to shooting you a little while ago." Wu took a seat on the couch. "Why the hell didn't you duck after the first shot? It's a good thing I decided to keep an eye on you while I'm off duty. What were you going to do, stand there all night until he hit you?"

"He wasn't shooting at me." Corinne sipped her drink once more. She held the drink up to the light, studying its amber color. It appealed to her eye. She set the glass on the bar, awaiting Wu's reply.

"What do you mean? From where I stood, it looked like a damned good imitation of shooting at someone to me."

She raised her gaze to meet his before answering. "No, it really wasn't. I knew I wasn't in any real danger from the first shot. I'm not sure I can really explain it, but no, he wasn't trying to hit me, much less kill me. Besides, I think he had made another fake attempt earlier tonight. I really believe he's only trying to scare me off this case, whoever *he* is." Corinne explained the incident with the Ferrari to Wu, who listened without interruption.

"I thought about it a lot after I damaged the Lamborghini. We were doing nearly a hundred miles an hour between slowdowns for traffic. If he wanted to kill me, a simple nudge would have done the job, but he never crashed into my car, never even came that close to touching it. He made sure we both had enough time and space to maneuver around other cars. He could have easily smashed into my car, and sent me spinning into traffic, one of those barriers, or off the road entirely." She paused to sip her Scotch. "At those speeds, a crash would have almost certainly been fatal for me, especially since the airbags are defective, or rigged not to work, I'm not sure which, but they never inflated. Anyway, the more I thought about it, the more I concluded that he never *really* tried to drive me off the road. He drove carefully. He knew exactly what he wanted to do. I have to give him credit for that." She held up her drink in a mock salute. "Maybe I underestimated his driving ability. Who knows? Maybe he is a better driver than me. Only my panicking caused me to crash into the barrier along the exit, not his driving skill. He didn't force me into that crash. No, he wasn't trying to kill me, only scare me."

Wu's frown spoke his doubts louder than if he had yelled them at Corinne. *She's right, though, at those speeds, even the slightest mistake, or miscalculation could have cost both of them their lives. Would someone risk that simply to scare her? I doubt it. Maybe Corinne had underestimated her own driving skills.* "What about the shooting?"

She took another long drink of the Scotch. "The same, I'm sure. Think about the circumstances. I wore my sister's yellow jacket to the wake. To boot, I had parked under a bright light. There's a full moon tonight, and hardly any clouds. I must have shone brighter than a flashing neon sign to him, and, if you remember the scene before you tackled me, I stood between him and my car. If he had really shot at me and missed, the bullet should have hit the Lamborghini, not the car parked next to it, and definitely not twice. Not even an amateur could miss with that set up. No, he shot at the Ford, not me."

"You took one hell of a chance, but, even if he wasn't trying to hit you, why hit the Ford, and not your car? Do you think he simply loves beautiful sports cars?"

"No, but I'll give you odds his boss told him not to damage me, or that car."

"His boss? Who, may I ask is that, Oh-Miss-Know-It-All?"

"My guess is my former boyfriend and owner of the Lamborghini, The One and Only Paul Camarazza. Who else?"

"Former? You mean I've finally convinced you the man is truly evil, and not good enough for you?"

Corinne raised her drink in another mock toast. "No, I convinced me, with the help of Paul's underhanded behavior and lies. Can you believe he showed up tonight at the funeral home, supposedly looking for me. I don't buy it. I don't know what his connection is with all this yet, but he's still lying to me. I can sense it. He knows a lot more about what happened to Monica and Sage than he's admitting."

"So, you think he's the one popping shots into cars to scare you? If it is, he cleaned up after himself. There were no cartridges, or any other evidence that anyone had even been on the roof, much less fired a weapon there."

"Oh, no!" Corinne shook her head, and then had to grab the bar as she teetered to the left. *Whoa, my head's spinning! The effects of the alcohol, I guess. It feels good though, doesn't it, Corinne? Better be careful, though. Remember you don't tolerate alcohol well. That's why you limit your intake. I fooled Paul, but, even then, the small amount of alcohol won, putting you to sleep until Wu came knocking. Better watch your intake closer for a while. All these events are proving too much for you to handle even without alcohol.* She studied her glass. *Looks harmless, though.*

"Paul would never shoot at anyone from that distance, not his style. He strikes me as a more face-to-face, confrontational attacker. My money's on Kevin, his chauffeur. Paul told me tonight that Kevin had already left for New York on a family emergency. I don't buy that lie either."

"Do you have any idea how we're going to prove that Kevin's the one who shot at you?"

"We have to find him here in Washington with his rifle. Your lab boys should be able to compare one of its bullets to the ones fired at me, if you can recover the bullets, that is."

"Don't worry, I've got that covered, but how do we find him?"

Corinne thought for a few seconds, and then held up one finger. "As a matter of fact, I think I know a way of finding out where he's hiding. I'll work on that tomorrow."

"Good. My men are digging those bullets out of the car right now"

"They should compare them to the one that killed John Zachary while they're at it. I wouldn't put that murder past Paul and Kevin either."

"Good idea. I had planned to do that anyway, since Zachary testified against your boyfriend...I mean, former boyfriend. Maybe that's why he wants you off the case so badly. Maybe he's afraid you'll find out how he managed to find the location of the safe house, and that he had ordered Zachary killed."

"Maybe." Corinne held up her empty glass. "Drink?"

"No, I'll pass, but how about a rain check after this whole affair is over?"

"Sure." She poured herself another Scotch that she knew she shouldn't have. The first drink had given her a buzz. She studied the liquid, trapped inside the clear crystal as she hooked a long curl behind her ear. "Did your lab boys come up with anything else useful?"

"A couple of things: first, both your sister and Camarazza's two hoods were killed using the gun found alongside Sage Browning's body."

"Sage killed everybody?" Corinne placed her drink on the bar, abandoning it to join Wu on the couch.

"Sure looks that way, but we're still left with the question of why?"

"If we can make a connection between her and Paul, we might be able to answer that one. Any luck with my phone list?"

"That's the other bit of news from the lab. I've got the complete list right here. Our search would have been a whole lot easier if we could have used the lab's computers, but since our investigation is off the record, and they're not supposed to be helping us, I had them print out what they could without leaving anything that could be traced back to them. No reason to get them in trouble too, if we get caught with information we shouldn't have. " He reached into his inside jacket pocket to retrieve several folded sheets of paper, giving Corinne an unintentional glance at his weapon in his belt holster. "Who do you want to start with?"

"Let's start with Sage. She seems to be at the heart of all this. Let's see who she called."

Wu shuffled through the papers, and then spread Sage's call list on the coffee table. Corinne ran her long, slim finger down the numbers, her head now pounding, her buzzed mind trying hard to concentrate on the series of blurred numbers before her, hoping to find one she recognized, one that would give her a clue to Sage's involvement in these murders.

"Some kind of computer glitch occurred at the lab, or so they said. They may simply be covering their asses in case things do go south. Anyway, they claim they couldn't get the names associated with the numbers, but they promised them as soon as the problem is fixed...maybe. They told me someone had gotten into the system, and tried to erase several files, including those we needed, someone one who really didn't know what they were doing. Anyway, I've got the lab boys, as you call them, jumping at my every command. They'll find the culprit, if one exist, and will get us those names eventually."

"They're afraid of you. Maybe Mr. Center clued them in on how mad you can get, or maybe he's the hacker trying to block our progress on orders from above. At this point, I don't trust anyone."

Half way down the list, Corinne stopped her finger. "Wait a minute! Look at this. Sage called a lot of numbers with the New York long distance exchange, and several with the Connecticut and New Jersey ones. I learned tonight that she came from Connecticut before moving to New York. I wonder if she's got relatives in those states." She restarted her finger's trek down the list. "None of the others ring a...whoa! I'll be damned!" She pounded the paper with her finger. "That's Paul's private number in New York. Why the hell would she be calling him?"

"Let's see how many times she called that number.' Wu ran his fingers down the list, and onto the second page. "She called it once a week, except for last week. See, she called him every Monday, but last week she added Thursday and Friday."

"What time Thursday?" Even with the paper right in front of her, Corinne couldn't get her eyes to focus on the small print.

"Eleven thirty two...for ten minutes. Why?"

"Paul told me tonight he first heard the details of the murders of his men Thursday night. I wonder if she told him."

"If she did, then, maybe she is the killer. The murders were reported to us Thursday evening at 6:15, but we didn't release the names, or any of the other details such as the cocaine at the scene, or the 'NY' on the mirror until much later in the weekend. The only way she could have passed those on to Camarazza Thursday night is if she had been there when the murders took place."

"So, Sage did kill those two." Corinne sat back, and closed her eyes. "But why did she do it, and why tell Paul about it if she did? Paul told me they worked for a company he oversees, but he had no reason to kill them."

"Maybe we should ask him those questions, if he hasn't left town already."

"He said he would call me again before he left." She glanced at Wu. "I'll ask him. You can count on that."

"Better be careful." Wu placed one hand gently on Corinne's forearm. "If he thinks you're getting too close, he may send his gunman after you again, only this time, he won't have him miss."

She nodded her head once, as slow as she could. Even the diminished motion increased her headache. The effect of the liquor caused her voice to crack and slur. "I'll bet those two men called the same number from their hotel room before they were murdered."

Wu shuffled the papers until he found the records from the motel. "Right on the money. They called it right after they checked in on Thursday morning. It's the only long distance call they made."

"I wonder if Paul's number appears on either of the senators' lists."

Wu spent a few moments checking.

Corinne examined Wu's squared off features as he conducted his search. She felt the alcohol doing its job, sensing it warm her body, and making her both lightheaded and happy all over. Surprisingly, her headache had begun to lessen. *Yeah, dumb cop, but definitely handsome. I wish I hadn't taken that drink. It's making me giddy and terribly sleepy. Corinne, you're an idiot for even considering liquor. I don't know why you keep trying it. It makes you act reckless.*

"That number doesn't appear to be on either of their lists." Wu pushed the papers away, and turned to Corinne, "That doesn't really mean anything, though. If either of them wanted to talk to Camarazza without leaving any traces, they could have simply used a disposable cell phone, and then tossed it. I'm afraid we can't prove anything either way. I'll get the names that correspond to the rest of these numbers eventually. Maybe that'll help."

"How about my sister's list? Is Paul's number there?"

Wu lifted Monica's phone list. "I don't see it."

"That doesn't surprise me." Corinne risked sitting upright, daring to test the effect on the lessening pain in her head. It didn't worsen. She took Monica's list from Wu. "Look at this. There's another New York number. Let's see who answers that line."

"We can do a reverse check on that with the computer, if you want. I'll check to see if the station has gotten the names by now. They were supposed to call me, but you never know."

Corinne punched the numbers into her cell phone, and waited while the phone rang four times.

"You have reached the Dickerson Detective Agency," the female voice said. "We're out of the office at the moment. Please leave your name and number, and we'll return your call as soon as possible."

Corinne disconnected, not bothering to leave a message.

"It's another detective agency. I'll call them tomorrow."

"You're going to have a busy day tomorrow. I guess I'll get going. I'll call you tomorrow to see how you made out." He headed toward the door. "Besides the phone calls, what's on your agenda?"

"I want to talk to some of Monica's friends to see what they know."

"I've talked to most of them already. Your sister didn't tell them much about her work. The one closest to your sister is a weirdo named Jacqueline Kant. You may want to start with her."

"Weirdo?"

"Yeah, she's into all kind of meditation and psychic stuff. She served as your sister's meditation teacher, at least that's what she called it."

"I'm not sure I follow you."

"Well, it's simply that..." Wu paused, rubbed the back of his neck, and then squeezed his neck muscles. "...Well...she's really weird...and rumor has it that she is also...a lesbian."

"Are you saying my sister and she were lovers?" Corinne stared at Wu, trying to read his expression. *Maybe the alcohol is affecting me again, but I can't read anything in his expression, good, or bad. Are you a homophobe, or simply trying to get a rise out of me? No, that can't be it. He doesn't realize I know more about my sister's way of life than I care to. Lesbian? Ha! If she ever kissed another woman, my lips would have lit up brighter than a Broadway sign, broadcasting the fact directly to me. No, she's never had a lesbian experience.*

"No, I'm not, not in the least. Ms. Kant denied knowing anything about your sister's activities in any of her investigations. She insisted her only connection with Monica was as her meditation instructor. I thought she had lied to me. She's covering up something. I figured that if they were lovers, she could have had something to do with her murder, maybe a romantic triangle. Anyway, she refused to say more. She's a cool one. Believe me. Maybe you'll have better luck with her than I did. I've got her address right here."

He sat on the couch again, and copied the address and phone number on the top of Monica's phone list. Corinne slid closer to him. The light scent of cologne drifted off him. She didn't recognize the brand. She placed her arm gently on the sleeve of his coat. The muscles beneath were large and hard. She squeezed gently.

"Interested in collecting that rain check?" She lowered her head, and rolled her eyes upward to meet his. She let her lips grow into a demure smile.

"Is that the liquor talking, or you, Corinne?"

"Both. No! I've only had two. No, make that one. The other is still on the bar, untouched. Besides, it's early. What do you say we spend some time together, discussing something other than murder?"

"Why the sudden change, Young Lady?" He ran his fingers through her thick hair. It felt soft as fine silk. "I thought you hated me."

"Ha! You hated me. Remember? I threatened you and your case because I had the wrong boyfriend."

"I get it now. You've lost faith in that old boyfriend, and you're expecting me to be your catch on the rebound, as they say." *Oh, I want you, Babe, want you more than any woman I've ever met, and I'm not exactly sure why, what attracts me to you, but I want you under different circumstances, normal circumstances, whatever that is between a simple police detective and a gorgeous, highly trained nurse. I should know better than to get involved with someone involved in an investigation, but somehow this feels different, feels normal, allowable, but is it? I don't know, and I don't really care at the moment.*

"With the proviso that I'm betting..." Her words became increasingly slurred. "...I'll be better at picking my new boyfriend this time around. Interested in participating in that experiment? It'll be our new TV reality show...without an audience, of course. We'll title it: 'Physical

Therapist Nurse Gets Physical to Find New Boyfriend.' Remember, I'm that nurse, and, as a medical professional, I know what's best for you."

"But do you know what's best for you? Maybe I should come back later when you've sobered up, cooled down, and had a chance to reconsider linking up with a hard-nosed police detective."

"Later won't make any difference, Hank. I can call you Hank, can't I? So, unless you find me ugly, or still hate me for being so naïve when I invaded your town, shut up, and take your medicine. Be a good patient. That's an order!"

She pulled him to her, and allowed their lips to touch, gently at first, then harder, releasing her pent-up passion. *No need to worry about sharing what I experience with you anymore, Monica…no more blocking my emotions.* She wrapped her arms around his neck, and let herself truly engulf him, squeezing him tightly against her body. She let herself be free to explore and explode for the first time in her adult life. *Where you are, Monica, you probably already know how I feel: hurt, alone, vulnerable, and yet full of passion, and hungry for love, hopefully true love for the first time.*

Her thoughts of Monica faded as Hank's hand found her breast.

CHAPTER 29

Corinne awoke late the following morning to the smell of coffee. Her head pounded. Hank had left, but she found a note on the fridge: "Had to get to HQ early. Breakfast in microwave. Heat for one minute. See you tonight? Hank."

She sighed. *All business; no mention of last night at all. Not even a "Wonderful Night" compliment. Blasted cop! He really is dumb, doesn't even know how to sweet-talk a lady.* She yawned and stretched. *Oh, well, maybe he's simply not good at expressing himself. Maybe he's inexperienced, unseasoned, so to speak. I guess I'll have to forgive him if that's the case. Maybe he simply doesn't know how to treat a real woman. He needs a good education, and I'm precisely the one who can teach him.*

While the food cooked, she poured herself a black coffee, took two aspirin, and sat at the kitchen table. "Well, Monica, I believe that's the first time I've kissed a man that you haven't known about it at the same instant. Oh, it felt so good not fighting the desire to let myself go, not trying to hold back my real reactions, my real feelings. What do you think, Monica? Is he worth the time and effort? I think so."

She took a sip of the coffee, put her hand on her left temple, feeling the slightly smaller lump, and tried to suppress the pounding beneath it. It didn't work. She dialed the number for "Regentco," Paul's corporate headquarters in New York.

"Regentco. Carol Riggins speaking. How may I help you?"

"Hi, Carol, it's Corinne. Has Paul checked in this morning?"

"Oh, hi, Corinne, no, I'm afraid not. Isn't he still down there in Washington with you?"

"Yes, but he's supposed to try to find Kevin for me. Paul gave him a few days off, and now I need him. Paul said he'd check with you to see if he had called."

"Oh, I see. Well, as far as I know, Kevin hasn't checked in the last few days. Someone did call first thing this morning looking for him, something about damaging some Ferrari he borrowed, but, otherwise, I haven't heard a thing."

Corinne grinned widely. *I guess he can't drive any better than me.* "Any idea where he might be staying down here, favorite hotel, friends, anywhere I might be able to reach him?"

"Have you checked the City Limits Inn on the outskirts of Washington? He's stayed there before."

"No, but I will. Thanks for the info."

Corinne next dialed Wu's office, leaving the information about the motel with Sergeant Doyle who had answered Wu's extension.

She then dialed the Dickerson Detective Agency. To her surprise, John Dickerson answered. "This is Corinne Day, Monica Day's sister. I believe my sister called you recently." Corinne could hear a file drawer open and the quick rustling of papers.

"Let me think. Oh, yes, now I remember. Yes, she called looking for some information she had asked me to gather for her. I hope it proved helpful to her."

"Can't really say. You see, someone murdered her last week, and stole that information from her office."

"Murdered? Oh, I'm sorry to hear that. You say you're her sister. I never actually met her. She got my name from a mutual acquaintance years ago, and we've used each other as an information source for our respective cities. We've talked on the phone, but never managed to get together. How can I help you?"

"I'm investigating her murder. I don't know if it relates to the case at all, but I need to know what you told her."

"That's easy. It wasn't top secret, that's for sure. She wanted to know about a woman named Sage Browning, whether she had a record, that sort of thing."

"Did she...I mean, have a record?"

"Well, yes, but it wasn't easy to find. Your sister had already checked the usual channels, police records, Internet sites, you know, that kind of public record thing, and found nothing. She asked me to dig deeper. So, I checked the old newspaper files. Finally found her in the police blotter. She had been arrested a total of four times on prostitution and drug charges. Last arrest occurred about six years ago."

"What happened to the arrest records at the police station? Shouldn't those arrests have been recorded there, and shouldn't there have been some court records?"

"Beats me. Someone obviously didn't want the arrests discovered, I guess, and arranged for both her arrests and the trial records to magically disappear. Maybe she did a few favors for someone on the force, or in the courts here. Maybe she had a few connections in high places, or maybe the mob. Who knows?"

"Did you find anything else?"

"Only that she used to be Paul Camarazza's girlfriend. They were never married as far as I could find. Have you heard of him?"

"What?" Corinne had screamed into the phone. "Are you sure?"

"My sources are absolutely sure. Your sister provided a photograph of her. I found some Camarazza gang members who identified her for me."

Corinne pushed her coffee away, and laid her head down on the table. She felt the muscles in her stomach tighten, the taste of acid crept into her mouth, burning her chest en route.

"Are you still there, Miss Day?"

"Yes," she sputtered into the phone, "who is this Paul Camarazza anyway?"

"You mean you've never heard of him? I guess you don't read the newspapers much, do you?"

"No, at least not the news sections. I'm usually too busy reading professional journals, and attending meetings. I hardly ever read the papers, except for the headlines I see on newsstand on the street, and then, only if I think to look at them. I don't even listen to the news on TV, or radio. It's too violent for me." *And by avoiding the news, I guess I made myself blind to his involvement in crime, as well as naïve about our relationship. I am so stupid!* "Please, tell me about this Camarazza."

"Extremely smart man, college degree to prove it. Came from a family of mobsters. Rose to the head of the family here in New York about ten years ago. He's suspected of being involved with most of the gambling, prostitution, and drugs on the East side here. Almost got caught a few times, but always managed to worm his way out of any problems. Never convicted. He gives everyone the appearance of a fine, upstanding citizen like Bruce Wayne from the Batman comic books, but, unlike Bruce Wayne's alter ego of the law-abiding Batman, in real life,

Camarazza's alter ego is no better than a common hood, only smarter, and a hell of a lot more dangerous."

"Do you think he's the one who buried the information on Sage?"

"Probably. He's got the connections downtown, and certainly is capable of tremendous deceit."

"Tell me about it," she mumbled while rubbing a lone tear from her eyes.

"Excuse me? I didn't quite hear that."

Corinne ignored his question, but did manage to raise her head, staring off into the distance. Nothing, however, came into focus, except her shattered life and ego. "Do you happen to know who he's dating at the moment?"

"Oh, yeah, as a matter of fact, I just found that out a few days ago. A colleague brought it to my attention. Her name sounded familiar, but I'm having trouble remembering why. Anyway He's got her...I think she's a physical therapist, or nurse, something like that...wrapped around him all the time." The rustling began again. "Can't remember her name at the moment, but you may have seen her on TV, or in magazines. She did something great for some clinic here. I guess it put her on the map in medicine. The hospital milked it for as much publicity as they could. Anyway, she's been seen with him a lot around town. Oh, yeah, I remember now. Her name was Day, same last name as you and your sister. I'm surprised I didn't remember that. Don't know what she sees in him beyond his money. He's got no redeeming qualities from what I hear."

"Maybe he's got a lighter side."

"Yeah, and maybe the Devil's got a lighter side too. I can tell you this much. If she continues to hang around that devil, she'll get burned, and probably badly. I doubt if she realizes she's playing with that much fire."

"Probably not." Corinne wiped the now-gushing tears from both cheeks. "If she's as smart as you imply she is, she'll probably see through him eventually."

"For her sake, I hope she catches on before she gets hurt too much."

"Too late for that, I'm afraid,"

The patrol car pulled up to the City Limits Inn in front of room 125 without benefit of flashing lights, or siren. The two officers exited the car, one brandishing a shotgun, the other his pistol. Sergeant Doyle had radioed them that a man answering the description of Kevin Bent, a suspect in the murder of John Zachary, had registered there under the name of Robert Dillon, and that they should consider him armed and dangerous. He had emphasized that they should exercise extreme caution in approaching him, and that they shouldn't underestimate Kevin Bent's expertise as a killer.

As the first officer's head rose above the roof of the car, Kevin squeezed the trigger. The bullet struck the officer above his right eye, killing him instantly. The other officer quickly aimed the shotgun at the door, but a short burst from Kevin's rifle stopped his assault, a series of bullets smashing into his head.

Kevin then ran to his rented Cadillac, and carefully drove out of the rear entrance of the parking lot, racing away from the motel as Hank Wu's car flew into the front entrance of the same lot.

Jacqueline Kant had agreed to meet Corinne for lunch at a Café in the Northwest section of Washington, telling Corinne the restaurant had become renowned in Washington for its fine food and Scandinavian décor. Corinne arrived early, and had chosen a table on the veranda. After a ten-minute wait, Corinne spotted a tall, thin, pale woman who, after checking with the hostess for Corinne's table, skipped toward her, reminding Corinne of a child without a care in the world. Her curly, ash brown hair bounced in tune with her steps. She wore a brightly colored, floral dress and a waist-length, white sweater. The loose fitting dress looked both fashionable and comfortable. Her long neck stretched above its high neckline, exposing a large Adam's apple that slid up and down as she skipped. A wide grin grew as she approached the table. A pair of pink, plastic glasses completed her dazzling appearance.

Her long, thin fingers encircled Corinne's hand, her grip surprisingly strong for her build. "I'm delighted to meet you, Corinne. I'm Jacqueline Kant. Please call me Jackie."

"Hi, Jackie, thanks for agreeing to meet with me on such short notice."

"No problem." Jackie plopped into the seat directly across from Corinne, placing her bright yellow purse between them on the table. "I had planned to call you anyway. I missed Monica's wake and funeral. Can't stand the stupid things. We were best of friends. I'm sure she would understand. I hope you do, too. You are her duplicate…beautiful beyond description."

Corinne blushed. "Thank you. I do understand about the wake and funeral. I hate them too."

"I'm glad we agree, then." She waved her hands in front of her. "I left the caterer to handle the post-funeral lunch, and went to a bar with a friend. Got stoned out of my mind. Best thing I could do for Monica. She always took care of me, you know. We were best of friends. Did I already mention that? I'm glad you're going to find her killer."

"Any ideas who that might be?"

"No, unfortunately." She eyed Corinne over the top of her glasses. "I thought the police had closed the case already, though. From what I read in the papers, some woman Monica had been investigating murdered her. I gather you don't believe that."

"No, I don't." Corinne clenched her fists. "There are too many things wrong with that explanation. There's got to be more to it than a simple murder. That's why I asked you to meet me."

The waitress appeared to take their drink orders, a Perrier for Jackie, and a Club Soda with lime for Corinne. Corinne wanted to remain clear-headed, and still had a residual headache from her Scotch and head bump, although lessened by aspirin. When the waitress left, Corinne leaned across the table. "Did Monica discuss her last case with you? Did she mention any names, or places, anything at all? Did she mention being in danger?"

"Afraid not. I told the police that Monica didn't discuss any of her cases with me, or with the other members of my class."

"How do you know she didn't talk with the other students?"

"Because I grew to know your sister better than any other student." She took a long drink as soon as the waitress placed the glasses and Perrier bottle on the table. "She wouldn't discuss business with anyone, believe me. I'm one-hundred percent sure of that."

"How close were you to my sister?"

"Extremely close. I believe I became her closest friend here in Washington."

"What about boyfriends? Wouldn't she have confided in them if she thought she were in danger?"

"I doubt it. She did have some new lover. Wouldn't even tell me his name. I always imagine him as some bigwig politician, or philanthropist, but, no, she wouldn't have gone to him for help. She would have come to me first. I'm sure of it. She trusted me, and knew she could depend on me." She took another sip of her drink. "No, if Monica had felt any inkling of imminent danger, she would have called me, and only me. I would have been furious at her if she hadn't."

"Then, you don't think she realized she had put herself in danger?"

"Not until it had already become too late, anyway."

"I'm as surprised as you that she hadn't confided in you. Were you...?" Corinne sputtered.

Jackie leaned forward, her expression becoming dead serious. "Listen, Corinne. I know what you're having trouble asking. So, I'll make it easy for you. No, your sister wasn't a lesbian. We weren't lovers."

"I...wasn't asking that at all."

"Oh, yes, you were, even though you already know the answer. I served as your sister's meditation instructor, and became her best friend, nothing more. I gave her instructions designed to increase her awareness of another person's emotions...other than those she could sense from you, of course. I understand you became skilled at hiding your emotions from Monica. Not many people could have accomplished such a feat, considering your intimate connection with your sister."

She waited for Corinne to comment, but when she didn't, and only blushed, Jackie continued. "Anyway, I taught Monica how to enhance that sensitivity. Almost anyone can learn it. For example, I sense fear as well as great loss in you. I also sense feelings of inferiority, anger, and loneliness." She reached across the table, touching Corinne's hands lightly, causing a chill to spread up Corinne's arm. She then squeezed them gently. "I sense fear of what you might learn about Monica's life, fear of discovering that you may have contributed in some way to her death, fear of failing to discover the truth about her murder, and fear of having to live with that the rest of your life."

Corinne jumped up, as if a bolt of electricity had struck her. She felt momentarily paralyzed, her gaze frozen to the woman who she now recognized as every witch she had ever seen in a Disney movie. Jackie's gaze had become both hypnotizing and enticing, drawing her further and further into her power.

Jackie folded her arms across her small breasts. "How close did I come?"

"Bull's-eye," Corinne admitted, lowering her gaze from the witch. She sat down again. "But, in truth, what difference does it make? What you sense in me won't help me find my sister's killer."

"Maybe not, but two things come to mind. First, as to your feeling of guilt, if your sister had felt danger for an extended period of time, she would have called me, and I would have detected it anyway even if she hadn't, almost as clearly as you. One of us would have felt that danger in time to prevent her murder. So, I'm thoroughly convinced your sister had no idea danger pursued her, at least not for a long period of time anyway. Therefore, she never felt a need to confide in me beforehand, or contact you through your 1-800-psychic connection. So, if you detected any hints of fear from her, it probably occurred close to her death, not days, or weeks before."

Corinne relived the horror of her last connection with Monica. She clenched her fists again.

"Therefore, you couldn't have prevented her murder. You didn't fail her. Second, as far as your fears of failure are concerned, they are the same things your sister expressed to me when she first set herself up as a private detective here in Washington."

"What? What do you mean?"

"That you and your sister are more alike than you care to admit...I mean beyond those gorgeous looks of yours. I'm sure if it were you who had been killed, she would be experiencing the same emotions you are right now."

Corinne took a long drink. "I can't believe that. We were identical twins, linked by birth and genetics, but we are so different. Monica always had so much more insight than me, and events you could have no knowledge of have recently pointed how naïve and stupid I can be. No, not Monica! She had much more insight into the world than I ever had."

"That may be only because she developed a quicker response to those worldly events, and became more skilled than you at both expressing herself, and reacting to whatever circumstances she confronted. Unlike you, she never tried to hide her actions, or emotions. She learned from them, from the mistakes she made. Monica told me you hid your emotions for reasons she never understood. By not expressing those emotions, you set up a wall between you and that world you mentioned. It made your sister seem the extrovert and you the introvert, hiding behind a self-created wall and all your fancy, book-learned degrees."

She took a deep breath before continuing. "You succeeded in medicine because you followed what you had learned from your textbooks in college and nursing school, not only the ones containing medical knowledge, but also the ones that taught how to be a leader. You manipulated the people you dealt with until they followed your rules, your lead without exception. You did it with no hint of emotions. You worked your way up until you became head of that clinic, but only because you were helped by another's lead, Monica's. You had become so dependent on Monica for both your true feelings and direction in that world of yours that you sought her guidance for almost everything. I should know, Monica consulted me frequently on what advice she should give you. Monica gave you all the direction she could because she loved you, and knew that you thought you needed it. However, she knew the truth: she wasn't any more talented than you concerning life, or decision making." She rolled her eyes. "She simply 'beat you to the punch,' as the saying goes, at experiencing life to its fullest, of taking chances, of expressing her emotions, of making her own mistakes, and recovering from them…learning from them. She knew that one doesn't need talent to live, but one should always live through one's own talents. You were afraid to do that. She wasn't."

"Do you also have a Doctorate in Psychology?"

"No, but I always see things for what they truly are, and, at the moment, I see a woman in a great deal of pain, struggling against enormous odds, as well as against the ghost of a supposedly superior sister."

Corinne still couldn't tear her eyes from the witch. "Okay, I'll bite. What do you think that woman should do, Doctor Kant?"

Jackie laughed at the whimsical barb. "Let your sister go." She took a deep breath, closed and opened her eyes twice. She lowered her voice, her tone taking on a somber note. "Oh, Corinne, Monica told me how much you shared. I can't imagine how alone you must feel after all those years of always having your connection with her." She leaned forward. "But now, you have to let her go. Learn how to think for yourself. You may feel alone for the first time in your life, but, if you want to be successful at your investigation, you've got to adjust to that. If you do, you have a good chance of coming out on top. If not, you're going to be eaten alive by whoever killed her."

"What do you mean by 'eaten alive?'" Corinne's hands were now shaking noticeably. She placed them on her lap, out of sight.

Jackie leaned forward again. "Simply that whoever killed Monica conned her into believing that nothing that she had uncovered presented a danger to her, but, in reality, it did. She had been investigating that Sage woman for over a year…over a year, and not one sign of any danger. Then, without warning, Monica is murdered. Your sister had no inkling of what might occur, had no idea what she had gotten herself into, who she had upset." She paused, examining the empty Perrier bottle. "Your sister knew how to handle an investigation, to say nothing of herself. She had the reputation of being a top-notch private detective, one who pursued an investigation until she had uncovered the entire truth. That persistence cost her dearly."

"I still don't understand what that has to do with me being eaten alive by the killer."

Jackie sighed deeply, leaning back in her chair, and closing her eyes for several seconds. When she finally opened them again, she talked slower and more hushed. "The police gave up on the case days ago. You haven't. You're being as persistent as your sister, but your mind is not focused on your goal alone. You're distracted by thoughts of Monica and her absence. If you continue your investigation, I have no doubt you'll discover the same thing your sister did, maybe more. If you do, you'll become the killer's next target. I respected your sister and her judgment. I loved her as a friend, tried to make her more sensitive to the projections of others, but she still got in trouble. You've got to remember, you're not Monica. You don't have my training to make you sensitive to others. If, without that sensitivity, you try to think as Monica did, and act as Monica, the detective, did, you'll end up as dead as she is."

"So, again, what do you suggest, sensitivity training?"

"No, that would take too long." She leaned toward Corinne again. "Start using the logic of the famous physical therapist, nurse and, clinic redeemer, Corinne Day. Monica supported you, but you promoted you. You succeeded at all those medical tasks, not Monica. She represented your support team, your cheerleader, but she wasn't the one who succeeded. You were. Now, use your God-given brains to pursue that killer, but go beyond that. Use all your talents, medical and non-medical, maybe even some Monica didn't possess. Apply those to your investigation. That's the only way you'll ever solve Monica's murder, and stand a chance of coming out alive."

Jackie sighed. "If you're right, and there's more connected to her death, you have to be careful. The closer you get to an explanation, the more danger you'll be in, and, like Monica, you might not recognize it. You can't trust anyone, and it's imperative that you protect yourself at all times, from all sides. Remember, you're not your sister. You're not a licensed private investigator. You're not trained in detective skills. What you are is a highly intelligent, highly motivated leader and problem solver, the same attributes Monica possessed. She became successful applying those talents to her own profession. You can do the same to your investigation, but coming from a different viewpoint and direction. Apply your own talents to solving her murder. In other words, you've got to become proactive, pretend the investigation is a patient, and you've got to develop a plan to help that patient go in the right direction to find a cure, or, at least the right treatment. Give that patient some fancy diagnosis, and then prescribe the most appropriate treatment."

She shut her eyes as Corinne's blank look remained unchanged. "Listen, Corinne, what I'm saying is that you must find out what started Monica down the road to death. Once you determine that direction, you can then follow that lead, using a different approach than your sister's, prune out anything that's distracting and, therefore, unnecessary to your case, and, if you do all of that while remaining conscious of the fact that you're Corinne, not Monica, I believe you stand a good chance of solving her murder, maybe even proving the police wrong."

Jackie's eyes opened wide. "One more thing: Stop being the lonely victim, lost without her sister, and become the aggressor, outfox the opposition as only as you can."

Corinne finished her drink, and signaled the waitress to refill them before speaking. She quickly recounted the events leading up to the two attacks the previous night.

"That's exactly what I mean. Suppose they were really trying to kill you. They would have succeeded already...twice. If you're going to survive long enough to solve this thing, then you'd better start believing there are bad guys out there who are trying to cover their tracks, to say nothing of their asses, and start hunting them rather than have them hunt you."

She held up her new bottle of Perrier in a toast. "Outfox them. Become the hunter, instead of the prey, Corinne. The days of the helpless female are gone, Honey. You are a good example of that with all you've accomplished in your field, but you've got to be able to extend outside the medical profession now. Get your head out of the medical textbooks, and into life, the life you've been avoiding. You've got to be flexible enough to apply yourself totally to this investigation, and forget everything else. Remember Monica, and what she taught you about life, how she loved life, and tried to experience all it had to offer, while remaining true to her upbringing...including all her experiences with you. Use those memories in your investigation, if you must, but don't let them distract you, or interfere with your own forward motion in this case. Don't look back. Look ahead, and remember, become the hunter. Stop being the hunted."

"I'm not sure I can be a hunter," Corinne admitted with down-turned eyes.

"Sure you can. If you couldn't, you wouldn't be here now. You would have given up already, and gone home to New York. Another thing, I'd advise you to carry your sister's gun. The bad guys obviously mean business. So, you'd better be prepared to fight back." She patted her purse. "I carry one, and I'm not investigating anything."

"Sure, I can carry my sister's gun, and I know how to use it, but I'm not sure I can think of myself as a hunter. I'm only doing this investigation because there's no one left to do it. I'm sure if Monica were in my shoes..."

"Stop right there!" Jackie held up her hand. "There you go again, talking about what Monica would do. Haven't you listened to a word I've said? It doesn't matter what she would do. What she did got her killed. What matters is what you're going to do. Leave Monica out of the investigation, except for being your motivation."

Corinne lowered her head as well as her voice. "But you were right. I always felt inferior to Monica and her successes."

"Look, you came here for information to help you catch a murderer. Unfortunately, I don't have any that would help. I already told that to the police. Your sister missed several lessons recently. So, I hadn't even talked to her for the last couple of weeks. As a matter of fact, I had planned to call her to find out why she hadn't attended class. Then, I heard she had been murdered."

She paused, again examining her drink. When she spoke again, her voice had an even slower tempo. "Understand, Corinne, the real reason I agreed to meet with you has to do with the fact that your sister confided in me that you had this inferiority complex...specifically about her and her supposedly superior abilities."

"It's not a complex," Corinne objected, more harshly than she had intended. "I'm a nurse, a physical therapist. I have been trained in psychology. I work with brilliant psychiatrists when need be. I don't have any complex. I should know."

"All right, Corinne. Don't call it a complex. I'm neither a medical professional, nor psychologist. So, I'm not in a position to argue that one. Let's say that you simply felt that Monica had more...now, what did you call it? Oh, yes, Monica had more 'insight' than you did. Anyway, Monica knew it wasn't true. I mean, for crying out loud, Corinne, your sister bought a big tower computer to solve all her data storage problems, and then couldn't get the damn thing to work, but she kept it anyway. It's probably in her office right now, taking up space, not solving her data storage problems at all. I finally convinced her to buy a laptop with a large hard drive, and she used it sparingly and reluctantly, I might point out, preferring her little pieces of paper, her sticky notes, scattered all over her desk. Now, I ask you, is that showing insight? She wasted a ton of money, to say nothing of time, trying to learn how to use the damn computers. She hated computers, if you can believe that of anyone in this day and age, and she had two in her office. No, believe me, she had many faults, many shortcomings, and I'm sure you do too, but being inferior to Monica isn't one of them."

"I wish I could believe that."

"You'd better. It appears that your life depends on it." She leaned forward again, and again reached for Corinne's hands. Corinne slowly placed her hands into the witch's for another reading, wondering what she would sense this time. "Your sister made me promise to talk to you if anything ever happened to her. So, I'm here, trying to do my best. I loved your sister, and will miss her more than you can imagine. You're a duplicate of her physically, but you aren't her. You're different. I'll say it one more time. Let Corinne out of that shell, and you'll do fine. End of lecture."

She looked Heavenward, and added, "Okay, Monica. Mission accomplished."

Jackie then returned her gaze to Corinne, her eyes now appearing softer, more normal, and less witchlike. She smiled. "Now, I think we should eat before I starve to death."

Corinne shot her a quizzical look. "Tell me one more thing, and then I won't ask you anything else. Did my sister ask you to talk to me before, or after she died?"

Jackie laughed, a belly laugh that made the other restaurant patrons turn to see what had caused such an uproarious commotion. "Before. Despite what you may have been told, I can't really communicate with the dead."

"Maybe not, but you sure do one hell of a job communicating with the living."

CHAPTER 30

Corinne sat in her sister's office, her elbows on the desk, her chin resting in her hands. The phone rang, but she didn't bother answering it. *I don't want to talk to anyone about anything. I've got too much to think about, too much for my mind to digest. The only things I don't have enough of are clues to solve Monica's murder.* Frustrated, she blew onto the phone as if it were a candle she could blow out. It didn't work, its ring loud and persistent. On the twelfth ring, she reached for the receiver. "Damn you, Monica, didn't you even own an answering machine?" She looked with distain at the receiver before speaking into it. "Hello."

"Miss Day? This is Special Agent Collins. I thought you'd never answer. I've been calling all day."

"I went out."

"Investigating, I hope."

Corinne yawned. "Yes, but I'm not sure I'm getting anywhere. I spent some time with a friend of my sister's."

"Learn anything useful?"

"I think so, but not in the area I had expected, not directly related to Monica's murder anyway, but she did manage to give me an in depth analysis of my feelings toward Monica and my sister's attitude toward me."

"What is she, another self-proclaimed psychiatrist, or a psychic in touch with your sister's spirit from the other side?"

"I'm not exactly sure which myself, but she had a ton of advice for me. I may even be able to use some of it." Corinne huffed her frustration. "That's enough about me, though. What'd you call about?"

"Wu told me about the attacks on you. Are you okay?"

"Sure, I think they were only attempts to scare me off."

"Wu told me you'd say that, but I have to agree with him that you should be more careful, maybe carry a gun as Wu suggested. You know how to use one?"

"Yes, I had several on the farm in Connecticut where I grew up. I actually prefer rifles, but I became an excellent shot with handguns as well. I even beat Monica at a county contest when we were twelve."

"That's good, but remember, your targets may be shooting back this time. So, be careful, and don't take any chances. We need you in one piece. I encouraged you to do this investigation. I'm responsible for your well-being."

"Now, that's the second time you've shown concern for me. Is it genuine yet?"

"Well, it's getting there." He paused. When he spoke again, his speech had a more deliberate tempo. "Please don't take this wrong, Miss Day, but I did some investigating on my own, and my sources from New York describe you as a naïve woman who had her head buried in the medical journals, and lived at the hospital more than her apartment."

"I'm afraid that's true. Not much I can do about that now." She huffed. "It seems to be analyze Corinne day. Anything else about me, Oh Great FBI Psychiatrist Collins?"

"I am sorry, Corinne, I don't mean to add to your burdens, or hurt you, but they called you more than naïve; they called you blind to reality. I would have thought that would be a rare breed, all intelligence and no world sense, no common sense, I guess."

"Hey, back off; that's enough! I received advice from one amateur analyst already. I don't need another on my case."

"I'm not trying to analyze you, Miss Day, simply understand you. I'm trying to figure out how you think, how you got into the situation with Camarazza in the first place. I guess what I'm trying to say is that maybe I do believe now that you really didn't know much about your boyfriend."

"Former boyfriend," Corinne corrected.

"Okay, former boyfriend. At least you finally found out he's beyond a scoundrel. He's a hardened criminal not worthy of your time." He paused briefly. "I guess maybe I came down on you a little too strong the last time we met, huh?"

"Apology accepted."

"I wasn't apologizing. I simply wanted to let you know what I had learned about you, that's all. I'm still keeping an open mind on the subject. That's all I'm saying."

"Men! I know all I need to know about me. I've lived in this body my entire life, and I also know more about me than your sources will ever find out. You don't need to tell me what your men found out about me back in New York, and I really don't give a damn what you think about me...ever. Now, did you call about anything else, maybe something more useful and more applicable to my investigation? I've got work to do, and you're wasting my time."

"Okay. Please calm down. We're both on the same side. I did have another reason for calling. I called Judge Jacobs, and she's agreed to talk to you. Give her a call at the number I gave you."

"Okay, will do. That's already on my to-do list today anyway."

"She's only meeting with you because she knows me, and owes me a favor. Be careful what you say. Remember, she's a federal judge. If you come on too strong, she won't tell you anything. Believe me, she'll respond to a soft sell, but will clam up with a hard push. Trust my judgment. I've dealt with her before."

"I'll keep that in mind. Anything else?"

"Not for now. Keep me informed."

"Will do."

Corinne opened the top drawer of the desk, and retrieved her sister's gun. "Everyone thinks I should be carrying you, but I'm not so sure that's the right thing to do yet." She removed the magazine and replaced it several times. The weapon felt comfortable in her hand. She sighted the computer screen, placing her finger gently on the trigger, imagining the screen exploding as the bullet blasted through it. "I should blow a hole in you for all the damn good you've done me. Can't even get a cursor out of the computer attached to you. I know your hard drive is fried, but it's no wonder my sister gave up on you, You Outdated, Electronic Dinosaur."

Replacing the gun in the drawer, she jumped when the phone rang again. "You're nerves are shot, Corinne." She reached for the phone. "You've got to calm down, if you're going to be effective in this investigation. Control, control, control." She took a deep breath, allowing the phone to ring two more times before lifting the receiver. "Hello."

"I thought you might be there, Corinne," Paul said. "How's the investigation coming?"

She snapped her eyes closed. *Oh, no! You're the last person I want to talk to right now, but I do have questions for you, things only you can answer.* She sighed. "It's coming."

"You don't sound convinced to me. Listen, Honey, why don't you come back to New York with me tomorrow, take a break from all this. You've been under a terrible strain. I'm worried about you."

"Sure you are. Tell me, how's Kevin these days?"

He responded without hesitation. "Kevin? I told you he's in New York. Don't you remember?"

"Oh, I remember all right, but I thought I saw him on a rooftop last night."

Again he replied with no delay. "Couldn't have been him. He's in New York. Now, come on, Honey. You're not yourself. First, you think you saw me in a Ferrari, and now you think you saw Kevin on a rooftop. You're not yourself. I'm worried about you."

"I'm worried about me too."

"Then, come home with me. Take a rest. We'll come back when you're feeling better, when you're stronger."

"I think I am home, now, right here. I feel strong now, and I certainly don't need a rest. What I need are answers from people, starting with you."

His voice grew louder, angrier. "I told you everything I know already."

"Somehow, I doubt that. Now, tell me what your connection is with Senator Stern."

"I told you I met him for the first time at that wake. I paid him my respects. That's all there is to tell."

"What about your girlfriend, Sage? Did you tell me everything about her too?" Corinne could picture him sweating.

After an extended pause, he said, "Oh, you found out about that. I had hoped to spare you that pain. Okay. You wanted the truth. Here it is. I knew Sage back in New York years ago. She got into a little trouble with the law, and I helped her by getting her a lawyer. She felt grateful, and, well, we dated a few times. It never developed into anything really serious. We never got really close, as you and I did after she left."

He waited for Corinne to say something. When she didn't, he continued, "One day she decided to go to Washington, and that's the last I heard of her until I saw her on the floor in your sister's office. Can you imagine my surprise? I go there to meet you, and there's Sage, dead. The night you spotted me at her wake, I really had gone there looking for you, not Sage. I had no intention of going to her wake, or funeral. I guess I was in shock from seeing her again. I had no idea her death would affect me the way it did. That's why I jumped when you first spoke to me that night."

"Then, you didn't know whose wake I had gone to?"

"Hell, no, I happened to be driving by that funeral home on my way to a meeting that night when I spotted my Lamborghini parked out front. So, I stopped to talk to you. Sage's happened to be the only wake there that night. When I saw her name posted at the door, I panicked, and hurried to find you. I didn't want to tell you I had dated her. I didn't want to hurt you. I had really hoped to get you back home before you found out. I didn't see any reason for you to know that some former girl-friend of mine had killed your sister. I really don't want to lose you, Corinne, especially over some past affair that means nothing to me, and that has absolutely nothing to do with our relationship now."

"You really expect me to buy that pile of crap?"

"It's the truth, Corinne. It may sound a little farfetched, but I swear it's the truth. Why the hell would I want to make up such a story anyway?"

"You tell me. I'm not good at reading minds, or seeing through bullshit."

"Come on, Corinne. Give me a little credit for having some brains. I know you're no dummy. You're a hell of a lot smarter than I'll ever be, and you've got all the degrees to prove it. I had hoped that my little deceit might spare you some pain. Now that the truth is out, I really want you to return with me to New York. Let's leave all this unpleasant-ness behind."

Corinne threw a pencil at the computer screen across the room, striking it with the eraser, wishing she had fired Monica's gun at it in-stead. "Okay, let's pretend for the moment that your story is at least plausible, and now there are no secrets between us. Tell me something else. Why are you so insistent that I return with you? It can't be for my health. I never felt better in my life. If your old girlfriend did kill Mon-ica, then there is no killer on the loose to threaten me, and I'm not in any danger."

She waited for him to comment. She heard only silence. "I've found out that you managed to cancel my consult here, so, I have no pa-tient to worry about here in Washington. That frees me to pursue my in-vestigation. Back in New York, my colleagues are seeing all my patients. There's no reason to rush back. I've got all the time I need to finish what I've started. So, explain to me again why you don't want me to stay,

Mister Manipulator. Are you afraid I might uncover more uncomplimentary things about you, more of your lies maybe?"

An extendedly long pause followed before Paul cleared his throat, and spoke again, his voice deeper, more serious. "I guess I'm afraid you might want to stay here. You've already referred to it as your home. I lost one girl to this city. I don't want to lose another, especially not one as beautiful as you. You mean a lot to me, Corinne. I love you."

Corinne closed her eyes tightly. *That's a big, fat lie. You love only you. I can't believe you could say you love me, lie to me again, and so easily.* Her voice cracked, growing louder as she spoke. "Not a good enough reason, and you know it. If you really loved me, you'd stay to help me instead of trying to manipulate and scare me into going with you. You wouldn't ask me to leave before finding the truth. You're the one with all the contacts down here. Why aren't you offering me their help? No, I'm staying. There's no debating that. I am going to get to the real story behind my sister's death, and no one…did you hear me, Paul…no one is going to stop me."

"Oh, I hear you loud and clear, Corinne. You don't have to yell. I disagree with what you're doing, but you've left no doubt about your intentions. If you need anything, I'll be in New York only a phone call away. Don't hesitate to call. Believe me, Corinne, I wish you luck. Give me a call when you find whatever it is you think you're looking for. Bye, Corinne."

Corinne didn't bother with a "goodbye.'" She pointed the gun at the phone. "Bang."

Paul sat back heavily in the couch. He had hoped he could reason with her, hoped he could somehow persuade her to return to their life in New York. He had underestimated her determination. He slammed his fist onto the couch's arm. "Damn! The bitch isn't coming."

Kevin pulled his .45 from his shoulder holster, and began caressing its barrel tenderly. "You want me to take care of her? The cops are already looking for me, but I can avoid them easily. I can hit her when she least expects it."

Paul stood, and stomped to the bar without uttering a word. He poured whiskey into a shot glass, downing the entire drink in one gulp. He glanced at Kevin, and poured another drink.

"I want you to go on a vacation for a few weeks on some tropical island of your choice, all expenses paid. I've got a few other loose ends to clear up here myself, and then I'll head back to the city. Call me when you get to the island."

Kevin nodded.

Paul snarled, the snarl morphing into a huge grin. "On the way to the airport, make her your final job here. Kill her, and use your friend there to make it personal.... from me."

CHAPTER 31

Corinne found Nellie transcribing notes when she entered the reception area of Senator Stern's office.

"The senator is expecting you. Go right in. I'll announce you."

Senator Stern rose when Corinne entered. He wore a neatly cut gray suit, white shirt with a button-down collar, and a loud, gray and pink striped tie.

She took a moment to look around the office before accepting his outstretched hand. The beige room had one wall covered with prints of the last two Presidents. On the opposite wall were photos of the Senator, posing proudly with several other people. Corinne recognized some as famous actors, others as senators, but there were several who were unknown to her. The parquet floor appeared highly polished, and looked slippery, although she had no difficulty traversing it with her leather-soled shoes. The furniture, consisting of three large, brown leather chairs, a couch beneath the presidential prints, and his large oak desk, were overpowering in such a small office.

"Thank you for seeing me, Senator. I realize this isn't the best time, but it's important."

"I know it is, Miss Day. First, let me say how sorry I am about your sister."

Corinne took out her notebook. "Thank you. Did you know her?"

"No, not personally, but I knew Senator Jackson had hired her to investigate Sage's background."

"I gather you had no objection to that investigation?"

"No, of course not."

"Did Senator Jackson keep you informed of my sister's progress?"

"No, I didn't need any updates because I knew that your sister wouldn't find anything."

She tapped her pen on the notepad. "How did you know that?"

"I knew the real Sage, a wonderful woman, hard worker, loved by everyone. She couldn't have done anything dishonest in her past. Besides, she told me everything about herself, and she never mentioned doing anything off color, much less illegal. She would have confided in me, if she had. She wouldn't have risked my career trying to hide something. I would have forgiven her anyway, and worked around any such indiscretion. She knew that. I trusted her honesty then, and I've got no reason to think otherwise now."

"Then, how do you explain the fact that it appears that she murdered my sister and then reportedly committed suicide? Would the Sage you knew do that?"

"Well, to be honest with you, Sage wasn't exactly herself the last few months. She had been under a lot of pressure both at work and in her private life."

"Oh, what kind of pressure?"

"We were preparing a massive Presidential campaign. She became committed to spending all of her spare time to make it successful."

"And in her private life?"

"Listen, Miss Day, Sage and I were lovers. There's no denying that. We had plans to marry before the election. Couple the pressures of an upcoming Presidential campaign with all the hassles of wedding plans, and you can see how someone could easily crack under the strain. I'm afraid her personality compelled her to work harder than any woman I've ever known. She strove for perfection in everything, and would settle for nothing less. Eventually, that probably contributed to her suicide."

"But why shoot my sister? As far as any of us know, she hadn't found anything negative about Sage."

"That's because there wasn't anything negative to find."

"Then why shoot Monica? It doesn't make any sense."

He rubbed his eyes. "There are some things going on here that you don't have security clearance to be told, Miss Day. There are things you're not privileged to know."

"Security clearance? Why should I need that? We're not talking terrorist acts, or anything involving national security. We're talking about a simple murder and suicide. Granted we're both personally involved, so, it's an emotionally charged issue, but that doesn't make anything about it so secret to that it should be raised to that level. Where does a security clearance fit into any of this? I don't get it."

Senator Stern stood, and paraded in front of the prints of the Presidents. "All right, let's take it from the beginning. Your sister had been hired to do a simple job, search the background of both Sage and myself. She did a good job of that, and came up empty, but, in the process, she stumbled upon some information that is highly secret..."

Corinne huffed. *This sounds like a rehearsed speech.*

Senator Stern glanced at Corinne for only a second before continuing. "...and that you're not privileged to know."

"Is that why they searched my sister's office before her murder?"

He stopped his march to turn toward Corinne. "I don't know anything about that. Who told you it had been searched?"

"The police, but, please, don't let me interrupt. Continue with your story."

The parade started again. "Maybe Sage searched your sister's office. I don't know. I've always wondered why she had gone to your sister's the day of the murder. I thought she might have been looking for any information your sister had found about her, got in a fight with her, and, during the fight, her gun fired accidentally. I warned her not to carry that gun. People are always getting killed accidentally with those damn things. They shouldn't carry them."

"But how did Sage know about the information my sister discovered? Was Sage one of those who had been privileged to know, as you put it?"

Senator Stern stopped the march again, and spun toward Corinne, glowering at her. The respite from his parade proved only temporary, his march starting again as if Corinne hadn't interrupted him. "Sage could be a resourceful woman. I'm sure she came by it by chance, maybe when your sister interviewed her. I'm not one hundred percent sure. In any case, Sage recognized its importance immediately." He glanced at Corinne.

Sounds more fairy tale than truth to me. "Go on with your story. I'm listening."

"I figure Sage panicked after shooting your sister, and left without the information. She went back for it when she thought she wouldn't be caught, while everyone attended your sister's funeral."

"Okay, if you believe that, explain why she killed herself."

"Now, there I'm a little shaky."

You're a lot shaky, if you're asking me to buy this cock-and-bull story.

"My guess is that she figured getting caught for your sister's murder would have hurt my political career, maybe have even ended it. I mean, think about it, a Presidential candidate whose fiancée kills a detective while trying to recover top-secret information involving that Presidential candidate. The trial would have been unbearable for her." He glanced downward, his voice dropping with his gaze. "I wish you had gotten the chance to meet her. You would have enjoyed knowing her, I'm sure." He shook his head, as if clearing the cobwebs. "Anyway, the news media would have had a field day, crucifying both of us. Of course, she knew that I would have defended her through it all, even at the cost of my career. She knew the voters would be leery of a man who picked a murderer as a future wife and possible First Lady."

Corinne closed her notebook, and placed it in her purse. "Sounds altruistic enough to me, but it's also a lot of bullshit. The story of you two being involved leaked even with her dead, and everyone thinks that she's a murderer. All the news programs carried it at least for a day or two, and I don't see your political career falling to pieces. If your story is correct, she predicted the wrong outcome, and died needlessly. I don't buy it."

Senator Stern hurried back to his seat. "It's the truth, the only truth, Miss Day. Sage sacrificed herself for me. If you want to believe something else, fine. It doesn't make a whole lot of difference to me. Your sister's dead, and so is the woman I love. We've both suffered a devastating loss. Can't we simply leave it at that, and let this whole thing die away?"

"I'm afraid there's more to it than that, Senator." She crossed one leg over the other pulling her skirt down over her knee. "I understand Sage had plans to leave Washington with your son, and you knew it. That information doesn't require security clearance, does it?"

He slammed his fist onto the desk. "Damn! Why can't you people let Sage rest in peace? What does it matter if she had an affair with Tom? You'd better drop it, Miss Day, or else."

Corinne pushed back a curl that had fallen across her eye. *How far can I push him before he simply kicks me out of his office, or finds some excuse to have me arrested on some trumped up charge?*

"Is that a threat, Senator?"

"No, it's friendly advice. Sage, Tom and I were trying to work things out. My son seemed to think Sage had decided to accompany him, but he's wrong. She changed her mind. She decided to stay with me, and go through with our wedding plans. I had hoped to spare Tom that knowledge now that Sage is gone. His knowing wouldn't serve any purpose. So, I'll have to ask you to keep it confidential for Tom's sake, if nothing else. You can at least grant me that much, can't you."

Corinne thought for only a second. "Agreed."

"I think Tom would have eventually understood Sage's decision. Of course, he would have been hurt when he initially found out, but I really think that when he finally realized Sage and I were still madly in love, he would have come around. Now, I'll never know. I really wish Sage had come to me for help. I'm sure she shot your sister by accident. It couldn't have happened any other way."

"Maybe, and maybe she had tried to contact you before she killed herself, but couldn't find you. Do you remember where you were at the time of Sage's death?"

"Want to check my alibi, right?"

"It had crossed my mind. Well?"

"Let me think for a moment. Oh, yes, I believe I attended your sister's funeral. I had turned my cell phone off so its ring wouldn't disturb any mourners."

Corinne's eyes opened wide. "You were there? I didn't see you."

"I went in Senator Jackson's limo. I decided not to get out at the last minute, and forgot about my cell phone's ringer until later…and, before you ask, she didn't call me at that time. There were no texts from her and absolutely nothing new on my voice mail. Check my phone records, if you wish." He took a deep breath. "Sage had promised to meet Tom there to tell him of her decision to stay with me. She didn't know I planned to be there, but I wanted to be close in case she, or Tom needed some moral support. She never showed. Now, if you don't mind, I have a full day ahead of me, and this interview has taken a lot out of me."

Corinne stood, and extended her hand. He reluctantly took it, grasping and releasing it almost as soon as he touched her.

"Thank you, Senator, for your time and candor. I may have to talk to you again. Can I call you?"

"Sure, providing it doesn't involve anything requiring that security clearance we talked about. Forget all references to the information you're not privileged to know." He sat down and pointed toward the door. "Nellie can set up any future appointment you need. She knows my schedule."

Corinne spoke to Nellie on her way out. "Did Senator Jackson's car come here to pick up Senator Stern, or did he use his own car to attend my sister's funeral?"

Nellie consulted the senator's appointment book as Corinne peaked over her shoulder. "Neither, the senator didn't have an appointment to meet Senator Jackson at all that day. He had been scheduled to attend a crime committee meeting, but it had been cancelled. If I remember right, the senator said he had some work to do, and left the office early. I didn't see him the rest of the day. Why? Is it important?"

"Probably not. Thanks again for setting up the appointment with the senator. I owe you."

As Corinne headed for the stairs, she wrote in her notebook:

1-Check Senator Stern's story of being in limo with Senator Jackson.

2-Find out what I'm "not privileged to know."

CHAPTER 32

After leaving Senator Stern's office, Corinne hurried to the courthouse, and her appointment with the superior court judge. Arriving early, she sat in her chambers for fifteen minutes before the door behind the desk flew open, and Judge Jacobs, a tall African American, whose robes made her appear chubbier than her actual slight frame, charged into the room, flopping into her seat in one fluid motion. Corinne judged her age as early sixties. Corinne chuckled to herself. *I can't believe women Justices still wear those awful-looking robes.*

Above a deep frown, Judge Jacobs's eyes rapidly scanned two sheets of paper on her desk, at the same time trying to find her hands, hidden somewhere in the robe, totally ignoring Corinne's presence. When her hands finally popped out of the folds of the garments, she unhurriedly folded her spindly fingers together, pushed the two sheets aside, and glared at Corinne. "I haven't got time for pleasantries, Miss Day. The only reason I squeezed you into my busy schedule is that Special Agent Collins asked me for the favor. I owe Dave, but I'm in the middle of a case, and don't have much time. So, get on with it. I understand you're investigating your sister's murder."

"Yes." Corinne's voice remained steady and firm, although she felt nervous, talking to a judge for the first time. "And I don't believe what I've been told about it."

"What, exactly, have you been told, and what do you not believe?"

Corinne explained all she knew about her sister's murder, finding Sage's body, and the information provided by both senators. "I don't believe any of it. I think there's a huge cover-up going on in the case."

"That's a serious allegation. Do you have any proof of what you say?"

"None that you would issue an arrest warrant on yet."

"Then why are you here, and what do you expect me to do about a simple murder and suicide, and your unproven supposition?"

"I need to know why you issued the search warrant to the FBI to clean out my sister's apartment and office."

The judge leaned forward, her frown increasing. Her eyes became slits. "What do you mean by 'clean out'?"

"They took every scrap of paper, and went through every page of her notebooks."

"That's what a search warrant is for, Miss Day. They were trying to determine how much your sister knew."

"But they did more than that. They seized every file she had, and they even erased all her computer files, destroying her hard drive in the process. They also wiped the place clean of fingerprints."

The judge's expression remained unchanged.

"Doesn't it bother you that they took things and destroyed files not related to your warrant? Doesn't it bother you in the least that my sister's murder occurred right after the FBI search, and that there might be a connection between the search and her murder?"

"Coincidence, Miss Day. From what I understand, Sage Browning killed her for other reasons. There are no connections."

"That's what they want us to believe, but I think there is a connection." Corinne leaned forward, resting one elbow on the desk. "Sage knew Paul Camarazza, the crime boss from New York. They were lovers."

"Maybe that's why she killed your sister. Maybe your sister discovered that relationship, and Sage killed her to keep that information secret. She certainly had reason to want that information buried. Didn't she?"

"Maybe, but there are some things that still need explaining. For one, Sage's gun had been used to kill two of Camarazza's men a few days before my sister's murder."

"So, Sage had killed before. That supports the theory that she killed your sister, whatever her reason."

I'm obviously not getting through to you. Why am I the only one who can see that the facts don't add up, that they don't make sense? Okay, I'll try a different approach. "You issued a warrant for a search for her apartment and office. I assume they gave you proper cause, or you wouldn't have given it to them. The FBI team took everything that she could have possibly used to record information, all her papers and even her electronic media. Who knows what else they took? Special Agent Collins told us he personally incinerated everything they found."

The judge's facial expression changed to quizzical. "Did you say *incinerated?*"

"That's what he said. His superiors ordered him to incinerate everything without examining its contents."

"He never told me that. They were supposed to find out what your sister knew, and talk to her about it, warn her off before any damage could be done. They sent their best team. I know most of them. I can't imagine them destroying evidence, for any reason."

"That's what the FBI director ordered. That's what the team did."

"Dave never told me that."

"Your Honor, please don't take offense at this, Special Agent Collins said he tried to tell you, but you wouldn't listen. He thought...maybe you were involved in the cover up, or were afraid of your involvement because you had issued the original warrant."

"No, I guess I simply didn't listen to what Dave tried to tell me. My mind must have been elsewhere. What else didn't I hear?"

"Did you know that team has been disbanded? All the members, including Special Agent Collins were sent to different parts of the country."

Judge Jacob's speech became slow. "Dave did mention he had been transferred."

"He thinks they transferred the entire team to prevent them from exposing what they had done."

"But why?"

"Don't know yet, but it probably has to do with the information they were after."

"That information is delicate and extremely dangerous."

"So delicate it cost my sister her life?"

"You're being melodramatic, Miss Day. You haven't told me one thing that connects her murder to that information."

"Maybe that's only because I don't know what the information is. Senator Stern says I'm not privileged to know what my sister found, but I think it's the key to this whole mystery."

"What mystery? As I understand it, everything occurred exactly as you described: Sage killed once, your sister discovered it, and so, Sage murdered her. Then, she killed herself, maybe out of guilt. Who knows? Not much of a mystery in my mind."

"Yeah, I've heard that account. It's the soap opera version. I think there's another version."

"Which is?"

"A major cover up is underway to protect someone high up in government. It has to be someone with a lot of power and the knowledge to use that power to control and use all the forces involved in this case."

"Forces? What forces?"

Corinne pointed at the judge. "You, for one. They deceived you into giving them the pretense of a legal warrant to get into my sister's things. They told you a made up story about my sister finding something concerning national security. You bought it, but you weren't the only one. Someone tricked the FBI Director to go beyond what you ordered, and destroy all the evidence. He then transferred all the agents involved out of the area so we can't easily talk to any of them. Whoever's orchestrating all this then had the police commissioner order Captain Patelli to close the investigation using that made-up chain of events you just rattled off. Someone's caused all these events to sound unrelated when, in reality, there's a link between them, a link that points to someone high-up who knows how to use people, including you. Again, no offense intended."

"The FBI Director *has* taken an unscheduled vacation to Europe, and is nowhere to be found, according to Dave."

"That doesn't surprise me. He doesn't want to be questioned about his part in all of this. Someone's pulling all the strings, including yours very carefully, and getting exactly the results he wants."

Judge Jacobs slammed her fist on her desk. "No one pulls my strings!"

"Now, doesn't my version sound as plausible as the official version, maybe even more plausible? The main difference is that mine has a mastermind behind it who's trying to cover something."

The judge studied Corinne for a few seconds before speaking. "You really believe what you say, don't you?"

"Yes, I do, and I believe my former boyfriend, that rat, Paul Camarazza, is somehow involved. He's tried to scare me back to New York twice, once by having a car nearly force me off the road, and the second time by having one of his hoods shoot at me."

"Shoot at you? Did you report it?"

"Detective Wu is investigating it now."

"I know Wu. He's good. What does he think about all this?"

"He's the one who talked me into carrying on the investigation...he and Special Agent Collins, that is."

The judge stroked her chin, and closed her eyes for several moments. "You do realize, Miss Day, the danger in all this if you're wrong, don't you?" She leaned toward Corinne, and lowered her voice. "If the information your sister discovered is as devastating as they say, and leaks out because of your investigation, many lives could be put at risk. You have no concept of how big this whole thing really is. Your investigation may be downright dangerous to this country's national security."

"What if I promise not to tell anyone else, not a single soul?"

"Not good enough. I haven't got time to get clearance on you either. Besides, with your affiliation with that gangster, I doubt you'd pass anyway."

"Can you at least tell me who asked for the warrant? Was it the police commissioner, the FBI Director, Senator Stern, Senator Jackson, or someone else?"

"Can't tell you that either. Sorry."

"You've got to at least give me a place to go next. Maybe I can unravel this mystery without knowing the exact details of what they claim my sister discovered, but I'm at a dead end if you don't tell me something. Anything would help at this point. If you don't, whoever is pulling those strings has won the battle."

"There are many battles in a war, Miss Day." She drew in a deep breath, blew it out slowly. "I guess you plan to persist until you win that war."

"Those are my intentions."

"Then discuss it with Senator Jackson next."

"I'll put him on my agenda. Thanks."

"Keep me informed, Miss Day. I'm going to pull a few strings of my own. Let's see what I can stir up."

"That would help a great deal."

"Remember your promise not to tell a soul if you do discover something that may affect national security. I'll expect a report from you no later than tomorrow night. Understood?"

"Yes, Your Honor," is all Corinne could say before the judge stood, and hurried through the door, her gown flowing behind her like a giant superhero cape.

"Still hate the robes, though," Corinne muttered, as she placed her notebook into her purse.

CHAPTER 33

Aaron Center entered Wu's office after knocking once. He found Wu staring at the whiteboard, shaking his head, and rubbing his chin. "You look like you lost your best friend? Anything I can do to help?"

"Sure, all you have to do is give me enough information to crack this case."

"I'm trying. That's why I came by. You were right. The rifle bullets fired at your girlfriend that we pulled out of the Ford matched the ones that killed Zachary."

At the mention of the word "girlfriend," Wu's head spun toward Center, his eyebrows rising high into his forehead, and his complexion turning a brilliant red. "She's not exactly my girlfriend."

Center chuckled. "Better tell that to the office grapevine. They've got you sleeping with her already. Next will be a wedding ring."

"Right!" Wu wrote on the whiteboard: "Rifle used to kill Zachary and frighten Corinne- same- ? Same Perp- ? Kevin Bent?"

"Better add Officers Malone and Stargel to Bent's murdered list."

"We knew he killed them already. They never even got a shot off, damn him anyway. Same weapon, I assume?"

"The same, and add Senator Edmond's name too."

Wu spun away from the board. "Senator Edmond? You mean?"

"Yup, the same weapon."

"Wow! This thing *is* a lot bigger than it looks. That's what Monica Day said to me just before being murdered, but what could that thing be? What the hell is the connection between Senator Edmond and the other murders, and what's the motive behind it all? What's the end game?"

"Motive's your area of expertise, not mine; however, if you're asking my opinion, maybe the senator rubbed Kevin Bent's boss the wrong way."

Wu began rubbing his chin again. "Or maybe they simply wanted him out of the way permanently. Wasn't Senator Edmond the major opposition to Senator's Stern's run for the Presidency?"

"That's what the newscasters reported, and, if you believe all the political hype, he had a decent chance of beating him. What are you implying, though, that they killed him to clear the way for Senator Stern's run for President? That's a huge allegation."

"I don't think we can eliminate any possibilities right now, even an attempt to place someone they could control in the White House at the expense of another senator's life."

Center tilted his head. "Who are the *they* that you mentioned?"

"My guess would be organized crime, and that probably means Paul Camarazza." Wu circled Camarazza's name, and then returned to his desk as Captain Patelli entered.

The captain read the whiteboard quickly, noticing the newly added elements, and glared at Center. "What the hell's going on here?"

"Uh, I stopped by to report some ballistic data to Detective Wu. I'll be leaving now."

Wu's gaze jumped from Center to the captain. "Yeah, thanks."

Captain Patelli headed toward the board. He picked up an eraser, placing it against the board, and hesitated, reading the newly added materials once again, as if that would make it clearer to him. They made it too clear.

"Erasing it won't make it disappear, Bill. Even if you suspend me, or fire me, the investigation goes on, no matter where it leads."

"I had no intention of erasing all of it, only the wrong parts."

"Wrong parts?"

"Yeah, my name, for one. It's not good for morale to have the captain's name on a suspect list, even if it's among so many dignitaries."

"Then prove to me it doesn't belong there. Help me solve this thing."

"Help you? I ordered you off this case. I closed it, and yet you continued your investigation behind my back. Who the hell knows how many department rules and regulations you've broken? Yet you still expect me to help you?"

"The Bill Patelli I once knew would do exactly that."

"You really think I'm hampering your investigation?"

"Aren't you?"

"No, I'm not. How long do you think you can go on with your private investigation without my finding out about it?"

"I had hoped long enough to solve it."

"Not in my precinct! I've known about this from the start."

"Let me guess. You heard it through the grapevine that Center mentioned a few minutes ago, right?"

The captain laughed. "Yeah, the grapevine, but I had to pretend I didn't know, or else you would have had the PC and maybe even Director Higgins of the FBI down your throat, instead of me watching from a distance."

"You could have clued me in to the subterfuge."

"No, you work better if you think you've got free rein."

"And if I screwed things up, I couldn't take you down with me, right?"

"Oh, come on, give me a break. I could have nailed you days ago if I had wanted to suck up to the higher-ups, and then I wouldn't have had to worry about you screwing up anything."

"Maybe. So, why talk to me about it now?"

"I got a call from some judge named Jacobs. That murdered PI's sister has got her all stirred up about some cover up involving these murders."

Wu muttered, "Good job, Corinne."

"This judge says she wants the case reopened. I guess your girlfriend has everyone hopping, and covering their asses. Is that what you wanted?"

"I want anything that'll help solve this case."

"Well, anyway, you're officially back on the job. Is there anything I can do to help your investigation? Do you want more men assigned to you?"

"Not at the moment, Captain, but I'll check with you if I do."

"By the way, word on the street is that there's a contract out on the Day woman, and this time it's for real. You'd better warn her."

Wu quickly grabbed his phone before the captain finished speaking, and began dialing. "Thanks. I'll call her right away."

"Oh, and about this entry, I still think it's bad for morale." Captain Patelli then erased his name from the board one letter at a time.

"I'll keep that in mind the next time."

Corinne entered her sister's office, and, feeling exhausted, leaned against the door. She had difficulty keeping her eyes open, her lids as heavy as lead. As a yawn overtook her, and she stretched her aching arms above her head, tears of fatigue began to form in her eyes. She rubbed them away without thinking.

Forcing herself to walk before she fell asleep against the door, she headed for the chair behind the desk. As she walked, she massaged the back of her slim neck, trying to relieve the tension that had built up there, causing the muscles to tighten, and now causing her head to throb.

I don't know how you kept up this pace, Monica. It's worse than pulling a double shift at the hospital. How the hell did you keep sharp, investigating Sage and Senator Stern all those months when you kept coming up empty? I'm so damned tired and frustrated I could scream. I've got nothing but theories to go on. I guess Judge Jacobs had it right: I've got no real evidence, only feelings and theories. As your friend, Jackie, advised me, I've got to rethink what we already know, and try to get a whole new perspective on things, but, right now, I'm too damned tired to even think straight. Sleep is all I want, but I need to work, not sleep. I need to think. I have to stay awake a little longer.

She fought the desire to close her eyes, to give in to a peaceful, mind-clearing sleep. The short journey across the room seemed to take forever. Finally achieving her objective, she allowed her eyes to close and her arms to fall limp at her sides. She kicked off her heels. With great effort, she put her feet on the desk, allowing her skirt to slide up her smooth shins and stop well above her knees. She took several deep breaths. "I give up. Maybe a little sleep will help."

Her cell phone rang before sleep could overtake her.

"Damn!" She didn't move, allowing the phone to ring three times before she reached into her purse, retrieved the device, and flipped it open without checking the caller ID. "Who's this, and what the hell do you want?"

"It's Hank. I'm glad you answered."

She opened her eyes, and placed her feet on the floor. They still hurt, as did her head. Using her elbows for support, she braced her chin with her free hand. "I'm afraid I fell asleep. What's up?"

Before Wu could answer, a movement caught Corinne's eye. She tried to focus on the closet door. *Did that doorknob just move?*

"We got some information that there's a contract out on you, and this time it's for real, no more near misses. Whoever it is wants you dead."

Corinne's tired, but now wide-open eyes were glued to the closet door. *Did it move, or did I imagine it?* She focused on the doorknob. It started turning again. Her heart raced, aggravating her headache. Her breathing quickened, but she felt air-deprived, couldn't suck the air in fast enough to calm her suddenly alarmed body. She felt lightheaded. *Stop panicking this instant!* She reached for Monica's gun, as she continued staring at the doorknob. Her hand searched for the weapon, groping the interior of the drawer. *Oh, my God! It isn't there.* Her hand desperately searched the perimeter of the drawer, but still found no gun. *Oh, shit! He's got the gun.*

"Corinne, did you hear me? Is everything all right?"

"No!" Corinne quickly searched the other drawers. They were all empty. *What am I going to do? If he comes out, I'm as good as dead.*

The doorknob continued its relentless rotation.

Corinne then knocked as hard as she could on the desktop. "Come in," she yelled, "it's open."

The movement of the doorknob froze, and then reversed.

"Corinne, what the hell's going on? Who's at the door?"

"Oh, hi, Detective Wu, come on in," Corinne said, keeping her voice loud for the benefit of her visitor. "Have a seat. I'll be with you in a minute."

"Listen, Love," Corinne said into the cell phone, "the police are here, so I'll have to run."

"Is someone there with you?"

"I'm afraid so."

"Don't do anything stupid, Corinne. No heroics! I'll have a car there in no time."

"I hope so. Let's plan that get-together as soon as possible. I'll give you a call as soon as I get a chance." She paused briefly, pretending to listen to a reply. "Okay, that's fine with me. Listen, I have a handsome police detective here at the moment, so, I'll have to hang up before he puts me in handcuffs. See you soon."

Corinne closed her cell phone, making sure it snapped loud enough for her closet audience to hear.

"Now, don't say a word, Detective," she said, slowly standing, and rolling her chair noiselessly out from under her. "It's my turn to talk." She strode around the desk, ignoring her screaming feet, and keeping her eyes riveted on the doorknob, praying that it would remain motionless until she could get to safety. "I've got a few things I want to tell you, and I don't want any interruption. Understood?"

Corinne paused when she arrived at the front of the desk. The exit seemed so far away, so inaccessible from where she stood. Her hands trembled. Her mind raced. *Will he notice the nervousness in my voice? Can I keep him fooled long enough to get to the door? How long is it going to take the police to arrive? Should I risk running right now? Wouldn't he hear me running, sense my panic, and come out shooting? Might he do that anyway?*

She took her first tentative step toward the door, hoping the floor wouldn't squeak under her weight. "All we have to go on is theory and a long suspect list. I mean, there's Sage, Paul, Kevin, the two senators, Tom Stern, the PC, your captain, and the FBI Director...what's his name? Oh, yeah, it's Michael Higgins."

She had taken only four nervous steps during her speech. She had surprised herself by remembering all the suspects with the fear and fatigue surging through her body. She had reached the halfway point of her journey, the relative safety of the outer hallway. *Did the door handle move again? I'm not sure.* She kept her eyes glued to it, afraid she might see the motion that could turn out to be the last motion she would ever see before she felt the bullets slamming into her body. The knob remained motionless. She breathed a sigh of relief. She continued her trek, quickening her pace.

"All those names," she continued, "and no real proof of what actually happened. That's bothered me, and I think I know how to get some answers."

She had reached the door. She turned the deadbolt and the doorknob simultaneously.

"I have something to show you, Detective. Wait a minute while I get it."

She had barely finished her sentence when the doorknob turned abruptly, and the closet door sprung open. As Corinne yanked the door open, she saw Monica's gun, held by a gloved hand, being shoved into the room. At first, it pointed at the desk. Finding the seat empty, the hand swung toward her as she darted out of the room, the gun firing almost simultaneously with her exit. The bullet shattered the glass on the door, and buried itself in the wall. Corinne ran as quickly as she could down the stairs, heading for the front door. As she bolted through the doorway, a second shot rang out. The bullet whizzed by her head, blasting into the doorway molding, sending small pieces of wood flying into the air and into her hair.

She hurried down the cement stairs, taking two at a time, fully expecting another shot to be fired, however, she heard nothing. She ran to the Lamborghini, and hunched down behind the car, staring at the doorway she had traversed, expecting her assailant to charge through at any moment. She tried the car door, but found it locked. Her keys were in her purse in Monica's office. She had forgotten to grab it in her haste to get out of the office. She peered over the car once more, staring at the front door, but no one appeared.

She panted heavily, and her arms continued to tremble. She couldn't stop shaking. She looked up the street, spotting, at long last, the flashing lights of a speeding police cruiser.

It screeched to a stop near her, and two policemen, armed with shotguns, jumped out, and joined her by her car.

"He's inside. He shot at me twice. He came out of the closet of my sister's office."

"It's okay now, Miss," one of the officers said. "We're here. You stay here. Detective Wu told us to tell you he'd be right behind us." He turned to his partner. "Cover me. I'm going in."

One officer ran toward the building as his partner trained his gun at the door. A second police car screeched to a halt behind the first. The newly arrived officers joined the policeman at Corinne's side. When the first officer reached the front door, he positioned himself on one side of the door, and awaited his partner, who ran to the other side. One then entered the building, the other following as soon as his partner signaled that the initial hallway had been cleared. The door closed behind the second officer with a bang.

CHAPTER 34

Wu's car squealed around the corner, skidding to a stop behind the police cruisers. He dashed toward Corinne, gun in hand, eyes surveying the office building for any signs of the intruder. He knelt next to her, placing one arm around her shaking shoulder. "Are you all right?"

"Getting shot at...is getting to be a habit...a habit I want to break...soon...no, now." She managed a small, but shaky smile, the pounding in her chest starting to subside. Her breathing eased, but her throat remained dry, her voice raspy and shaky.

"What happened? That scenario on the phone scared me near to death."

"Someone...in...closet...started shooting at me. Your men...went in after him."

As she finished, the two officers came out of the building.

"It's clear," one officer yelled. "The shooter is gone. He probably used the back door. We'll drive around to check out the back alley."

"Okay," Wu said as he helped Corinne to her feet. "Ready to go back in?"

"I think so." On weak and wobbly knees, she began a sluggish trek up the steps, supported the entire way by Wu. At the doorway, she silently pointed to the bullet hole in the molding. She did the same at the entrance to the office, being careful to avoid stepping on the splintered glass. "Lousy shot." Corinne made her way toward the closet.

"Don't touch anything in there," Wu ordered.

"I won't." Corinne peered into the closet, and finding the gunman gone, sighed with relief.

"This is exactly what I called to warn you about. Kevin got away from us at the motel. He killed two of my men in the process."

"Oh, no!" *That adds two more victims to the veil of violence that seems to have exploded into my life. Oh, God! Where and when will this horror end?*

"Kevin must have been ordered to kill you this time. No more fooling around with near misses."

"I'm not so sure Kevin did the shooting." Corinne raised her head, and opened her bloodshot eyes. More tears of sleep clouded her vision. She wiped them with the back of her hand.

"Why not? He's number one on my list."

"Not his style, for one thing. If we're right, and he did kill John Zachary, and try to frighten me off, why would he change his method? Why not use his rifle? That way, he'd be less likely to expose himself to capture, and more likely to succeed."

"I don't know why he'd change. Maybe he's ditched the rifle so we won't catch him with it, or maybe Camarazza told him to make it personal so you would know who ordered the hit. You know, 'From Paul with Love. Bang, Bang, You're Dead.' Who knows how these criminals think? By the way, speaking of that rifle, you were right. The bullets from the Ford matched the ones that killed John Zachary, and, get this, those same bullets matched the ones that killed Senator Edmond."

Corinne flopped down heavily into her seat. "But, if Kevin did ditch the rifle, why steal my sister's gun to shoot me? If he's so good at killing people, I'm sure he's got others to use...probably big ones at that."

"Oh, he is good at killing. Kevin Bent has a long rap sheet in New York. He's suspected of a bunch of gangland style murders, but the New York police have never been able to make a charge stick."

"Paul's probably helped him there."

"Probably. You seem to be full of explanations at the moment, Detective Day. Are there any other reasons you think it may have been someone else shooting at you?"

Detective Day? I don't feel much like a detective at the moment, private, or otherwise. "Well, now that you ask, why wouldn't he simply ambush me outside the building with either a rifle, or handgun? Why risk coming in here? And what about the fact that he shot at me, and missed...twice? Granted, I ran for my life, but if he's a professional killer, I don't think a moving target would bother him much. If Kevin had come out of that closet, I think I'd be dead right now."

"Okay, let's say it wasn't Kevin. Any ideas who it might have been?"

"No, not really, but what interests me more is why he didn't shoot at me sooner."

"I don't follow you."

"Well, whoever shot at me, simply hid when I first came in. If he wanted to shoot me, he could have done it easily as soon as I came into the room, but he didn't. He waited to see what I did, or maybe what I intended to do, and that involved napping. That would have given him the opportunity he may have been hoping for, a chance to leave. When I didn't make any noise for a few minutes, I'll bet he figured I had either left, or fell asleep. I'll bet he planned to sneak out. I don't think he came here to kill me. I think he came here looking for something, when I showed up unexpectedly."

She ran her fingers through her hair, hooking it behind her ear this time. She knew she needed to run a comb through it, but didn't have the energy, and really didn't care about her appearance at the moment. "Your phone call woke me up almost as soon as I had fallen asleep. When I woke up, he had already started turning the doorknob slowly. I think he tried to open the door without making any noise. He didn't want to wake me. Otherwise, why not simply throw the door open, and start shooting? When I found Monica's gun missing, I had to think of something that would buy me some time to get out before he did come out shooting, because that's what I thought he wanted to do."

"Is that why you pretended I had knocked on the door?"

"Exactly! I figured if he thought you were here, he wouldn't dare open the door."

"But he opened it anyway."

"Yes, but not at first. So, either my acting got worse, which is possible, of course, or I said something that made him desperate enough to come out shooting, even though he knew he would then have to deal with an armed detective."

She began retracing her steps as she talked, gently pushing Wu out of her way. "I spoke about the mystery we're dealing with in this case, and mentioned all the suspects, and he stayed put. He didn't care who graced our list, I guess. He came out only after I said I had something to show you. That panicked him."

"Something to show me? I wonder what he thought you had?"

"Probably the same thing he had come looking for. He came here to find whatever that thing is, not to kill me. It all makes sense. There must be something still hidden in this office, something Monica discovered that led to her murder and all the subsequent events in this case. She must have hidden it really good somewhere in this office to have it not be discovered yet."

"But this office's been searched twice, once apparently by Sage and once by the FBI. They didn't find anything that we know of. What the FBI didn't destroy, we removed, and examined. Our lab found nothing, nothing at all. We stripped this place to the walls."

"I know, but that intruder came back for another search. Is it possible the FBI, Sage, and your lab team missed something?"

"I suppose, but I can't imagine how. Have you got any ideas on where to begin looking, because I don't."

"Not really." Corinne went to the middle of the room, and slowly rotated, searching every sector of the room for any hint of a hiding place, trying to see something new, something different. Her eyes landed on Monica's tower computer. "How about that useless computer? Even Jackie Kant didn't understand why she kept it after she got her laptop. Any chance it could still have some information on it?"

"Not according to my experts. The hard drive's been fried."

"Look. One of the screws came loose from the cover." Corinne bent down, and picked up the small screw. *All right, Little Screw, how about giving me some kind of inspiration on that hiding place.* She waited for the inspiration to hit her. *Nothing? Oh, well.* She chuckled. "I guess those computer experts aren't so expert at screwing things back together, are they?" She snapped her head in Wu's direction. "You know, I found a note in one of my sister's computer books that supposedly had been signed by me."

"Oh, yeah, I remember that. I flipped through it at the apartment the other day. You wrote something about computers being capable of hiding information as well as safes, and something about using the book as an entry into the world of the computer's hidden files."

"Correct, and using a book on computers is probably good advice, except I didn't give her the book, and the handwriting appeared to be Monica's, not mine."

"Why would she write a note to herself?"

"I'm not sure. When I first saw it, I thought it strange, but shrugged it off as unimportant, but she had left a message for me with her friend, Jackie. Maybe she left me another message, saying she kept her secret files in there." She pointed to the computer.

"But what good does that do us? It doesn't work anymore. There's no way to retrieve any of the data she may have hidden on it in its present condition. It's gone forever."

"Monica couldn't have simply meant the files hidden on the hard drive. Everyone, including me, would know to look there. I presume that's why they erased her hard drive...eliminate the data. Besides, we know Monica hated computers. So, again, it begs the question, why keep this old clunker? Maybe she meant something other than the information hidden on the hard drive." She thought for a few seconds. "She did mention the word 'safe' in the note. I wonder if she meant a physical safe, instead of an electronic one." She pointed at the computer again. "Maybe she put something in there for safe keeping and for me to find."

"But that doesn't tell us why your sister decided to hide whatever it is in the first place. Why not simply put it in a real safe, or give it to that weird friend of hers?"

"Maybe Monica didn't want to endanger her, or anyone else for that matter. So, she hid the information here, and then left me a note in case something happened to her."

"That assumes she knew how dangerous the information could be in the first place. If not, she may have simply hidden it before she knew what she had. Then, when she figured it out, she called me, but the murderer got to her before she could retrieve it, or even tell me about it."

"That would mean the information is still here, probably inside this box." She pointed at the computer once more. "Maybe my intruder figured that out too, and had begun to take the computer apart when he heard me coming down the hall. I'll bet your computer experts didn't forget to tighten that screw. The intruder loosened it."

"There's a quick way to find out." Wu displayed the screwdriver on his pocketknife. "Don't get your hopes up, though. I saw the insides to this thing, and there didn't seem to be anything out of the ordinary hidden that I could see, and certainly no compartments big enough to hide something."

As Wu worked on the remaining screws, Corinne leaned against the desk. "You know, if there is something in there, it'll be the second time Monica has helped me since she died."

Wu paused at the last screw, and looked up, not knowing what to say. He decided to say nothing.

"I really loved her, Hank."

"I know."

He lifted the cover from the base, exposing a mass of electronics and wires, but nothing that would be considered a file of any type he recognized. He turned over the cover, something neither he, nor the computer technician, had done at headquarters. Inside, taped to the top of the cover, he found a brown envelope. He pulled it off, and held it up toward Corinne. "Bingo!"

Corinne looked Heavenward, smiled widely, and winked. "Thank you, Monica!" She rushed to Wu's side, and grabbed the envelope from him before he knew what had happened.

"Thank you, Monica," Wu echoed, "wherever you are. Thank you."

Corinne dumped the contents of the envelope onto the desk, her heart racing with excitement. "Let's see what we've got: photos and a thumb drive."

The first few 5X8 photos were of Sage and Senator Stern, sunning on some crowded beach. In one, they held hands as they climbed aboard a Jet.

"They look happy," Wu said.

"Maybe these were taken before the split between the two of them. I don't see any of the senator's son yet. Wait a minute. Here's one of Tom and Sage, boarding some yacht. Look at this." Corinne pointed to the next photo in the pile. "That's Senator Stern hiding behind that crate on the pier."

Wu chuckled. "Guess he did a little investigation of his own."

"He claimed he knew of Sage's affair with Tom. I guess this proves he told the truth."

There were two men in the next photo.

"Who are they?" Corinne asked, holding the picture so Wu could see it better.

"James Wyman and Chuck Florentino, the two guys who were murdered last Thursday night, and that's the motel where they were killed."

"Here's another with one of them holding the door open for Sage." Corinne flipped the picture over. "It's dated Thursday, September 13th, seven PM"

"We were right then. Sage went there, probably to kill them."

"Apparently my sister followed her there, but she must have left before the shooting, but why wait until Sunday to call you if she had proof that Sage had been there?"

"Well, if your sister did leave before anything happened, she didn't know any murders had taken place. The story made the late edition Friday, but the complete story appeared in Saturday's paper, although it had been reported on network news almost as soon as we got the call. The names of the victims and all the other details weren't released until late Saturday. So, those wouldn't have appeared in any of the media until Sunday morning. Your sister may have only made the connection on Sunday when she either saw a report on TV, or read the morning paper. So, we were right. She didn't know what she had when she put these in her improvised computer-safe."

"Get a load of this shot. It's marked with the same date and time. That's Senator Stern, and he's looking right at the camera. He must have also followed Sage to the motel."

"Or driven her there."

"He sure looks mad. Do you think he'd kill Monica over this photo?"

"Possibly, but remember, if he followed Sage there, and left before the murders, he's not guilty of anything that happened at the motel, and, unfortunately, we have no evidence of his involvement with your sister's murder either. We need more proof to pin anything on him."

"Look at this. It's a picture of Sage, Senator Stern, and Paul. They did know each other. Paul swore he hadn't met Senator Stern until Sage's wake. He lied again."

"It's an outdoor café. What's Paul handing Stern?"

Corinne studied the photo. "Maybe a check? Boy, how I'd love to see the front of that."

"Maybe I can get our lab to enlarge it enough to read it. I'll bet it's a large contribution to his political campaign, and I'll also give you odds that that contribution won't be found on any of the senator's books either."

"Maybe it's a payoff for services rendered. Both of them have some major explaining to do."

"Now, don't go jumping the gun on this, Corinne." Wu rested his hand on her neck, drew her closer. "All it proves is that they knew each other, not that they committed any crimes."

"It proves that we're right," she snapped, pulling away from his grip, "and I'll bet either one of them could tell us what happened to my sister...who did it, why the cover up, who invented the story that prompted Judge Jacobs to issue that warrant...all of it."

"That's probably true, but we're going to need more proof than these pictures to convince a judge."

"Oh? We'll see about that." Corinne reached for her phone, and dialed Judge Jacobs' number.

Corinne spent the next few minutes explaining the attack on her, and what they had found.

"That's good work, Miss Day. Your investigation is proceeding nicely. I want to see those pictures when you get a chance."

"Any chance we could get a warrant to arrest them, or a search warrant to look for more evidence at this stage?"

"No, all you have are a few photos. Photos can be faked all too easily. No, you're going to need some living, breathing witnesses who can testify that they saw them together at the crime scene. You've got to find out what that piece of paper is they're exchanging. It may be a check as you say, but it could just as easily be a laundry list, or merely the restaurant menu. For that matter, it may be a check for his half of the meal they shared. You simply need more evidence before I can issue any kind of warrant based on that piece of paper. Remember, we're dealing with a United States Senator here, not some lackey drug addict with a long arrest record. I'm not going to have the senator arrested until we have a firm case. Besides, none of this proves any of them committed any crime, or cover up. You've simply got to do more digging, Miss Day. I've reopened the case for you, and made sure Detective Wu is in charge again. That should make it a little easier for you. Now, it's up to you to collect more evidence. Keep me informed."

"Yes, Your Honor. I'll be sure to do that."

Corinne closed her phone and her eyes. She rested her elbows on the desk, placed her chin in the palms of her hand, deforming her cheeks in the process. She decided the position had become all too familiar. *I'm getting nowhere, but what else can I do? Nothing!* Her gaze shifted to Wu. "You were right. We need more evidence."

"I'll get the lab up here to go over the closet again." Wu gently massaged Corinne's back. "Maybe this time there'll be some prints we can use."

"He wore gloves." Corinne raised her eyebrows so she could see Wu, but made no effort to raise her chin from her hands. "There are two other things I think we have to do, though."

"Oh? What?"

"First, I'm going to talk to Senator Jackson. I think he's been orchestrating what some of the others have been telling me, or not telling me for that matter. He may be more deeply involved than he's let on."

"Want some company?"

"Not for this. I think he'll be more open with me alone." She forced her head off her palms, stood, stretched her arms over her head, and then stumbled toward Wu. Physical exhaustion had overtaking her, but she knew she had more to do before giving in to sleep. She placed her arms around his neck, ready to collapse at any moment. His touch brought back memories of their night together. She wanted him, wanted to be taken by him, and then fall asleep in his arms, the peaceful sleep of lovers. *Not now, though, no sleep, and no sex. How could I even think of that? How could I think of anything but working on solving Monica's murder? Pleasure comes later, much later.* She looked up into Wu's eyes. "I think I'm going to need your help for the second part of my plan, though."

"Oh? What might that be, Young Lady?" He hoped it had something to do with her bed once more.

"I think we should break into Senator Stern's office later tonight to see what we can find."

"What? Are you crazy? That's illegal!"

"But we've got to know what his connection is with all this. All I want to do is to look around a little. Maybe we can find something that will be the key to solving this whole affair. Maybe it'll give us another direction to go in. We can worry about the legalities later."

"Yeah, while we do time in jail. The judge said no search warrant. That means we can't go in there uninvited."

Corinne turned her back to him. "Well, the senator *did* say I could return to talk to him whenever I wanted. I think I'll go there tonight, and find the door conveniently open for me."

"If the senator catches you there, do you really think he's going to buy that stupid story?"

"No, of course not, but he won't catch me. I saw his schedule, and he's delivering a speech later tonight on the other side of town. It'll be late. His office staff will be gone by then. I've got to get a look around in there. Care to join me?"

Wu thought for a few long moments, and then turned her around, held her at arms-length. "Listen. I would love to be there with you, but I'm a police detective, an officer of the court. I've sworn an oath to uphold the law. I can't stomp on the law the way you want me to, even if I think it's the only way to gather evidence on a case. I simply can't."

"Fine, but you're not going to talk me out of it."

"Wasn't going to try. Tell me what time you're breaking in, and I'll join you a few minutes later. After all, I am the investigating officer on this case. So, let's say that I had planned to go there to help you interview the senator, thinking you had arranged an after-hour appointment with him. I'll simply find you already inside, but we've got to make it a fast search. If we do get caught, I'll have to be the good police detective, and arrest you for breaking and entering. Even so, that may not fly. We'll be in real trouble then. We may both end up behind bars. So, you'd better hope we don't get caught."

"We won't, and I promise we'll make the search quick." Corinne hugged him, her large, pleading eyes raised toward his. "Now, could you tell me the easiest way to break into his office without setting off any alarms? I'm new at being a criminal."

CHAPTER 35

Corinne parked the Lamborghini outside Senator Jackson's office ten minutes before her scheduled meeting with him. She scanned the rooftops for any signs of Kevin. Not finding him, she rushed into the building, slamming the door behind her.

She took the crowded elevator to the senator's office on the fifth floor. Upon entering, she found it larger than that of Senator Stern's, and much more impressive. Its large furniture seemed a better fit for the size of the room. She also preferred its mauve walls to that of Senator Stern's dull brown paneling. It gave the room an overall warm, comfortable feeling. Her low heals clicked loudly on the tile floors.

Senator Jackson limped toward her with his hand extended. "Hello, Corinne. I understand you've created quite a stir so far."

"Is that so?" She accepted his hand, but refused to smile. She couldn't help staring at his gate.

"Don't let my limp bother you." He pounded his leg with his fist. "Sometimes it's good; sometimes it's not so good. Today is one of those not-so-good days. I've gotten used to it. Your sister didn't seem to mind."

Corinne blushed. "Sorry. I didn't mean to stare, but it does appear to be a lot worse than the last time we met."

He headed back to his chair. "It's worse when I'm tired, and I've been very tired lately. I don't think I'll ever catch up on my sleep."

"Could it be that there's something on your mind? Maybe something bothering you that you need to get off your chest?"

He halted his progress, froze for an instant, and spun to face her. "You're good, Corinne. You don't miss a trick, do you?"

"Well?" Corinne felt in no mood for idle chitchat, and made no effort to answer his rhetorical question.

He resumed his plod toward his desk, finally taking his seat, and extended his leg before he spoke. "Judge Jacobs says she's ordered Monica's murder investigation reopened because of you. You must be persuasive."

"Not as persuasive as you, I'm afraid, Senator. I tried to get that same judge to do something else for me, but failed miserably, but you were able to convince her to issue the warrant to search my sister's office, right?" *Come on, Senator. I don't know for sure that you're the one, but you're the most likely candidate. Confirm, or deny. I don't care which, but give me an answer, so I have a new avenue to pursue.*

He interlocked his fingers, and stared at his hands. "I'm afraid that's true, but I had to. You must understand I had no choice. I had to protect…" He paused, searching for the correct phrase.

The pause persisted too long for Corinne. "Protect who, or what, Senator?"

"…protect…innocent people. There were lives at stake. There still are."

"Somehow, I find that hard to believe. All I keep hearing is that if I learn this top-secret information, people will die. I don't buy that. You're covering up for someone, maybe even yourself, and it may have been at the cost of Monica's life."

His jaw fell. "You can't believe that. I would never knowingly do anything that might even remotely jeopardize your sister, even if it meant exposing me to danger or political ruin. I loved her."

"I've only got you to tell me that now, don't I? No one else even knew that you were getting that serious with her."

"But that's the way your sister wanted it. I even swore my closest staff to secrecy about our dating."

"Why? Would more innocent lives have been lost if the news got out?"

"No, of course not. You have to stop being so cynical, and listen to what I'm saying. It comes directly from my heart. I really loved your sister with my entire being."

"Oh, give me a break! You asked for that warrant before Monica had been murdered. You expect me to believe you loved Monica, and yet you convinced Judge Jacobs to issue a warrant for Monica's things? You expect me to believe you did that to the woman you loved without first asking her to relinquish the information to you. That's what a true lover would have done in that situation, not what you did."

He stared at her for several seconds. "I suppose I deserved that. I had thought about doing exactly that, but I couldn't."

"You couldn't because Monica didn't have any secret information concerning national security. My sister couldn't hand over something she didn't possess. Am I right?"

The senator expression remained blank.

"Not answering yet? Want me to tell you what you were really looking for? You wanted a set of photos we found that include your beloved Senator Stern."

"Shit."

"You knew those photos would have effectively destroyed your Presidential hopeful's chances. They would have proved him to be as crooked as most of the people I've met in this vile city." She narrowed her eyes. "Are you one of them?"

"Me? Ha! I'm not in any of those photos. You can't prove anything against me."

"So, you admit the photos exist, and were what you were really after with that trumped-up search warrant." Corinne jabbed an accusatory finger at him.

"No, I simply know I couldn't be in any such photos, but you seem to have all the answers already. What else do you think you know?"

"I know that my sister would have gladly turned over anything that would have endangered innocent lives, including those photos, whether it involved national security, or not, but no one ever asked her because the photos didn't expose anything related to a threat to national security. She may, however, have had good reason to withhold information from you. Maybe she figured what you were up to. That's why you had to suddenly invent that national security scam. You had to figure a way to get into my sister's office to get those photos. You were trying to protect the ass of whoever it is that you're covering up for…probably your beloved presidential candidate, Senator Stern."

The senator closed his eyes, but remained silent.

I wonder if he's trying to invent a plausible story. How good a liar are you? Are you as good as Paul?

He sighed deeply. "If that's true, why would I bother with a search warrant at all? Why not simply search her place myself? I had access to her office. She had given me a key. Why would I risk getting both a federal judge and the FBI involved?"

"Good question. I've done most of the talking so far, Senator. Why don't you answer that one?"

"I can't." He began drumming his fingers.

"Maybe you should think of an answer. That way, you'll have something to say when Judge Jacobs questions you in court." Corinne matched his rhythm with her fingers.

He stared directly into her eyes. "I haven't done anything wrong, and I certainly didn't do anything to harm your sister. As a matter of fact, I tried to protect her."

"You're making no sense." Corinne placed her hand gently on his. "Listen, if the information Monica had will really endanger anyone at all, I promise not to tell anyone, not even Detective Wu, but you've got to tell me. I have to know what really happened to Monica, and why. I won't quit until I find out everything anyway. It might as well come directly from you."

She paused, squeezing his hand harder.

"How about it, Senator, for Monica's sake, from the beginning, the whole truth?"

A small tear appeared at the corner of one of the senator's eyes. His hand trembled slightly. He cleared his throat before speaking. "Okay, Corinne, but you've got to believe that I loved your sister."

She patted his hand. "I think I do."

"I already told you everything up to the point that I left for California, so I'll start there. I received a phone call from Frank...Senator Stern...that Friday. He sounded upset. He told me he had been in some important negotiations...secret negotiations...involving..." He paused and took a deep breath, "...the Middle East."

"You mean the Middle East peace negotiations going on right now?"

"More than that, Corinne. A new leader is about to mount a coup in one of those countries. You don't really need to know which one, do you? I mean, which country really doesn't matter in your sister's murder now, does it?"

"No, I guess not."

"The other Middle-Eastern countries fear the new leader is going to be too much of an aggressor, worse than any leader in that part of the world has ever been, worse than Hitler, maybe the Anti-Christ, but certainly someone who would upset the balance of powers within the region. They're afraid he'll use his military power to overrun their countries and beyond. We're afraid he'll renew the aggressions and wars we've worked so hard to deal with for so many years."

He took two deep breaths. "Those countries have asked for our help. Frank told me he had been working with them for months, and that only the President and Secretary of State knew of his negotiations. You see, the other Middle-Eastern countries, even those who hate us, wanted this new leader stopped, but they couldn't assassinate him for a whole list of reasons, including the risk of causing a major conflict involving all of them. They wanted a political solution. Frank said he finally had a chance to have all the parties involved agree to a plan, but they would only agree if the United States' involvement in the plan was never revealed. Certain parties in the negotiation threatened to back out, and deny their involvement if word leaked out. That would have destroyed the entire plan, and made war inevitable. Frank had fostered an uneasy alliance, and one that could collapse at the first hint of trouble."

When he hesitated, Corinne smiled, hoping the gesture would encourage him to continue.

He placed his hand over hers. "Frank had seen your sister snapping pictures of him Thursday night during some of those negotiations. He feared your sister might sell the photos to some reporter, or at least break the story online, revealing all the envoys' identities at the same time. That's how I knew I couldn't possibly be in those photos. I never became involved in the negotiations."

He stared at Corinne, expecting her to speak. She remained steely eyed

"Anyway, I did suggest we ask her for the digital camera and photos, but Frank insisted that didn't go far enough. Now, I really wish I had had the courage to call her. I acted so stupidly." Another tear joined the one traveling unchecked down his cheek.

"What else did Senator Stern say concerning Monica?"

"He felt that talking to Monica would only show her the importance of the photos, and further encourage her to release them to the general public, maybe through social media the way others have done, thinking they were doing good for the country when, in fact, they were doing just the opposite."

He removed his hand from Corinne's. "You know, I think you're right. She would have handed them over to me no matter what damaging information they contained…if I had only asked."

"Probably. Please continue."

"Frank asked me to call Judge Jacobs to get a search warrant for her apartment and office to confiscate the evidence. We would have had to talk to Monica later anyway to guarantee her silence about the meetings, but we were sure she would have agreed to that, especially since she wouldn't have had proof of any allegations she made subsequently."

"Why did you have to be the one to ask the judge for the warrant? Wouldn't it have been more logical for Senator Stern to talk to Judge Jacobs, since he had been conducting these alleged negotiations?"

"I know Judge Jacobs personally. Senator Stern doesn't. We both were afraid it would take too long to go through the normal channels to check the facts in the case against your sister, too long to confirm the importance of those photos. Frank insisted he couldn't risk the delay. So, I made the call."

"Were you surprised the FBI took all her files, and destroyed them, or is that what you asked the judge to approve?"

"I still don't know why they destroyed everything. I asked for a warrant to search for those photos, nothing more, I swear."

Corinne closed her still weary eyes. "I think Senator Stern didn't want anyone looking specifically for pictures of negotiations with Middle-Eastern leaders because there were none. You see, Senator, if the FBI examined the photos they found to be sure they had the correct ones, they would have stumbled on the real reason for the search, pictures of Senator Stern with a known criminal, Paul Camarazza, rather than any national leaders or representatives. They would have exposed his connection with the criminal world, as well as his lies about those photos. That discovery would have probably spelled the end of his run for President."

Senator Jackson remained silent.

"So, Senator Stern convinced Director Higgins that even his most trusted Special Agents didn't have a high enough security clearance to see the photos. They, as Senator Stern recently told me, weren't *privileged to know* that information. So, those agents were instructed to collect everything indiscriminately, and destroy it without ever looking at any of its content."

Senator Jackson closed his eyes, but still didn't speak.

"Then, to be sure they didn't report anything they might have inadvertently seen to any of their superiors, Senator Stern had Director Higgins transfer the entire team."

He raised his head. "How do you know that Frank...Senator Stern...is behind all this? How can you prove there really are no negotiations?"

"For one thing, I can prove that my sister couldn't have possibly taken any photos of negotiations that Thursday night. Among the photos we found was a shot of Senator Stern at the motel where we believe Sage Browning killed two of Camarazza's men. He probably followed Sage there, and spotted Monica taking the pictures. My sister had written the time on the back of the photo when she printed them as 7 PM. She couldn't have taken any photos of negotiations that night. If she had, they would have been hidden with the others we found. There were none. As to Senator Stern, we know that he delivered a speech at eight o'clock across town, and stayed there until after eleven. So, Senator Stern couldn't have led any negotiations. He didn't have a spare minute. No, Senator, there were no negotiations going on that night involving him. He lied to you."

Senator Jackson lowered his head again, and clenched his fists tightly. "I can't believe Frank deceived me."

"I'm afraid there's more. Later that weekend, I believe Senator Stern heard about the murders at that motel. He knew my sister would eventually make the connection with Sage, and would go to the police. Then, the photos of him with Camarazza would be found. So, even if he were innocent of the murders at the motel, his connection with the criminal world would be exposed. I believe he invented the Mid-East story, called you, and began manipulating everyone to get the story straight, so everything pointed away from his involvement. Then, using his contacts, he got the case closed as quickly as possible."

She squeezed the senator's hands, feeling their tension and trembling as his nails dug deeper into his palms.

He sniffed a few times. "Maybe I've known all along about Frank's involvement. I should have known. There's no excuse. I kept denying it. I guess you're right. He used me."

She released his hands. "He may have used you one other time, Senator. He claims he stayed in your limousine during my sister's funeral. Did he?"

He looked at Corinne through the tears that now flooded his eyes. "No, he asked me to say that after Sage died. He swore he had been alone in his office at the time, and feared that someone might accuse him of having something to do with her death."

"And you agreed to provide his alibi? Why? Didn't you see he had manipulated you?" Corinne suddenly thought of the way she had been used by Paul, and remembered that she hadn't suspected anything at the time either. She had been as naïve as this man, now crumbling before her, and yet she had accused him of not recognizing the deceit of another. *You should talk, Corinne. You should be the last one to accuse another of that. How could I be so insensitive to Monica's lover?*

He opened his hands toward her, as if pleading for mercy. "You have to understand. At the time, I believed everything he had told me, from the Middle East negotiations right through to the alibi. I had no reason to suspect him of lying. I've known the man for years. He's always been honest with me, as far as I knew." He lowered his voice to barely above a whisper. "I thought he'd make an excellent President. I guess not."

"No, he definitely would not."

"I can't believe how wrong I have been about him. I guess I'd better talk to him, and get him to explain a few things."

"I'd rather you didn't. I haven't got all the pieces to this puzzle sorted out yet. I need a little more time to gather evidence, and I need to do that before he realizes we're on to him. I don't want to give him a chance to destroy that evidence. We still haven't proved he's done anything illegal. Once we do, then we'll get Judge Jacobs involved again. I'm reporting to her now."

"All right, but I think I'll give her a call myself. I owe her some explanations, don't I?"

"I guess. Tell her I'll give her a call tomorrow morning."

She opened the door to leave, but leaned on the doorframe instead. "Thanks for your honesty, Senator."

"You know, Corinne, Monica and I were planning a big wedding. She had planned to have you as her bride's maid. She would have made a beautiful bride...and wife. I loved her so much. Do you believe me now, Corinne? That's important to me."

"Yes, Senator, I believe you."

"Can you ever forgive me for getting her involved in this mess in the first place?"

"Of course I can. I can see how my sister could love you. Don't blame yourself for what happened. You're not really responsible for any of it. Neither of us are. I realize that now, and I hope you do too. We've both suffered a loss, and we both feel guilty, but I really think Monica would forgive us, and want us to move on."

He smiled, a small smile, but it was all he could generate at the moment. "Maybe the two of us can get better acquainted when this is all cleared up."

She gave him a broad smile. "That sounds like a great idea. Let's get together, but not to discuss this morbid affair. I'd really love to hear more about you and Monica. What do you say?"

"I'd love that too, Corinne." He reached into his pocket to retrieve a key that he tossed to her. "That's the key to your sister's apartment. She also gave me one to her office, but I lost it a couple of weeks back. Now, go get some answers for us."

"That's where I'm headed right now, Senator."

CHAPTER 36

Corinne parked the Lamborghini on 1ˢᵗ Street, N.E., a few blocks from the Senate office building. Before exiting the car, she surveyed the area for any hint of danger. None came into view, no sign of Kevin, no shadow lurking along the rooftops, no rifle barrel pointed in her direction. Rushing to the side of the building, she peered around the corner down Constitution Avenue. Nightfall had arrived, and, with it, diminished activity on the street, although the streetlights lit the area as if it were noon.

She glanced at the lights. *I wish those damn things were off.* She frowned. *I don't know how successful I'm going to be at this breaking and entering stuff. I've got a degree in physical therapy, not second story thievery. I don't know the first thing about breaking into someone's office, or how to get around the alarm system. Hank's basic instructions better work, but I really doubt I'm going to be able to get in before he arrives.* She shook her head. *Stop being so negative, Corrine. You've got to get a look in Senator Stern's office one way, or another. All the evidence points toward him.* She closed her eyes, and tried to ease her breathing. *This is an extremely major risk I'm taking. If I'm caught, the senator will undoubtedly press charges. Judge Jacobs would then take great pleasure in personally arranging a long visit to some distant prison, if she doesn't send me to some mental hospital first. It's too late to worry about that now. I've got to do this. It's the only way I know to get the evidence I need.*

She walked without incident to the Hart building. After checking the area one last time, she tried using the lock pick Wu had given her. Even with the instructions he had provided, she found the tool awkward to handle. A grinding noise sprang from within the mechanism, but the lock held. *Damn it, Hank! I told you I'd never be able to do this. I can't even get by the first door.*

"Better let me handle the breaking and entering." Wu laughed, as he came out of the shadows, and climbed the stairs behind her.

Startled, Corinne jumped, and spun around. "I thought you were coming later, after I had broken in."

"I said I would be arriving after you, and so I have. I figured you wouldn't be able to break in without me. Besides, I managed to get a key to the place."

"Great! I hope the lock still works after all my probing. What about the alarms? Do we still have to worry about tripping one, or were you able to shut them off as planned?"

"No problem! I already checked with the alarm company. I arranged for it to be turned off for the night. They've been told we're making some upgrades to the building, and won't be using the alarm until morning."

"Neat trick, but how did you manage to convince them without all kinds of codes?" She closed the door behind them, and used a flashlight to guide them to Senator Stern's office.

"It's easy when you know the alarm service owner. He owes me a favor." Wu used another key to open the Senator's door.

"Does everyone in this God-forsaken town owe everyone else a favor?"

"Just about." Wu closed the blinds, and turned on the lights.

Corinne began her search with the desk. Papers and files cluttered the top. She tried the drawers, but found them locked. She used a letter opener to pry the center drawer open. It contained letters addressed to the senator, which she scanned quickly, but didn't bother reading. There were also a few folders that contained papers about people whose names and pictures meant nothing to either her or Wu.

Another drawer contained a gun, a brass key, and a broken necklace.

"That's Monica's gun. Isn't it?"

"That would be my guess, same make and model, anyway." Wu lifted it with his handkerchief.

"So, Senator Stern did shoot at me in Monica's office."

"It looks that way."

"I've seen this necklace before." Corinne lifted it using a handkerchief in imitation of Wu. "It's the one Sage wore in the pictures we found in Monica's office."

"The marks on her neck were probably caused when he yanked it off her." Wu examined the necklace for any residual blood, but found none.

"This key must be the one Senator Jackson lost to my sister's office. See, it matches my copy exactly. I'll bet he's been using this to keep track of what Monica had discovered about him."

"Your sister probably realized someone had been going through her things, maybe even stealing things. That may have forced her to hide her photos where they wouldn't be found. That would explain her use of the tower computer. As you suspected, she probably wrote that note to herself in the computer book for you to find, depending on you to decipher its cryptic content. Smart woman."

"I guess..." Corinne stopped mid-sentence, and stared at the door.

"And what exactly is going on here?" Senator Frank Stern stood in the doorway, his hands on his hips. He turned, speaking over his shoulder. "Look at this, Tom. We've caught ourselves some thieves." Senator Stern threw his coat down in front of Corinne. "What do you think you're doing in my office?"

Wu reached for his badge. "Senator Stern, let me explain."

"There's nothing to explain. It's obvious what you're doing. I think I'd better call the police. What do you think, Tom?"

Tom joined his father.

"I am the police." Wu flashed his badge with one hand, while he hid Monica's gun behind his back with the other.

"I know who you are." I assume you have a search warrant. May I see it, please?"

Wu's hesitation gave Senator Stern an inkling of Wu's position. He stormed at Wu, stopping inches in front of him. He held out his hand. "Give me the warrant."

"He doesn't have a search warrant, Senator. I broke in to look around, and he saw the lights on, and came up to investigate."

Senator Stern grabbed the desk phone. "Nice try, but I don't buy that, and I'm sure the Police Commissioner won't either."

"Before you dial, Senator, you'd better be ready to explain what you're doing with my sister's gun." She reached behind Wu, and produced the weapon.

"You were obviously planting it here when we arrived."

"But that's not true, Dad. We both watched them open the drawer, and take it out. They were surprised when they found it. So, how did it get there? What's going on?"

The senator returned the phone to its cradle, and scowled at his son. "Now, don't you start. They're criminals. They broke into this office. How can you believe anything they say they found? Maybe they planted it before we arrived, and then pretended to find it, so they could later truthfully say they discovered it there together. I'm telling you they can't be trusted."

"You're not answering his question, Senator," Corinne said. "Tell your son where you got my sister's gun, and what you did with it when you found it."

"I didn't do anything with it because I never found it. You two came here to plant evidence that would implicate me, and got caught in the process."

"Implicate you in what?" Wu asked.

The senator turned away from his inquisitors. "Tom, don't listen to them. I don't know what they're talking about."

"In that case, Dad, call the police, and have them arrested. What are you waiting for?"

Senator Stern made no move toward the phone. Instead, he lowered his head, and closed his eyes.

"He's afraid we'll tell them what we know already," Corinne said.

"What's that?"

Senator Stern gripped his son's shoulders. "Listen to me, Tom. They're going to lie to you. Don't listen to them."

"I want to hear what they have to say, unless you're going to call the police, and we do it at police headquarters. Either way, I'm going to hear their story."

"But they don't know anything."

"We know that an intruder stole this gun from my sister's office, and then hid in the closet when I unexpectedly arrived. When that intruder heard me say I had something to show the police, he came out of the closet, and began shooting at me. He fired the gun twice." Handling the gun with the handkerchief, Corinne removed the clip and counted the bullets remaining. "Thirteen. Two missing." She replaced the clip, and handed it, along with the loose bullets, to Wu.

Wu placed the gun and bullets in his jacket pocket. "Ballistics performed on the bullets we dug out of the wall will prove that this gun is the one fired at Corinne. Unfortunately, Corinne's attacker got away, and took the gun with him. Now, it shows up in your desk, Senator."

Tom glared at his father, and pointed at Corinne. "You shot at her?"

"Don't believe them, Tom. They're making it all up."

"Ballistics don't lie, Senator," Wu said. "It's only a matter of time until we prove all of what we said. So, you might as well admit everything. Tell us, tell your son, exactly what happened."

"Why would I shoot at you, Miss Day?"

"Because you thought I had found the pictures of you with Paul Camarazza. You claimed you never met him before the funeral. You lied. You've known him for a long time. My sister found out, and probably confronted you with it. Later, she took a picture of you at the motel where Sage shot two of Camarazza's men."

"Sage wouldn't shoot anyone," Tom yelled. "I told you that already."

"See what I mean, Son. These two are liars. You can't believe anything they say."

"I'm sorry, Tom, but it's true. My sister took these pictures minutes before those two men were murdered." She handed him the photos. "Your father then went with you to give his speech. That left Sage alone with Camarazza's men, and she shot them. It's the only explanation that fits the facts, I'm afraid."

"That's ridiculous," Senator Stern said. "Everyone knew Sage as a fine, honest lady. She couldn't commit a double murder."

Tom sobbed with each breath. "Oh, no, I can't believe this. Sage did admit to me that she had done some awful things back in New York. She never admitted to killing anyone. Maybe those guys threatened her. Maybe she killed them in self-defense. Otherwise, I agree with dad. She couldn't commit murder." He handed the photos back to Corinne without looking at them again.

"It could have been self-defense," Corinne said. "We may never know. In any case, your father then arranged for Senator Jackson to get a search warrant from Judge Jacobs to search both my sister's apartment and office for these photos, and maybe others that implicated him. Using that warrant, the FBI cleaned all the evidence out of both places, destroying anything they found."

"Ridiculous!" Senator Stern walked to his son's side, one arm wrapped around him.

"Your father," Corinne continued, ignoring Senator Stern's exclamation, "then went to talk to Monica at her office. Maybe he even planned to threaten her with Sage's gun to get her to hand over the pictures. However, when he got there, he found Monica already talking to the police on the phone. Your father panicked, and shot her. Isn't that right, Senator?"

"That's preposterous, and all conjecture. You have no evidence of that, or you'd have an arrest warrant with you right now."

"You're his alibi for that Sunday afternoon when my sister died, Tom. Can't you see that your father manipulated you exactly as he manipulated Senator Jackson, Judge Jacobs and the FBI?" She waited, allowing Tom the time to absorb her conjecture. *I hope he believes me.*

Tom remained silent, his gaze jumping back and forth between Corinne and his father.

"Now, tell me the truth, Tom," Corinne said, "were you with your father that day?"

Tom still did not answer.

Corinne sighed. "Need more to convince you? Okay, but this next part is going to hurt, Tom. Believe me, I wish it weren't true. Your father told me that Sage had planned to cancel your trip together, and tell you that you two were finished forever."

"That's not true! It can't be." Tom cried openly. "Sage bought our tickets. I still have them."

"I know," Corinne said. "I believe your father tried to convince Sage to stay, but couldn't. So, he placed the gun to her head, and shot her to make it appear that she took her own life."

Senator Stern took his seat behind the desk. "Again you're only guessing. You've got no proof whatsoever."

"You then placed the body in my sister's office, using this key, a key you stole from Senator Jackson, to get in. We found it in your desk with the gun. Finally, you arranged for the Police Commissioner to pull everyone off the case, and have it closed quickly, before any incriminating evidence concerning you surfaced."

"Preposterous! At the time they say Sage killed herself, I had gone to your sister's funeral with Senator Jackson."

"No, you didn't, Senator," Corinne said. "Senator Jackson admitted you weren't with him then. We've explained to him how you manipulated everyone, including him, in this case. He won't lie for you anymore."

The senator dropped his head onto his forearm, and mumbled, "You still have no evidence. It's all speculation."

Sobbing, Tom walked toward his father. "You're not denying it anymore. All you keep saying is they have no evidence. They are right in one thing at least. You weren't with me on Sunday. Sage and I were together, planning our getaway. I can't believe you did all this. Tell me it's not true. Tell me, please." Tears reappeared in both eyes, as he awaited his father's denial, praying harder than he had ever prayed before that his father would be able to explain it all, make all their statements lies, errors in deduction, make it all a bad memory of misunderstandings.

"You can't believe anything they say. They really don't have any real evidence."

"How about this?" Corinne asked, holding up the necklace. "You pulled it off Sage when you shot her, didn't you, Senator?"

"That's Sage's necklace. I gave it to her for her birthday. Dad, talk to me, please. What the hell happened?"

"Listen to me. You can't believe them. They've really got nothing connecting me to either the PI's, or Sage's death. I've been very careful..."

"Careful?" Tom screamed his disbelief. He eyes sprang open. His jaw fell, as his whole life came undone before him. *I've lost Sage, the love of my life, to my father's political ambition and by his own hand, no less. It can't be. It simply can't be.* He flushed, and his muscles quivered. He took a step toward his father. "You did kill Sage. You son of a bitch!"

CHAPTER 37

An infuriated Tom Stern flew over the desk, his first crushing blow landing on his father's chin, knocking him and his chair onto the floor. The two men rolled around as Tom continued his barrage of punches, pummeling his father with a non-stop bombardment of fists, knees and feet. Blood gushed from his father's nose, the corner of his mouth, and the corner of one swollen, red eye, but Tom refused to stop. The entire attack lasted less than a minute, but the damage and fury of the attack made it seem like hours to the senator who, although receiving a terrible beating, refused to counterattack, choosing, instead, to block as many of the incoming blows as he could.

"Stop it," Senator Stern yelled, as the punches continued to rain down on him. "Tom, get a hold of yourself."

Undeterred, Tom continued his barrage of punches. As the blows continued to land, Wu pulled Tom off his father, only to be greeted by a punch to his stomach. It doubled Wu over slightly, but he maintained his upright stance until Tom pushed him down, and rolled him to one side. The maneuver surprised Wu, who could only go where he had been pushed, landing unceremoniously on his back, knocking the wind out of him. Tom delivered one last, hard punch to his father's chest, and then rolled on top of Wu, pinning him to the floor. From there, he continued to throw punches at his father with his free hand, as Senator Stern struggled to crawl away from his son's non-stop assault.

"I'll kill you, you son of a bitch," Tom yelled.

"Tom, let them up," Corinne pleaded, gently touching his shoulder, while leaning away, ready to execute a quick escape if he turned his anger toward her. As she had expected, he pushed her back brusquely. She barely managed to keep her footing.

Wu finally managed to get a hand free, grabbed a fistful of Tom's hair, and yanked him to one side, out of reach of his father, and in a position where Tom couldn't throw any effective punches.

As Tom slowly stopped struggling, Wu maintained close contact, and a strong grip on his captive. He finally managed to maneuver his body between the two combatants. As he looked toward the senator to see what damage had been done, he didn't notice Tom's hand, making its way into his jacket pocket, removing its contents. Tom then hurriedly placed them in his own pocket, and immediately stopped all resistance, going limp in Wu's arms.

Senator Stern fought his way to his feet, and applied a handkerchief to his bleeding nose. He stumbled, distancing himself from Tom and Wu. He spat blood onto the floor. His blurred vision cleared slowly.

Tom began to cry loudly. "God damn you, Dad. I hate you. How could you kill the woman I loved?"

Sensing the fight going out of Tom, Wu slackened his grip. "Are you going to be all right, now, Tom? Can you control yourself if I release you?"

"Yes." His voice shook with each syllable. "I'm sorry. I can't believe all this. I've never been so mad in my entire life." He looked at his father through his tears, as he and Wu helped each other to their feet. "Why, Dad? Why?"

Senator Stern spoke through the handkerchief. "Tom, what this bitch said isn't true, none of it. I'll explain the whole thing to you when we're alone. There's a whole lot more to this than these jerks know." He turned to Corinne, and pointed to the door. "Now that you two have caused me all these unnecessary problems, I want both of you out of here now. You have nothing that'll hold up in court, and nothing that would convince a judge to issue an arrest warrant. All you have are conjectures and planted evidence." He lowered his hand when he noticed how much it quivered. His nose had stopped bleeding. "I found that necklace after Sage left the office last week. Besides, you haven't presented any evidence that Sage had it on when she killed herself. Those pictures you're so proud of could easily have been faked on any computer. The gun and key you pretended to discover are inadmissible in court because of the way you illegally obtained them, anyway. Everything you have that supposedly incriminates me is either fabricated, or had been planted by you. In any case, all of it is inadmissible. Admit it. You've lost."

Senator Stern reached for the phone. "Now, I'm going to see that both of you pay for all this. I'm going to report you directly to the Police Commissioner, Judge Jacobs, and my lawyer. We'll see who has the real power in this city. I'll make both of you sorry you ever came here. Now, get out."

"I'm not sure that's such a good idea, Senator," Wu said. "Suppose your son loses his temper again. You could be hurt worse than you are now. Why don't you come with us to headquarters? We can straighten this whole affair out there."

Senator Stern slammed the receiver into its cradle. "I'm not going anywhere with you, unless you're arresting me with a proper arrest warrant. Believe me, you'll never be able to get another one when I get through talking to your superiors. You won't even have a job. As to Tom, he's not going to be a problem anymore. Are you, Son?"

"No." Whimpering, Tom trudged to the other side of the room. He sat down, turning away from the others.

"See. I can handle him. Now, go, and leave us alone."

Corinne glanced at Tom. "Will you be all right, Tom?"

"Yes." Tom turned toward Corinne. "Leave me alone with my father. I know what I'm doing." He placed his hands in his pockets, and hung his head low, appearing totally cowed.

No one noticed the movement of his agile fingers reloading bullets into the gun clip in his pocket.

As Corinne and Wu left the office, Senator Stern threw his arms around his still seated son, the two men weeping loudly together.

Corinne slammed the door. "Damn it! He's going to get away with it, isn't he?"

Wu placed one arm around Corinne's shoulders as they walked down the hallway. "It looks that way. We've proven he has no alibi for either murder, and we know he had motive, but we haven't linked him to either murder with any hard evidence that we can use. I'm afraid he's right. He's been very careful. I really wish now that we had been more careful with this little escapade. I shouldn't have agreed to an illegal search, but I really didn't think you'd find anything important, certainly not your sister's gun and key. If I had insisted we wait until we could secure a proper search warrant, then everything we found could have been used as evidence. As it stands right now, he's right. We lost, and it's my fault. I didn't use my head."

"Isn't circumstantial evidence enough to arrest him?"

"I doubt it, but I think that's the only avenue left. I'll talk to the captain, and I think we should both talk to Judge Jacobs. Maybe they can persuade the DA to follow up on this, and maybe find other evidence. It's our only hope at this point."

"I guess you were right. We shouldn't have come here, but…"

Before Corinne could complete her thought, a gunshot rang out from within Senator Stern's office. Wu patted his jacket pockets.

"Monica's gun is gone."

"Oh, my God," Corinne screamed, as they both ran back down the hallway.

Wu beat Corinne to the closed door by seconds. Wu drew his gun, threw opened the door, and knelt on one knee, gun aimed into the room, ready to fire. Corinne stood over his shoulder.

Tom Stern stood above the body of his father, lying at his feet. Senator Stern held Monica's gun loosely in his right hand, smoke still streaming from the barrel. A wound in the senator's right temple oozed blood and gray matter.

Corinne ran to Tom's side. "What happened?"

Tom looked up at them through eyes overflowing with tears. "He confessed to it all. He killed your sister, Sage, and shot at you. He said he couldn't stand an investigation, and what it would do to him and his career." He glanced at Wu. "I guess he took the gun from your pocket during our struggle. He must have reloaded it while we were distracted. After he confessed, he told me he loved me, put the gun to his temple, and pulled the trigger. It all happened so fast. I couldn't stop him."

Corinne checked for a pulse, knowing that with that type of head wound, she wouldn't find one. "He's dead."

Tom hurried to the desk chair.

Wu lifted the weapon from Senator Stern's hand by the barrel using a handkerchief. Corinne leaned over to Wu as he stood again, and whispered, "How do we know who took the gun from you, and reloaded it?"

Wu looked down at the body, returning his weapon to his holster. "We don't, but does it really matter at this point?"

"No, I suppose not. I don't see how we'd ever prove it anyway, but my bet is Tom killed him, the same way his father killed Sage."

"You're probably right. There might be a way, though. I'll call the CSI team. They can check Tom for gunshot residue. They can also check the bullet casing for any residual fingerprints. That may tell us which of them reloaded the gun, but I would suspect we're not going to find much in the way of evidence. Like his father, I'll bet Tom is both careful and smart."

Out of the corner of his eye, Wu spotted a movement at the opened door. He saw the .45 automatic before he recognized Kevin. Wu shoved Corinne aside, sending her flying across the room, and reached for his gun, as he dove for cover behind the desk. Kevin fired twice, hitting Wu in the chest. He fell back across the desk onto the floor.

Tom sat up with a start at the gun's discharge, and flung himself to the floor behind his father's desk, barely avoiding the tumbling Wu. Tom then plastered himself against the desk, as Wu's body rolled by, stopping when it hit the wall.

Wu's shove had sent Corinne to the floor adjacent to Senator Stern's body. She saw Kevin's gun as it fired and Wu falling. Smiling, Kevin turned his gun in Corinne's direction, his movement in slow motion.

Corinne searched for something to use against Kevin. She spotted Monica's gun where Wu had dropped it when he had spotted Kevin. It now lay between her and Senator Stern's body. *Does it have another bullet in it, and can I reach it before Kevin shoots? It doesn't matter. I have to try. It's my only chance.*

In one rapid, fluid motion, she grabbed the gun, aimed it at Kevin's chest with as much speed and accuracy as her shaking hands would allow, and pulled the trigger twice.

CHAPTER 38

Four additional gun blasts, fired in quick succession, jolted the air in Senator Stern's office. The two bullets fired by Corinne traveled true, striking Kevin mid-chest a moment before he fired again. The impact of Corinne's bullets caused Kevin's shot to fly high, the bullet whizzing over her head to strike the wall behind her. The final shot came from Wu's weapon. It had fallen to the floor as he fell. Tom had seized it, and fired at Kevin, missing his target as Kevin fell backward through the doorway.

Corinne scrambled to her feet, keeping her weapon trained on Kevin as he collapsed. Concerned about Wu, she turned her head to find him crawling from behind the desk, brandishing his backup weapon that he had retrieved from his ankle holster. Wincing, he grabbed his gun from Tom's shaking hand, struggled to his feet, and ran toward Kevin, rubbing his chest the entire time. He kicked Kevin's gun away from his hand, and checked for a pulse.

"He's dead. Nice shooting."

Corinne ran to his side, placing a concerned arm on his shoulder. "Are you all right? I thought he shot you."

Wu took Monica's gun from Corinne, and tapped his chest with his thumb. "Bullet proof vest. Still hurts a ton to get shot, though. Thought the Kevlar might come in handy with this guy taking shots at you all the time. How are you?"

Her hands were shaking, as were her knees. She felt her chest pounding as her heart raced. "I've been better. How about you, Tom? You okay back there?"

"Yeah...I'm...fine." He made no effort to stand, preferring to lie behind the safety of the desk.

"I'd better call this in. Why don't you see what you can do for Tom? He sounds a little shaken up."

"And I don't?" Corinne took a few wobbly steps in Tom's direction, unsure her legs would really support her for the entire trip. "When we're done here, I'm going back to my sister's apartment, and sleep for a month...right after I gulp down a whole bottle of Scotch."

"Want some company?" Wu asked, dialing his cell phone.

"I'll think about it."

The investigation into Senator Stern's suicide and the subsequent shoot out with Kevin Bent had lasted long into the night.

Wu escorted Corinne down the hallway. "You can leave now. There shouldn't be any charges filed on our little escapade, thanks to Judge Jacobs' intervention, and Tom's insistence that we were justified. Captain Patelli made me promise not to break any laws ever again, but, believe me, I'm not eager to go down that road again soon, anyway. They'll probably have more questions for you and Tom in the morning, but they're satisfied with your stories for now."

"It won't change by morning. What we found, and what happened is exactly what I told them. Did they find anything that could help us prove any of our speculations?"

"Remember me telling you how smart the Stern men were?"

"Of course, and I agree with you fully. What are you getting at?"

"The CSI team found only smudges on the cartridges from Monica's gun, so we don't know who re-loaded the clip. Tom fired my weapon at Kevin. He missed, but he now has GSR on his hands from that. There's also GSR on Senator Stern's hand, but we don't know if he fired the weapon himself, or if Tom held the gun, and the residue got on the senator's hand when the gun discharged during a struggle. It could have happened either way. Now, we'll never know."

"So, Tom probably fired your gun so he couldn't be accused of firing Monica's gun. He really thought fast on his feet."

"The team is still looking for even the slightest clue that could give us the answers, but I doubt they'll find anything. These Stern men *are* really smart."

"Not smart enough to stay out of trouble altogether though. They seem to be involved in an awful lot of corruption." She stretched up to give him a light kiss on his lips. "Thanks for all you've done for Monica and me, Hank."

He smacked his lips, and ran his tongue over them leisurely. "That tastes awfully good to me. Now, as the lead detective on this case, I'm supposed to tell you not to leave town, Miss Day."

"I'm too tired to go anywhere but straight to bed with my bottle of Scotch. So, you can tell your boss I'm going nowhere fast. See you later?"

"As soon as I'm done here, I'll come over. Save some of that booze for me."

Corinne made her way back to Monica's apartment, her mind spinning with the day's events. Once inside, she leaned heavily on the apartment door, the steel cooling her forehead. She felt physically and mentally exhausted again. She backed away from the door, and stretched her neck. Everything hurt. She turned toward the small bar, throwing her purse on the couch, and placing her keys in her pants pocket. During her journey, she pulled her blouse out of her jeans, allowing the shirttails to hang loose. She couldn't wait to take off her clothes, and fall into bed, but first, she had promised herself a drink, and drink she would. *Only sip a little. Don't want to be totally drunk when Hank arrives.*

I wonder if Monica ever shot anyone. I realize in my case, it was self-defense, but that doesn't matter. I still took a life. My entire professional career has been dedicated to saving lives, and reducing patients' pain, both physical and emotional. I never thought I would ever deliberately try to kill someone. Just the thought of it nauseates me. Besides my training, it goes against everything the Church taught me growing up. I know it was self-defense, but... It was self-defense. It was self-defense. No matter how many times I keep telling myself that, it still bothers me beyond belief. I hope, and pray to God that I never have to do it again.

Arriving at the bar, she began to unbutton her blouse, but stopped abruptly after the third button when she sensed someone else's presence. Reflected in the mirror behind the bar, she spotted a man, hiding in the shadows. She froze when she realized he had a gun. She stifled an inrush of air, and then turned around. "Hello, Paul." She didn't bother buttoning her blouse. "I thought you were in New York."

He walked farther into the light, his patented, broad smile plastered in place. He wore his usual dark-blue suit with a crisp white shirt, and sported a new blue tie. He had an unlit cigar in the breast pocket of the jacket.

She leaned on the bar for support, allowing her eyes to scan him, trying to find the reason she had initially been attracted to him. She couldn't. *That's exactly the outfit one should wear to commit a murder. At least my murder will be a formal affair.*

"I am in New York, and I have witnesses to prove it."

She tried to add as much disgust to her statement as she could. "I have no doubts of that, *Mister Camarazza*. By the way, who is your new girlfriend, anyone I know?"

"You don't miss a trick, do you? You don't know her. She's a secretary in one of my corporate headquarters. Her name really doesn't matter, unless you really need to know."

Corinne starred at him through disinterested eyes. *You beast! I won't give you the satisfaction of thinking I'm the least bit upset by your current love interest.* "Mind if I make a drink? I've been promising myself one all evening. This has been one long day."

"No, go ahead. Drink all you want." He kept the gun fixed on Corinne as he spoke. "Help yourself to as many drinks as you want. That'll even help my plan."

Corinne hesitated, cringing at the word "plan." As she proceeded to pour herself a Scotch, she asked, without looking up, "What, exactly, is this plan of yours?"

"You're going to jump to your death from your sister's balcony." He pointed to the open slider. A gentle breeze caused the flimsy curtain to billow noiselessly into the room. "A high blood alcohol level will reinforce the idea that you became distraught with everything that has happened, and decided to end it all. So, have a few."

"Thanks. It's nice to know you still care. Can I pour one for you? Why not light that cigar, and make yourself comfortable?"

"No, no, we want them to find only one glass, yours, and no trace of any cigar smoke. No, you were drinking alone before you jumped. They'll be no traces of me here when I leave."

"Suit yourself." Corinne sipped the drink, keeping her eyes fixed on Paul, but refusing to look at the gun. The liquor tasted good. "Where's your new boyfriend, The Meddling Detective Wu?"

She looked into her Scotch. *That's a good question. Where the hell are you, Hank? You said you'd follow me here in a few minutes. Hurry up! I can only nurse these drinks for so long before Mister Crime here shoots me, or tosses me off the balcony. I need some help...now.* "He's probably still investigating your chauffeur's death."

"Kevin? He's dead? I sent him to kill Senator Stern tonight. Did he?"

"He didn't have to. The senator killed himself."

"Humph. I didn't think he had it in him."

"I guess he did." Corinne decided not to mention her suspicions about the senator's son. "Kevin came in right after we found the senator's body, and died in a shootout with the police." She also thought better of mentioning who actually killed Kevin.

"That's too bad. I appreciated his work as a chauffeur."

"And hit man, too, right?"

"Yes, he had many talents. He always followed orders to the letter."

"Like when you had him shoot up the car next to me without hitting me, or your vintage Lamborghini?"

"Exactly! I also had ordered him to kill you today. I guess he failed me there."

"Looks that way. If I'm supposed to be dead already, why are you here with this elaborate lemming-jumping-off-the-balcony routine?"

"I know how resourceful you can be. I thought you might avoid Kevin's attempt. So, I'm here as a backup. If Kevin had killed you, I would have simply disappeared. Since he didn't, you'll die by my hand, and then I'll disappear. Actually, I prefer it this way."

"Glad I could oblige."

A loud knock at the door froze Corinne's drink halfway to her lips.

Paul rushed to her side as she returned the drink to the bar. He placed the gun barrel against her cheek. Yanking her toward the door, he whispered, "Get rid of whoever it is, or I'll kill you both. Understand?"

She ignored his question, and reached for the doorknob, not bothering to check the peephole. Paul positioned himself behind the door as Corinne opened it, his gun ready for any subterfuge.

"Hi, Hank." Corinne placed a restraining hand against his chest, preventing him from either coming in, or pressing against her. "I know I said you could come over, but I'm awfully tired, and I simply want to collapse in bed. What do you say you come back for breakfast tomorrow?"

Hank frowned his disappointment, but did note the fatigue in Corinne's eyes and in her stance; however, he also detected something else there that he couldn't readily identify. *Is it fear?* "If that's what you really want, Corinne." He slowly reached for her shoulders.

Corinne pushed his hands aside, put her finger to her lips, and opened his jacket wide enough to find his gun. "It's what I really want, and need, Hank." She quietly reached for the gun, after mouthing the word "Paul," and pointing toward the door. She noiselessly removed the gun from its holster, and placed it in the waistband of her pants, covering it with her blouse.

Hank lifted her blouse, and, with one finger, moved the gun's safety to the "off" position. "Sure you'll be okay?"

"Positive. I'll be fine after some much-needed sleep." She patted the gun. "Thanks for all your help this evening."

"Okay, but I won't be far, if you need me."

"I know." Corinne removed the keys from her pocket, gripping them so they wouldn't jingle. She then handed them to Hank, who handled them in the same manner. "I'll call you if I do."

"Bye." He then mouthed "good luck," as he turned, and headed down the hallway.

"Bye, Hank." She closed the door to find Paul, still standing there with the same, dumb smile of impending victory. Corinne ignored him, and hurried back to the bar. She grabbed her drink, as Paul listened for Hank's fading footsteps. When he cautiously opened the door to confirm Wu's departure, Corinne placed the gun on the top shelf of the bar, out of sight, but within easy reach.

Paul closed the door, and locked it before returning to his station in the center of the room.

"You're a good actress, Corinne."

Better than you know. She took another sip of Scotch. "No use getting anyone else killed."

"Good thinking."

"Before I take my lover's leap, would you mind telling me some things about this whole affair?"

"Not as long as you keep drinking, and don't try anything."

"What do you expect me to try, drink my way out the window, and float to safety?"

"That would be unique. You would become Corinne Day, the first flying physical therapist." He guffawed, but continued to point the gun at her. "Keep drinking. Where do you want me to begin my story?"

"Start at the beginning, when Sage left you, and came here to Washington."

He laughed even louder this time. "That's not the beginning, and Sage never left me. I sent her here."

"Why?"

"I got the idea almost a year before that. I had watched the police jail a number of my friends and relatives on all sorts of raps. I decided not to go down that same road. I wanted some inside sources and lots of power, but not simply at the local level. I wanted real power, Federal power."

"Is that where Senator Stern enters the picture?"

"Yes. With a little information from some of my sources here, I determined that he would be the most likely candidate for the Presidential nomination of his party, and that he had a good chance of winning too. So, I had a friend of mine, named Ross Martino, do some research. I believe you met his Ferrari on the beltway."

"With Kevin at the wheel?"

Paul chuckled. "Yeah, I told him to scare you, and not cause a crash. You almost destroyed both cars when you panicked. You should be more careful how you drive borrowed cars, you know."

"I'll keep that in mind. What else did this Ross Martino tell you about the senator?"

"Well, besides the usual public relations stuff, he loved gambling, good food, good times, and he had taken a bribe, or two during his career, nothing big compared to a lot of other politicians in Washington, mind you, but they were there for the finding, nonetheless."

"Exactly the kind of person you wanted to get to know, right?"

"Precisely, but I wanted more. I found out his friends were telling him to marry before the campaign. It's good for the image, I guess. Anyway, Sage and I were dating at the time, nothing serious though, really."

"Your sordid relationships don't matter to me anymore." Corinne added some Scotch to her glass even though she hadn't emptied it. *I don't know how much more of your crap I'm going to be able to have thrown in my face before I vomit my guts out, and shoot you on the spot, You Dirt Bag.*

"I made a deal with Sage. She agreed to come down here, and, using the background information on Frank that my friend provided, make herself available to the senator. I told her to try to get him to fall in love with her. Her secondary task involved gathering any information she could from his crime committee activities, and passing that information on to me. She did a great job there. Eventually, she introduced us, and I took it from there, giving his career a much-appreciated boost, money, contacts, that sort of thing. For all that, Sage got the chance to be a powerful senator's wife and possibly the Nation's First Lady." He looked up at the ceiling for a moment, then back to Corinne. "Imagine me with a direct contact in the White House, looking out for my interests first."

"Sounds scary, if you ask me." Corinne held her drink up in a mock salute to him, but did not take an accompanying sip. She felt the effects of the Scotch coursing through her, warming her insides, but didn't want to become too impaired. *I need to be able to shoot straight.* "Why the hell did she agree to do that? She would have had to marry a total stranger, someone she might not even love, get him involved with you and your crime family, and end up stealing information about his committee's activities. It makes no sense for her to agree to all that, unless you had something on her. What were you holding over her head, an axe?"

"Nothing so crass. I actually didn't have to force her to do any of it. She did it all willingly, after I agreed to help her with a little problem she had. You see, Sage's only living relative is a mentally challenged brother who lives with some friends in Connecticut. Sage didn't want him sent to an institution for permanent care. She had been providing the money for all his needs, until the economy collapsed, and she lost her job. That's why she turned to crime in the first place. I simply agreed to set up a trust fund that provides him everything he'll ever need, and for the family taking care of him to be well compensated. She also got her police records destroyed, and got the chance to become a Washington lady of leisure. She won all around."

"So, what went wrong with your plan, my sister?"

"Oh, she became part of it, for sure. I got her name from Ross. He knew Senator Jackson, and had been in on the senator's discussion of his plans for Senator Stern, including having a private investigator research the senator's background and all his contacts. He thought your sister would be perfect for the job, especially since she had a semi-famous sister who worked in my hometown of New York."

Corinne stared at Paul, wide-eyed, open mouthed, and speechless for a full minute. *I can't believe how evil you are.* "You mean to tell me that you were interested in me only because my sister had been chosen to investigate the senator?"

"Yes." He puffed out his chest like a proud rooster. "That's why I helped your career along with a few bribes, and I even arranged for that clinic of yours to survive. I also went out of my way to ensure that you got all the credit and publicity for that. You soaked it all up, and never suspected a thing." He bowed toward her mockingly. "You have me to thank for almost all your success in New York."

She sucked a large gulp of air, and held her breath, speaking only after the pain in her gut subsided a little. She blew the air out, as a tiny tear emerged from one eye. "I don't believe you. Why all the manipulation in my life?"

"Out of the goodness of my heart."

"Oh, give me a break." She couldn't help herself. She took a large swig of her drink.

"Okay, I thought knowing the PI's sister might come in handy, and decided to give your career a much-needed boost. After all, I have an image to uphold. I only date winners, not losers."

Corinne slammed her drink down hard on the bar, spilling most of its remaining contents. "Or women you intend to use." She scowled at him. "Handy for what?"

"I figured that if your sister did discover something juicy about the senator, or Sage, she would tell you, and you would tell me."

"So, that's why you kept showing up at every event I attended. I'll bet you didn't really appreciate opera, the plays, or the concerts we attended, did you? You went only on the pretense of meeting me by accident, and I fell for it, and naively fell for you." She looked up. "Heaven forgive me!"

"Oh, don't get me wrong, Corinne. I did eventually learn to enjoy some of the operas, and I did grow to appreciate your company...well, your body."

"And it still shows in the delicate way you point that gun at me." Corinne again saluted him with the little she had left of her Scotch.

"You're as sarcastic as ever, Corinne. You know, that's one of the things I grew to respect about you. You've got spunk."

Unmoving, Corinne stared at him. *Give me half a chance, and I'll show you some real spunk, delivered courtesy of Hank's gun, You Scumbag.*

CHAPTER 39

Corinne mopped up the spilled Scotch with a towel, and stored the damp towel on the shelf holding Hank's gun, resisting the temptation to simply seize the weapon, and shoot it out with Paul. She refilled her glass, took a small sip, and looked at the gun still aimed at her. It had hardly moved during their entire discussion. The alcohol had frayed her nerves. *I've already drunk too much, and I know I shouldn't drink any more, especially if I want to use Hank's gun with any degree of accuracy. I really hope I don't have to use it against Paul though, scumbag that he is. I've already shot one man...killing him. I don't want to do it again.* She placed the drink to her lips, pretending to take a sip. She couldn't taste anything, anyway: her throat felt scorched and tight.

I hope you're outside listening, Hank, and I hope I can get the whole story out of Paul before he figures out what I'm up to, or I'm one dead lady. "So, I gather everything went smoothly at first with your 'put-a-spy-in-the-White-House-courtesy-of-Paul Camarazza' plan until last week when things starting falling apart. What happened?"

"There were some things I couldn't control, or couldn't have foreseen. For one thing, Sage fell in love with the senator's son. Up to that time, she had been a great help to me and to Senator Stern. She kept feeding me information as planned. She even managed to discover the whereabouts of that bum Josh Zbronski, or John Zachary, as he called himself around here. By then, I knew she had stooped to feeding me information only to convince me of her commitment to my plan, but I knew she had her own agenda. I wouldn't have let her run away with Frank's son, even if she hadn't been killed."

"Now, that's true loyalty to an employee." Corinne offered him another salute.

"Oh, I appreciated her as an employee...while she remained loyal to me. I have to admit that. Her information kept me out of jail on at least one occasion."

"But I thought there were two episodes in the last year where the police thought they had you, but you were able to sidestep them, and avoid prison."

"That's right. You're well informed. That other time, the information came directly from Senator Stern, or Frank, as I had started calling him. We had become old chums by then."

"Then, you did manage to get him to sell out to you. What kind of price did he have?"

"Not as much as you might imagine. I had, of course, contributed large amounts to his campaign, both legally and under the table, and to his favorite charity, himself. Then there were the boats, cars, and casino connections I provided at no cost to him, but the power I provided attracted him most."

"Power? How much more power is there in this country than a senator on his way to the Presidency?"

"Much more, Corinne! You are naïve, aren't you? Senators and Presidents have people to answer to, their constituents, the press, the law, congress, and others. I answer to no one. I am the boss, period. What I say goes…without exception. That's real power. I offered him access to that power. I told him he could have the best of both worlds, all the legal power of the Presidency and all the illegal power of the criminal empire in this country."

"Criminal empire? What criminal empire?"

"The new one Frank and I were going to form. Using his political power and the Crime Commission information, we were going to literally take over every criminal organization in the entire country. We would run drugs, gambling, prostitution, government graft, and everything else illegal, all from the White House."

"You mean to tell me he bought into that crock of bull? That would make him even dumber than I thought."

"Oh, it's not bull. I think it'll really happen eventually…with me controlling everything. I'm working on it with another senator already."

"You don't waste any time, do you?"

"I've got to keep moving forward, if I'm going to be ready for the Presidential campaign kickoff. That's why I'm really disappointed with the way things went with Sage. I mean, we put a lot of work into getting Frank into the White House. We even had Frank's major opposition removed from the running, and now, I've got to do everything all over again from the beginning."

"What? Do you mean that your orchestrated Senator Edmond's assassination too?" She sighed. "I suppose Kevin pulled the trigger."

"That's right. I told you, he's an excellent shot, never misses with that rifle of his."

"Sage is a good shot too, apparently. What forced her to start killing people?"

"She got nervous that I had become suspicious of her. I guess I'm not as good an actor as you were with your Detective a few minutes ago. After Sage fell for Tom, her reports became less frequent, and sketchy at best. Even the senator noticed a change in her before he finally caught the two of them together, but by then, everything had started to unravel. Your sister had pictures of Sage with Tom, Sage with the senator and me, and who knows what else? Then, somehow, your sister discovered Sage's background. Sage knew she had to get out before your sister released her information. She also knew I would come after her as soon as I realized she had reneged on our bargain. So, she arranged to run away with Tom. I hear they were making arrangements to take her brother with them, along with as much money as they could get from his trust. Ross got wind of it, and called me. I sent two of my best men to confront her, and bring her back to New York, by force if necessary. She called me later to tell me they had been killed in a drug shoot out. Of course, I didn't believe her."

"She killed both of them."

"Yes, I'm afraid she did. That's why I had to come down here that weekend. I had to see what I could salvage."

"But why the elaborate scheme to get me down here with you? Why not simply come alone to do your dirty work?"

"I needed you to introduce me to your sister. I thought if we went out with her socially, she might tell us what she had discovered. I can be persuasive, you know, and if I did get her to share that information, I could either convince her to stay quiet or…"

"Or kill her, right?"

"Believe me, Corinne, I had hoped it wouldn't come to that. Apparently, Frank had his own plan to get the information from your sister. He used a key he had stolen from Senator Jackson to search your sister's office, and even came up with some photos and a thumb drive, but he became increasingly fearful that he had missed something, maybe a second thumb drive. I guess he caught your sister talking to the police, and shot her with Sage's gun. Then, he arranged to have any traces of his searches, as well as any evidence he had missed, erased by professionals. He had become good at deception...almost as good as me."

Corinne simply continued to stare.

"He then came up with some story about Middle East negotiations, and got the FBI to clean out her office and apartment to ensure no information remained, but then, he became obsessed with the idea that even they had missed something, something that would eventually come back to haunt him, prevent him from becoming President, or force him to step down once he had attained that office. I know he went back to your sister's apartment several times to search the place."

"I know. I caught him there once, and he shot at me. He may have been smart and good at deception, but he didn't have Kevin's talent when it came to killing people. He missed with two shots."

"You know, I really didn't think he had it in him to try to kill anyone, but he surprised me. When you and I stumbled on Sage's body, I knew he had done it. He had become insanely jealous when it came to her. I'm surprised he didn't shoot his son too."

"Maybe he would have eventually, or maybe family meant more to him than a girlfriend. Who knows?"

Paul continued his narration, ignoring Corinne's speculation. "Somehow, he then managed to have the police close the case, and covered his tail. I really thought that would be the end of my problems. After all, I still had a chance of having my pliable contact, my own puppet in the White House. I still remember how happy I felt at the time."

"But I really messed up that plan, didn't I?"

"Yeah, you wouldn't listen to me. You had to meddle. Even my little attempts to scare you off didn't work. You somehow managed to get the case reopened, figured out who killed your sister, and backed Frank into a corner so he killed himself. Then, you managed to avoid Kevin's real attempt on your life. It wouldn't surprise me if you contributed to Kevin's death too. Yeah, you screwed things up for me real good, Corinne."

Corinne began weaving back and forth slightly, pretending the alcohol had taken affect.

"You should have been an obedient little girl, and come back to New York with me."

"Little girl," Corinne yelled, her weaving disappearing instantly. "Is that what you think of me?"

"You'll always be my naïve, little girl, Corinne."

"How sweet..." Corinne curled her lips into a giant kiss..."but oh, how revolting."

Paul didn't bother returning the kiss.

Corinne stood with her hands flat on the edge of the bar's surface. "Now, tell me what makes you think you're going to get away with all the deceit, manipulation, and murders?"

"Because I have the brains to pull it off." Paul tapped his temple gently with the barrel of the gun.

As soon as the gun reached Paul's head, Corinne dropped her right hand from the bar's surface, and grabbed Wu's gun. In one fluid motion, she yanked the weapon off the shelf, braced both elbows firmly on the bar, and pointed the gun at Paul. She aimed for his chest. *I doubt I stand much of a chance of hitting your minuscule heart, if you have one at all, no matter how many times I shoot, but I'll give it my best attempt. So, you'd better not move.* She said nothing, however. She rested her index finger firmly against the trigger.

Paul froze, losing his smile in an instant.

"Don't." Corinne spoke through gritted teeth. Her lips barely moved.

"I know you well, Corinne, maybe better than you know yourself. You're a nurse. You're dedicated to saving lives. You won't..." Before finishing the sentence, Paul jerked his arm down in front of him, and pulled the trigger.

CHAPTER 40

Both weapons fired in tandem, Corinne's gun providing the first blast, followed almost instantly by Paul's. Corinne's bullet struck Paul in the chest, buckling his knees, and causing his shot to sail over her head, shattering the mirror behind her.

As soon as he heard the shots, Wu used the key, and burst through the door, brandishing his backup pistol. Keeping his weapon trained on Paul, he kicked Paul's gun away. Wu checked for a pulse. "He's still alive, but barely." As he called for an ambulance and backup, he watched Corinne drop the gun to the bar, and gulp the last of her Scotch.

For the second time that evening, a man she had shot lay at her feet. *I killed Kevin. I wonder if Paul will become my second victim. Funny, I don't feel the least remorse at shooting him. I don't really care if he survives or not. He really deserved to be shot after all he's done. Either way, though, I sincerely hope he becomes the last man I will ever have to shoot.*

She turned toward the mirror behind her, its smooth surface no longer whole, but, instead, replaced with sharp edges, blasted into shards by the violence imposed upon it by the bullet. In its still reflective, but broken surface, she no longer saw the brainy and beautiful medical professional she had once been, seeing instead a defeated, shattered woman. Her life of excess, fast cars, thousand dollar meals, handsome, shallow men, late-night parties, drug and alcohol induced stupors had been without foundation, without substance, and worst of all, without lasting significance.

She began to sob, this time not for a deceased sister, but for what she had deteriorated into, what she had allowed herself to become, an emotional recluse, afraid of her own feelings, afraid to share them not only with her twin, but also with any other human being, and the warped, sinful road that took her down.

"Monica, please forgive me. I lost touch with you long before the connection between us vanished. You were right. I had ignored all your warnings about my emotional isolation, and the abnormal, sometimes-evil direction my life had taken. I not only tried to hide my emotions from you, but I also used it as a shield against the world. I became increasingly dependent on others, especially you and Paul, for help with that frightening world. I guess I've developed a dependent personality disorder. Can you believe it, Monica? The supposedly brilliant nurse with all the training in psychology didn't even recognize her own malady as it developed."

She took a deep breath, blew it out slowly. "I really thought I could avoid the pain associated with emotional commitment and the mistakes associated with decision making. I turned out to be so wrong. When I locked you out, I locked out life, truth, God, everything that had once been important to me. I became too good at it. I made a huge mistake."

She closed her eyes, wishing it would shield her from the reality of her life-destroying blunder. It didn't. When she next opened them, the devastated woman remained. "I chased all the wrong things for all the wrong reasons. I'm sorry."

With a shaking finger, she caressed the reflection. "Please forgive me, Monica. I should have allowed us to grow closer, learned from our shared experiences, instead of hiding from them, isolating myself from you, living so far away, and making it a one-way communication highway between us.

"Hank had been right; I should have been in Washington for you, visited you more often, grown closer to you, learned more about you and your way of life...and loved you more...deeper. I know my actions contributed to your death. No one will ever convince me otherwise. By not growing closer to you, I abandoned you, left you to die alone, not sensing my presence, or my love. I'm so sorry. Monica, please forgive me, and pray for me. Your intervention with God may be my only hope for redemption."

"Corinne, are you all right?" Wu asked, approaching when he heard her conversing with the mirror.

Corinne turned to him with puffy, mournful eyes that, although blurred by tears, were seeing the real Corinne Day for the first time. "No, I'm not." Bypassing his proffered hug, she stood over Paul, and added, "But with Monica's help and a lot of forgiveness from God, I will be."

Allowing Hank's arm to encircle her, she closed her eyes once more, and leaned against his chest. "Thank you," she muttered as she passed out.

CHAPTER 41

The next evening, Corinne and Wu stood on the balcony of Monica's apartment, silently watching a brilliant, red sunset for several minutes. The cool breeze blew Corinne's hair gently. She turned into the wind to catch its full, refreshing effect.

Wu put his arm around her waist, and whispered, "When this thing's finally settled and Paul's behind bars, are you going to go back to living in New York?"

Corinne couldn't tear her gaze from the spectacular sunset. She shrugged her shoulders. "I have to. I can't simply walk out on my life, no matter how tempting that may be. I have patients, colleagues who depend on me, and clinic responsibilities. I can't simply abandon all of them for personal, selfish reasons."

"There must be other physical therapists who could cover those patients, and help your colleagues. Believe it or not, Corinne, that clinic would survive without you."

Corinne turned to him. "Oh, I'm sure that's true, but, for now, I owe it to them to return to the city. I made a commitment to them, and I simply can't renege on that." She stroked his cheek. "Listen, Hank, my whole life has been turned upside down these last few weeks, not only because of Monica's death, but with what I discovered about myself." She turned, facing the sunset once more, and leaned heavily on the railing. "I've changed, Hank. I'm not the same woman anymore, not the same woman you met and fell for anyway." She looked to the sky with its changing colors. "It may sound hokey, but I really think all these events were directed by some power greater than me. Who knows? Maybe Monica acted from Heaven, or my Guardian Angel finally got through to me, or maybe even God Himself tried to show me the evil of my ways. I've had too many close calls for all my escapes to be simply luck. No, it's got to be more than that, and, if someone, or something did make an effort to intervene on my behalf, then there's got to be more to my life too, more that I can accomplish, and definitely a different direction for my life to take." She looked Heavenward. "I can hope that's true, anyway."

She stared into his eyes. "I have to go back to New York, back to the beginning, examine how I got so perverted, get myself straightened out, and start fresh. I've got to find the real Corinne Day. Does that make any sense to you?"

Wu pulled her closer. "Well, to be honest, no, but if you understand it, that's good enough for a dumb detective in love."

"That's part of the problem, Hank. I don't know if I understand any of it either, including my feelings for you." She lowered her gaze. "I feel damaged, used, and old. I'm different, changed, but I can't explain how, or what I've become."

"You mean, you're not Corinne Day, the Superwoman of the psychology and physical therapy anymore, able to leap tall hospitals and mere, mortal men in a single bound? You've discovered you're human like the rest of us."

"That's part of it, I'm sure, but I think it's deeper than that. I'm changed inside, and I'm frightened more than when I confronted Paul and his henchmen. Does that make any sense?"

"Sure, those were physical threats, something you could plan for, react to, and overcome. I think you're afraid of facing life's unknown future without Monica's presence. There is no way you can plan for that."

"I wish I could."

He held her at arm's length. "Listen, to me, Corinne. I'm not a counselor, or a philosopher, but I'll try to give you what wisdom I can. Camarazza deceived you because you were naïve, and he certainly caused you a lot of pain, but that's in the past. Learn from it, and move on. There is more to life than pain, and much more to look forward to…there's play, love, and companionship to name only a few of life's benefits. Look to the future, not your past. That future lies here in Washington…with me, not back East. You'll find yourself here just as easily as you will in New York."

"But I wasn't simply naïve, Hank. I became sinful. I wanted what Paul had to offer. I turned my back on my moral upbringing. I made myself blind to Paul's lies and manipulations. I never realized how evil he really could be, and how easily he used me for his nefarious purposes. I even blocked out Monica's warnings. Now, I don't know what direction my life will take other than away from that evil, but I think I've got to return to New York to find out. I've got to start building a new, stronger foundation for that life, and I have to start there."

"Nefarious? Wow! That's a big word."

"Yes, a big word for an even bigger evil."

"Are you talking about Paul, or the Devil?"

"Both; Paul did the Devil's work on Earth, and I fell for his deceptions, and helped with some of that evil, including getting Monica killed."

"You can't blame yourself for that. It would have happened anyway. Even Monica didn't see it coming. As for the rest of the case, you handled yourself remarkably well under pressures that would have crushed many people. In this detective's humble opinion, you couldn't have done any better than you did. I'm sure you'll be able to sort out all of life's future problems on your own with that same strength."

"Thank you, Doctor Detective Wu. Who says cops are dumb? Some are as smart as psychiatrists."

He sighed. "I'm not that smart, but I am willing to help you in any way I can…but I can only help you if you stay here."

"You've helped me a lot already." She kissed him lightly.

"Okay, now that I've helped you with your problem, I have one of my own maybe you can help me sort out. I have this girlfriend I'm trying to persuade to stay in Washington where I can keep an eye on her, and enjoy her company, but I'm not getting through to her. Do you have any idea how I can accomplish that?"

She smiled. "You're persistent; I'll give you that much. Listen, Hank, I appreciate what you're trying to do for me, and I'd love to stay, but I have to go back. It's going to take me a long time to resolve all my issues, and I think I have to do it alone, away from Washington with all its bad memories, and, unfortunately, away from you for a while. Besides, I need to go back to New York to have access to the resources I may need to accomplish all that."

"Sounds like you're going on a retreat for a counseling session with a psychiatrist and a priest."

Corinne laughed. "My associate in research, Doctor Winter, is a psychiatrist. I definitely intend to talk to him. As to the priest, I haven't seen one in years, but I think I should go back to Church and to confession if I want to finally understand this new Corinne Day. That way, I can get the forgiveness I need, and maybe a chance to start over with a clean slate in both my heart and soul. Who knows? I may be able to find the original, childhood Corinne under this bruised exterior after all."

"And finally understand what she really wants in life, including where she stands concerning Detective Wu?"

"Exactly!" Corinne pressed her head into his chest, and hugged him. "Thank you for all your help, Philosopher-Detective Wu, and all your understanding."

He tilted his head, and frowned. "You know, you really should be in the witness protection program. The Camarazza family will be after you. My New York colleagues told me that Paul apparently kept the rest of his family under his thumb, and didn't allow them free access to that power and control he loved so much. So, they really don't like him, and are probably going to be happy he went away, but that doesn't mean they won't come after you, especially if you testify against him. As they say, 'mob-blood is thicker than water.'"

"I don't think witness protection will be necessary. If you're right, and they really *are* happy to have Paul out of the way, I should be safe. Besides, I know the vice president of Paul's main corporation, which is probably really a front for his criminal activity. He's ambitious, and will probably be one of those who will be especially delighted to have Paul out of the way. I'm sure he'll be happy for the opportunity to grab the reins of the organization, and run it the way he sees fit, as illegal as that may be. He won't care what I did to Paul. So, I think I'll be safe."

"I still think he may come after you. You can't predict how the mob will react."

"Not one hundred percent, I agree, but the odds are in my favor. If I'm wrong, and I sense any danger at all, I'll call you, and you can ride into New York on your white stallion to save me."

"Okay, it's a deal. To be truthful, the way you handled yourself down here, they'd be smart to stay away from you. They should probably fear you more than the law."

"I don't know about that, but I'll be careful in any case." *Is my bravado justified? Can I really handle any new situation I confront? We'll see. I need to take things one step at a time…no more hasty decisions, or outlandish behavior.*

"Could I possibly convince you to come back here for a few visits while you're trying to figure out what's going on in that pretty head of yours? After all, all you've seen is the darker, seedier side of Washington. There is a brighter side, and I'd really love to show it to you."

"That's an invitation I may not be able to pass up."

"I hope not, or I'll be forced to get Judge Jacobs to issue an arrest warrant for you, and I'll have to go to New York to pick you up personally."

"You don't need an arrest warrant for that." Corinne placed her arms around his neck. "For that matter, I wouldn't object to being picked up right now, *if* you're strong enough to handle a new, stronger woman, that is."

He swept her off her feet, and held her close, as if she would float away if not for his tight embrace. He kissed her full on the lips. Their hearts beat in unison. As their lips parted, and their gazes met, he moved toward the doorway. He rocked her gently in his massive arms, hoping she would find the closure she sought, and become a woman without a care in the world, his woman, his lover, and, eventually, his wife. "I'm not sure I can handle you, Corinne, but I'm definitely willing to give it a try."

As if on cue, a strong breeze blew the light curtains aside, inviting them into the apartment, and allowing them easy, unfettered access to its inner security, warmth, and comfort. The breeze carried with it the sweet fragrance of lilacs.

Corinne took one last look at the sunset through the open doorway, sniffed the air, smiled, and winked. "Goodbye, Monica, I want to thank both you and God for all the help." She then pressed her cheek against Hank's chest, her smile broadening with the knowledge that she had finally started on the road to recovery, to discovering the real Corinne Day and where her future lay.

> Happy is the man, who finds Wisdom,
> the man who finds understanding!
> For her profit is better than profit in silver,
> and better than gold is her revenue.
> Proverbs 3:13

####

ABOUT THE AUTHOR

Bill Rockwell is a retired physician. He has written many medical articles, including a Chapter in a medical textbook on allergies. His other novels are a vampire love story, *Generation Z, Birth of the Zompire*, and an inspirational fantasy, *Heaven's Conflict, The Rise and Fall of Angels, A Novel*, the story of God's attempt to redeem his wayward Archangel before casting him into Hell. Bill lives with his wife in Connecticut, and loves to travel.

NOTE FROM AUTHOR

Thank you for reading my novel. If you enjoyed this book, please review it on Amazon and/or the book websites you frequent. Also, tell your friends who might enjoy my writing. For more information about my future novels, follow me on Facebook (billrockwellauthor) or Twitter (@bill_rockwell), or visit my website (http://billrockwell.net) to read summaries and the first chapter of all my novels.

Please enjoy this brief excerpt from *Heaven's Conflict, The Rise and Fall of Angels, A Novel*, available since Fall 2014:

CHAPTER 1

AT THE EDGE OF HEAVEN,
ABOVE THE ABYSS OF HELL

With a grimace, Lucifer strutted across the battlefield until face-to-face with Michael. He glared into the Archangel's eyes.

"Is that what this represents to you," Lucifer sputtered, "a personal battle between the Evil Lucifer, former Archangel, now the damned demon, Satan?"

Michael didn't flinch, nor divert his eyes. "No, not personal! What you're trying to do here is evil, and my forces...the forces of God...are here to stop you. It's not personal. Call it whatever you wish. It's still Good versus Evil, and, if that means me against you, so be it."

Lucifer screeched as he lunged at Michael...

To read the rest of this Chapter visit http://billrockwell.net

Not Privileged to Know

Made in the USA
Columbia, SC
25 May 2017